THE PULL OF THE PAST

THE PULL OF THE PAST

The Finale of The Luna's Pack Trilogy

L M LISSETTE

Dreams In Ink

For the wild ones who have lost their freedom and the organizations
still fighting for the rights of the remaining few.

Contents

I

Despite the blazing summer temperatures, the birds in the barren trees have been singing nonstop for hours. My father lies along my legs, staring beyond the cliff's edge, while Bastian sleeps under my head. I bring them here the day before my mother's birthday each year. Although it's been over seven years, our birthdays still sting like we lost her yesterday.

My name is Annalisa. Like my mother, I am the Luna of wolves. My father, Tarq, is still the Alpha of our pack. Bastian will take over for him when we marry. I gave my father permission to join my mother a few times, but he promised her that he wouldn't leave me. Secretly, I'm glad he's still here, but I know he misses her.

Slipping my fingers through Daddy's fur, I look beyond the cliff. The view is different this year. It hasn't rained in over six months, so everything is dead in the valley. "Neala said the guards' storage is running low," I whisper to my father.

Disturbed by my voice, Bastian rolls onto his side with a sigh. He stands watch around our birthdays so I can help Daddy with his emotions. He's exhausted.

"*We might need to make a run to the ranch,*" my father suggests, resting his chin on my knee. "*We can bring some beef down for the kids until the rains return.*"

"Brock says it hasn't rained down south either. He told me the bayou is drying up," I tell Daddy, wiping the wet fur under his eyes. "Have you ever seen it this bad?"

"*Grandpa said he's been through a few droughts but never like this.*" My father lifts his head, looking at the songbirds. "*I've been coming up here for years. These birds never sing unless you or your mother are with me.*"

"I pretend they sing for her."

"*So do I,*" he says, chuckling. "*I just didn't want you to feel left out.*"

I'm unsure how I'd get through days like this without my father. Giggling, I tug his fur. "Do you remember when that bird flew into the house?"

My father rolls onto his side and lifts his paw for me to rub. "*Your mother with that broom,*" he says, chuckling. "*She yelled at me when I caught it.*"

"Daddy, you killed it," I say, lifting my eyebrow.

"*But it wasn't flying around the house anymore, was it?*" My father's smile rings through his voice.

"*She somehow combined a disapproving head shake with love,*" Bastian adds. He curls around to poke my cheek with his nose.

"She had a lot of practice," I tell him. "Daddy's always been a goofball." I close my eyes as Bastian rubs his whiskers over my face. "Ok, Bass, what story do you want to hear this year?"

Bastian only knew my mother for about six months, but they were very close. It was too difficult for me and Daddy to talk about her when we sat here the first year. Bastian told us about his memories with her the entire time. We cried a lot, but eventually, he had us laughing. I believe we began to heal that day, and my Alpha was responsible for it.

Bastian rests his head on my father's hip. "*You said you call Tarq 'Daddy' because of your mother,*" he starts. "*Can I hear about that?*"

I rub his ear between my fingers and squeeze my father's paw. "That was one of Mom's favorite stories." Rolling to my side, I slip my hand between the Alphas and push small, unnoticeable bursts of heat to them. "I was six years old when I saw my first bear. She had two adorable cubs with her."

My father chuckles and rolls to put his head on my hip so he can look at us.

"I could pet wolves, so naturally, I thought I could pet the bears," I say, giggling. "The cubs ran, but their mother rose onto her back legs like she wanted to hug me. Daddy ran in and attacked the bear. Mom grabbed me, but I still saw him fighting that bear who only wanted to be my friend."

Bastian's lips fluff a few times. His greatest strength is honesty, so I know he's trying desperately not to laugh at my naïve thoughts and behavior. My father isn't worried about my feelings and continues chuckling.

"I don't remember ever calling him 'Pa,' but Mom said I kept telling her my Pa was a scary monster. So, she told me my father is my mighty protector," I say, smiling. "She said Daddy was everything I needed him to be and would always protect me even when I didn't know I was in danger."

"And I always have," my father says, closing his eyes as another tear falls.

I curl my fingers and scratch his hip. "They started teaching me about different animals, and it just became normal to call my greatest protector 'Daddy.'"

"So, *you never got to hug a bear, huh?*" Bastian asks, letting out his laughter.

"No," I answer sadly. "I even cried when Daddy tried to put on a Winnie the Pooh movie."

Bastian lifts his head as my father laughs hysterically. *"What's Winnie the Pooh?"*

"You'll find out someday when we bring about the future Luna, my Alpha," I say, scratching his chin. "Until then, let's just say he was a friendly bear that deserved a hug."

Bastian tucks in to lick my cheek with the tip of his tongue. *"Every-one should experience your hugs at least once."*

We while away the rest of the afternoon recalling tales of my mother's time as Luna. I've always enjoyed Bastian's stories because they help me understand why they were so close. Bastian had suffered a horrendous childhood, and my mother and father rescued him from his abuser. That man cost me my mother and great-uncle, but his evil is forever gone.

"*She spent so much time telling me stories in those paddocks,*" Bastian recalls. "*One day, she told me the same story about the day she met Neala three times in a row.*" He chuckles, curling his front leg over my lap. "*She didn't think I was listening, but I was. Luna and Neala were my favorite people at the time, so it was my favorite story.*"

"*She loved you both very much,*" my father says, looking toward the setting sun. "*Take comfort that you'll see her again, but for now, daughter, we should get you out of here.*" He rolls to his feet and howls for Grease.

Bastian moves before me as I sit up. "*Tarq's right, Ayls,*" he says, bumping his nose to mine. "*We need to get home.*"

I might be the Luna, but these two wolves are the head of my security. This is one of the few battles I will never win against them. The gathering for my mother's birthday is widely known, so they require me to be safely at the lake, surrounded by wolves, for the duration of the festivities.

"I love you, my Alpha," I tell him, kissing behind his whiskers.

"*I love you too.*" Bastian lifts his leg into a hook for me to pull myself up with.

* * *

Although we made it home late last night, I still wake up at sunrise. Edith and Anthony always cook us breakfast on my mother's birthday, so the sound of pans clanging filters up the stairs. I have an Alpha on each shoulder with my arms around their necks. Pulling my fingers through their fur, I let them sleep while I listen to my wolves.

Nate is giving Matthew orders for tonight. Most of the junior guards on Ash's morning run are whining about the distance. Brock is in the south with Rachel and Chase. They've picked up a young wolf that met my mother while we were down there. I giggle as Brock argues that she's not old enough to be a Luna's guard.

A knock brings me back to the bedroom. I lift my head as the door opens, and I can't stop my smile when my eyes land on Grandpa Bruce. "Hey, kiddo," he whispers.

I slip out from under the Alphas and jump off the bed. "I'm so glad you made it back in time," I whisper back, flinging my arms around his neck. "Where's Grandma?"

"She was dying for a bath," he says, smiling.

I lead him from the room and down the stairs. "Let's let them sleep," I say, hooking our arms. "Were you able to find Davis?"

Grandpa Bruce pats my hand and guides me into the kitchen. "We found him." He pulls out a stool, and Edith slides me a coffee cup.

Anthony leans over the counter to kiss my cheek. "Good morning, little Luna."

"We don't have long before they notice I left, Grandpa Bruce," I remind my grandfather. "What did you find out?"

He tucks my hair behind my ear. "There's no rain, Ayls. He said even some of the river is too shallow now for most boats." My grandfather is a stunning wolf that refuses to age. His dark brown hair is getting long, so it falls into his eyes as he looks down at me. "He's going to stay north in case you need him. We should look at going west."

"Bastian said there was plenty of hunting, but that was years ago," I say, sighing. "How do you know it'll be the same."

"I choose to have faith that the land will provide."

"Grandpa, I can't move the whole pack on faith," I grumble.

"Kade and Gaine are supposed to be back soon," Anthony offers, clanging his spoon on a pan. "You know that wolf can't stay still. You should consider sending him to scout."

Smiling, I reach out for his hand. My mother told me to trust Anthony's tactical advice, and he's never been wrong. "Do you agree?"

"Little Luna, you have a lot of hungry wolves," Anthony starts, squeezing my fingers. "If the rains don't come back soon, you won't be able to feed them. Anything is better than starvation."

"Edith?" I look to my mother's good friend and our resident witch.

"Annalisa, I'm a witch, not Mother Nature," she says, winking.

Grandpa Bruce looks up at the ceiling as it creaks under the weight of at least one of the Alphas. "Give them the day," he whispers, turning to me. "The flowers bloomed this morning. They look lovely."

There's a loud commotion, and furniture slides across the floor upstairs. I rub my eyes as clattering on the stairs turns into loud thuds and a crash. Edith grins broadly when Bastian snarls behind me.

"I'm faster. Get over it," my father boasts, pulling my head back to kiss my temple. "Good morning, daughter."

When Daddy releases me, the arms that wrap around my waist make my nerves try to jump out of my skin. Bastian tucks into my neck as I blast heat into his forearms. Mom allowed Bastian to shift around me as his birthday gift last year, and Daddy helped him overcome the bond's pull. I can't stop my nerves from responding to him, so he has to be the strong one if he wants to shift around me.

"Your father broke your hammock," Bastian whispers in my ear.

Daddy clicks his tongue. "You're the one that landed on it."

"Whose fault was that?" Bastian laughs, moving away from my neck.

"You're the dumbass that got in my way." My father pulls on his shirt and takes over cooking for Anthony.

I love them both with all my heart, but they are like two mighty toddlers when they get together. I lean against Bastian and listen as the others plan the day's events. Our festivities don't follow a schedule. We offer food to our wolves who come to pay their respects and make ourselves available for those who want to talk or need help.

I turn around on my stool and melt into Bastian's chest. His heartbeat is as steady as my father's and calms me during even the most trying times. My nerves relax under my skin as we allow them to enjoy his touch. Bastian is beautiful, and I love to watch him as a wolf or a man, but nothing compares to the feeling of his protective arms.

I pull away from Bastian's chest and reach for his cheeks, holding his hair out of his eyes. His muscles are tense, but his gaze is filled only with love. Pushing a small amount of heat straight to his face, I lick my lips and try to pull him to me. I have dreamed of kissing Bastian since we were teenagers, but something stops us every time.

Daddy clears his throat behind me. "You need to let your guard eat, daughter," he says, making me scowl at his interruption.

"I brought the eggs from the guards' storage," Grandpa Bruce tells me. "The lake looks pretty low."

We knew the fish wouldn't last long with the water level declining, so I limited fishing a month ago. The Alphas' notably larger frame takes a lot of protein to maintain. The only way to decrease their food consumption was to change them to a high-protein diet. Edith found some books to help us understand their needs, and my father has enjoyed playing with the recipes.

"We're gonna make a trip up to the ranch after the memorial," Daddy says, sliding a plate of eggs before Bastian.

Edith cuts a block of cheese into sticks, handing a few to Daddy and piling the rest on Bastian's plate. "Only a quarter of the herd I sent to trade with the militia made it," she says, frowning. "And then only half the chickens survived the ride back."

Bastian holds his fork up to my mouth. "Ayls, you should eat some of this," he pleads. "You need your strength too."

"I'm strong because I have you," I whisper, brushing my fingers over his cheek.

"Aw," Edith gushes.

"Father present," Daddy grumbles.

Giggling, I accept the food from Bastian and help Edith slice the rest of the cheese.

* * *

My mother's altar never ceases to amaze me. As Lunas, we can't smell the scents our wolves can. Bastian says I smell like his favorite fruit. My mother smelled like flowers. My father would lie around smelling roses when he was a little boy, but later developed a refined sense of smell and preferred lavender, jasmine, and honeysuckle. So, naturally, that's what my mother smelled like.

The altar is stone with a metal grate for the flames to come through when we burned her body. My father etched her name and date of birth on the side as part of his healing process. Lavender, jasmine, and honeysuckle grow over it for just one day on her birthday, and the smell is overwhelming.

I don't doubt Mom visits us because I often hear Daddy talking to her in his sleep, but today is when I feel closest to her. The number of wolves who need my help dwindles each year. They stop by to celebrate my mother, and I love hearing their stories, but we know she wouldn't want us to continue to cry at her memory.

Trish waddles a bit as she approaches Bastian and me at sunset. Her mate, Jinx, braces her back for support. Pregnant and struggling, she shouldn't be on her feet, but they wouldn't miss this event. "If losing your mother didn't kill me, this baby doesn't have a chance," Trish says, smiling.

Edith holds out a bowl of boiled chicken. Trish has been having trouble with food, and Edith learned the boiled meat trick from Grandpa and Uncle Miles. I take the bowl and help Jinx ease his pregnant wife to the ground.

I link our arms as Bastian leaves to shift, and Daddy sets out the lanterns. Bastian started this tradition a few years after Mom died, and it quickly became popular. Daddy limited it to family and close friends when we began shouting so everyone could hear us.

"Alright, I'll go first," my father calls out, settling our small group. "Annalisa was four when I built the cattle pens up at the cabin. Darya told her she could pick out the cows." He chuckles, shaking his head. "So, we packed up our excited toddler and hauled her across the basin.

"Edith gathered some of her milking cows in a little pen for Annalisa to choose from. Right beside it was the meat pen with a few steers. Darya brought her to the cows, but she kept wandering over to the steers. By the end of the afternoon, Annalisa had her mother performing weddings for the cows and agreeing to take them all home with us. Somehow, Darya convinced one of those cows to let Annalisa ride it."

I giggle, vaguely remembering my cow ride. "You started shifting so I could ride on your back after that."

"It was either that or bring that damn cow down from the mountain because you were not getting on a horse." My father rubs his forehead. I remember he used to like telling stories about Grandpa shooting him. He said it's not as fun without Mom around to complain or try to correct him.

Ash and Neala tell their stories when Bastian returns. He slides in and pulls me back against his chest. It's easy to get lost in his touch. My mother explained the strength of the bond's pull, but I didn't fully understand what she said until I first felt it. If I hadn't laid in Bastian's arms on that train, I probably would've realized my mother was saying goodbye. Maybe I could've stopped her.

Bastian begins to hum, pulling me out of my thoughts. Pushing some heat to him, I focus on the current story.

Neala's favorite tale about Mom is a short trip they took with Ash to a neighboring wolf village. There was a young couple having trouble with their child. They asked my mother for help, but she told them Neala was the right person to ask. They could not convince their child to bathe and often had to scrub him by force. It turned out that the child had never seen a dark-skinned wolf.

"Ash told him that when he refused to bathe, Luna made his skin turn dark," Neala says, laughing. "Luna was so mad at him. She spent the whole afternoon with that kid coming back increasingly dirty, asking if he could look like Ash."

"And five years ago, at 18, his parents passed, and he joined the junior guard," Ash adds, smiling.

"I never managed to get dirty enough for Luna to change me," Jinx says, chuckling. "It took me years to figure out that it was just the color of his skin."

Anthony tells of when Uncle Miles tried to kill Mom, and Edith recalls her wedding day. I'm not as emotional as my mother, but I love hearing about their wedding. Edith wasn't allowed at the ceremony, so Anthony fills in those details. I reach for Daddy's hand and give him a few small bursts of heat when Anthony recites their vows.

"I'm ok," Daddy whispers, kissing my cheek. "I meant every word. Your mother would rather see our smiles."

Each year gets more manageable, and he feels calm as he listens to what he still says was the happiest day of his life. Bastian told me years ago that my strength comes from my family and my father is the strongest man I know. He will be full of life again tomorrow, driving us all a little crazier each day. But today is reserved for my mother. It's the one day every year that is just for her.

Ash breaks the seriousness with a story of my mother tripping in the mud with a milk bucket while staying at the cabin with Bastian. Grandma tells us of the day I was born, and Grandpa Bruce recalls the night my mother shot Dax because I kicked her bladder. It's always been his favorite story.

"I didn't have Luna for as long as most of you," Bastian starts, tightening his arms around me. "But every moment was a blessing. I didn't know how important she would be to me until the day I woke up to her climbing into my deathbed. I had given up on life. A weak man had crushed my will to live."

Bastian slides his hands up my arms and across my chest to pull me against him. He leans over my shoulder to put his cheek against mine, slowly exhaling. Tucking into my neck, my Alpha takes a deep breath before he's ready to continue.

"She hummed to me for hours while she rubbed my pads," Bastian continues quietly. "Luna thought I was unconscious, but I listened to her until she fell asleep. She was the first angel I'd ever met, and I couldn't give up while she was with me.

"Then she introduced me to a Luna of my very own. I will forever be thankful for the life she gave me." Bastian squeezes me tightly again and takes Neala's outstretched hand. "Luna brought together the team that taught me to be strong so that I could be near Annalisa. You're all bonded, so you know how hard this is."

Anthony clicks his tongue. "Not a wolf," he points out.

"Nobody's perfect, Anthony," Bastian replies.

My father chuckles beside me until Anthony punches his arm.

"My mother taught me a lesson when I struggled to find perfection among my wolves," I say, reaching back for Bastian's cheek. "She showed me that our family, friends, and packmates are perfect in their own ways. They will be strong, protective, and goofy." I reach for my father's hand. "They will be fierce, passionate, and supportive," I whisper, pulling Bastian until his cheek rests against mine.

Closing my eyes, I take a moment to regain my composure. Bastian's hum starts, and I feel a hand brush across my forehead, slipping down my cheek. I open my eyes with a sigh, half expecting my mother to be sitting before me.

"Even if we don't have all we want," I continue, smiling. "Our lives are filled with the perfect blend of what we need." I release my Alphas and reach both hands out to Anthony. "Even you, Anthony. You have blessed our lives for many years and provided us with unmatched support for which we will always be grateful."

Anthony kisses my knuckles. "Yeah, well, you're still not at the tippy top of my list."

"I suspect that spot is reserved for Edith," I say, winking. "I'll find a way to be ok with that."

Something about tonight feels different. As our group shares stories, I notice the air isn't as thick as it normally is for this event. The smiles are brighter, and the laughter is lighter. Even Bastian seems more relaxed than usual when we spend time together in his human form.

Listening to them laugh reminds me of conversations I had with my mother. She repeatedly said she was happiest while her wolves were enjoying themselves. I'm not sure I ever fully understood that until tonight. There's a warmth in my heart when I look at their smiles. I feel a peace wash over me from the sound of their laughter.

Once all those gathered around the lanterns have told a story, my guards rotate in, one at a time. When Nate arrives for his turn, he bumps my cheek with his fingers, and an overwhelming sense of comfort washes over me. *This is what Mom was talking about.*

"I had the pleasure of being the second wolf to meet the Luna," Nate starts, sitting in the center of our circle. "We didn't know she was the Luna, but she smelled so good and had no clue what we were. Dax had us settled into a certain way of doing things, and Darya had issues with it from the beginning. Even then, she showed us her compassion and caring. Darya's legacy began that day, and I couldn't be prouder that I was there to witness it."

Wolves age more gracefully than humans, but Nate's hair has turned gray, and he's sporting a few wrinkles. His wolf has a gray muzzle, and his hands are rough from years of working for Grandpa, but his touch is gentle as he takes my cheeks and pulls my forehead to his.

"You are every bit as amazing as she was, my young Luna," Nate whispers. "You will find a way to guide us past our trials. We trust in your love."

These wolves are forever making me cry.

Nate kisses my cheek and shakes Bastian's hand before returning to his post. The stories continue as our group thins until it's just five of us. Anthony and Edith lie together while I rest my head on my father's stomach. Bastian lays his head on my lap, looking up at the stars.

"I want to marry your daughter, Tarq," Bastian whispers, making me smile.

My father inhales sharply. "I know you do," he answers. "Let's figure out how to feed the pack before holding an event requiring a feast."

I hold a hand out to each Alpha. "Life is an endless series of adventures," I whisper. "We will make it to the other side as long as we have each other."

2

With my guards' storage quickly running out of food, we set out for the ranch the following day. Typically, we can fill the reserve areas throughout the summer to keep larger families, teenagers, and older wolves fed throughout the colder months. If it runs out while it's warm and they require less food, they will not survive the winter.

Leaning against a tree, I rub Grandpa's medallion between my fingers. The full moon is in a few days, and I hope he has some advice for us because Daddy and I are out of our league. Grease paws at the creek bed. She's thirsty, and the once ample water supply that contained fish and offered life-sustaining hydration to all our crops is now as dry as the basin.

Matthew bumps my hand with his nose. *"We should go, Luna,"* he urges. *"There's nothing here for us anymore."*

He means this watering spot, but it reminds me of Grandpa Bruce's suggestion. "Maybe you're right, Matthew," I respond, hooking my fingers under his jaw. "Where's my Alpha?"

"Right here," Bastian says, sliding his arms around my waist. "You looked like you needed to talk, so I thought I'd ride with you."

I turn to look up at my Alpha. "I would love that."

He helps me into my saddle and swings up behind me. "The guards at the shack say their well hasn't dried up yet," Bastian says quietly. "They haven't eaten in three days, Ayls." Sighing, he tightens his grip on me.

"You're the best hunter out here now," I whisper. "Could you try to track some game for them tonight? Maybe you can find something to hold them over."

"Sure," he answers, pulling me back to rest his chin on my head.

"Grandpa Bruce brought up the mountains again," I say thoughtfully.

"There was a lot of food out there," Bastian tells me. "With fewer people, they didn't have the numbers to feed that we have here. What does Tarq think?"

I lean forward and turn to look into his eyes. "Grandpa mentioned it during the last full moon," I say, cringing. "It didn't go over well."

"But things are worse now," Bastian points out. "Ayls, I've been hungry. It's not the legacy I want to leave behind." He slips his hand over my cheek, searching my eyes. "I like it here at the lake, but not enough to watch our wolves die for it."

Bastian is emotional about many things, but he lacks the attachment to our home that we have. This is not the first time he's mentioned leaving the area. As an accomplished hunter, he knows all the best places to find game. If he can't feed our wolves, we're in serious trouble.

"My father's family has been here for many generations," I say. "Daddy travels a lot, but the lake has always been home. It's where he spent time with Grandpa and lived with Mom." I pinch the bridge of my nose. "Bastian, I don't know what to do, but I'm sure my father will not leave willingly if I decide to move the pack."

"Maybe Edith could knock him out," he suggests with a smile as he tangles his fingers in my hair.

Truthfully, the love Bastian and I share scares me. His grip on my hair is firm, and this is him controlled. Despite my fear, I nearly kissed him once. Bastian felt himself losing control when I got too close, causing him to shift in my arms and cut me with his claws. I rub my fingers under his lower lip and gently blow onto his face. His eyes roll closed as he sighs, easing the tension in his grip.

"How can I help you?" I ask when he opens his eyes.

"Ayls, I just want to move on with our lives," Bastian answers. "When Luna said I could shift, she gave us her blessing. I want to have our ceremony. You deserve that."

"Daddy is just asking us to wait on the wedding, Bass. Our pack will want to celebrate," I say, trying to explain my father. "Waiting until we're married to bond is not a pack law or tradition. I don't mind waiting for the wedding until the rains return."

Bastian squints his eyes and chews his lip. I remember my mother telling me multiple times that I needed to learn my wolves. She also told me this wolf was the most important. Bastian is about to admit something and is afraid of my reaction. He'll still say it, but I must give him time to prepare. Turning around to face forward, I relax against his chest and thread our fingers.

"I'm scared," he whispers, ducking to put his head beside mine.

I am a Luna before I'm someone's mate. Whether he's my Alpha or not, I am this wolf's Luna. "Can you tell me why?"

"Ayls, I killed Bones," Bastian whispers, causing me to hide a gasp. "Your mother was in that militia camp, and it took me almost two days to get to her after she asked for help. I charged straight into the base and ripped through every man within my bite. Tarq didn't even realize I was there until he heard the screaming. That horse was following him and got in my way.

"I tore his head off. I could only think of one thing, and I killed everything in my way until I reached your mother." Bastian stops and leans away, waiting for me to look up. "I crave you. Everything in me wants what's mine, and I want to rip your clothes off and take it. I feel myself losing control and turning into that wolf that killed your mother's horse."

I slide my fingers over Bastian's cheek. "Daddy hated that name," I whisper. "He's never liked any of the names I chose, but that one he especially hated. Did my mother ever tell you why I chose it?"

As kids, Bastian got us hooked on the tales my mother would tell us during the quiet times. We no longer tell many stories, but they are the best way to soothe his troubled mind. He holds my hand to his face and kisses my fingers.

"No," he replies with a shy smile. "I avoided the subject. Tarq said it would be better if she didn't know."

"I can't speak to that, but she is why he had that name," I say, smiling. I lean against him and watch the trail ahead of us. "I was ten. My mother was leaving again, and I was so mad at her. She never took me on any of her trips. I followed her to the horse field, crying and screaming at her, just throwing a fit.

"She stopped at the fence and looked over the herd. This tiny black colt was jumping around like he was the biggest horse in the field, and his mother just put up with his shit. My mother pointed to him and asked if I knew why the mare tolerated his behavior and didn't run him off."

I stop and think back on the lesson I was too mad to understand at the time. My mother taught me many things while I was too pissed off to care. I'm thankful she tolerated my childish attitude and still tried to teach me.

"My mother said, 'All this is to prepare that little horse to take on the world as an adult. The fight he puts up today will strengthen his bones for tomorrow.'" I rub my hand over Bastian's arms, and he tightens them around me. "I want to be with you, Bastian. I want our bond."

Bastian has many great qualities. He will charge blindly into any danger to save me from a bad situation. He will do this while murmuring in my mind to keep me calm. But Bastian is also honest to a fault, and I know it burned him from within to keep that secret. I might have felt differently about it as a teenager, but today, I'm thankful he saved my mother and gave me a memorable six months with her.

"I love you," I whisper, turning my head and tucking my forehead under his jaw.

"I love you too," Bastian responds as his hum starts.

* * *

Bastian stays with me for the rest of the day. The sun is setting when we arrive at the shack. The boulders usually covered in honeysuckle vines are now bare, the vines brown and shriveled.

"I'll take Grease to the stalls," Bastian offers, helping me from her saddle.

I stand with my chest to his, looking up into his eyes. It's a hot evening, but this is the first time I've sweat all day. I've never been with a man, but I'm pretty sure this is my body crying out to Bastian, wanting his attention. I rise onto my toes, bringing my lips closer to his.

Bastian's growl builds quickly, and he pushes me away. "Annalisa," he says through his teeth with his eyes closed. "Stop making this so hard."

I watch him drag Grease behind the shack to the horse stalls. Fighting this bond is becoming increasingly difficult. For the millionth time, I wish my mother were here.

"You're wishing for your mother, aren't you?" Anthony says, approaching from behind me. "I hated how she could figure a way around everything."

I produce a weak smile as I turn to face him. "What do you think she'd say now?"

"I think she'd tell you that love is the answer," Anthony says thoughtfully. "I hated her for just as long as I loved her. Do you want to guess when I was happiest?"

"It seemed like things were so easy for her," I say, sighing.

Chuckling, Anthony puts his arm around my shoulders and guides me toward the shack. He points at the boulders where Bastian is peeking out to watch us. He's back to being a wolf to lessen the pull of our bond. "Looks like your wolf is going hunting. Why don't we talk? Your father prefers the world to see you as the untouchable Lunas, but your mother struggled too, and it's not fair to hide that from you."

"During our Christmas in the south, she told me she had made mistakes," I say, remembering our last holiday together. "She quoted Daddy. It was something about how we fix them that counts."

"In the beginning, when your mother first met these wolves, she had no idea what she was doing," Anthony says, grinning. "She spent almost all her time with your father as a wolf. She was obsessed with him. She studied his fur and paws, asked about the humming, and loved just staring at him. She connected to him as a wolf.

"You've had years with your wolf but have only wanted the man he becomes. It's almost as if the wolf was in your way, and you just want it gone so that you can have the man." Anthony studies my face. "I believe you love your wolves, but you've forgotten to love the wolves they become."

Considering his statement, I squint and reflect on my time with Bastian. The image is the same when I think of him or when he's in front of me. I was picturing the 16-year-old holding me on the train many years ago. He's older and more beautiful now that we can spend time together, but it's the same. I'm putting his human face on his wolf. I cover my mouth, realizing I've been causing this delay and Bastian's fears.

Anthony sits on the porch step and pats the spot beside him. "Tarq left your mother before they were married. Did you know that?"

"He what?" Shocked is not a strong enough word for my feelings.

"Yep," Anthony says, nodding. "The ancient Luna did something to them, and he got mad. Said some cruel things to your mother and ran away in shame." He puts his arm back around me and pulls me to his shoulder. "She was pretty sick trying to grow you by then—spent a week recovering from the whole ordeal. That was the first time I held her while she cried."

"How did she convince him to come back?"

"She said she remembered to connect to his wolf," Anthony responds, rubbing my arm. "You're in love with a man who depends on his wolf to protect you. When you hold the man, his wolf is between you. You have to find a way to calm the beast within." He leans his cheek on my head. "Does that make sense?"

"I never thought I'd be having this conversation with you," I say, giggling.

"Someone had to," he scoffs. "He's gonna tear you apart if you don't figure this out." Anthony nods toward where Bastian had been sitting. "That boy loves you. You've waited like your mother wanted. Connect to his wolf, and you'll find a way."

Looking up, I kiss his cheek. "Thank you, Anthony."

"You're welcome, kiddo," he says, pulling me up. "Now, you might want to claim that bed before your father gets done with the guards. It's not as big as the one at home."

Anthony hugs me one last time and turns toward the guards' bunk-house. He's right. Daddy typically kicks Bastian off the bed, and I curl up on the floor with him.

I step onto the porch, leaning over the railing to watch the grounds. Bastian jogs across the yard with something hanging from his mouth. "What did you find, my Alpha?"

"A couple of rabbits and a squirrel," he answers. *"It's not much, but at least they'll eat tonight."*

"Do you remember those old ledgers at Edith's house?" I ask, not really caring if he does. "I wonder if any of them have a gardening chart. Maybe there are some vegetables we could grow that don't require much water."

"It's worth a shot," Bastian says. *"If I'm the best hunter, and this is all I can come up with, we're in serious trouble."* He jogs toward the bunkhouse. *"Let me drop these off. I'll be right back."*

I watch him as he leaves. Bastian's gate is smooth, but his hind legs lift higher than most of my wolves. They almost seem to prance. He's holding the squirrel by the tip of its tail, so he has raised his head to avoid dragging it on the ground. Bastian's fur is thicker over his shoulders and along his ribs than my father's coat.

I can remember appreciating his beauty in the beginning. My mother walked with him in hand to introduce us until she lost control of him. Bastian had charged up the hill. His stunning presence was overwhelming. The first time I touched him, I felt a hot wave spread over my body and thought it was my imagination.

Anthony was right. I let resentment build over the years. I wanted my Alpha, not the wolf with fur and claws. I need to spend time with my wolf and learn to connect to him again. After all, that's who I fell in love with.

"You alright, Ayls?" My father's voice pulls me out of my head.

I smile as he steps onto the porch. "I think I forgot that Bastian is a wolf, Daddy," I tell him, cringing.

My father shakes his head and sits on the railing, looking down at me. "What gave it away? The fur or the tail?"

Clicking my tongue, I rub my eyes. "Daddy, can you please help me understand what Bastian's going through?" I straighten my back and lean my forehead on his shoulder. "I know this must be weird, but you are the only other person that's been where he is. I need help to understand it."

"Wolf," he mutters.

"What?"

"We're wolves, Annalisa," Daddy says quietly. "We're not 'people' or 'men,' we're wolves. It's an instinct, daughter, not a want." He puts his arms around me, holding me close. "That wolf feels a pull anytime you're near that tells him to take what's his. You feel the nerves just under your skin. He's feeling them from deep within, and they reach for you with so much force that it borders on painful."

I put my ear to his chest to listen to his heartbeat. "How did Mom help you?"

"I don't know," Daddy says, sighing. "But you aren't her, and Bastian is not me. You have to find a way through this together." He runs his fingers through my hair and tugs at the tips. "Why don't you two take the bed tonight? Spend time with the wolf you love and forget about the man he becomes for a little while."

"I love you, Daddy," I whisper, hugging him tightly. "Thank you."

My father kisses my head and lets me stay against his chest while I consider his words. I understand why my mother trusted their council so much. Anthony and Daddy are some of the wisest men I know. Teamed up with Bastian and our companions, they're unstoppable.

I pull away from him and look into his eyes. "Daddy, I want to call Brock and Chase back up here," I say. "I feel Brock's absence, and I'm guessing you are feeling Chase's."

Inhaling deeply, he cups my cheek. "You are the Luna, sweetheart. If you want them to come home, then call them back. They are doing important work down there, so make sure you do it for the right reasons."

"Chase traveled with Mom all the time, didn't he?"

"Well, yes, but the Luna line was already in place," he says, taking my other cheek to hold my face. "You were already born. There was no danger of ending the line."

"You'll not be traveling without me," Bastian says firmly.

I move as much as my father's grip allows and see my wolf stepping onto the porch. "Ok," I say, pulling Daddy's hands from my cheeks. "Why don't we talk about this later? Thank you for your counsel, Daddy." I lean in to kiss his cheek.

He gestures toward the door, eyeing my Alpha. "Have a good night."

Bastian bows to my father before joining me in the shack. *"What was that about?"*

"I'm considering having Brock and Chase bring the southern wolves up here," I tell him, sitting on the corner of the mattress. "They're not faring any better down there and still have the rebel bands battering them. I don't want to lose any more wolves to the stupidity."

Bastian sets his chin on my knee. *"But we can't feed them, Ayls."*

"Do you remember Brock complaining about the little girl that pulled his whiskers? He was pissed because he said she was a wolf and should know better." I slide my hand over his head absentmindedly. "That's the kid that's bothering him now. She's 16 and wants to join my guards. Bass, what if we lose them?"

"Let's find a way to feed the wolves already here before we add to the numbers," Bastian suggests. *"I'm not sure I could watch more go hungry."* He steps onto the bed and slides his nose along my jaw.

Pushing my fingers through the fur over his shoulders, I wrap my arms around him. I can't remember when I last nuzzled my face into my Alpha's coat. Growing up sheltered at the lake, I always spent time with my friends in their human form. The only time I was around wolves was for the full moon.

Bastian is not the only wolf I've let down. I've failed my entire pack by not connecting to who they truly are. "I think I need to be taught my place," I say, quietly giggling.

Bastian pushes me onto my back. *"Seems as good a place as any,"* he says, chuckling as he lays his head across my chest.

I rub my thumb over the short hairs on his chin. "I was thinking about the day we met earlier," I murmur. "I remember you lying your head in my lap. I had no idea what I was doing."

Lifting my eyes to the ceiling, I narrow them in thought. My mother started teaching me, but most of my experience was with my father and Grandpa. I hadn't even handled Uncle Miles because he was always with my mother. I was frozen with my hands over Bastian's head, unsure what to do.

"I nearly burst waiting to feel your touch," Bastian tells me. *"I'd been waiting a month to meet you. I was so scared you wouldn't want me."*

It crushed me when Bastian told me what the Blood Pack's Alpha had done to him. I struggled to find my breath as he detailed the four years he'd been tied to a wall in a basement. He'd been beaten, starved, and humiliated until he had no confidence. Bastian was sure no one would ever love him. I held him and cried into his fur for hours.

Once I calmed down, he told me about his time with my mother at the cabin. He depended on her presence to remind him he was safe. He wouldn't let her out of his sight. My father gave him the courage to spend time away from my mother, first with Daddy and then with Neala and Ash. I was missing my mother so much when he told me, and his story somehow made me feel closer to her.

"Come here, Bastian," I say, scooting from underneath him and laying my head on a pillow. "I will always want you."

Bastian crawls up the bed and slides in beside me. I roll toward him and curl his neck so his ear is against my chest. His hum starts as he releases a deep sigh. Bastian stretches his front leg over my ribs, relaxing against me.

"Would you mind staying a wolf for a while?" I whisper.

Bastian shifts his head slightly and licks his lips. *"Are you ok?"*

"I am, sweet wolf," I tell him. "There is so much pressure on us right now that we could use a little break. I want to spend time with my Alpha without the added stress to bond." I slide my fingers through his fur. "Does that make sense?"

"I think that's a good idea," Bastian answers, snuggling closer to my

chest. *"Have you noticed how everyone stares at us now? Like we'll be wearing a sign saying we've bonded when it happens."*

"I haven't, but now I'll be watching for them," I say, giggling. I rub the leg Bastian has over my ribs. "Why don't you tell me a story?"

"What story could I tell you that you haven't heard?" he asks. *"Shoot, you've been there for most of them."*

"That might be true," I say thoughtfully. There's one story that I've asked for a few times, but he refuses to tell me. "I want to hear about the day you met me."

"Ayls, you were there," Bastian whines.

"Please, Bass," I beg. "I want to hear how it felt for you."

Like my father, Bastian hides things he believes show his weaknesses. His honor is important to him, and his pride is untouchable. I hope that if I can understand how he is feeling, I can find a way to help him.

"Your mother was my rock," Bastian starts just as I'm ready to give up. *"She kept me calm all day while we worked in hand. Bruce stayed with us and coached me to see through her aura. I was doing ok until you laughed."*

"Oh," I say accidentally. I didn't mean to disturb Bastian, but I don't remember laughing at him.

My Alpha lifts his head away from my chest to look into my eyes. *"It was about something in the field, but it scared me,"* he admits. *"I wanted you so badly and just knew you'd reject me. I started to back up and pulled away from your mother."* Bastian rubs his nose over my cheek. *"She just knelt and waited for me to remember that my life had changed. Bruce sat beside me, remaining quiet so I could decide to return to her on my own.*

"I remember just standing there, frozen. Everything in me ached, wanting to be with you," Bastian says, sighing. He rests his muzzle over the side of my face, making my eyes close. *"Your grandfather rammed Tarq, and I suddenly needed to help him. I started pulling your mother up the hill. I didn't have a plan, but I wanted to defend your father. Then you looked at me."*

Bastian's hum hasn't stopped as he recalls our life-changing evening from his perspective. I trail my fingernails through his fur, giving him this needed time and hoping he'll continue. I take a deep breath and recognize his scent for the first time in a while. Bastian's scent is the same as a wolf or man. Although I can't describe it, it suits him perfectly.

"*Something took over that I can't explain,*" Bastian starts again. "*You were mine, and I intended to take you by force if necessary. I yanked against your mother until she let me go, but Tarq stopped me. I'm not sure anyone else could have.*" With a sigh, Bastian slips the tip of his tongue over my skin. "*I was going to hurt you.*"

"It's alright, Bass," I whisper, knowing it took everything in him to admit that. "You can stop if you want to."

"*Your father stopped me,*" Bastian says. "*But it was your mother who helped me regain control. She settled me as I lay beside her. And your touch. Ayls, it was magical. I wanted to feel it over my whole body. Your touch reaches my soul and eases every insecurity my past created.*"

I tighten my arms around his neck. "I will always be here for you, my Alpha."

"*And I am forever yours, my Luna.*"

"Thank you for telling me," I say. "You were the most beautiful thing I'd ever seen." I nuzzle my face into his fur. "You still are. Thank you for reminding me."

"*Sleep, my Luna,*" Bastian whispers. "*We will find our way.*"

3

Grease is trained to follow my guards, but she's always been partial to Bastian. He stays close so she can find him in the dust as we charge across the dry, cracked terrain of the basin. We control this entire area, and guards are stationed along the outskirts. I'm relatively safe here, even out in the open, but Bastian continuously looks back to check on me.

I can't see much with the dust cloud my guards out front create, so I spend most of the long ride studying Bastian. After my mother's death, Neala taught me how to assess my wolves' bodies and what to keep an eye on regarding Bastian because of his past. She showed me how to extend his pads to inspect his paws and ensure they didn't stiffen.

I spent much of the first years slipping my fingers through Bastian's fur, memorizing his muscle tone. He would hum as I rotated his joints, feeling for any stiffness or popping. I made it a point to study their dietary needs and establish a balanced diet to keep them fit and healthy. Their diet affects every part of their lives, including their joint health.

Watching my beautiful wolf run steadily before us, I begin detecting a limp. It's slight, so I wouldn't have noticed if we hadn't been running at this continuous cadence for so long. He's been offering his food to the other guards. It's a noble gesture, but his body can't handle a lack of nutrients due to his past.

After running through most of the day, we slow to a walk as we reach the tree line on the opposite side of the basin. I step out of my saddle and hold my hand out for Bastian's muzzle. We wait a moment, allowing Anthony to catch up to us.

"Without bringing up age, you've been around a while, Anthony," I say, smiling. "Have you ever seen it this dry?"

Anthony puts his arm around my shoulders. "I did a lot of traveling with the militia in the old days," he starts, squinting thoughtfully. "I do remember some fires in the north one summer. Wiped out thousands of acres of farmlands. Corn, I think. The crop was pretty dry. Went up like that." He snaps his fingers to show the quickness.

"Well, we don't have to worry about losing crops," I grumble. "They're already dead."

"There was another assignment that took me south," Anthony continues. "It was a swamp down there, but it was all dried out. I'll never forget the smell of rotting cattle mixed with salt water."

Bastian curls around my hip to look up at Anthony. *"Does he have any advice?"*

"Let's talk about this when we get to the cave," I tell him, rubbing his jaw. "I heard Kade was back, so he should be waiting for us."

Bastian sighs, rolling his eyes. It didn't take long for Kade to grow on me, but my Alpha only tolerates him at best. I was overjoyed when Gaine finally agreed to marry him. Kade is the perfect blend of a wolf who follows the rules but lives in his own little world. I enjoy his company, but the skills he acquired being Tynan's enforcer make him extremely useful when I need someone to travel outside our boundaries.

"I heard he tried moonshining last time he was home," Anthony grumbles.

"Gaine blew up his still," I say dismissively. "She wasn't interested in that life."

Bastian chuckles. *"He was so mad."* He rubs his head over my hip. *"I'll admit, she's been good for him. She doesn't take any of his crap."*

"No, she does not," I say, giggling. "I know we didn't have the easiest of starts, but I like having Kade around. He reminds us that there's always another way."

"I don't see how he hasn't been shot yet," Anthony says, lifting an eyebrow. "He's an ass, and his damn wolf literally shines. He's an easy target."

"Anthony," I start, trying to maintain a straight face. "If Bastian hasn't killed him after what he did to him, I'm pretty sure Kade's officially won everyone over."

Anthony squints and drops his arm from my shoulders. "He hasn't won me. You're the only reason he's allowed to live in my presence."

I shake my head, listening to Bastian chuckle. "I appreciate that, Anthony."

"Anything for you, kiddo," he grumbles.

Daddy says Anthony is somewhere between 55 and 60 years old. He will never see me as anything other than a kid. Anthony should be staying home at his age, but he promised my mother he'd protect her family.

We stroll along together, enjoying the moment. Bastian slips his tongue over my fingers to settle himself and remains quiet as I listen to my father position the guards for the evening. By the time we approach the cave, Daddy's already dressed and leaning against a boulder, waiting for us.

"Can you two care for the horses while I talk to my father?" I ask, looking down at Bastian. "I'll be alright, Love." I kneel to kiss his nose, and he nuzzles my cheek before leading Grease into the cave.

"He's limping," Daddy says as soon as they disappear.

Sighing, I lean against the boulder beside him. "You noticed too, huh?"

"He should probably ride tomorrow," he suggests. "That cliff is a bitch."

I wrap my arms around his waist and let him pull me to his chest. "Bastian will be staying a wolf for a while, Daddy."

"I think that's a good idea," my father says, kissing my head. "You probably could've picked better timing, though."

I giggle into his chest. "I spent so much time wanting to hold the man he becomes that I forgot to love the wolf." I twist my face in thought. "You are all beautiful wolves. I'm not sure when I forgot that."

Daddy chuckles and directs me toward the cave. "It'll come back just like the rains. Kade's been waiting for you. He's got something for us."

This cave is long, and the fire pit is further inside than I'd like. We can hear Kade and Anthony carrying on as soon as we step through the mouth. Kade might be a favorite of mine, but he annoys Anthony. I'm pretty sure he does it on purpose.

"You might be shiny, wolf, but your shit stinks just like the rest of us," Anthony growls.

"See, you've got me all wrong," Kade responds. "I'm not saying I'm better than everyone. I'm simply saying that I'm better than you."

There's a stunned silence in the cave, and a tight smile spreads across my face as I picture the many hues of red Anthony must be turning. I pull my father along before Kade says anything else. He's an acquired taste that Anthony would rather burn than serve for dinner.

I find Bastian by the fire and let my father deal with the bickering men in the horse pens. I sit beside him and slide my hand over his face. My Alpha looks exhausted, but his eyes are sweet and gentle. I pull his muzzle to my cheek and close my eyes.

"I love you," I whisper, feeling my chest tighten.

"You are the reason my heart beats, Ayls," Bastian responds, sliding the tip of his tongue over my ear. *"How are you holding up? Kade said he brought some steaks with him."*

"Good," I say, smiling. "You'll be able to eat tonight."

"No, Ayls," Bastian says, pulling away. *"I meant for you. I know how to handle hunger."*

I raise my eyebrow. "But your body does not, my beautiful wolf. What did you hurt?"

"It's just my paw, Ayls," he says, holding it up. *"It gets stiff sometimes."*

I reach for it. "My mother has something written about paws and stiffness. She was adamant about ensuring the toe pads extended when she pushed on the center pad." I push on Bastian's and notice how little they move. "Give me your other paw."

"I'm just tired. I'm sure once we reach the ranch..." his voice trails off as

I stare at him with my hand out, waiting for his paw. Sighing, Bastian rolls onto his side and lets me inspect his pads side-by-side.

"Luna!" Kade shouts, making me jump. "Shit, I've missed you!" He crashes onto me, squeezing tightly and groaning for effect.

"Kade," I whine, straining to breathe. "What the hell?"

He releases me and sits up, eyeing Bastian. "So, look, I think I should have a title. You know? Make an official position for me." Kade leans against the cave wall and stretches his legs out. "Maybe I should even be called 'Sir.'" He rests his head back and closes his nearly-silver blue eyes.

Kade's gorgeous. There's no other way to describe him. His black hair perfectly cups his face, and his skin is flawless, except for the judgment scar on his chest that he received from my mother. Whether smiling or frowning, his face is stunning. Kade is serious when he speaks but moves on dismissively, knowing the answer will always be "no."

I'm not sure how to respond to him. I know he wants a job, but Kade is a mess, and I'm not sure anyone else has acquired the taste I have for him. "Kade?" I wait for him to open his eyes. "I love you."

"Well, that's obvious," he says, shrugging. "I'm totally lovable. But I'm bored, Luna. I need to do something. Use my skills, woman!"

Sighing, I relax into Bastian and begin rubbing his pads. "How was your trip, Kade?"

"I don't know how you convinced that woman to give me a chance, but she is spectacular," Kade says, smiling. "I have never hunted with someone so vicious. Your father's bringing up a little gift from the wife and me. I heard hunting hasn't been so good down here."

"And yet, that doesn't answer my question, Kade," I grumble, lifting my eyebrow.

"I still don't understand why you like him so much," Bastian chimes.

I push firmly on my Alpha's pads, and he rolls onto his shoulder with a groan. "Did you find anything useful?"

"Luna, food is useful," Kade scoffs. "But I didn't find any rain. Every-where is dry." He smiles, sitting up and pointing toward the back of the cave where Daddy is approaching. "Your wolf is losing muscle, though. That'll do him some good."

Bastian is nearly asleep, but his nose starts wiggling, and he takes a few deep breaths. *"Ayls, that's buffalo."* He lifts his head and watches my father and Anthony carry a large, cured shoulder toward us.

"They called them 'bison' up north, but I didn't notice a difference," Kade says. "That's the third one my woman took down. I was bloody stuffed. Figured the Alphas might like some, so we stole a wagon."

I click my tongue. "Kade, could you try to make friends instead of enemies?"

"Nah, Luna," Kade says, waving his hand. "I nabbed it from the militia. It's all good."

Bastian pulls his paw from my hand and sits up, pushing me upright. His stomach growls as my father lowers the large slab. Kade had left the leg attached, ensuring they had meat and marrow.

"Anthony has some steaks to cook for you," Daddy says, kissing my cheek. "I'm gonna shift," he continues in a whisper, nodding toward Bastian. "It'll be easier to convince him to eat if he has company."

"Thank you, Daddy," I whisper back. As he leaves, I pull Bastian's muzzle to my lips. "That is for you and Daddy. He'll be right back." He moves closer to nuzzle my cheek, and I whisper, "I know that's why your feet are stiff. Stop trying to hide things from me."

"How could I ever hide things from you, Ayls?" Bastian responds, chuckling.

Pulling the fur under his throat, I leave him to join Kade on the other side of the fire. He extends his arm for me to slide under. Kade is oddly likable, and I struggled to understand how Gaine could deny him when he found her.

Besides my Alpha, Kade is second only to our companion. Harboring anger and resentment toward him would be easy. Kade knowingly left my mother on the train and didn't free her from the compound the night before she died. He held me countless times as he told me about the conversation they had in the end. Watching my father lose my mother broke him. It took months for him to come back to the lake.

Chase gave Kade the wing off the kitchen with Daddy's blessing, and he stayed with us for about six months before he stopped needing me. He didn't take long to request my help to get through to Gaine. Blessing their union was one of the happiest moments of my life.

Anthony returns with the steaks and places them in pans over the fire, pulling me out of my head. I fold my legs on Kade's lap and curl against his chest. He leans his cheek onto my head and rubs my arm while we watch my father join in on Bastian's feast.

Bastian and Daddy have kept a strict protein diet of poultry, eggs, and dairy at my request to maintain most of their muscle mass. All my wolves need grand amounts of food to fuel their bodies, but the Alphas are much larger and require more. Grandpa calls them the "bodybuilders of wolves," whatever that means. This red meat is a treat for them, and if I'm being honest, I'm tired of hearing their stomachs growl.

Relaxing in Kade's heat, I watch my father and Bastian enjoy their meal. Daddy's never had buffalo, so my Alpha points out all the areas he thought were the tastiest and shares some of each. Rabbit is Bastian's favorite meat, but he is eating this meal similarly. He takes long licks of the muscle tissue with his eyes closed before tearing it off.

The sizzle of Anthony's cooking is overwhelmingly loud until he removes it from the fire. The Alphas' hums filter in as they finish the meat and gnaw on the bone, attempting to get to the marrow. The muscle and fat might have been delicious and filling, but the marrow is packed full of the nutrients I want them to have.

Kade leans forward to take some plates from Anthony. "Give it here, guys," he tells the Alphas. "I don't want to listen to that all night." Kade pulls a knife from his pocket and hands me the plates. He told me Uncle Miles taught him everything he knows about knives. A master never reveals all of their secrets, so I bet Miles was amazing after watching Kade with them.

As Bastian approaches me with a thick bone, I settle the plates across my lap. "How's your stomach, Love?" I ask, taking the bone. My Alpha has a loud hum that embarrasses him, but I enjoy hearing it.

"I will always give to those in need, but I really don't like being hungry,"

Bastian admits. He nuzzles my cheek before sliding down to my neck. *"I miss peaches."* His tongue slips over my skin as he exchanges the flavor of the meat for the taste of me.

"I'm sure they will come back with the rain," I murmur, appreciating his attention.

"Or there will come a time that I'll just need to eat you," Bastian says quietly. He takes another lick and slides the front of his muzzle across my shoulder so his short front teeth rake over my skin. *"I've missed this. You smell so much better when you heat up."* Bastian takes a deep breath. *"Like fresh peach pie."*

Giggling, I push him away. "You just ate half of that massive shoulder," I tell him, shaking my head. "You've had plenty."

Bastian jams his nose back against my neck. *"Have you ever known me to be full?"*

I know he's playing, but he has a point. My mother used to call Daddy a "bottomless pit." I couldn't disagree with her, but now I realize it's an Alpha thing.

I flick my eyes toward my father, suddenly remembering he's here. He used to reprimand Bastian when he would act like this, but since Mom released my Alpha from his vow, he's backed off. It doesn't make it any less awkward. I'm relieved to see him bothering Anthony for some of the cooked meat while Kade finishes splitting the bones for them.

"I've missed relaxing together," I whisper.

"Mm, me too," Bastian says, continuing to taste me.

"Here, Bass," Kade says, holding out one of the bones. "Haven't you two bonded yet?"

"I hardly think that's any of your business, Kade," I scoff. "Stay in your lane."

Kade chuckles. "What does that even mean? Never mind. Look, it's easy," he continues, popping a chunk of meat into his mouth. "You just put your skin against his, and your bodies will take over. All you have to do is enjoy the ride. You're overthinking, Luna." He kisses my temple. "Get out of your head and let him blow your mind."

By the time Kade stops talking, we're all staring at him. He just says whatever comes to mind and never considers his audience or the consequences. Most of the time, it's funny, but I'm sure Anthony and Daddy are picturing his death. It's probably quite bloody.

"Kade," I say slowly, trying to figure out how to respond. I sigh and furrow my brow. "There are no words."

Kade nods. "I know, Luna," he says. "Just let me know if you need any help."

I may get used to Kade's dismissal of boundaries one day. That's apparently not going to be today. "Why don't you tell us what you found out on your trip, Kade?" I suggest, hoping that changing the subject will snap him back into reality.

"We talked to a few farmers up in the flats," he starts, instantly switching gears. "They were trying corn like they usually grow. It only requires a small amount of water, but they couldn't provide even that. Some of them switched to a kind of bean. Lima, I think they called it. Gross, but it attracted game looking for something green to eat."

Kade digs in his pocket, producing a few flat, light-green beans. I turn them over in my hand while the handsome wolf takes another bite of his meat.

"My grandmother used to put those in her stew," Anthony says, tapping his plate to draw attention to the fact that I've ignored mine. "I have to agree with the idiot. They're disgusting."

Kade brandishes his knife with a raised eyebrow. "You won't have to worry about taste when I cut your tongue out."

"Both of you, stop," I grumble, still studying the beans. "Most beans are high in protein and iron." I'm mainly talking to myself. None of them have cared enough to learn their dietary needs. "Are these all the seeds you got?"

I glance up to find Kade looking at Bastian quizzically. My Alpha has finished his marrow and is participating in his favorite pastime—licking my skin. I barely notice it anymore.

Grabbing Kade's chin, I pull his eyes to mine. "The beans, Kade. Is this all you got?"

Kade narrows his eyes. "I brought your wolves meat," he scoffs. "I can't do everything, Luna. You're gonna have to contribute a little."

I rub my eyes and sigh. "I'm glad we get to have these little talks."

Kade grabs me up in his arms again, squeezing tightly. "Me too, Luna." He kisses my head and cradles me against his chest.

I'll eventually get the information I need from him, but I'm tired, and everything is grinding my nerves. Bastian is still humming, and his rhythmic licking has slowed. It won't be long before he's asleep. I bite into a chunk of meat while watching my father push Anthony's leg with his paw. He'll never be too old to beg for food. I smile when Anthony casually gives him a piece.

These men, along with Chase and Brock, are my trusted advisors. I will be confident enough to move forward without discussing a plan with them one day. But for now, I rely on their counsel. I might wish we were a little faster at getting to final decisions, but I love them as they are.

Kade and I silently pick off the same plate as the Alphas wind down completely. Bastian rolls his body against my leg and falls asleep. Daddy finishes off the rest of Anthony's meat and joins Bastian. He rests his chin over my Alpha's shoulders and wishes me goodnight as his eyes droop. Anthony bows his head and leaves to sleep near the horses, deeper in the cave.

This is my favorite time with Kade. When he lived with us, we would sit on the porch swing for hours at night while I caught up with my traveling units. I spent much of that time pulling his negative emotions and helping him to feel whole again, but we talked a lot.

Kade is wonderfully nonjudgmental. He'll talk in circles, make jokes, and avoid emotions, but he will answer my questions somehow. He arches his back against the wall to stretch his chest as I unbutton the top of his shirt. Kade carries one of two pieces of my mother still in this world. I hold the glass pendant that hangs with Grandpa's medallion against the handprint on his chest. Edith had encased some of my mother's ashes in it for me.

"I don't think she'd have the answers either, Ayls," Kade whispers.

"I try to channel her sometimes," I whisper back. "I pretend we're talking and wait for her to tell me what to do."

"Does she ever come up with anything good?"

"We're going hungry, aren't we?" I grumble quietly.

Kade squeezes me and rests his chin on my head. "Your mom never thought of herself," he starts thoughtfully. "She was cold, tired, and in pain, and all she could think about were the things that would benefit others."

"But she was right, Kade," I whisper, tracing my fingers over her handprint. "Those wolves needed us, and Chase did help you find a new purpose."

"And I'm good at it when you let me do it," Kade scoffs. "So maybe you need to tie yourself to a tree for a few days in the freezing cold."

"Kade," I whine. "Please try to be serious."

He slouches to cradle me more comfortably without disturbing Bastian. "You've lifted your mother into sainthood," Kade starts. "She was smart, resourceful, and beautiful. She was not a saint or an angel. You are all those things and maybe more... if you give yourself a chance."

"She'd probably be mad at you if she heard that," I say, smiling.

Kade sighs with a groan. "Nah," he whispers. "Everybody loves me. She's no different."

"I don't know about love, but she certainly trusted you," I say quietly, recalling that night. "Maybe that's where she started going wrong."

"There's no need to be mean, Ayls," Kade scoffs. "She was right then, and you should probably start trusting her instincts. She put your life in my hands, trusted Bastian to protect you, and knew the pack would be safe with you. Was she wrong?"

Kade is cunning, funny, beautiful, and reliable, but these qualities can't compare to his best attribute. I don't know how he does it, but the man is always right. It's hard to dispute most of what Kade says. Sadly, his need to self-promote typically follows his correct statements, and he disguises his brilliance with an idiotic declaration that he is the king of something or another.

"When you went south a few years ago, what was your impression of the wolves?" I ask, changing the subject.

Kade begins to hum when I place my hand over his mark. It's the only time he hums to my touch. "They're weird, Ayls," he whispers. "They spend more time with the dead than the living." He rubs my arm before resting his hand over mine. "And the cemeteries... What's with the cemeteries?"

"Kade?" I whine, giggling.

"Ayls, you're better off not mixing that voodoo shit into the land of normal," Kade adds, rubbing his chin over my forehead.

Sighing, I roll my eyes. "Noted," I whisper. "But why are they constantly battling the militia and rebels? This has been going on for years. Is the land that rich?"

"The only rich land around here was where Tynan buried his gold," Kade says, chuckling. "And now it's poor."

"That doesn't really answer my question," I grumble.

"It doesn't? What was the question?"

I dig my fingers into my forehead and mash my lips together, aggravated.

"You know? That is one thing you definitely have in common with your mother," Kade remarks. "You two have the same anger issues. You should really do something about that."

Disturbed by my tension, Bastian pushes against my side to roll me toward Kade and lays along my back before returning to sleep. He might not like Kade, but he's used to sharing me with him when he's around. Kade scoots far enough that we can lie down with the wolves beside the fire, and I roll to lay on his chest, throwing my leg over his.

"This will be part of our discussion tomorrow, Kade," I whisper, threading my fingers with his over my mother's mark. "I will be asking for your opinion. It might be nice if you have one that doesn't include the words 'crazy' or 'voodoo.'"

"I'll try, Ayls," Kade whispers before kissing my forehead and heating his body to lull me to sleep.

4

Although it's more of a mountain trickle these days, we fill our canteens and water the horses at the mountain spring before taking the cliff trail in the morning. Daddy leads us with some of my older guards that he plays ball with while Bastian is distracted in the rear.

Kade and I walk behind Anthony's horse. I have given up on getting anything useful out of him. Our conversation started with me asking if the creek at the ranch still had water. I'm sure Kade thought he answered me, but he has somehow turned this into a long discussion about why living in the Kotas would be a dumb idea.

"Honestly, Luna," he says, turning to me. "If you stand on a rock, you look down on all the land. You can see for hundreds of miles." He pauses as if expecting me to respond. "There's nothing. A whole damn land of nothing."

This is my world. I spend most of my time completely dumbfounded by this wolf. He keeps talking, and it only gets worse. Eventually, I will tune him out and consider the possibility that I might be dreaming or perhaps having a nightmare. But ultimately, I'll settle on the fact that I'm insane for always wanting him around. Something about Kade just makes me adore him.

"Just don't ever send me there again," Kade finishes. "And don't be sending my wife. You know I'll follow her, and that's just mean."

"Kade?" I say, looking up at him.

"Yeah?"

"I love you," I say, laughing.

Kade slips his arm around me. "I know you do," he responds.

We move beside Anthony and stand in the horse's shadow as he rests on one of the flat shelves. Kade leans against the cliff wall, pulling me to his chest.

"Would you consider going west for me?" I ask, looking up into his eyes.

"What? Like, beyond the river?" Kade asks, wrinkling his nose. "Oklahoma? Or worse... Nebraska?" He shakes his head with a look of disgust. "Luna, I need mountains or trees, or I could settle for a butte. Shit. Give me a hill, at least."

This is precisely why I love Kade. Anthony turns to stare at him, and I try to maintain a straight face, but I've reached my limit with Kade. "I was thinking further, Kade," I respond, laughing. "I thought you might enjoy scouting the Rockies for us."

"I could enjoy that," he says thoughtfully. "The oldies said the elk up there are quite large." Kade is about to turn this ridiculously awkward, but I can't think of anything to change the subject. "You don't want to send them too, do you?"

"Kade, it would be great if you would stop calling my grandparents 'oldies,'" I snap, rolling my eyes.

"Luna, those two are too much for anyone to handle," Kade complains. "I like to hear myself having sex. I can't with those two. They're like rabbits."

My mouth opens and closes a few times, but I end up just staring. Anthony laughs heartily while Kade maintains his rather serious expression.

"You'd understand what I mean if you bonded," Kade remarks, pulling me along to follow Anthony's horse as he resumes the climb. "You spent all that time convincing Gaine to give me a chance and finally got her to bond with me. Which was fabulous, by the way. All those other women? Terrible. I mean, positively horrible in bed."

And this is where I tune him out. Kade will continue to talk about his sex life like it's public knowledge, and everyone can't wait to hear the juicy details. I'm unsure why he thinks this way, but it seems to be normal for him.

Bringing my wolves' voices forward, I listen to Daddy and Ash as they begin positioning my guards around the field. They've reached the top of the trail well ahead of us because they didn't have horses to rest.

"Coming up behind you, Ayls," Bastian says, pulling me from my thoughts.

I stretch my chest as my mother taught me and turn to kneel to my Alpha. Bastian slides his muzzle over my cheek, humming and breathing me in. Matthew steps beside him and rests his chin on his shoulders.

"Are you guys doing ok?" I ask, scratching Matthew behind his whiskers.

"Besides listening to Bastian talk about you for the past four hours, we're fine," Matthew grumbles.

Hidden by my hair, Bastian laps his tongue over my neck several times. *"I may have missed you,"* he admits. *"Just a little bit, and it wasn't until after the trail's first 10 or 20 feet."*

"I love you too, sweet Alpha," I say, giggling. "Why don't you join us? Daddy already made it to the top."

Rubbing his muzzle over my face, Bastian only hums as an answer. Matthew watches him, a bit forlorn. I've had Gaine look for his mate, but she saw a wolf with fiery red fur, and no one in my pack has red hair. I secretly plan to have her look again during this trip. He's lonely, and I hate making him watch Bastian and me.

I move Bastian's muzzle to my shoulder and grab Matthew. Over the past few years, he's gotten used to my affection as I try to help him. I pull him to my cheek and hold him against me until he relaxes. *"I promise, Matthew, we will figure this out,"* I tell him.

The first time Gaine looked for his mate was at his request. It tore him apart. All known wolves are in our pack now, so it doesn't make sense to us. When I helped Brock, I knew he would eventually be with his mate. *I can't be sure Matthew ever will.*

"Come on, guys," I say, standing up. "I need the healing powers of the flower fields."

Kade walks with us for a while but ends up mounting Grease and leaving me with my guards. Bastian chews on my fingers while I talk to Matthew, pulling his anxiety.

"You seem to be doing well taking over for Nate," I remark, sliding my fingers along his jaw.

"If I don't do well, he yells at me," Matthew says, chuckling. *"I was hoping your grandfather could talk him into retiring."*

"Nate doesn't seem the retiring type," I tell him. "He was raised and trained under Grandpa, who was immortal. There was no 'retirement.'" I twist my face and look down at him. "I don't think that's the answer. Let's talk to Daddy about it later. He spent time with him realigning the guard after Mom died."

"He doesn't actually do anything with the guard anymore," Matthew grumbles. *"He just orders me to do everything."*

"Matthew, he's earned these rights," I remind him. "Nate watched over this pack under my grandfather. He handled my mother's protection guard when she first became the full Luna and helped my father and Chase maintain order among our wolves for years. The junior guard trained under him while Neala and Ash were away.

"Nate was the wolf placed in charge when we went south for my mother's last winter. And do not ever forget that he held our pack together while we all healed during that first year after her death. Nate has earned every bit of the respect he is given. You'd do well not to forget that."

Matthew lowers his head, pulling my hand. *"You're right, Luna,"* he says sadly. *"And he taught me everything I know. I think I might need to come around a little more often. I didn't realize this was bothering me so much."*

"I will always be here for you, Matthew," I promise. "I've never met a red wolf. I bet she's beautiful. We'll devise a plan to find her when the rains return."

Within an hour, we reach the wind-break wall that protects the fields from the high winds that batter the cliff. As Grease turns the corner, Kade halts her. He slides from the saddle and allows her to walk forward without him.

"So, there's something I haven't told you," Kade says, wincing. He takes my arm from Matthew and slows me. "The fields haven't fared well this season."

My breath catches as he guides me around the corner. I clutch my chest, looking over the dead field. Some brown stalks still stand tall, but most have given way to livestock and wildlife trudging through, searching for anything edible.

When everything went wrong and ceased to make sense, this field of flowers would piece my life back together. It turned dark into light, noise into silence, hate into love. It mended my broken heart when I missed my mother so much I couldn't breathe. Yet it lies dead and unrecognizable before me.

Despite Kade's best efforts, I fall to my knees, and Bastian slides his head under my arm. He's been to this field with me many times. I've told him every story I could think of that happened in this field. We had a few full moon gatherings here, and Grandpa told us about the night he died when he and Mom spent time here before she came back to life. I know it will come back with the rain, but I needed it now.

"Ayls, I know you love this field, but we have to go," Bastian urges somberly. *"River will have dinner and a bath ready for you by nightfall. We're already running behind."*

River is Gaine's sister and our historian. A few years ago, Edith was able to take her off the last of her suppressors, but she still struggles with her abilities. I had suggested that she move to the cabin so I could have easier access to her, but Daddy nearly killed me with his eyes, so I'm thankful she declined. He boarded the cabin up shortly after that, ensuring I wouldn't try it again.

"Bass," I whisper with a sigh.

"I know, Ayls," he says quietly. *"I never spent time here with her, but I always felt like she was with us."*

"We were here when you escaped that psychopath," Daddy says, approaching us from the dead field. *"We sat among the flowers while we*

taught you how to show us where you were. She was so happy to be getting you back."

Bastian rubs his muzzle against Daddy's and hooks his neck over his shoulders as my father nuzzles me. This is how Daddy reminds me that my mother always saw beyond what was in front of her. She would call it the 'bigger picture,' but I prefer to consider it something beyond my sight.

"Thank you, Daddy," I whisper. I kiss him behind his whiskers and reach out to Kade, who helps me stand. I hook my arm with his, gesturing toward the ranch. "Let's get going. Maybe we can make it before dark."

My wolves let me walk in silence through the dead fields. My boots crunch over the brown stems, breaking them to sever any hope of recovery. I close my eyes to let Kade and Bastian guide me. I recall the past when my mother was dealing with struggles. After militia attacks, the rebel bands, her illness, while she was helping Bastian... I may not have known what was happening then, but I remember one thing—she closed ranks.

"Brock?" I call out to my companion. I search through my wolves' voices without letting them all in. Brock isn't responding, so I listen for a wolf to help me find him. When I find one, it causes me to groan. *"Myla, I need to talk to Brock."*

"Luna? Is everything ok?" the teenager asks.

"Myla, I don't need assistance. I need to talk to my companion," I grumble. *"Will you please ask him to shift when he can?"*

"Yes, Luna."

I open my eyes to see the sun falling behind the trees to the west. "I think we better ride the rest of the way, Kade," I say, looking up at the wolf.

He whistles for my mare and tosses me into her saddle. Once Kade swings up behind me, I nod to Bastian, and he darts forward, leading the charge toward the ranch.

* * *

It's dark when we arrive. Edith placed a gem ward around the cottage, so anyone wanting to pester Gaine about finding their mate would have to do it in their human form. Since only a few wolves are marked to cross its barrier, most duck inside the guest house to shift while we continue past.

Kade's wife enjoys handing him over to me when I visit but misses him when he stays away. I smile as Gaine meets us in the yard. Her mate slides off my horse and scoops her into his arms. Kade leans her backward, cupping her cheek and kissing her sweetly.

Gaine smiles, tearing her green eyes off Kade to welcome me. "Luna, I thought you'd never get here," she gushes.

I take her outstretched hand and allow her to kiss my cheek. "I'm sure it had a little more to do with Kade than myself, but I appreciate the welcome just the same."

"I did miss him a little," she says, smiling. "Come on, River's been busy, and then we have boiled some water for you."

Edith's dining room is only big enough to accommodate six people, so Daddy made an oversized outside table for them a few years ago. It's set so my Alpha and I would sit at the ends, but since Bastian isn't shifting, Daddy takes his place.

Once all my wolves are ready, we take our seats and enjoy a meal of beef and buffalo. They've prepared potatoes, long beans, and black-eyed peas. River sits beside me between refilling bowls as my wolves empty them. Bastian drapes his head across my lap and hums as I hand him pieces of food from my plate.

Anthony sits opposite River. He knows my wolves tend to check out when there is food in front of them, so he keeps me close and stays vigilant while they enjoy their meal. His start with the pack was rocky, from what I was told. Although they first hated each other, my mother somehow won him over. I've only known this version of Anthony and enjoy his steadfast demeanor.

I reach for his hand, pulling his knuckles to my lips. "Thank you, Anthony," I say, smiling.

"For what, kiddo?" Anthony asks.

"For always being here when they're preoccupied," I answer, gesturing to my feasting guards.

Anthony smiles and pats my hand as he follows my eyes. The drought has been harder on them than most. My guards have been monitoring and assisting all the wolves living around the lake. While the resident wolves are conserving their energy and attempting to balance consumption with use, my guards are more active and eating less. It's not been easy to watch them lose weight.

"We've slaughtered the last of the steers for you to take back to the lake, Luna," River tells me as she sits. "Edith sent us the herd requirements. We still have the two bulls and 45 head of cows for breeding."

"How were the droughts handled in the past?" I ask, passing Bastian another piece of meat. His head has become quite heavy, and he's begun licking my leg between bites.

River frowns. "I'm sifting through the information," she starts. "They grew potatoes and some kind of bean. Kade told me they are growing lima beans up north, but I'm unsure if that's what it was."

"I thought you could see all this?" I usually send word ahead when I need information. I've never been part of the search process, but since River is supposed to simply know about the past, I assumed this would be easy.

"I'm sorry, Luna," River says sadly. "It's not as simple as one might think. The entire time comes up when attempting to find out how an event was handled in the past. I have to search through killings, squabbles, battles, parties, and everything in between."

"It's been exhausting for her," Gaine adds. "A few days ago, I found her laughing hysterically. I thought she was going crazy again. After what she said she saw, I'm still riding the fence." Gaine lifts her eyebrow at her sister.

I furrow my brow, turning back to River. "What did you see?"

"It was nothing, Luna," River responds, glaring at her sister. "The stress is getting to me, and I've not slept well."

Kade scoffs. "A unicorn is not 'nothing.'"

Ash spits his drink across the table, causing Matthew to throw a chunk of potato at him. I'm glad to have something distracting the group's eyes from my confusion. I close my mouth when Bastian taps my arm with his paw. I hadn't even noticed he'd lifted his head from my lap.

"Can I have some room, Love?" Bastian looks down at my chair.

Barely noticing my movements, I slide over to make room for Bastian's paws. "Had you fallen asleep? Were you dreaming?" My eyes shift to River.

The young historian turns a deep shade of red. "I must have been," she spouts. "There's no such thing!"

River is older than me, but her vulnerability makes me see her as a child. I believe it's because she struggled with her gift so much in the beginning. When she sees strange things in her visions, she fears we will assume she's going crazy again. So far, even the weird stories have turned out to be true. *But this one is a little too far-fetched even for me.*

"Perhaps it was a play or something to entertain the children," I offer as a possible explanation, looking toward my father. He's sitting quietly with his fingertips together. His eyes narrow in thought as his index fingers rub over his lips. "Daddy?"

My father takes a sharp breath and shakes his head slightly. "We have enough to worry about without trying to decode mythical mysteries," he says.

"Luna, I will look back through the periods for you," River declares. "I'm sure you can understand how I was a bit unnerved by what I saw."

"I understand, River," I say, patting her hand. "I appreciate anything you can find for us."

"We've started a crop of potatoes and planted most of the lima beans we brought back," Gaine chimes. "We bred the cows early for more milk, but it will be a while before their calves come."

"We can package the rest of the beans for you to plant closer to the lake," Kade adds. "The beans are healthy, but the northerners mainly used them to attract game. They can be poisonous if not cooked correctly, so plant them away from the cabins. I wouldn't want the kids to get into them."

I rub my forehead. The candles flickering on the table make my eyes want to close. "Alright, why don't we resume this in the morning?" I suggest. "It's been a long ride, and I think these full bellies could use a rest."

Bowing her head, River stands and collects my plates. "We have a bath ready for you in the guest house, Luna," she says. "It should be cool enough by now. Please enjoy your evening."

"Thank you," I respond, cupping her cheek. "Daddy? Are you staying with us?"

My father hasn't lost his quizzical expression. "No, baby," he says, forcing a smile. "I'll stand watch. Get some rest."

After a quick goodnight, I let my Alpha lead me to the small guest cottage beside the main house. I lean on the door as I close it and sigh quietly. "Unicorns?" I ask, frowning down at Bastian. "This is not the time for her to flip the crazy switch."

"Let's not jump to conclusions," Bastian says, nudging me toward the bathroom. *"I've seen your father snarl, but that doesn't make him mean."*

Smiling, I let him direct me to the tub. "Oh, he can be mean," I say.

Bastian pushes the bathroom door closed and pulls some towels from the rack to lie on. *"You know what I mean. I could see you being right,"* he says, settling on the floor beside the tub. *"There's a drought, food is running low, the children are hungry... Entertaining them would be a good distraction from their troubles."*

"I suppose you're right," I say, pulling my boots off. I sit on the tub's edge to untie my vest and pause before releasing the last string. "Are you ok? Should you turn around?"

"I like to see you," Bastian says quietly, licking my leg. *"You're beautiful."*

"I don't understand how you're able to see any of me with my aura," I grumble, loosening the last tie. My vest slips down my arms before falling to the floor.

Bastian sits up. *"Your aura does indeed block some of my vision,"* he says, moving closer. *"What I can see looks delicious."* He stares into my eyes as he tilts his head slightly and laps his tongue over my stomach so slowly that time seems to stand still. *"Like warm peach cobbler,"* Bastian says, humming loudly.

My eyes roll closed as my hands find the sides of his face. A whimper escapes while I exhale and seems to urge Bastian on. He moves within my hands to take another taste of me. His tongue is wetter this time, and his saliva runs down my skin. Bastian pushes against me when he wants more, but I'm on the tub's edge now.

"Shit!" I shout as I fall backward into the water. "Bass, seriously?" Laughing, I push my hair from my face.

Bastian slides his nose over my wet skin. *"Stop tasting so damn good,"* he somehow grumbles whimsically. He pushes his towels around to mop the splashed water while I remove my soaked bottoms.

"Thank you for letting me have time with Kade," I say, setting my shorts over the side of the tub. "He offers different views that help me put things into perspective."

"He is unique. I'll give him that," Bastian says, pulling out the last dry towels to lie on. *"Kade is one of our wolves. We have a past, but I will show him the same love I offer the rest. Your wolves are always safe with me."*

"How did I get so lucky?" I ask, smiling as I lay back. The hot water soothes my sore muscles as I slowly rub a rag over my skin. When Bastian doesn't respond, I look over the tub's edge. He leaves his chin on the floor but shifts his eyes to me. "Are you ok?"

"I'm just thinking, Ayls," he says, closing his eyes. *"Your mother talked about the bigger picture a lot. Do you get the sense that something is pushing us?"* He lifts his head to touch his nose to my cheek. *"Like we're supposed to be somewhere else?"*

I slide my hand over his jaw and lie back. "Honestly, I feel like we're being punished." I poke at the water with my fingers. "Or maybe I'm the only one being penalized."

"Sure," Bastian says, chuckling. *"Let's just make this all about you."*

I giggle and lie my head back, closing my eyes. It's easy to turn the blame on myself. I haven't been perfect. I was worthless for nearly a year after my mother's death. My father was hardly any better. Nate and Bastian governed and helped the pack while I figured out how to exist without her.

When I snapped out of my depression, my wolves were ready to welcome me with open arms as if I'd never abandoned them. That's the absolute perfection that is my pack. My wolves choose love over hate and anger every time. *No. There's no way anyone or anything would ever curse them like this.*

* * *

I'm startled awake when I'm lifted from the tub. My nerves announce that I'm in Bastian's arms, cradled against his smooth chest. He heats up to dry my body as he carries me across the cottage to the bedroom. Bastian rubs his cheek over my forehead, and I slide my hand up his neck to his jaw.

My body comes to life when he starts growling. "Easy, Bass," I whisper. "Please just let me feel this."

I open my eyes to see he's stopped beside the bed. Bastian's eyes are closed, and his jaw is clenched, but I detect his hum underneath his growl. My fingertips trace his jaw and finally rest on his lips.

Bastian opens his mouth to exhale, and I can't stop myself. I lift my lips to his and finally take the kiss I've wanted for so long. Bastian's grip on my body threatens to break me, but his mouth is gentle against mine. His tongue licks my lip, causing my mouth to open and let him in.

I push into Bastian, pulling on his neck and letting my nerves respond to him. There's something natural about how his tongue feels sliding over mine. The tension in his grip dissipates as we melt into each other. When Bastian's eyes open, they are gentle and kind. Smiling, he sweetly kisses my lips once more before lowering me to the bed.

"You should sleep," he whispers.

I slide my hand over his cheek. "Stay with me."

"I will never leave you."

Bastian lies on the bed with me and pulls me under his chest as I'd seen my father do so many times with my mother. I rub my face against his skin, breathing him in. His weight is as comforting as it is foreign.

As his body heats, I drift to sleep, knowing tonight has changed everything for us.

5

❧

"Ayls?" Brock's voice wakes me with a jolt at sunrise. *"Is everything alright?"*

Bastian tightens his grip and pulls me further under his chest. His growl builds as I feel him move to glance around the room, looking for the threat. I'm unsure how I ever felt safe before, but this is how I want to sleep for the rest of my life.

Knowing we're not in danger, I slide my hand along Bastian's ribs. I'm upset they aren't filled in with muscle as they should be but excited that I can touch him without his body tensing. I close my eyes as my stomach tightens and rub my lips over his skin, just wanting to feel him against them again.

Realizing there is no threat, Bastian lifts off me and looks down. We have similarly colored sandy hair, but his brown eyes are lighter than mine. A smile plays across his lips as he studies my face. I reach for his shoulders and pull myself up the bed to put us face-to-face. I hadn't noticed how naked we were while we slept, but I am acutely aware of it now.

Bastian lets out a shaky breath as his hand slides up my back, and his fingers tangle into my hair. His lips gently press against mine, and his hum starts, making me smile. I part my lips, waiting for his tongue and matching his movements when he gives it to me.

"Bastian! Annalisa!" Brock shouts. *"Are you ok? Alpha!"*

I push my forehead into Bastian's, attempting to catch my breath. *"Brock, we're fine. Give me a minute."*

"Ayls?" my father grumbles. *"Why is your companion waking me up?"*

"Sorry, Daddy," I apologize, rolling my eyes.

Bastian searches my face for an explanation. I'm positive that this never happened to my mother. My father would have put a stop to it instantly.

"It's Brock," I explain to Bastian. "He called out to Daddy when I didn't answer."

Although it irritates me that he finds this interruption humorous, Bastian's gorgeous smile has no equal. He reaches down for my leg and pulls it over his hip.

"It's not funny," I say, smiling back at him as he chuckles.

"Love, we have all the time in the world," Bastian whispers against my lips. "Don't rush. You only get one first for every experience. I want you to enjoy them. You asked to feel me last night. Let me do this for you."

I lift my chin to kiss him. "Well, I am enjoying your kisses," I say, smiling.

Bastian pulls my thigh off his hip and digs his fingers into my skin. "I'll admit that I want so much more of you." Bastian pauses to claim my lips, making me gasp. He pulls away and licks my top lip. "We don't have anything to do today, right?"

I can see myself getting lost in his kisses, but we can't keep Brock waiting. "Bastian, stop kissing me," I tell him, pulling away. "We need to talk."

"Then you need to put clothes on," Bastian whines, rolling out of my arms to dig in the drawers beside the bed. I shield my face as he throws clothes at me before shifting with a huff.

"Is this you pouting?" I ask, untangling the clothes.

"That depends," Bastian says, folding his legs under his body to appear smaller. *"How adorable do I look?"*

"Quite," I answer, winking.

"Ok, then, yes." He places his chin on my leg as I sit up, pulling a shirt over my head. *"So, what do we need to talk about."*

"I'm going to call Brock back," I tell him.

Bastian tilts his head as he lifts it. *"Why?"*

"We've been talking about my mother and wondering what she would do," I start, stepping into the shorts. "The one thing she always did when facing a problem was close ranks. I've felt like something is missing and realized it's him. I need him here with us."

"Ok, but it's gonna take them a while to get back here," Bastian reminds me.

Brock has been gone for a year. I have felt his absence every day, but eventually, that empty spot in my life began to feel normal. My companion takes over for Bastian when he's away. Brock goes with me if I want to walk around the lake while Bastian's busy. When it's Bastian's turn to stand watch at night, Brock sleeps in my bed, even if Daddy is with me. Things aren't right without my Alpha or companion nearby.

My mother told me that the Luna would claim their companion through a blood bond in the past. I love Brock but couldn't imagine our life together without Rachel. She comforted me after Mom's death, and I will be forever grateful for her.

Bastian rubs the front of his muzzle over my cheek. *"Are you ok?"*

"I think I've missed them more than I thought," I say, opening my arms for him and lying down as Bastian rolls to his side. "I always wondered why Mom was so close to Chase."

"I miss him too, Ayls," Bastian admits, nuzzling my face. *"Let's bring him home."*

"Brock?" I call out, snuggling into my Alpha.

"Is Bastian with you?" Brock asks.

I smile at the sound of his voice. *"Yes, he is,"* I answer. *"We would like you to come home."*

"Ayls, this is bigger than us," Brock says. *"Chase is shifting. You need to get Tarq. This requires his counsel."*

"Alright. He stood watch last night," I tell him. *"Give him time to wake up."*

Bastian pushes my head away from him with his nose. *"All hands? This can't be good."*

* * *

We'll find my father asleep in the house. Besides Kade, he and Bastian are the only wolves marked to pass through the ward's barrier without shifting. However, the ranch is easiest to inspect as it sleeps, so Bastian and I spend the morning checking the grounds. We start behind the house in the quietest area where the creek winds through some trees. The water is barely a stream now and a bit dirty, but at least it's still flowing. We follow it to the cattle fields, where we find Gaine and Kade checking some cows.

"Hey, Luna," Kade says as we approach. He kisses my cheek, and Bastian bumps his nose into Kade's fist. "The cows aren't great, but they're still alive."

"We're just making the rounds, Kade," I say, cupping his cheek. "I love watching you two work together." I take Gaine's hand. "Can you try to look for Matthew's mate again while we're here? I'm pretty worried about him."

"I can try," Gaine replies, cringing. "I couldn't get near him last night. He didn't take the answer well last time."

"We're talking about unicorns now," I scoff. "Red wolves aren't that far off, are they?"

"There is that," Kade chuckles.

"Do you mind if I borrow your husband, Gaine?" I ask, hooking my arm with hers. "Something has happened, and Brock requested a meeting with my father. I'd like Kade to join us."

Gaine furrows her brow. "Sure," she says, nodding. "Let me know if I can help."

I pat her hand and reach for Kade. "You'll need to shift."

"Sure, Luna," Kade says, winking. "Your father kicked us out of bed this morning. I'll meet you there." He kisses my cheek and nods toward the house.

I turn away from them and glance down at my Alpha. "You know, my father really does act like a bratty little kid."

Bastian chuckles, but I'm being serious. Anthony always calls him a spoiled brat, and the more I think about it, the more I realize he's right. When we enter the house, my wolves are spread out around the living room, sleeping on the couch and chairs. Matthew is sprawled out in front of the fireplace with his face jammed into a pillow.

My father would have walked through the house after standing watch and muscled his way into Edith's large bed, pushing Gaine and Kade to the very edge. And that's if he even allowed them to remain on the bed. I open the door to find him entirely stretched out with his face buried under a pile of blankets to block out the light from the open window. No one would have fit on the bed with him splayed out this way.

"Daddy? You know this isn't your bed, right?" I say, trying not to laugh.

My father jumps a bit, startled by our intrusion. *"Annalisa,"* he grumbles, sighing.

I'm pretty sure that was the start of something, but his leg twitches as he falls back asleep. I climb onto the bed and lie against his back. As I slide my hand over his neck, he lifts his head from the blankets and lays his muzzle beside my cheek. Bastian steps onto the bed from the other side, laying his jaw on Daddy's shoulder.

"I'm ok, kids," my father says. *"I'm just tired."* He yawns and licks his lips. *"Did you need me?"*

"The companions requested a full meeting," I whisper.

Daddy sighs. *"That can't be good."*

"Probably not, but I've ordered Brock to come home," I tell him. "I won't order Chase unless you want me to."

"Annalisa, you are the Luna," my father says. *"I'm not in command. I am only here to advise while you need me."*

"He's your companion, Daddy," I snap. "I want my companion with us. If you want yours, I will call him back."

My father only closes his eyes, ending the discussion. My mother's death severed their bond. Chase helped me with him initially, but we realized that his presence made it more painful for Daddy, so he moved out.

I tighten my arms around his neck. "Alright, Daddy," I whisper, dropping the subject. "Why don't you make room? I've asked Kade to join us for this meeting."

After some coaxing, my father moves enough that I can lie down with them on either side of me with their jaws draped over my shoulders. I pull my fingers through their fur, letting them relax. The ranch is one of the few places we visit where they can let their guard down.

As the door is pushed open, I lift my head, and my shining silver wolf joins us. He steps onto the bed, sliding his paws between me and the Alphas until he's looming over me. I smile broadly, trying not to laugh as he crouches to stick his nose in my face. Kade licks my cheeks and rubs his whiskers over my skin, waiting for one of the Alphas to yell at him.

"Seems I might have permission now, Luna," Kade mumbles, sticking his nose to my neck.

"Get off my daughter, Kade," Daddy grumbles.

"Her wolf or not, I will kill you, Kade," Bastian adds, lifting his head to bare his teeth.

I giggle as Kade pokes Bastian with his nose. "Alright," I say, scratching his chin. "Quit playing around, shiny one."

"Say what you want, but this shiny coat is a chick magnet," Kade says. He steps back and waits for me to hook my leg so he can lie down. *"You know you want me."*

"What I know is that you don't want me, so stop acting like you don't love your wife," I respond, lifting my eyebrow.

"Yeah, I kinda do." Kade lies between my legs and drapes his neck over my thigh to poke Daddy. *"Wake up, old man. It's time for you to silently judge me."*

"I already am," Daddy grumbles.

Bastian chuckles. He loves listening to Daddy and Kade bicker.

"Are you all ready to start this?" I ask, shaking my head at them before reaching back out to my companion. *"Brock, we're all here now. What's going on?"*

"Luna, we're moving the pack west," Chase answers before Brock can. *"It'll be slow. We only have a few horses left."*

Daddy lifts his head. *"Hold up. Why are you moving them?"*

"And how?" I add. The southern wolves are comprised mainly of older

generations, as most younger wolves moved north to the lake in search of their mate. They have strong ties to the land and heritage. They are as protective of the dead as they are the living. I've tried to bring them closer several times.

"*The rebel groups in the area have pushed the militia too far,*" Brock tells us. "*The militia poisoned the water sources, killing off the game. Even the food we can find is dying.*"

"*It's made its way into our water,*" Chase continues. "*I met with the elders yesterday, and we all agreed. We're leaving in the morning.*"

"*Give us a minute,*" I tell them. I slide my arms from under the Alphas and sit up to pull my fingers through Kade's fur. I always expect it to feel like metal. "Where can they go?" I ask my advisors.

"*They can't go to Texas, Ayls,*" my father warns. "*Their healer was the wife of the militia's Commander there. He put a bounty on her head for helping us.*"

"Important information," I grumble. "Thank you, Daddy."

"*What about the boat?*" Kade asks. "*Where's the coyote?*"

"*His boat isn't big enough for everyone,*" Bastian says thoughtfully. "*We could send him down to help them cross. It would probably be safer for them on the west bank, right?*"

"*Surprisingly, the kid makes a good point,*" Kade remarks.

"*You're about to wish my judgment would return to being silent,*" Daddy growls.

"Can we please not fight and consider the big picture, guys?" I say, looking at the wolves. "They were short on food but at least had some water. Now they have nothing. If they stay, they will surely die. To the east, they will only find war. The militia would expect them to head straight for us."

"*Bruce said the river was low, but there'd be water for them,*" Bastian adds.

I point in his direction. "Yes, and where there is water, there's game."

"*I can find the coyote and send him to help them,*" Kade adds.

This brings up another point that I need to discuss with the Alphas. "I want to send Kade west," I announce.

"*Fine,*" Daddy says. "*He can go with Davis to help.*"

"No, Daddy," I say, rubbing his ear with my fingers. "I want to send him toward the mountains. Something is telling us to leave. The land doesn't want us here anymore. We need to find where we belong."

Daddy shakes his head. *"Annalisa, your mother is here,"* he says firmly. *"I'm not leaving the lake. I will not leave her."*

"Daddy, she's not here anymore," I say privately to him, leaning to place my forehead on his head. *"Mom is in our hearts. She will be with us wherever we go, and we will join her when our time ends."*

Bastian curls behind me to slip his muzzle under Daddy's neck. This simple act is how the wolves show support. By taking away their sight, they honor the neck's owner with their trust and respect. Since no wolf is stronger than an Alpha, it's the highest honor one could receive from them, and they do not take it lightly.

Kade waits for them to have their moment before he speaks up. *"I can start heading west within the week,"* he says quietly. *"Getting to the river and finding the boat will take a few days. You don't have to decide where I go from there right now."*

I slide my hand over his head and cup his jaw. Kade is resourceful and cunning. He has connections that reach much further than I have ever tried. Even next to these two powerful Alphas, Kade is the proudest wolf I have ever met. He was not used to showing an Alpha respect when he came to live with me. His personal growth is awe-inspiring.

"Thank you, sweet wolf," I whisper.

Kade licks his lips, watching Bastian rub muzzles with Daddy. He nudges his nose toward them, but Daddy lifts his lips. Kade's ambition often rears its ugly head at the wrong time. He is desperate to connect with the Alphas so that he won't need my protection from them.

I rub the Alphas' chins and push on Kade until he backs off the bed. *"Let's give them a moment, Kade. I want to check on your wife's progress."*

Kade slips his muzzle into my hand as I close the bedroom door. Some days are more challenging, and I've pushed my father again to discuss leaving the lake. He'll fall asleep cuddled up with Bastian, and feeling my mother's presence, he'll calm down.

The living room is empty when we walk through it. I allow Kade to pull me outside and guide me around the property, looking for his wife while I speak to my companion. Brock attempts to tell me I'm selfish for wanting him to return to me, but he drops it when I suggest he leave Rachel to help Chase.

We find Gaine by the creek behind the house. She and her sister sit with Matthew as he lies in the grass. I stop Kade to watch them for a moment. Gaine is looking at Matthew curiously while her sister rambles quietly. Matthew is stretched out with his arm over his eyes.

I pull Kade back with me and kneel when Gaine looks up and puts her finger to her lips. We stay out of sight while she continues to listen to her sister. Kade relaxes with me and puts his jaw on my shoulder.

"You need to stop pushing them, Kade," I say, leaving my eyes on his wife.

Kade leans against me until he knocks me over. *"Then I'll push on you,"* he says, chuckling.

I put my arm out for him. *"I'm being serious. Some days, it's like she just died yesterday. On other days, it's a distant memory. I loved her, but she was everything to my father. Bastian agreed to forgive you with the pack judgment, but my father never agreed to forgive you for leaving her there."*

Kade sighs, tucking his nose into my neck. The tall, dry grass sways quietly around us, shielding us from the world. Kade would have made an excellent stand-in for my companion if I could ever get him to stay still for long enough.

"Kade, have you ever thought about having kids?" I ask, hoping to pull him out of his head.

"I think I screwed enough kids up, Ayls," Kade scoffs. *"That woman doesn't deserve to watch that."*

"You have so much to offer another generation," I say. *"Don't shut the door on something Gaine should be allowed to experience because of fear."*

"I'm not afraid of anything," Kade grumbles.

I turn to rest my cheek against his muzzle, raising my eyebrow. *"Don't lie to me."*

"Ayls, I just figured out how to be something other than a womanizing asshole," Kade says, nuzzling my cheek.

"Oh, you did? When do I get to experience that?" I giggle, rolling into him.

Kade tucks his claws away from my skin. *"I don't know. Maybe tomorrow."*

"I love you, Kade," I say, giggling.

"Everybody loves me, baby," he says, tucking his head under my chin.

I'm unsure how long we lie there, but I'm deep in thought when something brushes against my head. Startled, I look up to find my Alpha. *"Hi, Love,"* I say, smiling.

"Tarq's asleep. I left him with Anthony," Bastian says, licking my cheek. He pokes Kade with his nose as he lies down with us. *"What's going on with him?"*

"He's just wishing he were you," I say, smiling.

Kade huffs. *"Woman, stop your lies."*

I giggle, scratching his shoulder. *"I think it's time for us to find out what Gaine has learned."*

* * *

After Gaine reported still only seeing a red wolf, Matthew stomped off. Generally, she sees their human forms when she looks for mates, but Matthew's mate is only in wolf form and bright red with dark tips.

"Maybe she's a blonde but somehow dyes her fur red?" Gaines suggests as we walk around the brown grazing fields. "Luna, there's never been a red wolf."

Sighing, I look out over the dried stalks. Bastian and Kade are horsing around in the distance. I hook my arm with Gaine's. "There's never been a silver wolf either," I say, smiling. "Yet, you married one. We might not understand what is before us, but that doesn't mean it isn't there."

"What about the unicorn?" Gaine says, scowling. "She's adamant about seeing it. She tries to look around it, but it rears up at her. Hooves strike. It's blocking everything."

"My mother accomplished a lot without a historian," I grumble. "We should be able to do this."

"I'm sure we'll figure it out," she whispers. "I'll keep working with River."

"Yeah," I say slowly. "About that." I cringe slightly and look back at the wolves. *"Guys, come here."* I wait for the wolves to join us before speaking to all of them. "I'm sending you two west," I announce. "I need you to scout toward the mountains for us. And I need you to do it quietly. My father might not be ready to leave the lake, but I need to know if it's an option."

Kade nods and rubs his muzzle over his wife's hip.

"My grandparents will go with you to the river," I add to Kade's dismay. "While you find the barge, they can help you pick the best route since they've been to the mountains before." I kneel to my silver wolf. "Take this opportunity to learn, Kade. Grandpa Bruce healed Bastian. He can help you."

* * *

We tour the grounds for the rest of the afternoon. Gaine chooses a few wolves to stay at the ranch while they are gone, and I send for Grandma. We pick the basin cave to rendezvous for the full moon gathering before they head west. I smile at how easily things are piecing together.

I sit on the fence at sunset, watching my wolves. Gaine places food on the long table, and everyone grabs bites between playing around and roughhousing. My father and Anthony are still missing, but I hadn't expected them tonight. Anthony will have put my father back together by morning.

"He is a beautiful man, isn't he?" Gaine asks, eyeing Kade as she hands me a plate.

I smile crookedly. "What's worse is he knows it," I say, giggling.

Gaine shakes her head. "You and Bastian seem to be doing better. Are you finding your way?"

"We're trying," I tell her with a smile. I pop a steak strip into my mouth as I watch Bastian share a buffalo hip with a few guards. "I heard you had an exciting hunt while you were gone. Kade was quite impressed."

Gaine turns a slight shade of pink. "Luna, I was hungry," she says, giggling.

"Well, we appreciate the meat," I say, nodding toward my Alpha. "Bastian's been dropping weight even with how careful I am with his diet."

"You might need to relax a little bit, Luna," Gaine suggests, leaning against the fence beside me. She gestures to our group. "You're trying to control so much that you have no time to enjoy anything. Look at them, playing and having fun. See how light they are?"

I follow her gaze and look closely at our group. The wolves are working together on the hip and happily talking about hunts and different cuts of meat. Those in human form are laughing and playing. When Bastian looks up at me, I clearly see the joy in his expression, and my chest instantly aches.

My hand clutches my shirt as I slip off the fence and pass my plate to Gaine. I barely hear her tell me goodnight as I step toward my Alpha. The closer I get to him, the more alive my body becomes. My ache for him spreads until it consumes me.

I reach out as Bastian approaches, melting me in his gaze. "Shift," I whisper.

Shifting into my arms, Bastian lifts me to his hips and gives me easy access to his lips. My ache begins to ease as his tongue massages mine. He marches across the yard to the cottage and pauses only to slam the door shut, closing us away from my guards. I claw at my shirt, yanking it over my head as we cross the living room.

Bastian lays me on the bed and slides his hand down my leg to push my boot off. His tongue laps over my neck before moving to my jaw. My Alpha's teeth glide across my skin until he nips at my lips. "Are you sure about this?"

"Bass, I've been trying to rule over everything in our lives," I whisper, tracing my fingers over his face. "When I stop, my body tells me it wants you. I'm listening now."

Bastian rubs his mouth over my stomach as he lifts off me to remove my shorts with my other boot. He slowly crawls over me, blowing on my skin and causing me to shiver. When Bastian begins to shake, I pull him back to my mouth, and his muscles' tension eases as he settles into our kisses.

Once he's relaxed, Bastian introduces his body to mine. At first, my nerves turn off as something pops painfully inside me. I gasp, wincing, but Bastian stops and gives me a moment to catch my breath. He's gentle when he starts moving again, and my nerves return to life, asking for more of him.

I didn't know what perfection was until I met Bastian. He continues to prove that he is my everything every day. His touch remains sweet and gentle throughout the night. After each exploding sensation, Bastian allows me to rest and slide my hands over his body while he tucks into my neck to enjoy my touch.

I sigh as we end the night with him rolling protectively over me. His chest blocks the light from the nearly full moon filtering through the glass doors. Although it's impossible to describe, Bastian's scent grounds me when I feel like I'm spiraling. Tonight, it eases my soul, sending me into a peaceful slumber.

6

⚬∾⚬

In the morning, we travel the long way through the fields instead of using the cliff trail. I ride quietly beside River, watching my father and Anthony. They were talking about some of their memories of Mom before we left. It's part of the process Anthony uses to help my father, and I would love to hear them, but I'm stuck listening to the insane ramblings of my broken historian.

River refuses to shift because her father told her that the information is easier to regulate in her human form. Since she struggles with her gift in general, the thought of it being out of control scares her. I wish she'd shift so I could filter her voice into the background with the rest of my wolves.

"It's chestnut," she says, continuing to drone on about the mystical unicorn she swears she sees. "It's beautiful, but I think it's hurt."

My eyes drift to my gorgeous wolf as he walks beside Grease's shoulder. Crossing my arms over my saddle horn, I study how his fur moves with each step. His shoulders roll under his skin, making the fur ripple in waves. Bastian's coloring is sandy, like my father's, but he has dark stripes of shorter hair. His ears keep flicking back to me, and I smile when he trips, signaling he's just as distracted.

"I smell pie," River says, reminding me she's there.

"What?" I scoff, annoyed.

River smiles. "The unicorn," she replies. "It smells like a sweet pie."

I love my wolves, but I've never been good at handling her craziness. "That's just great," I grumble.

I drop from Grease's back and step beside Bastian, slipping my fingers through his fur. He rubs his muzzle over my hip before licking my thigh. I smile as his hum starts. Bastian steps closer, trying to slide his jaw into my hand, but steps on my foot, tripping me.

Shrieking, I fall forward, tumbling over his shoulders and rolling onto my back. Bastian chuckles and lies on top of me. He rubs his muzzle over my face, sneaking a taste of my neck.

"I want to put my mouth all over you," Bastian says whimsically. His growl mixes with his hum as his words cause a wave of fire throughout my body. *"I want to rub my hands over your skin and ensure it never forgets my touch."*

Bastian's rubbing his whiskers over my jaw, but I feel a muzzle against my forehead. *"Mm, Luna. You smell hot,"* Kade says.

I giggle, grabbing Bastian's face as he lifts it to snarl at Kade. "When my mother was teaching me how to handle my wolves correctly, my grandparents had just bonded," I tell them. Bastian eases the pressure he's putting on my hands. "I remember them ignoring my mother and her lesson so they could cuddle. She was so annoyed." I chuckle, scratching Bastian's chin. "Now I understand."

"Kade, leave them alone," Gaine barks, standing over us. "Or shall I remind you that I nearly starved to death when we bonded?"

"Don't believe a word out of her mouth," Kade says. *"I brought her food."* He licks my forehead. *"She liked it when I cleaned it off her."*

I stare at the silver wolf looming over me for a moment. "Kade..." I start, trying desperately not to laugh. "That's not..." I shake my head. There are no words for this man right now.

"You're the one that wants him around," Bastian reminds me.

"And yet, you're all I can think about," I say, smiling.

"I'm distracted too, but it's not safe, Annalisa." I'm unsure why my Alpha is suddenly concerned. There hasn't been an attempt on my life within our boundaries for so long that I no longer carry my mother's bow.

"Kade! Bastian!" My wolves back up as my father storms toward us. "Get off my daughter!" He reaches for my hand. "Get your ass back on that horse. We don't have time for this." He throws me into the saddle and jumps up behind me. "Let's go, Bass."

Bastian darts forward, taking Grease with him. I look around my father to watch the rest of the group grow smaller as we leave them behind. Daddy doesn't run them hard but keeps Bastian moving fast enough that he's panting by the time we slow and needs to stick to the shade to cool off. He pats my leg and swings down from Grease.

"Was that really necessary, Daddy?" I ask, joining him. I kneel to Bastian and run my hands over his shoulders. "Are you ok?"

Daddy pulls me up by my arm. "He's fine, baby," he says. "Come on. Let's talk." He waits for Bastian to set up in my hand before walking toward the cave. "Did you ever hear about the second time your mother and Uncle Miles spent time together?"

"I don't know," I snap, staring at my Alpha.

"They shared a love that even I don't understand, but that's not how they started out." Daddy sighs, gathering himself for a moment. "He tried to kill her the first time, but the second encounter was about a week after we bonded. I couldn't get your mother out of my head. My favorite thing was putting her in my mouth."

"Ok, Daddy," I say, wrinkling my nose. "I'm not... Just no, Daddy."

"Annalisa, shut up and learn," my father scoffs, making Bastian chuckle. "I led your mother to the trees behind Edith's house. I teased her. I circled her. And then I convinced her to give me the necklace that allowed me to shift despite the curse. I pinned her to the tree."

I click my tongue and cringe. "Daddy, I don't want to hear this."

"I'll admit I'm a little uncomfortable now," Bastian says, still chuckling.

"It was only a few minutes later that your mother was slapping me to stop because your Uncle Miles was behind me," Daddy continues, ignoring me. "No need to picture us. Think about that area of trees by the creek behind Edith's house. Anything standing out?"

I'm struggling to get past my mother and father engaged in things out in the open, but the moment I do, my mind wonders what that might be like with my Alpha. My father raises his eyebrow at me. *Shit. What was the question?*

"That's an isolated grove," Bastian says, saving me. *"There's no way he'd have been able to sneak up on them."*

I look at my father quizzically. "He was there the whole time?"

"Exactly," Daddy says, nodding. "We were so distracted that neither of us noticed him." He shifts his eyes between me and Bastian. "Thankfully, he wasn't there to kill her, but it would've been easy if he were. Danger can come from anyone, anywhere."

"I'm sorry, Daddy," I whisper.

"Baby, this isn't a lesson for you." My father pulls me down to kneel before Bastian. My Alpha tucks his chin to his chest, made nervous by my father's display. "While you were too distracted to listen to River's babbling, she told you something significant that even I didn't know." He cups Bastian's chin and guides his nose to my cheek. "Do you notice anything different?"

Bastian sniffs me gently but then pushes his nose against me, sliding it down my neck. Daddy chuckles when his hum kicks on. He puts his finger to his lips as my brow furrows.

Bastian jams his nose into the base of my neck and slides his tongue over my skin, slowly taking a taste. *"What is that?"* Bastian asks whimsically, falling limply against me.

"Daddy?"

"I'm pretty sure that's maple syrup," my father says.

"I don't understand," I spout, sitting back on my heels. "My scent is changing?"

Daddy pulls Bastian's nose away from me and waits for his eyes to open. "Sort of," he tells us. "River told you that the Luna becomes pregnant when she bonds." He cups my cheek. "You are pregnant, my child. Your life is extremely precious right now. You can't afford to be distracted."

I look down at my stomach. I always knew I would bring the next Luna into this world, but I imagined it would be later in life. Maybe even at a more convenient time. Perhaps I would've waited to bond with Bastian had I known. But his detection of a different scent says it's too late to take it back now. She's coming, and we need to protect her.

I rub my stomach as Bastian touches his nose to my cheek. "I'm going to name her Boulder," I whisper.

"I hate you," my father grumbles, pulling me to my feet.

I burst out laughing, clinging onto his arm. "No, you don't, Daddy!"

"Well, I love you a little less right now," he says, looking at me from the corner of his eye. "Let's get going. I wanna have a good seat when you tell your grandfather he's old as hell."

* * *

Daddy trades places with Bastian so we can spend time together while he guides Grease to the bluff behind the cave. Bastian protectively wraps his arms around me, holding me against his chest. He had one of the worst childhoods I have ever heard. I'm unsure what he's thinking, but I know he will kill anyone threatening to make this baby even frown.

After Daddy takes Grease into the cave, Bastian and I wander to the bluff alone. The cliff wall lines one side, and the trees create a natural barrier around the rest, except the wide trail leading back to the cave. The mountain spring still weakly trickles along the trees. We sit in the center of the clearing, facing the creek bed.

"You're not actually going to name my kid 'Boulder,' are you?" Bastian asks.

"No, Bass," I say, giggling. "It's a joke. Ash told me about Daddy's conversation with Mom regarding the names I chose for the horses."

I rub my fingers over Grandpa's medallion as the sun sets. Daddy wants tonight to be family only, so he tells my guards to stay back. Kade's complaints make me smile as he attempts to declare his importance. I kiss my mother's ashes before pulling the necklace off and setting it before us.

"I wish I could talk to her," I whisper.

"She hears you," Bastian answers, leaning back on his hands so I can recline against him. "Brock said they left this morning. Chase is going with the pack to the river, but Brock and Rachel are coming straight home."

"I should've been paying attention," I mumble. "I was so busy trying to ignore River." I consider what I had heard her say. "Bass, did you ever hear any stories about unicorns?"

Bastian frowns when I look up at him. "I think I read a few books when I was a kid. Why?"

"They were always white, weren't they?" I ask, rubbing my fingers over his arms.

"Yeah, I think so," he says quietly. "What's this about?"

"River said it was a chestnut," I tell him.

"I've always loved the red horses," Grandpa comments, appearing before me.

Smiling, I hold my arms out. "Come here, Grandpa."

He steps into my arms and lets me bury my face in his thick black fur. As a kid, I sat for hours talking to him but never truly appreciated his stunning presence. Grandpa was a beautiful man too. He had black hair and soft stubble the only time I saw his human form.

"Why are we talking about horses?" he asks, backing away to face me.

I lift my eyebrow. "Unicorns, actually."

"Ok," Grandpa says slowly. *"I'm gonna need some context, sweetheart."*

"It's nothing, Grandpa. Only fairy stories."

"I'm going to leave you with Dax, Love," Bastian says, kissing my cheek. "I'll get your father and shift."

Grandpa watches him leave before putting his nose to me and taking a deep breath. *"When did that happen?"*

"Grandpa, I am not discussing my sex life with you," I scoff.

"Ok, child. Gross," he replies, pushing me so I'll lie back. He crawls beside me and rests his chin on my shoulder. *"I've been gone for over a month. That long? A few weeks? You know your mother will want to know."*

I lay my cheek over his muzzle. "Last night."

"Oh," Grandpa says in realization. *"Now I understand."*

I giggle and roll to wrap my arms around him. "I love you, Grandpa."

My grandfather falls silent until Daddy and Bastian join us. We discuss the drought and possible locations that game might hide until the rains return. Daddy tells him about the wolves in the south and the poisoned waters.

"If they figure out how well it worked, they'll be trying it up here," Grandpa cautions us. *"You've made a lot of enemies by carving this land into wolf territory. They won't hesitate to destroy it to end your reign."*

I sigh, leaning into Bastian and reaching for Grandpa's paw. "Will we never have peace?"

"Your mother used to ask me that all the time," Grandpa says. *"I always hoped she'd see it eventually."* He lifts his head to nuzzle my cheek. *"I'll talk to your father. I never wanted to leave the lake either, but if it doesn't rain soon, your wolves won't make it through the winter."*

Grandpa lifts his paw from my hand and takes Daddy to talk closer to the water. I let their voices filter into the background to give my father privacy. Bastian and I are exhausted, so we appreciate the chance to lie together quietly. I'd prefer the protection of the cave, but I won't leave Grandpa.

Bastian lifts his front leg, allowing me to curl against his gut and bury my face into his chest. I used to lie like this all the time. I'm unsure why I stopped, but I'm glad to have it back. I pull my fingers through Bastian's fur, wondering if there would be a better way to raise our daughter and her Alpha.

Bastian calls Kade and Gaine to us as he lets his body heat up. I feel one of them lie against my back before I drift to sleep.

* * *

We haven't even seen the hint of a fog a week later. The lake is nothing more than a puddle of dead fish. We planted the lima beans in shady areas beside the lake, but only some have sprouted so far, and they are barely more than a few sad-looking leaves. Some of the children have resorted to hunting rats and bugs. Daddy says it's the hormones, but I spend more time crying than functioning as I listen to them ask if there will be any food soon.

Matthew has taken Bastian's place in the watch rotation as we spend most of our time reaching out to distant elders, looking for solutions.

They are all moving, either coming to the lake or meeting Davis at the river. Daddy was angry, but I told him about sending Kade and Gaine to scout the mountains. I talk to them every night, but they have yet to reach land that isn't barren or overcrowded with humans.

"I'll repeat myself—I wish we had a useful historian," Bastian grumbles. *"Have you ever wondered if she'd be functional if she'd just shift?"*

"Actually, I have," I answer. *"But I don't think we'll ever find out."* I relax on the porch swing, where I spend my evenings. Daddy made it long enough so Bastian could lie on it beside me. It's the same swing that Kade and I spent hours in when he lived here. *"I understand why Daddy doesn't want to leave. We have a lot of memories here. I like that I can look anywhere and see my mother, or Kade, or even you."*

"You'll always see me," Bastian says. *"Just open your eyes. I will always be with you."*

"Here, sweetheart," Edith says, pulling me out of my head and handing me a bowl of chicken. My stomach had started causing me issues a few days ago, and she put me on a boiled chicken diet. She pulls a stool beside the swing and sits, looking concerned. "Listen, guys, two of you need this diet to grow your little people. I'm hatching half the eggs, but we will run out. Especially without water."

Bastian's eyes rock from Edith to me before he bumps his nose against my belly. He's been incredibly aware of this baby from the moment we learned about it. My Alpha bumps my stomach randomly throughout the day and typically sleeps with his head draped over it while he hums. He doesn't want to shift. He says he's stronger as a wolf and wants to know we're safe. Edith said Daddy was the same way and that he'd relax after a while.

"How long do we have?" I ask, rubbing Bastian's jaw.

Edith shakes her head. "Two weeks, maybe. We can't make bread. Annalisa..." She sighs, and the concern written on her face says more than any words could.

Nodding, I take a deep breath. "We're out of time."

"We all love it here, but there's something in the air," she says, squinting. "Can you feel it? Sort of like we don't belong here?"

"Edith, I feel a lot of things," I tell her, sighing. "I feel the pressure to take care of this pack crushing me right now. We're losing this battle against an enemy we can't fight." I rub my eyes and nearly drop the bowl of chicken.

Bastian stops it from falling with his nose, and Edith takes it from my lap.

"You need to eat," she tells me. "It's your night with Trish. Jinx is on watch, and I want to spend time with my husband."

"Thank you," I whisper, knowing she's trying to help. "Give us a few more days, but you may want to start packing. I don't see our situation improving any time soon."

I watch as she walks down the porch steps and disappears around the stalls. Pointing my arrow at my enemy and letting it loose would be much easier. I could order my guards to cut it down and be done with it. Instead, they're conserving energy and staying cool because this enemy will kill them if they work too hard.

"Ayls, are you ok?" Bastian asks.

I lower my hands from my face and give him a weak smile. "I want to be," I say, taking the bowl from Edith's stool. "Does that count?"

"Not normally, but today, we'll make an exception." Bastian bumps the bowl with his nose, urging me to eat. *"Brock will be home tomorrow. Let's just look forward to that tonight."*

"I love you," I say, offering him some chicken.

"You heard Edith," Bastian grumbles, poking my belly. *"Feed my baby, please."*

I pop a chicken strip in my mouth, smiling. "Yes, my Alpha."

Bastian slides his tongue over my stomach, distracting me from my meal. His growl starts low but quickly builds as I heat up. I close my eyes and allow my body to appreciate Bastian's attention. For the past few nights, he's driven me to the brink of insanity by rubbing his whiskers over my skin. The swing jolts, and my nerves painfully push against the underside of my skin when hands slide up my thighs.

I open my eyes as Bastian lifts me by my legs and claims my lips, making me gasp. I was fooling myself, thinking I would be fine with him staying a wolf. Feeling my nerves relish his touch reminds me of the magic from our first night. I had only dreamed of what a bond would feel like. Nothing compares.

Bastian carries me into the house and kicks the door closed behind us. My body takes over, fueled by the need he creates, and my fingers dig into his neck. I part my lips to release a whimper, and Bastian pushes past them to slide his tongue over mine. He holds me against the wall beside the stairs.

I pull my shirt over my head, and Bastian sets me down to push my shorts to the floor. To be honest, one of my favorite things about loving a wolf is that I don't need to waste time removing his clothes. Bastian wraps my legs around his waist and waits for me to latch back onto his lips before pushing himself into me.

My Alpha was sweet to me during our first night together. He feels more needy tonight but stays gentle as he takes what I give. Bastian enjoys a taste of my skin and tongue while moving slowly enough that I can appreciate his attention. As my deepest nerves reach out, begging to feel his touch, my Alpha rolls my hips to give them what they want.

We call out to each other when my nerves explode in a joyous celebration until Bastian falls against me, pinning me to the wall with his body. I lay my cheek against his shoulder, sliding my fingers over his skin and listening to his hum. As Bastian begins to recover, his growl slowly builds, and he turns to grab my neck with his teeth.

A knock on the door makes us jump. "Luna?" Trish calls from the porch. "Ayls?"

Normally, Jinx will shift before Trish leaves the house to tell me she's on her way. I lean my head against the wall with a sigh, but Bastian doesn't stop his attack.

His growl deepens. "I'm not done with you." Bastian pulls me from the wall, climbs the stairs, and closes us in the bedroom. "She'll be fine," he says, laying me on the bed. "She can eat your chicken."

I giggle as he pushes into me and takes me away with a vision of rolling waves.

* * *

The sun has set by the time I wander downstairs to collect Trish. As Luna, having a best friend is not a good idea. They would only be another weapon to use against me. But Trish and I were close as children, and I could never abandon her.

I find my friend lying on my swing, watching the lightning bugs in the yard. "Thanks for the chicken," Trish says with a smile.

I sit beside her. "I'm sorry about the wait," I say. "Jinx normally tells me when you're on your way."

"He did," she says, rubbing her belly. "He made me wait for him to shift back so he could tell me he didn't reach you."

"Huh," I say, frowning. "I guess I was distracted."

Trish giggles. "It sounded distracting."

"Ok," I groan, moving so Bastian can join us. "I'd like you to see Doc Will tomorrow, Trish."

Bastian puts his arm around me and pushes the swing to rock us. "You should let him check you too," he suggests. "Edith may have gone through this with Luna, but it would make me feel better if Doc checked you, Ayls."

"Then we'll all go," I say, leaning into him. "He's been asking to see me for a few days anyway. There's just been so much going on."

"I heard Brock is returning to the lake," Trish says, smiling. "You must be excited."

I glance up at Bastian before nodding at Trish with a smile. "We've missed him and will be happy to have them both home," I say, squeezing her hand. "Perhaps we should get to bed so tomorrow will hurry along."

I pull them both to their feet, and Bastian stays behind to lock the house while I help Trish up the stairs to the bedroom. Her pregnancy exhausts her, and simple motions have become more of an exercise program. I fear a trip west would be a struggle for her. *Will I be in the same situation?* I rub my stomach.

"*I won't let anything happen to either of you,*" Bastian says from behind me.

I turn to see my beautiful wolf sitting in the doorway. Trish holds my hand as she lowers to the bed and rolls to lay her head on a pillow. I pull her sandals off and throw a sheet over her legs.

"*We need to talk to Doc about this trip,*" I tell Bastian. I crawl onto the bed beside Trish. "*We waited to see if the rains would return. Kade's idea with the plants might have helped, but it came a little too late, and we'll die waiting for those plants to grow.*"

"*I want to know how to ensure Boulder will survive,*" Bastian says, making me giggle. "*Stop laughing. I don't care what you call her. She's mine, and I want her.*"

Bastian steps onto the bed and lies down, facing me. He's staring at me as if he means business. I'm supposed to take him seriously. But I am Bastian's Luna and know him very well.

"*I might share her with you sometimes,*" I grumble, narrowing my eyes.

Bastian slides his slobbery tongue over my face.

"*I hate that Daddy taught you that,*" I say, scowling.

"*I am being serious, though,*" Bastian says earnestly. "*We've watched how hard this has been for Trish, and Edith says it's exactly how it was for your mother. What if your pregnancy is as difficult? I'll struggle to feed you, and it will only make you sick.*"

Bastian's fears are valid. Edith has been watching over me and caught all the signs before they became problematic, so I haven't experienced any difficult symptoms. Once we no longer have access to the only food I've been able to eat, our situation could quickly turn dire.

"*Ok, Love,*" I say, sliding my hand over his muzzle. "*I fear we have some difficult days ahead of us. Let's sleep and worry about the future tomorrow.*"

Bastian nuzzles my cheek before curling around to rest his jaw on my stomach. My mother told us we couldn't be selfish, but he's right. We must protect the next Luna by ensuring I'm healthy and fed.

What was it that my mother said? Oh, yeah. "This is a clear example of finding a mate and bonding at a very inappropriate time."

7

It's a quiet journey to the small medical office in the morning. Trish and I ride in Grease's light cart while Bastian and Jinx lead her down the well-worn road. I frown, listening to the wolves talk about playing ball. I put a stop to all games two weeks into the drought. I had promised it would only be temporary and that they would be able to play soon. Daddy told me I'd regret promising things outside my control.

From the beginning of this drought, I have felt unsettled. It's close to when I walk into an empty cave, feeling sure someone is watching me. Whatever it is, it isn't trying to kill me, but it does want me to leave. The lake has been our home my whole life. I don't know how to even imagine life anywhere else.

We emerge from the woods and stop before the little clinic. Bastian shifts to help us down while Jinx runs inside to shift in private. He holds me to his body as I drop from the wagon and kisses my lips once my feet safely touch the ground. My Alpha reaches for Trish, but she just smiles, shaking her head.

"Girl, I have no idea how you held out as long as you did," she says, giggling. Her eyes trail over Bastian's body. Edith's tea cannot heal scar tissue, so he wears all the marks of his past, but he is absolutely stunning. "Jinx is beautiful. But Bastian, you are something next level."

My Alpha chuckles. "Come on, woman," he says, raising his eyebrow. "If you take long enough, you'll have that kid right here."

"At least the doctor will be close," I say, laughing.

75

Bastian escorts us inside and leaves to get clothes from the back room when Doc Will gives him a disapproving look. He gives Daddy the same look, but my father intentionally irritates him and ignores the doctor's glares. Bastian's back is horribly scarred from his past, but I hardly notice as I watch him walk away.

"Where did he get all those scars?" Trish asks, stepping onto a stool to reach the exam table.

Sighing, I turn back to her with a small smile. "That's his story," I tell her. "Not mine." I quietly hold Trish's hand while Doc checks her heart and lungs. He gestures for her to lie down, but I stop him. "Let's wait for Jinx, please."

"Sure," Will says. "I had hoped to see you. I seem to have gone through all the blood I had."

Doc Will has been testing Lunas' blood for years. When my mother's family line was created, the old notebook stated, "Her blood shall heal them all." Doc is convinced that our blood is supposed to heal something, but it hasn't cured anything so far.

"You just took some before my mother's memorial," I say, raising my eyebrow.

"I know. I'm sorry, Luna," Doc says. "I've tried to be careful during this drought, but I seem to keep going through it faster."

"No," Bastian says, rejoining us. "She's carrying my child. You're done taking her blood."

"I heard Tarq truly emerged as an Alpha when he learned of his child," Doc says, cupping my cheek with a smile. "Congratulations, Luna."

"I don't understand why everyone is congratulating me," I huff. "All I did was have sex."

Trish laughs as she lies down, holding Jinx's hand. "That's the best friend I remember."

"I agree with her," Jinx says. "This kid has been a pain in the ass from the start. You got sick after just a few days."

I let them talk among themselves as Doc progresses with Trish's exam. I hadn't paid much attention to when Trish started getting sick. She was too ill to join us for a full moon gathering, and I sent Edith to check on her. Once her diet was changed, she joined us like nothing had happened. But since our pregnancies are not typical, the fact that they are so similar is unnerving.

Bastian notices that I've tuned them out and pulls me aside with a quizzical look. "What's going on? Did something happen?"

Taking a sharp breath, I shake my head. "No, Love," I say, squinting in thought. "I was just thinking about something. River is staying with Edith, right?"

Bastian nods.

"We need to see her when we're done here," I tell him, looking beyond him as Doc turns in our direction. "Looks like it might be our turn, though." I help Trish off the table and kiss her cheek. "Can you two wait outside for us? I'd like to talk privately with Doc."

Since we're so close, Trish knows better than to question me. She nods and pulls Jinx through the clinic to the front porch. Doc drags a chair next to the table as Bastian helps me into the space Trish had vacated.

"You're not here for a check-up, are you?" Doc observes, leaning back in his chair.

"You can look me over if you'd like, Doc," I say, waving my hand dismissively. "But I need your counsel, and I want this to stay quiet until I'm ready to announce it to the pack."

Doc Will scratches his graying beard. "Yeah, alright," he responds. That is the standard grumbly wolf response to everything they don't want to agree to but feel they have no choice. Doc's not a wolf, but he's heard my father say it so much that it's become part of his regular vocabulary. "How far along are you?"

"Ten days," Bastian answers. "Can you make sure my daughter's ok?"

Doc furrows his brow. "Bastian, I'm sorry, but your child is little more than a thought right now," he says, reaching for Bastian's shoulder but thinking better of it and pulling away. "We can make sure Luna is doing alright and healthy, but I wouldn't be able to check on your daughter for a few months."

I cup Bastian's cheek as he frowns. "The bigger picture, my Alpha,"

I whisper. "Let's take care of the many before we worry about the one." He leans his forehead on my shoulder as I turn back to Doc. "Trish is doing ok? You know, with the baby?"

"Her child is strong," he responds, nodding. "Trish is a bit dehydrated, but aren't we all these days?"

"Would she survive a long trip?" I ask as Doc stands to begin my exam.

Doc feels along my neck before helping me lie back. "Luna, a trip wouldn't be a good idea," he answers, lifting my shirt. "She's struggled, and now with the food shortage, no water or promise of its return... Travel would be reckless at best."

"What could we do to make it safer?" Bastian asks, watching Doc Will's hands closely as he feels below my waistband. "What are you doing?" Bastian's life experience has made him insanely protective of me from the moment he learned about the pregnancy. I suddenly became the glass case protecting his child. His building growl is from anxiety more than anger.

"It's ok, Bass," Doc Will says soothingly. "Your daughter is safely tucked away inside a few layers of Luna. I'm just feeling those layers to be sure they are doing what they're supposed to. Do you want to feel?"

I remain silent as Doc patiently shows Bastian everything he checks, teaching him what to feel for. Bastian stops growling and settles into his lesson. He holds my hand when he isn't feeling something in my stomach, and Doc smiles reassuringly whenever he asks questions.

"Your mother and I talked extensively when I first came to work for her, Luna," Doc says, holding up his finger in thought. "She told me a lot about her pregnancy. I have something you might get a kick out of. Hang on. I'll be right back."

I turn to Bastian as Doc leaves the room. "I'm not made of glass, Love," I tell him. "I'm the Luna and have a pack to care for. You need to find your inner Alpha and let him come out to play."

Bastian rubs his hand over my stomach and glances at me from the corner of his eye. "That's my child." This discussion was over before it started.

"I was making this for Trish, but I reckon you would like some too," Doc says, entering the room with a covered bowl. His eyes shift between me and Bastian. "Are we ok?"

I smile at Doc while rubbing my Alpha's arm. "Bastian's just nervous," I tell him. My stomach growls loudly even though I wasn't remotely hungry just a moment ago.

Doc laughs. "That's what I wanted to show you. Your mother said no matter what was going on, the moment her boiled meat came within reach, her stomach would growl. She said the best anyone could figure, the noise was you asking for some." Doc holds the bowl out to Bastian. "Here. Maybe feeding your small one will help you."

I smile as Bastian feeds me a piece of the chicken. It's a relief to see his face relax as he smiles back. Once I swallow, I turn back to Doc. "I need to move the pack west, Doc," I say, reaching for his arm. "Can Trish make that trip?"

"Luna," Doc sighs my name as he falls into his chair. "You're gonna move the entire hungry and dehydrated pack, and you're worried about one wolf?"

"I'm concerned about all of my wolves, which is why we are leaving," I tell him. "Even if the rains return tomorrow, which seems unlikely, they will not make it through the winter. Is she strong enough to make the trip?"

Doc doesn't answer right away. His eyes drift down to my stomach. Bastian returns to rubbing his thumb over it while waiting for the answer. I might as well have been asking about myself and our child. *I doubt Bastian will ever calm down.*

"It won't be easy on either of you," Doc Will starts, sighing. "Once you run out of water to boil it in, it'll become difficult to eat what food you **can** find. Your blood holds enough nutrients to keep you going for a few weeks, but Trish will suffer. Luna, that's hundreds of wolves."

"Can you have your office packed in a few days?" I ask, ignoring his concerns.

"Do I have a choice?"

"Not if you want to continue working with us," I answer. "I have a few things to take care of before I make the announcement, but we are leaving."

Doc nods, sadly looking around his office.

* * *

It takes us a few hours to travel back to the cabin. Bastian remains eerily silent the entire time. I escort the exhausted Trish to my bed and leave Jinx with some of Bastian's clothes to shift. My Alpha waits downstairs for me, anxiously pacing beside the couches.

"What do you want to see River about?" Bastian nearly bursts when I reach the bottom step.

"I think there's a pattern we've missed," I whisper, pulling him out to the porch. "Grandma got so sick with Daddy that Grandpa talked to the brother he thought he hated and risked a war between their packs. My mother was sick with me until they put her on the same diet Grandma needed."

Bastian leans against the porch railing to face me. "You think Trish is carrying our daughter's Alpha?" He raises his eyebrow curiously.

I step into him and rest my ear on his chest. "My stomach stays settled when Trish is nearby," I whisper. "Like the baby wants her close." I sigh, realizing how ridiculous this must sound. "I feel like I'm losing my mind. How is that even possible?"

Bastian breathes out a laugh and rubs my back. "I'll admit that it sounds strange, but we live a pretty remarkable life, Ayls." He leans back to cup my cheeks. "I am beginning to understand why Luna always smiled. We are surrounded by so much love and magic that it's impossible to stay focused on the bad things."

"Do you know about your mother's pregnancy?" I ask, rubbing our lips together.

"I'm not very interested in discussing my mother right now," Bastian says, his hum starting. He licks my top lip, causing me to open my mouth and accept his tongue.

I wrap my arms around Bastian's neck and whimper into his mouth. I love how he feels in my arms. There are nerves in my mouth that

I'd been unaware of until we bonded, and they are all reaching out to him now.

"You'll always be my little girl," my father grumbles.

I pull away from Bastian and smile as he pouts. "Daddy," I say, turning toward my recently shifted father. "If I'm required to be alright with seeing you naked, then you will need to accept seeing me kiss my Alpha."

Daddy scoffs, leaning against the railing. "What did Will say?"

I turn to press my back against Bastian's chest. "He doesn't think moving Trish is a good idea, but he's willing to help move the pack."

"Annalisa," my father says, clicking his tongue. "About your daughter, not your friend."

"She's too small to check," Bastian answers. "Doc did mention that Ayls' blood would sustain them for a while without food or water."

Daddy crosses his arms with a huff and looks away, twisting his face. He'd been hoping Doc would tell me to stay home. During the past week, he'd come up with every excuse to stop me from moving the pack, finally settling on my pregnancy.

"Maybe you could come with us, Daddy," I say, changing the subject. "I need information from River. You could visit with Anthony while we talk."

"Baby, you need advice from someone who isn't crazy," my father retorts.

We stare at each other until he sighs, rolling his eyes.

"Yeah, alright," Daddy grumbles before shifting and leading us off the porch.

* * *

Edith and Anthony live in a cottage near the lake, and River typically stays with them while her sister is away. Anthony is sitting on the porch steps when we approach. "Please tell me you've come to collect that crazy girl," he pleads.

"That bad?" I ask, sitting beside him and bumping our shoulders.

"Kiddo, there's fantasy, and then there's crazy," Anthony uncharacteristically whines. "That girl is beyond both, and I'm near my limit."

I frown. "She's still carrying on about the unicorn?"

"You know she is," Anthony scoffs, sighing. "Edith tells me we're leaving." He turns to my father, who's sitting on his other side. "You ok with that?"

Daddy hangs his head.

"Yeah, I didn't think so," Anthony says. "She's not a little girl anymore, Tarq. She's trying to do what's best for the pack. The militia have been pulling out of the bases around here for weeks."

"Where'd they go?" I ask.

Anthony handles all our surveillance of the militia. I assigned a team of our most cunning wolves to him, and they spy on the bases closest to us.

"I don't know," he answers, shaking his head. "Regular patrols recorded lower numbers, but they reported them abandoned this morning. The militia doesn't care about their soldiers, so it's pretty bad if they're gone."

My father rests his chin on Anthony's shoulder. *"He's right,"* Daddy grumbles. *"Just don't tell him I said that."*

I giggle and scratch his whiskers as I hug Anthony. "You got it, Daddy."

Leaving them on the porch, Bastian and I step into the small cottage. River smiles excitedly at us as she bounds into the room. I can only stare at her as she regales us with her unicorn tale. She doesn't notice my scowl as she drones on about its beautiful coloring and stunning features.

"River," I loudly interrupt her. "I really need you to focus on something real, please."

"But it is real," River pouts. "Or, at least, it was."

"Ok, but it's not now, and I need help with what is real right now," I state pointedly. "The mothers of the future Lunas and Alphas... I need you to tell me if they suffer similar issues when pregnant."

Edith's eyes widen. She sits beside River, rubbing her back. "Your

Luna needs your help, River," she says soothingly. "Take a break from your mystery to look at something for her. This is important too."

River sighs with a frown. We watch as she sits before us with her eyes closed. She shakes her head occasionally but never changes her expression. "The unicorn is changing colors," she finally mutters.

"River, I've heard all I want to hear about the damn unicorn," I growl. "I asked you a question."

Edith raises her eyebrow. "Easy, young Luna," she cautions. "Let's give her a moment to see if she can find her way back to the information you need."

I roll my eyes and lean against Bastian. Edith wasn't actually talking to me. She uses indirect reprimands to urge River to complete her tasks. It usually works, so I stay silent, hoping to receive an answer.

"They both became very ill," River says, scrunching her face and shaking her head. "The babies like to be near each other. It made the mothers feel better. They were able to eat." She takes a sharp breath and rubs her temples. "Something's not right. I don't feel good." She reaches out for Edith, falling into the witch's arms.

"I think she's done for now, Annalisa," Edith whispers.

Bastian sits up, pushing me with him. "Luna said they kept them apart," he says quickly. "We need to know when that starts and why."

"How would be nice too," I add.

Edith nods before shifting her gaze toward the door. I would never accept being excused in any other situation, but I appreciate the chance Edith has given me to duck away from River's insanity. Bastian and I quietly exit the house.

"Did you get what you needed?" Daddy asks.

I turn to find Anthony lying with his eyes closed against my father's shoulder and put my finger to my lips for Bastian. The ex-commander guarded Daddy for three days while he held my mother's body when she was killed. They frequently worked together when I was a kid, but since they returned from the mountains with her body, they have a connection that I doubt anyone understands.

"I think so," I tell him, tilting my head. *"Do you want to stay here for a while?"*

"He could use the company," Daddy answers.

Pulling Bastian down the steps, we leave Anthony and Daddy to relax. Once we're far enough away, I slow and look up at Bastian. "So, Trish is carrying our daughter's Alpha," I say thoughtfully. "Do you think we should tell them?"

Bastian tucks me under his arm. "We're about to tell hundreds of wolves that we are leaving the safe, secure home they have loved for many years." He squeezes me with a sigh. "Maybe we should give them a few days to digest that before we tell them they are about to raise the second most important child in our pack."

"You're probably right," I whisper. We step out of the woods beside the house, and I turn to lean onto Bastian's chest. "Let's take tonight to just relax. We'll tell the pack tomorrow."

"Ayls!" a voice I've been desperate to hear again calls from behind me.

I spin away from Bastian just before Brock grabs me in his arms. My tears instantly spring into action as I cling to his neck and reach for Rachel's hand. "I have missed you so much," I sputter. "You have perfect timing. I needed you."

Rachel puts her forehead to mine as I feel Brock reach for Bastian. I understand why Mom moved Chase into our house. Large pieces of my heart were missing while these two were away. I had forgotten what it was like to feel complete. I cling to Brock until he picks me up and carries me to the house.

Bastian sits on my swing and takes me from Brock. Our companion sits beside us to stay near me and holds his arm out for Rachel.

"I'm not used to sitting with you two like this," Brock says, chuckling. "Does this mean you finally bonded?"

"Like I stood a chance," I reply, giggling.

"She's pregnant," Bastian announces proudly.

Rachel excitedly claps. "Oh, yay! Precious cargo!"

"I'm naming her Boulder," I say, making them all scowl. "Doc says she's barely more than a thought, so let's talk about something bigger. How bad is it in the South?"

Rachel cringes and leans back to hide behind Brock. My companion frowns, pulling my legs over his lap. "Ayls, we lost a few," Brock whispers. "We didn't realize the poison had reached our waters until it was too late."

"But most of them got out of there?" I ask.

"Yes, Ayls," Rachel answers. "Even those that initially tried to protest the order have left. They realized that the land and water are no longer viable."

"Chase has been reporting that it's slow going," Bastian adds softly. "Many are older. Even as wolves, they struggle without food and water."

"I feel that," I say, closing my eyes. "Guys, we're leaving the lake."

Rachel gasps, and Brock starts to speak a few times but can't form complete words.

"We have not announced it, but it's time," I continue. "Hunting has been dismal at best, and we're nearly out of water." I look over our companion and his mate. "We butchered all but a few of Edith's cows. I want to have a gathering at my mother's memorial tomorrow. We'll feed the wolves who gather and make the announcement then. We leave in two days."

Brock takes my hand. "This could not have been an easy decision," he whispers. "I'm sorry we weren't here."

"You were where you were needed, Brock," I say with a small smile. "I'm just happy to have you home. I've missed our overly full bed."

We watch the sunset from the porch swing. Brock fills the time with stories of the different wolves he met. Rachel tells us about Myla, the young wolf who wants to join my guards. They had tried to leave her with Chase, but she followed them north until it was too late to turn back. She was unhappy about being left at the bunkhouse tonight.

They detail the condition of the land they had traveled through on their journey north. I hold their hands as they describe the hunger and devastation. My tears soak through Bastian's shirt as I pull their emotions and get as much information as possible. Nothing they provide can help us, but it is useful in its own way.

"At least we know we made the right decision to send the wolves west," I say soothingly. "Coming north to us might have been a death sentence for them."

"Kade will be reporting soon," Bastian says. "I'll make you some food and shift." He kisses my head and places me in his empty seat before leaving.

I wrap my arms around Brock and rub Rachel's arm. "Are you two ok?" I ask, looking at the dark circles under their eyes. Their cheekbones are pronounced, missing the muscle layer that covers them.

"We're just tired, Ayls," Brock says. "Maybe we'll head to bed while you talk to Kade. Has he found anything yet?"

My cringe is involuntary. "He helped Grandma and Grandpa find Davis, and then he and Gaine crossed the river. There have been a few small streams. Some were clean." I pause, sifting through Kade's information. He is a skilled hunter, a fast talker, and excellent with a blade. He can easily kill a threat and sweet-talk a local simultaneously. But he talks in confusing circles. "I don't believe he's found much for food."

Brock chuckles. "He's still Kade, I'm guessing." He leans his cheek on my forehead. "When he finds something worth sharing, he'll tell you."

My companion is a calmer version of Bastian. His dry sense of humor rears its head at the strangest times, but his heart is only filled with love. His brown hair has red highlights and has grown while he was away. It tickles my face as he leans on me.

When Kade calls out, I kiss their cheeks and send them to my room. Daddy calls the bed "extra-large." I don't know where it came from, but it's the biggest bed I've ever seen. Brock and Rachel lived in Chase's old wing before they left but often slept in our bed with us. I typically have at least four wolves comfortably lying in bed with me. Adding Trish and Jinx will be easy, especially in human form.

I hadn't realized how much I missed them. Bastian settles on the swing with me and bumps the bowl of chicken he'd brought me with his nose. *"Feed my baby, Love."*

"Yes, my Alpha," I reply, popping some chicken in my mouth.

"Alright, Kade," Bastian says. *"We're ready."*

"Well, *hallelujah,"* Kade grumbles, making me giggle. *"We reached the Ozark. A lot of people are drawn to the little bit of water here. I can't get close enough yet to see about fish, but there's no game."*

"We can't bring the pack to a heavily populated area anyway," I respond, frowning.

"And here I thought my night was going to be boring," Kade starts, sounding happier. *"I miss you, Luna. I think Gaine misses you too. She seems annoyed. When are you gonna come out and play?"*

Bastian lifts his head from my lap to place his jaw on my shoulder. *"Please let me kill him,"* he begs, gently licking my neck.

"You know I can hear you, right?" Kade scoffs.

I giggle at them. *"Stop it,"* I manage to say, kissing Bastian's nose. *"We are actually making plans to follow you, Kade. I'll be telling the pack tomorrow."*

Kade falls silent. He is a pain in the ass most of the time, but he knows when to rein it in. I've tried to make this decision seem easy for the benefit of others, but Kade is among the few who see right through me. This is the only home I've known. Leaving it is the hardest decision I've made yet.

"Are you ok?" Kade finally asks.

"I will be, Kade," I answer, sniffling as I look into Bastian's eyes. *"One day."*

8

Surrounded by the wolves I'm closest to, I fall into my most peaceful sleep in months. Bastian curls at my waist to lie near his daughter while I rest my head on Brock's shoulder and hold Rachel's hand. Trish sleeps behind me, realizing that my presence eases her stomach issues, and Jinx braces her back against his chest. Daddy even climbs onto the foot of the bed and nudges my leg until I make room for him.

I might have fallen asleep with a smile, but screams wake me in the early morning hours. Jumping up, I scare everyone around me. Bastian shifts, cutting my leg with his back claws. I hold my head in my hands as the noise takes over, threatening to burst out of my skull. I try to curl up, but my legs are stretched out for Bastian to close my wounds.

I can't make out what anyone is saying. It's all just loud noise roaring within my mind. My arms are pulled away from my head, and I recognize Daddy's hands as he holds my cheeks, pulling my forehead to his.

"Daddy," I'm pretty sure I whisper.

He pulls me into his arms, cradling me, and tucks in close to my ear. His beard fuzz and lips rub across my skin. I know he's talking, and I work hard to slow my breathing, attempting to find his words among the noise. My father sings when I need help calming. That has to be what he's doing, so I lean against him and try to find something in the noise with a rhythm.

Bastian mashes his muzzle between Daddy's shoulder and head to stick his nose in my face. He gently licks my skin before bumping his jaw against me in a pattern. I remember this. He did it when my mother died. All the wolves' voices came flooding in, terrifying me. He's tapping the beat of Daddy's song. I try to find him using the rhythm.

"How I wonder what you are," Daddy sings softly. "Up above the world so high, like a diamond in the sky."

"Daddy," I call out, sobbing. "Why are they all yelling?"

I look around and notice Trish and Jinx are gone. Brock and Rachel are clinging to each other with Bastian standing over them, pressing his weight down on their legs. As Daddy pulls away, the smell of smoke hits my nose.

"All I can smell is Ayls' blood," Brock growls, rubbing his face. "It's like she's on fire somewhere!"

I can't smell anything but the smoke. I grab Brock's jaw, turning his head so he's looking at me. "I'm right here," I tell him. "I'm not on fire. I'm safe."

Daddy yanks me off the bed. "You're not safe," he shouts. "Let's go. All of you."

He pulls me downstairs while Bastian shoves Brock and Rachel after us. Daddy opens the front door but slams it shut when smoke bellows through.

"Get her out of here," my father orders, looking at my wolves. "Bass, you remember what I told you. Take them straight to the bunker. Don't let her leave."

"Trish," I spout. "I need Trish! Where is she?!"

Daddy pulls my jaw. "Your life is more important than your friend's, Annalisa."

"She's carrying the next Alpha, Daddy," I sob. "She's important too!" I want to blame the pregnancy for this ridiculous crying, but I know it's because my wolves are still screaming, and I can't tune them out.

My father rolls his eyes. "Alright, I'll find them," he promises.

Brock pulls me to him. "I will bring them to you, Ayls," he whispers against my cheek. Rachel is shifting behind him, tearing her clothes in the process. "We will get them."

Five years ago, we were attacked while returning from Brown Lake. A rebel band set up an ambush, and I lost seven guards. Brock took advantage of how the screaming and shouting muddled up my brain and pulled me away before anyone could get near me. I realize that's what they're doing now, but I can't do anything to stop them.

Daddy opens the door and lets Bastian slip through before closing it again. "I will find as many as I can, Annalisa," he tells me. "You're getting on your horse and riding out of here. Bastian will keep you safe. Look at me," he orders, causing me to look into his eyes. "I love you. You're going to be ok."

I don't care about myself. I'm not hurt. My wolves are. I shouldn't be running away from them.

My father yanks the door open and drags me onto the porch. Bastian is standing by the step, holding Grease. She's jumping around and trying to get away from him. Daddy firmly grips my arm as he marches toward them and hands me to Bastian.

"I love you," my Alpha whispers before throwing me onto my mare's back. He shifts as he dives forward and darts toward the mountains.

The thick smoke makes it difficult to breathe. Once I start coughing, the tears really begin to flow. From what I can tell, Bastian is taking me toward the cabin. It's surrounded by forest, so I can't imagine it being any safer than the lake, but the distance is helping to quiet the screaming.

After hours of galloping at full speed, Grease stumbles to a stop beside the paddocks. I fall from her back, landing in Bastian's arms. The air is hot and thick with smoke. My wolves are screaming for me. Some seem to be looking for me; others are wanting my help. Their voices are so blended that I can't tell who I hear.

Bastian puts my feet on the ground and begins tearing boards from the gazebo where my parents were married. It's where I wanted to say my vows. I always dreamed I'd stand where my mother had and stare at my beautiful Alpha while I told him that he was my everything. As I stand frozen in this smoke, watching him tear it apart, it would seem he will be my only.

When he turns back to me, Bastian's mouth is moving, but I can't hear him anymore. Now that I've let my wolves flood back in, there's no silencing them. They all need me, and I'm too far away to help. I yank my arm away from Bastian when he reaches for me. My wolves are burning because they think I'm in that fire, and it's his fault. I'm miles away because he led me here.

Bastian lunges at me, grabbing my waist and throwing me over his shoulder. He pulls open a heavy lid and squeezes down a narrow opening. It's dark and somehow damp amidst the crumbling dryness. I don't want to be down here.

Once on my feet, I grab the ladder to climb back out, but then Bastian turns on a light. It's a small battery-operated lantern that probably won't last long. He steps toward me in the eerie blue glow with his head tipped down and his eyes pulling at my soul. His fingers slide over my cheek, claiming any attention I should divert elsewhere.

I lick my lips, wishing to taste his, and the voices are silenced the moment Bastian gives me what I want. He slips his hands under my shirt, releasing my lips to pull it over my head. I slide my teeth along his jaw and trace my fingers over his skin. Now I understand what my father was telling him. Apparently, my Alpha can silence my wolves, stopping my panic.

Being with Bastian transports me to where we are the only people. Nothing else matters but how beautiful he feels in my arms. He presses me against the wood plank wall and surrounds me with love. His arms provide all the comfort I need, and his lips excite every nerve they come near.

Bastian enjoys my body for hours. The lantern fails after a while, allowing him to explore me in the darkness. My nerves continue to fire no matter how exhausted I am. When my knees buckle, Bastian picks me up and holds me, pushing himself into me until my arms become too heavy to hold onto him.

My eyes close, unable to open, and my head nods heavily. Bastian pulls me from the wall and sits, holding me in his lap. I try to fold my legs, but nothing responds.

Bastian is moving me around when I hear him whisper, "Sleep, my Luna. I will wake you when it's over."

***

It's quiet when I wake. A dim light shines from above us. A shadow crosses over it, but I close my eyes and settle back into Bastian's heartbeat. I'm cradled in his arms as he sits on the floor with his back against the wall. My Alpha's body is heated slightly, keeping me warm while I slept and placating his child, as I'm sure I should be feeding her by now.

When a hand rubs over my back, I open my eyes to find my father kneeling beside us, covered in blood. I gasp and reach to feel his skin, searching for injuries in the low light. He pulls my forehead to his lips, stopping my panicked search.

"It's not mine, child," Daddy whispers. "We need to go. Can you get dressed?" He weakly smiles before climbing the ladder to leave us.

I turn to Bastian as he helps me stand. "What happened?" I whisper, feeling like my head is in a fog.

"I was here with you, Ayls," Bastian answers, helping me slip into my clothes. "I don't have the answers." He hooks my hands over the ladder's rungs. "Come on. Up you go," he says gently, nodding toward the opening above us.

My body is numb as I climb the ladder. Daddy takes my hand when I reach the top, pulling me against his chest. He's still covered in blood, and with the sweltering heat and haze of smoke, he's sweating, keeping it wet. It smears over me, but I still cling to him.

Wolves' blood smells of earth. My father is covered in the metallic stench of human blood. I want to be mad, upset, or commanding in some way, but my brain can only wonder why they hate us so much.

"I saved as many as I could," Daddy whispers as Bastian presses against my back. "Neala was injured, but Ash is looking for survivors. Edith is handling the tea supply and helping those that need it most." He stops, giving me a moment to settle as my sobs build. "Sweetheart, Brock found Trish. She needs you."

Daddy releases me and crouches to pull clothes out of a bag for Bastian. I lift my eyes to scan my surroundings. Once covered in long, flowering vines, the beautiful gazebo is now a charred pile of ruins.

As I turn to look behind me, my chest tightens, and I suddenly can't breathe.

The cabin my grandfather built, where my mother prepared for her wedding and took my father to spend time alone with him, where she healed the man I love, and where I hid so many of her items so they would never get lost, is gone. They took so much more from me than I ever thought they could. I might have been leaving in a few days, but knowing it would still be here was somehow comforting.

Bastian stays with me as I approach the crumbling beams still burning on the ground. He ensures my hands stay against him, allowing him to absorb my fire as it comes in aggressive waves. The true extent of my grief hits when I spot the remnants of a painting's frame. I try to dive for it in the rubble, but Bastian grabs me.

As I sob uncontrollably, we fall to the ground in the ash and soot. It was a painting of my mother. Kade is surprisingly artistic and painted it for me while he stayed at the cabin. Edith suggested it as part of his healing. I hid it from my father because I didn't think he could handle seeing her every day. I may not have seen it often, but it was the only portrait of my mother.

"Baby," my father says soothingly. *"We need to go. I haven't found a horse yet, so you'll need to walk. We can't stay here."*

"Are you sure you're ok, Daddy?" I mumble, attempting to channel my inner Luna.

"I'm fine, daughter," he tells me. *"That girl needs you, though, and it could take us a day to get down this damn mountain if I don't find a horse."* He sits back on his haunches to call out in case a horse is close enough to hear him.

"What happened to her?" I ask once he's done.

"Nothing happened to her," Daddy says, turning to lead us down the mountain. *"It's her mate. Jinx didn't make it."*

Clutching my chest, I allow Bastian to pull me after my father. The road is unrecognizable, but they try to stick to areas that are no longer burning. Bastian sings quietly to me as we follow Daddy, and I slowly let my wolves' voices come forward. I listen as they work together and report their position to my father when they move.

My guard units are what Grandpa calls "well-oiled machines." They work well together and have their own code that I may never understand. However, there is one thing I notice as they work. Voices are disappearing. When the third wolf they call for a report from doesn't answer, I've had enough.

"Daddy, what is going on?" I demand.

My father drops back to walk closer to us. *"Annalisa, there's still a lot of smoke,"* he starts. *"They somehow got your blood and put it on the fires they set. We're working on flushing the rest of them out, but we can't smell them. Your guards are overwhelmed with your blood's scent, and they are doing their best, but..."* His voice trails off.

"Militia?" I ask.

"They aren't wearing uniforms, but yes, I believe they are," Daddy answers.

I let him resume leading us down the mountain and begin listening to my wolves for specific information. There have been too many coincidences. I'm upset with myself for just putting the pieces together now. I listen until I hear Doc Will is with Edith in the field surrounding the barn. *Perfect. Maybe the barn is still standing. It's time I acquaint our old friend with a room my mother and I despised.*

* * *

We travel slowly on foot for hours before Daddy's call finally reaches one of our horses. It's an older mare that I used as a broodmare because she constantly came up lame on us due to an old injury. Luckily, she's having a good day. Bastian throws me onto her back and shifts to help Daddy guide us down the mountain.

As the Alphas organize the gathering of our surviving wolves, I begin searching for a wolf I know is safe. *"Kade?"* I ride quietly behind Bastian, waiting for an answer from my silver wolf.

"Luna," Kade says, sounding confused. *"What happened last night? I called to you. Tarq said you were busy."*

I look ahead at Daddy. My father has been the acting Alpha for a long time. He knows not to share news of attacks with distant wolves unless the threat is heading their way. Kade especially would have turned around and tried to come back to help. He would've never made it in time.

"There were issues," I say vaguely. "I have a strange question."

"I've been told I'm strange, so I'm probably the right wolf to ask."

"You said you followed my mother south and kept the militia off the river, right?" I ask.

Kade always pauses whenever I mention my mother. "Yeah," he answers quietly. "I tried."

"Kade, how did you know she was on the river?"

"Kerst," Kade scoffs. "Said he had a guy. Told him there would be a boat or a house, maybe."

"A houseboat?" I ask.

"Possibly," he says. "That fool was crazy, Luna. He probably got his information from a tree."

The Alphas slow as they reach the edge of the field behind what's left of Grandpa's house. "No, Kade. I think he got his information from a snake," I say, slipping from the mare's back. "Stay safe. I'll reach out when we're ready to leave."

Bastian drops to my side and pushes his muzzle into my hand. "Is there somewhere you want to go first, Ayls?"

"We need to see Trish and Brock," I tell him, rubbing my fingers over his jaw. "Then we need to go to the barn. There's something I need to take care of."

Daddy leaves us to help search for injured wolves since they've cleared this area a few times. We walk around Grandpa's house, surveying the damage. The roof collapsed, and the walls had caved under its weight as it burned. The trees behind it are still smoking, but the flames are extinguished.

Bastian leads me around the debris toward a storage locker we built into the side of a hill. "Jinx saved Neala," Bastian says quietly. "She was checking the bunkhouse. A tree fell on it. He was pulling her out when the roof collapsed."

If there is one thing I'm used to, it would be my wolves sacrificing themselves for each other. Jinx stayed with Neala and Ash in the bunkhouse after watching his parents die at the hands of a rebel group. They were his family just as much as Trish was.

Taking a deep breath, I step through the burned-out doorway and let my eyes adjust to the darkness. Rachel cradles Trish's head against her chest and rocks her while softly singing. Trish is sobbing uncontrollably against her, clinging to her shirt.

I kneel before Brock and lift his muzzle to my shoulder. "Are you two ok?" I whisper.

"We are uninjured," Brock answers, rolling his head to nuzzle my cheek. *"I wouldn't say that we're ok, though."*

"I understand," I say, frowning. "I'll take her for a while so you both can have a break."

I stand and move to the bed. Rachel sits forward and lets me slide my arms around Trish, pulling her to me. The heartbroken wolf latches onto me and loudly sobs against my chest. I rock and shush her as I lean my cheek on her head. The intensity of her emotion reminds me of Uncle Miles. I may never pull enough to drain her pain to a tolerable level.

I shift around to lie in the cot with Trish. Rubbing her back, I pull all the pain and heartache I can. Bastian lays his chin across her hip and nuzzles my hand when it comes close enough.

"I'll shift and go with Brock to search for survivors," Rachel offers.

"No," I say, stopping her retreat. "I need you to bring Edith to me. Find clothes for Brock and Bastian. This will not go unpunished."

Rachel doesn't have the status of the two wolves before me. She nods and steps toward the doorway, but Brock tilts his head. *"Ayls?"*

"When I'm ready, Brock," I say, nodding to excuse him.

Bastian stares at me until they leave, but I just shake my head. I know these wolves well. Our pack is our family, and someone has hurt them—killed them. They would not be able to stop themselves once their emotions take control.

I easily pull Trish's excess emotions once she falls asleep. Her breathing evens out, and her tears dry up. I continue holding her, listening to my guards. They've answered every check since we returned to the lake, so no more have been lost to the attack.

"Oh, Annalisa, it's good to see you safe," Edith gushes, entering the storage room. She kneels beside the bed and takes my hand.

I shift Trish around, cradling her off my chest so I can talk without waking her. "How are the survivors?"

Edith frowns. "Many are in bad shape, Ayls. We've run out of tea, and Anthony is with the guard, trying to find water to boil more. We kept the herbs underground so they were safe." She squeezes my hand. "It was so fast. I wish there were more survivors."

"You seem unharmed," I growl.

"I was bullied into drinking tea so I could help with the wounded," Edith responds, rolling her eyes. She lifts a small bag. "I grabbed a few pairs of shorts. Not much of the clothing survived."

I look beyond her to see Brock and Rachel standing in the doorway. "Give the guys a moment to shift," I tell Edith. "I'd like you to stay with Trish while we handle something."

She silently bows and steps out of the storage area so the guys can shift. Bastian wouldn't care, but Brock has a harder time and prefers privacy.

"*Whoever is with Anthony, bring him to the barn,*" I call to my guards once the guys have completed their shift. I've heard a few wolves mention the structure, so I'm sure it still stands. The dry straw fields surrounding it had died off to a barren dirt ground in the past few years. I'm thankful the building survived.

When Edith returns, she slides into my place with a quizzical look. "Is everything ok?"

I can't stop my disgusted expression. "At this point, Edith, I'm not quite sure why you would bother to ask that," I hiss. "Stay here with her until I get back."

Hooking my arm with Bastian's, I lead the wolves from the bunker. Brock and Rachel walk at a distance behind us, giving me a moment to talk to Bastian. "I don't like what you did," I whisper.

Bastian sighs, putting his arm around me to pull me close. "Ayls," he starts, narrowing his eyes in thought. "Can you try to consider the alternative? If you could hear them... If you experienced any part of what was happening... Could you have stayed away to keep yourself and our child safe? Or would you have run right into danger and possibly been killed?"

"I would've liked the choice," I tell him. "You took that away. I would expect better from you." I stop and put my hand on Bastian's chest. "You should've trusted me to make the best decision."

"I will next time," Bastian promises, leaning down to rub his lips against mine. "What are we doing?"

I lift my eyebrow and turn to continue through the charred trees. "We're going to hold court."

Bastian's stride hitches a bit before falling back in step with me. He knows what court is, but I've never had to hold it. My wolves work well together, and those humans we've taken into our fold have solid roots within our pack. Militia and rebel groups attack us, but there is no court. We eliminate the threat, bury the dead, and move on.

We leave the burnt forest and observe the dirt field full of injured wolves. Most are in their human form, but there are still a few standing guard as wolves. I see burns and abrasions. A few have slings, and many are frozen in shock. Bastian isn't willing to release me, so I touch those I can reach, offering my support and comfort.

Anthony unhappily marches toward us. "Annalisa," he hisses, grabbing my other arm. "I have shit to do. What am I doing here?"

I calmly look into his eyes and wait for his glare to ease. "Bring Doc to the cell."

Anthony knows of my dislike for the barn and the cell it contains. I've never used it, and neither did my mother. Grandpa had it built, and my Uncle Miles was the last person to be held there.

Brock and Bastian help kick some of the broken furniture and boards out of the way as we walk through the building. I've only been here once, but I'm the only one in my group who has. I let my wolves look around the room built with thick boards and reinforced with bars over any opening. The door itself is three times as dense as any other door they've seen.

Brock and Rachel move to the back of the room as a scuffling erupts in the front of the building. Bastian steps before me, shielding me from any danger that may be coming. I rest my hands on his back, letting them fire until he settles and starts to hum.

Anthony shoves Doc through the door straight toward me. He kicks the back of his knees, making him fall to the floor. Anthony might not know what's happening, but he knows it's bad if I order someone brought here.

"Doc," I say, smiling. "Good to see you made it through the fires unharmed."

"Yes, Luna," he whispers. "I was lucky."

"Lucky?" I ask, circling him. "You know? There have been a lot of 'lucky' occurrences over the years, haven't there? You see, Tynan's man and the militia knew my mother had gone south and that they were on the river. They were even tipped off that there was a houseboat."

My mother meant a lot to Brock and Bastian. Their growls build quickly as they understand my hints.

"There were five people besides myself that knew we were leaving the lake soon," I add, still circling the somber man. "And my wolves tell me my blood was burning in the fires. How did they get my blood, Doc? Did they rush to kill us before we could leave peacefully?"

"The only reason you're still alive is because your blood is supposed to be healing!" Doc sneers angrily. "They let you live so I could figure out your blood. Instead, you're just as worthless as the rest of your mongrels."

I lean down to look him in the eye. "My wolves are priceless," I growl.

I press my hands to his face, pushing all my heat straight into him. Doc's face turns red, and he screams so loudly that the remaining pane of glass shakes in its frame. His skin scorches to black, and he silences as his bones crumble. A few moments later, his body shrivels to ash as my hands shake in fury.

Anthony reaches out for me, but Bastian grabs my hands and pulls me away from him. "She's not ready for that, Anthony," he explains. "She'll hurt you."

I fall against Bastian, clinging to his shirt and releasing exhausting sobs. I always felt it strange that the militia knew we'd gone south. I never expected to find the enemy among us. I may have just killed a man with my bare hands, but today has a sense of completion. I have finally killed the last of those responsible for my mother's death.

9

Once regrouped, I ordered all my wolves to move west. Those closest to the lake gathered to assist the wounded. The death toll had crawled close to a thousand before it stopped. Each name hit me like a bullet, but Matthew came to tell me about Nate personally. Bastian stood close by as I fell into Matthew's outstretched arms and felt that loss.

After taking two days to mourn our losses, we're moving as a solid unit heading west. A few surviving horses returned, and we hitched them to a wagon carrying meat, clothing, and Trish. Grease was not among the horses we found. I've given up hope of finding her by the end of the first day.

"I don't want to tell Grandpa about the cabin," I whisper as Daddy lies beside me for the night.

"It's just a house, Annalisa," he responds, setting his chin on my knee.

I curl around to lay my head on his ribs. "It can't be easy to think about something you built being destroyed, Daddy."

"He's been through it before," my father says, sighing deeply. *"He built that hidden bunker after it burned down the first time."*

"Why wasn't I told about it?" I ask.

"Would you have used it?" He chuckles as I wrinkle my nose. *"That's why you weren't told."*

Sighing, I rub my finger over the bridge of his nose. "What else does Bastian control?"

"Your Alpha only controls your nerves, Annalisa," my father starts. *"Your*

nerves are what silences the wolves." He curls around to poke his nose in my face. "*It was for your own good.*"

"I know," I grumble. "I understand why you both did what you did, but it doesn't make abandoning my wolves any easier to swallow."

"*Someone will always want to kill us, Ayls,*" Daddy says, settling back against my legs. "*We're wolves. We are stronger, faster, and have unbreakable bonds. That will always threaten humans, no matter how often we explain that we only want peace.*"

I watch Anthony pass a canteen to River as he sits beside Edith. "Not all humans," I remark.

"*Yes, daughter,*" Daddy says quietly. "*Not all humans. How far has your scout made it?*"

Kade and I talk during the day now. He's reached the flatlands of Kans and spends most of his time as a wolf so he can move faster. Gaine has asked me several times if she can send him back to travel with us, but I know she'd miss him once he was gone. They have been a nice distraction from what I have before my eyes these days.

"He's in the flatlands," I tell him. "I want to keep the pack beside the river for a few days. They could use the chance to hydrate and relax. Kade said they found some food while there, but near Clayville, we can cross on foot."

Daddy rolls his eyes. "*That is not the name of that town,*" he grumbles. "*He's just the guy that owns the boat dock there.*"

I giggle and scratch his chin. He's right, but Clay likes that we call the area around his dock "Clayville." He's been trying to change the town's name for years. Clay is a human Davis saved a few years before he met my mother. He worked on the coyote's barge for years before my mother gifted him the small acreage my Great Aunt Rosalee owned on the river.

Bastian lies down behind me and throws his head over Daddy's hip. "*What are you laughing about?*"

"We were talking about Clay," I tell him.

"*We should make it to his place tomorrow,*" Bastian says. "*Are you ok? Did you have some water?*"

I reach back to push my fingers into his fur. "I had some," I answer. "It would appear Doc didn't lie about my blood's ability to sustain me, though. I'm doing alright."

I hear him talk to Brock, but his heat sends me to sleep before they finish the nightly report.

* * *

Trish walks with me for the final day before we reach the river. We hook our arms and discuss some fun stories involving Jinx as I unnoticeably siphon some of her depression. Her quiet giggle fades into calm silence after the fifth story.

"Can we talk about the baby?" I ask, patting her arm with my free hand.

"I wish Jinx could've met it," she responds, sighing. "He would've been a wonderful father."

"I don't doubt that," I say, smiling. "But you should probably get used to calling your little one 'him.' I spoke to River about our pregnancies."

Trish lifts her eyebrow. "How would she know anything about my child?"

"Well, it turns out your child isn't happy just being near any old Luna," I say, smiling. "He's happy to be near **his** Luna."

Trish stops and pulls me around to face her. "This pain in my ass is an Alpha?"

"Yes," I say, giggling at her dismay. "And from what I've gathered from history, you only get one shot at this. Bastian's parents couldn't have more children, and Grandma only got pregnant once."

"Aren't we supposed to keep them apart?" Trish is due in about four months. She's squinting and shaking her head, obviously confused. There would have never been a good time to tell her this after Jinx's death.

"I don't think we have to worry about that until they're born," I answer. "But maybe if we raise them together, the pull will be normal, and they can learn to overcome it before they are old enough to know what it is."

Trish tilts her head and shrugs. "Maybe," she says slowly. "Does this mean I'm your kid's guard?"

I scoff and giggle as I turn her to resume our walk. "A Luna's guard, you mean?"

"At least this explains why I have to keep stopping myself from putting my jaw in your hand," Trish says, joining my giggling.

We continue in silence for the rest of the morning. I am surprised to see the small smile Trish is wearing when I glance at her.

"Why does she look happy?" Bastian asks, joining us.

"It's a little weird, right?" I ask, tilting my head. *"I mean, I'm glad to see it, but still. We were talking about her child being the future Alpha."*

"Well, that would do it," Bastian announces, sliding his jaw into my hand.

I scratch his chin with my brow furrowed. *"Why?"*

"Her parents have been dead for years, Ayls," Bastian says. *"Jinx was her only family besides that baby. You just told her that her circle is about to become larger than she's ever experienced. When I learned who I was, I was much more excited about being Luna's family than an Alpha."*

"I guess you're right," I say thoughtfully.

"Luna?" my silver wolf calls out.

"Kade," Bastian growls. *"Horrible timing, as usual."*

I click my tongue at Bastian. *"How has your day been, Kade."*

"Eh, can't complain," Kade replies nonchalantly. *"Where are you at?"*

"We've nearly reached the river," I answer. *"Kade, where's your wife?"*

"She's sleeping," he answers, snickering.

I roll my eyes. Gaine is great at keeping Kade in check, but this happens when she gives up and joins in on his shenanigans. *"Kade,"* I say, taking a deep calming breath. *"I need you two to keep moving forward. Can you exercise your demons without knocking her out?"*

Kade and Bastian begin chuckling at the same time. *"Is that what we're calling it now?"* Kade asks.

Clearly, we're not going to have a productive conversation today. *"You should probably get some rest,"* I tell Kade. *"You need to get back on the trail the moment she wakes. It's not safe to stay still too long."*

"*Yes, Luna,*" Kade replies, still chuckling.

* * *

We reach Clay's by nightfall. The older man greets us with a giant smile and helps the Alphas load the leftover meat into his locker. There isn't much, and most is reserved for Trish and the children. He has large pots of water boiling near what used to be a thriving river. The few inches of water trickling over a vast sand bed could barely be called a creek.

Many of my wolves are severely dehydrated. They crowd around the first pot as soon as Clay lowers it and burn their tongues, desperate for water. Brock pushes them off it, asking them to shift while it cools.

"Sorry, Clay," I apologize to the chuckling man. "We haven't had much water for a while."

"I know, Luna," he says, taking my hand. "I have some pitchers that I've already boiled. This water isn't clean, but boiling it helps."

Linking our arms, I walk with him toward his small cottage. "I appreciate your assistance," I say, smiling. "It's been a difficult week."

"I heard," Clay says, pulling his arm away to wrap me in a hug. "I'm so sorry. I wish I could've helped."

I accept his embrace and watch my wolves over his shoulder as they pass the small tin cup to each other, sharing the water. "You're helping plenty now." I pull back and nod toward the thirsty wolves. "They needed this."

Clay sighs deeply. "Well, you're welcome to stay as long as necessary. If they find you again, I'll fight by your side."

"I appreciate that, Clay," I say, smiling.

I can't help shaking my head as he walks away to change out the water. Clay's gray hair and beard clearly display his age. His better years were spent working on Davis's barge. I'm sure his moral support would be appreciated, but he would probably just be in the way with his stiff gate and swollen joints.

"What are you smiling about?" Bastian asks, sliding his arms around me from behind.

Sighing, I lean back against him. It's been a few days since I felt his arms. I didn't realize how much I missed them. "I'm simply enjoying a safe moment," I answer, turning to look over my shoulder at him. I smile as he presses his lips to mine. "We've found no extra food, and this is the first freshwater we've had access to in days, but I still feel relief with each step further from the lake. Does that make sense?"

"Ayls, nothing makes sense right now," Bastian says, chuckling as he rubs his lips over mine. "Except that you smell amazing." He licks my lip, making me smile. "You taste even better."

"You can't eat me, so we should probably focus on food, my Alpha," I say, giggling at him. I turn back to our wolves. "Water will only get us so far."

"I'll take Brock out in the morning," Bastian says, kissing my temple as I relax back into him. "We'll find something."

Daddy builds a small fire beside the river bed for us and settles the rest of our wolves near the cottage. Clay offers to stand watch, sitting on his porch with a shotgun. I want to trust him, but I still post a few wolves and set up a rotation so they can all get some sleep.

Edith looks exhausted as she sits beside me and Trish. "How are you ladies feeling?"

My blood might sustain me, but Trish doesn't enjoy that benefit. Her cheeks are sunken, and there are dark circles under her eyes. I rub my knuckles over her cheek, causing her to smile weakly.

"I'm fine, but I'd like to see about something for Trish to eat and drink, please," I say, turning to Edith.

The witch nods and stands, leaving us to collect the requested items. Brock crawls behind us, bracing me with his shoulders and Trish with his hips. Bastian lies beside me with his head over my lap. Daddy, Anthony, and Rachel round out the rest of our group gathered around the small fire.

I hold my arm out as Matthew jogs near us. *Come here, Matthew,* I request privately so it seems more like his choice.

Matthew and I grew up together, and he's never been shy about asking for help, but he's kept his distance since the attack. Nate was his boss and mentor. That loss has been crushing him, and he's tried to hide it as best as possible. I don't force myself on my wolves, but I can't ignore his pain anymore. I wrap my arms around his neck and pull him down to me. Matthew's fur around his eyes is wet as I slip my hands over his face.

Nate spent time with the junior guards, training them whenever Neala was called away from the lake. Being an older wolf and part of Grandpa's trusted circle, Nate was well-known and loved throughout the pack. They all felt his loss to some degree.

My group remains silent as I pull Matthew's grief, making it easier for him to process his feelings and thoughts. Edith quietly hands Trish a small plate of beefsteak strips and a full canteen. I wink at her as she backs away to sit beside Anthony.

Once I sigh deeply and release Matthew's sorrow, my father clears his throat. "Your mother brought Chase here after Bristol passed," he says, looking toward the water. "They were gone for a month. He was determined to find her family and stay with them. So, Darya brought him here to wait for Davis's barge to come through and give him a ride."

Anthony lifts his eyebrow. "The barge doesn't come this far north."

"Yeah," Daddy says, chuckling. "Darya knew that. I think in the back of his mind, Chase knew too. But they still stayed here waiting for the boat all month until Chase finally healed enough that he was willing to return to the lake with her." Daddy scratches Matthew's shoulder and rubs his ear between his fingers. "This land has a way of healing wounds we can't see but feel just the same."

Brock rests his chin on Matthew's shoulder once he falls asleep and watches the rest of our group settle in for the night. "*Sleep, Ayls,*" he says. "*I've got you tonight.*"

"*I love you,*" I tell him as he gives me his muzzle for a goodnight kiss.

* * *

Rachel wakes me in the morning. She breathes heavily onto my face, stealing my breath. I smile as I open my eyes. She's the only one that wakes me this way. Brock just slides a slobber-filled tongue over my face, making me want to strangle him.

"Luna, can you help move Trish so Brock can go with Bastian?"

Matthew stirs as I move, but Trish remains asleep against my shoulder on my other side. Since becoming pregnant, she sleeps so heavily that Bastian says she'd sleep through my murder. I know he's joking, but he's probably right.

Bastian helps me lift Trish so Rachel can take Brock's place. Her brown coat is bleached at the tips and dry from her time in the south. I scratch her chin when Edith hands me a plate of meat for her.

"You should eat something before you go, Bass," I whisper.

"I'll eat on the road," he whispers back, leaning to kiss my forehead. "We're heading north along the river."

"Information only," I tell him firmly. "Do not put yourself at risk."

"Yes, my Luna." Bastian nods to my father and leads Brock behind the cottage where he can drop his clothes to shift.

Daddy sits beside my leg and stokes the fire. "You know he's gonna do whatever he wants," he grumbles.

"Do you want to go with him?" I ask, lifting my eyebrow.

"I do, but I'm going to stay here and make sure you two are safe," my father answers, matching my playful tone.

"Daddy, I want to marry him," I say, looking in the direction Bastian had gone.

My father rolls his eyes. "I told you that you need to wait."

"They need this," I hiss. "Daddy, our wolves are hurting. Let's give them something to celebrate before we risk their lives again. We will find them some food for a feast."

Daddy looks up at the wolves sitting on the dock with their feet in the mud. "Let's see what the guys find," he says, ending our conversation.

Trish and I walk along the river bed when she finally wakes. Rachel stays close but lies on the shore to catch a quick nap while so many attentive wolves surround us. It's nice to see Trish happily smiling as she rubs her belly.

"I think I'd like to name him after his father," she says quietly. "He will be strong and fair like those before him and sweet and caring like Jinx." She turns her smile on me as I hook our arms.

"I'm sure he will be a wonderful Alpha," I respond, leading her through the mud and rippled sand. "Are you hungry? Should we get you something to eat?"

"I'm ok for now, Ayls," Trish answers, still smiling. "How long will we be staying here?"

I study the same wolves my father was watching earlier. "The guys are trying to find enough food for us to hold a feast," I tell her. "I'd like everyone to have full bellies when we leave." I look into Trish's eyes. "I thought maybe we'd have a wedding."

"Bastian has been waiting a while," Trish gushes, giggling.

I nod, sighing. "He has," I agree. "And everyone could use a little bit of joy right now." I kick at the low water around our ankles. "Daddy said he wanted us to wait until we could provide a feast, so let's hope my Alpha finds us enough that I can bring him some joy too."

It's not long before Rachel calls us back to the bank, telling me we've traveled too far to be safe.

* * *

Once I finish talking with Kade, I've had enough of Brock and Bastian's silence. They aren't even talking to each other, which will never be normal. *Bastian? Brock? One of you better respond,* I demand.

Hang on, Ayls, Brock somehow murmurs.

With my fingers laced, I rub my thumbs over my lips and stare at the ground before me. As I rock slightly, my elbows dig into my folded legs, and I grow more tense with each passing second. Anthony touches my shoulder, making me jump.

We found a flock of sheep, Ayls, Bastian finally responds.

I sigh in relief and put my finger to my lips as Anthony sits beside me. *Are you ok?* I ask Bastian.

We're fine, but we're gonna need some help with this, he answers. *We'll be back in a few hours. Love you.*

"*I love you too,*" I say before turning to Anthony. "Bastian says they found some sheep."

"There was a herd of sheering sheep by the northern base," Anthony says. "They were civilian-owned, but Nate said one of his patrols found the owners dead about a month ago."

"Flock," Trish mumbles.

"What?" Anthony asks.

"A group of sheep is called a flock," she tells him.

Anthony stares at her for a moment. "Give me a minute, and I'll dazzle you with zebras before I murder you with crows."

He lets his face curl into a smile as we both lose control of our giggles. Anthony has perfected the grumbly old man routine but is collectively the pack grandfather. We all love talking to him, no matter how hard he tries to appear annoyed by us.

"Is a dazzle really a herd of zebras?" Trish asks, still giggling.

Anthony clicks his tongue. "You girls need better teachers."

"But we do know what a murder of crows is," I add.

"You would," Anthony scoffs.

Over the next few hours, we discuss different ways to prepare mutton and lamb. A few of my guards happily join us. Anthony lies back as he describes the difference between lamb and mutton chops. The meat changes to pork at the mention of chops.

Trish's favorite meat is pork, boar specifically. I can't tell the difference, but she whimsically describes how the meat creates a celebration in her mouth. They enjoy their favorite meats, but it wouldn't normally incite a spirited conversation that attracts the surrounding wolves to participate. There is no disguising my wolves' hunger, even with their laughter and smiles.

I relax back, lying my head on Anthony's chest while my wolves continue entertaining themselves with recipes and delicious experiences of the past. "This is your fault, you know," I tell him, smirking.

"They might be hungry, Annalisa, but they're happy," Anthony responds, throwing his arm over my ribs.

I follow his gaze and know he's right. This might be the first time since the attack that they are all smiling. There isn't one frown among the whole group. "Thank you," I whisper, reaching to cup his cheek.

"You're welcome," Anthony says with a small smile. "Why don't you catch a nap while you wait for your wolf?"

* * *

I'm the only one happy that I'm on a horse following the hunting party the next morning. Even Trish wrinkled her nose at the thought of dealing with her pregnancy alone. Bastian jogs nearly underneath the gelding I'm on, grumbling about how I'm determined to kill myself and that I'm needlessly putting his child in danger. *I do love my Alpha. I promise.*

Bastian slows the gelding as we approach the line of guards stopped inside the trees. Beyond them is a small field with about 30 sheep. I smile at the three little lambs, thinking about Anthony's feverish rebuttal about how lamb is better than mutton.

"*There are only a few soldiers,*" Brock tells the party. "*From what we saw, the militia has been hard on these people. I doubt any of them would make an attempt on this flock. There's a small camp on the east side.*"

"*We watched them for half the day yesterday,*" Bastian takes over. "*There are ten soldiers. I only see eight, so two are probably sleeping in camp. It should be quick and quiet if we spread out and take them out simultaneously.*"

I step down from my saddle as my wolves talk amongst themselves to break into smaller teams. Kneeling to Bastian, I pull his muzzle along my cheek. "Did you see a larger tree?"

"*Yes, my Luna,*" Bastian answers, humming. "*Your perch is close to their camp. Brock will be staying with you.*"

"Bastian," I start, raising my eyebrow. "Brock would be of better use beside you."

"*Annalisa, I did not want you to come with us,*" Bastian states, quite cross. "*I do not want you or my child in danger. I couldn't stop you from coming and will not be able to stop you from climbing into a tree, but I can post a wolf on you that I trained and know will defend you with his life.*" Bastian stares at me, waiting to see if I'll challenge him.

I know my Alpha well. This is not the time to assert my dominance. I sit back on my heels and pout like a child, letting him know he's won.

"*Stop making me smile,*" Bastian grumbles.

"Yes, my Alpha," I say, smiling.

Brock joins us as we venture to the tree beside the camp. Usually, I wouldn't go on hunting trips, but we don't typically steal whole herds or flocks. I'm the best shot, and with an eagle-eye view from a tree, my wolves are less likely to be surprised. Like anyone else, I will always do what is necessary to feed my family.

My Alpha and Brock get a kiss on the muzzle before I climb through the thick limbs. Bastian waits until I'm halfway to my chosen perch before leaving us. My wolves begin calling out their positions, finishing with my Alpha announcing he's beside the camp. He's chosen the closest target to ensure he'd be the one taking on multiple targets alone and nearby if I need his help.

I glance down to see Brock standing with his haunches against the tree, facing in the opposite direction. I pull an arrow from my pouch and work the tip into the branch beside me. Once it stays, I take another and nock it, setting my aim on the cot with an arm hanging from its blanket. Bastian said there should be two, but I can only see one.

I pull back on my string, waiting for Bastian's order. My eyes shift around the camp, looking for the second man. There's a canvas tarp tied to some trees to create a shelter, but no one is under it.

My wolves call "*Set*" to Bastian as he crawls forward on his belly toward the man on the cot. I watch my Alpha crawl around a bush and begin rocking his hips to set himself up for a pounce. Bastian is beautiful, and I love to watch him work. The dark stripes in his coat sway like ripples over water when he moves. It's mesmerizing and threatens to capture all of my attention.

But then the bush beside him moves. My aim suddenly shifts to the threatening foliage. My eyes squint as I try to find a reason for the movement. Bastian rocks back as he calls that he's set, and the bush comes alive. A man jumps out of it, diving toward my Alpha.

I release my arrow and catch the man in the calf, making him scream. *"Now!"* I yell to my wolves.

Bastian spins to take out the screaming man as I nock the arrow I'd jammed into the tree. The man in the cot sits up, pulling the blanket off his face. My arrow silently sails through the air in his moment of confusion and plunges deep into his neck. He gasps and claws at his throat before falling lifelessly back onto the cot.

I lean against a branch to look around for Bastian in time to see a man's head roll across the ground. My wolves begin calling, *"Done,"* indicating they've eliminated their target. Bastian steps out to where I can see him and glares at me as I climb down.

"This is why you shouldn't come with us, Annalisa," Bastian grumbles as I reach the ground.

Kneeling, I click my tongue. "I just saved you," I whine. "Why is that a bad thing?"

"Because all we can smell is you," Bastian points out. *"That man was horribly unwashed, but all I can smell is peaches and syrup!"*

I frown and hold my hand out. "I'm sorry," I whisper. "I didn't think about that."

Bastian pushes past my hand and buries his nose into my neck. *"Do you forgive me for the bunker yet?"*

"I asked Daddy to let us get married," I whisper to answer him. "This meat is for our celebration feast."

Bastian shifts, grabbing me in his arms. He spins around with his lips locked onto mine. When he pulls back, he smiles broadly. "I'm getting married, boys!"

IO

The hunting party moved quickly, slaughtering the sheep and haul-ing them toward the river. Other members of my guard pulled small rafts upstream to collect the carcasses and transport them with-out leaving a trail. I travel back with them, but Brock and Bastian lead the gelding around in circles for a while before returning to Clay's cottage.

In his excitement, Bastian announced to everyone who would listen that they would be attending a Luna's wedding. The air buzzes as our wolves joyfully discuss plans for the feast and party. I sit on the dock alone, ignoring them as I think about the wedding I wanted.

"You don't look very excited, kiddo," Anthony's voice makes me jump. He sits beside me, pulling his boots off to stick his feet in the mud. "Yep. That's just as disgusting as I thought it would be."

I giggle, bumping our shoulders. "It's definitely an experience."

Anthony puts his arm around me. "What's got your mind in a twist?" He shakes me slightly until I rest my head against him.

"I always thought I'd get married on Grandpa's gazebo," I say, frown-ing. "Nate would sing while Daddy turned me around the dance floor." Without warning, my tears begin falling. I look up into Anthony's eyes. "I wish Mom was here."

He wraps his other arm around me, allowing me to hide against his chest as I cry like a child for my mother. "I used to go to her altar to talk with her," Anthony whispers. "I did most of the talking, but she helped me through some pretty difficult times."

I smile at his attempted humor. "I remember sitting in the kitchen, rambling on about things," I tell him through my tears. "Mom just stared at me until I answered my own question."

"Yeah," Anthony says, nodding. "That's pretty much how our conversations go." He digs into his shirt near the collar and pulls his chain out. A crystal just like mine is attached to it. "She's always with me, too." He kisses the crystal and drops it back inside his shirt.

"What do you think she'd say?" I ask.

Anthony takes a deep breath and looks out over the riverbed. "I think she'd tell you the only thing that matters is the love you share with your Alpha." He kisses my forehead. "Your mother didn't care about getting married. It was your father that wanted it. So, I think if we channel your mother right now, she'd say, 'Just give the boy what he wants and let him be happy.'"

Giggling, I wrap my arms around Anthony to return his hug. "Now that sounds like her." I stay against his chest, collecting myself until I hear Bastian's voice among those talking by the cottage. Pulling away, I cup his cheeks. "Thank you, Anthony." I feel for his crystal through his shirt. "Keep her close to your heart. That's where she should be."

Bastian sits beside me and rubs my back. "I was thinking," he starts, inhaling deeply. "The full moon is in two days. Why don't we wait for Dax? He should be at the wedding."

Anthony smiles and pulls my cheek to his lips. "See? He deserves a wedding."

Leaning against Bastian, I watch Anthony collect his boots and retreat to the shade of the small trees along the bank. I relax into my Alpha's heat and remember my mother describing him to me when I questioned his behavior. She was right. He is perfect.

I turn to hold Bastian's cheeks. "I love you," I whisper.

"I know you do," Bastian murmurs, rubbing his lips against mine.

* * *

Wedding preparations start immediately. Since flowers are scarce, decorations are made from sticks and dried straw grass. Large wreaths and swags begin appearing along the pillars of the dock and on trees and posts close by.

Anthony enlists a few of my older wolves to assist him in the kitchen. They cook the beef for tonight before starting on the lamb for the reception feast. Daddy and Anthony agreed that cooking small portions inside would be better than cooking in large quantities outside and letting the smell travel in the wind.

Edith disappears into the back room of the cottage but comes out when she needs me to ask Grandma cryptic questions. When she wants to know where to find a reddish-orange rock and how to hollow it, I lift my eyebrow. As soon as I'm done translating Grandma's response, she disappears and only sends some of the kids out to find the items she needs.

Bastian is notably absent until he approaches me with a few thicker bones in his mouth. *"Hey, Love,"* he says, lying beside me. *"I'm going to leave the meat for the others tonight."* He lines a bone up with his teeth and slaps his jaw onto the ground, splitting it down the center.

"What have you been up to?" I ask, sliding my hand over his head as he digs the marrow out with his teeth. "I saw you disappear with Daddy."

"He knows you wanted to get married in the gazebo," Bastian tells me, handing me the bone. *"We were building you something to call your own."*

Smiling, I pull the loose bone shards from the piece he gave me. "You'll be there," I say. "That's all I need." I lay the bone before my Alpha and take the other half once he's finished.

"I like it when you talk to Anthony," Bastian says, allowing me to hear his smile. *"I don't know what he says, but he is much better at helping you through your thoughts than I am."*

I watch Bastian slide his tongue over the bones I'd smoothed out, thinking about his words. "Anthony has had a lot of practice," I respond. "He might work closely with the guard, but he has been an advisor for my mother, Edith, and me. He has years of experience."

Bastian licks his lips and moves on to the next bone. *"I should become his apprentice,"* he says, chuckling.

"You have your qualities, my Alpha."

Once Bastian finishes his marrow, he rolls onto his side and leans against my leg. He's exhausted from standing watch more than the others while we're stopped. Bastian enjoys one little luxury on the road that the others don't. When my stomach is upset, I ride in the wagon with Trish, and my Alpha rides with us. The wagon's bumping and rocking will often lull us to sleep.

His nap is short-lived, though. My stomach growls as Trish approaches with an oversized bowl of sautéed beef cubes, waking him. Bastian chuckles and bumps my belly with his nose. *"Quiet down in there,"* he tells his daughter. *"Daddy needs a nap."*

"Have you guys seen River?" I ask as Trish sits opposite Bastian.

"She's sticking to the smaller groups in the outer barrier," Bastian answers. *"Why?"*

"We need an elder to bless our union," I remind him. "She's the only one here. We'll need to make sure she's brought in."

Bastian rolls over, tucking his paws in to lay his head on my lap. My stomach growls again, making him nuzzle it. *"I wonder if that really is her causing that,"* he says, sounding tired. *"It sure would be nice to know."*

"I sent my grandparents to find someone to help us with River," I promise him. "Until then, let's pretend she's trying to talk to you. There will always be a special place in her heart for her Daddy." I pop a piece of beef in my mouth and tug Bastian's fur.

My Alpha rubs his nose over my belly. *"I love you too,"* he mumbles. *"Now let Daddy sleep."*

I shake my head as he lies back down on my lap. Once he's settled, I turn to Trish. "How are things going inside?"

"Anthony is a great cook," she gushes. "Why have you been hiding him from me? I thought we were friends."

I giggle, rolling my eyes. "Anthony is much more than that, but yes, he is a wonderful cook," I agree. "Has he finished with the beef?"

"Nearly," she responds. "Matthew was cutting chops for him. I think they'll cook those tomorrow. Anthony said something about a stew. He has Rachel and a few of the kids looking for dandelions."

"And Edith?" I pry. "Any idea what she's working on?"

"No," Trish answers quickly. "Why don't you take Bastian somewhere tomorrow? Tarq's told us many times about the day before his wedding. He took Luna to the cliff for a picnic."

I smile down at my sleeping wolf. "That's a good idea," I whisper to Trish. Letting my wolves' voices filter forward, I pick through each one until I find Drake, Matthew's right hand. *"Drake?"*

"Yes, Luna," he answers instantly.

"Can you take a small team and scout some areas on the river's west bank?" I ask.

"Yes, Luna," Drake responds.

Sighing, I shake my head. *"Would you like to know what you're scouting for, Drake?"*

"Sorry, Luna," he replies.

Drake is slightly older than us. He's been on my travel detail before, but we've never spent time together. I can't recall speaking directly to him before now. He's a solid wolf and would make a strong travel guard if he could stop being so nervous with me.

"I'm looking for a safe place to take my Alpha for the day where we could relax before the wedding," I tell him.

"We'll find you something, Luna," Drake replies more confidently.

Trish and I finish the rest of our beef as the sun quietly sets. She rolls toward me to put her belly against my hip. The worn-out mama wolf closes her eyes with a smile. Apparently, making an Alpha is hard work.

I listen to my wolves while Trish and Bastian sleep. Most are talking about the future and excited about seeing the mountains. A few have expressed their nervousness about crossing the flatlands. I have concerns myself, so I understand their fears.

I'm about to focus on those before me when I hear Ash and Neala scolding Myla. The young wolf wants to attend the wedding, but Neala explains that her behavior will not be tolerated around an Alpha or Luna. I frown, thinking about my mother. She accepted all of our wolves, no matter how they behaved. She even enjoyed her time with Myla.

"Neala," I call out, stopping her. *"Myla was a friend of my mother's. She is allowed to attend just like the rest."*

"Apologies, Luna," Neala starts. *"But you may want to speak with her first."*

"Send her to me," I order.

I smile as Daddy sits across the small fire. He enjoys Anthony's cooking, so a large bowl of meat cuts is in his hand. He raises the dish to me, but I shake my head and point to the plate Trish and I had emptied. Shrugging, Daddy bites into a piece.

"Drake tells me you're looking for somewhere to take Bastian tomorrow," Matthew calls out to me. I look around, spotting him in front of the cottage. *"It's not safe for you two to wander like it was for your parents."*

Nodding, I smile. *"Would you come with us then?"*

Matthew looks off over the riverbed. *"Yeah, alright,"* he grumbles. *"Let Bastian sleep tonight. I'll stand watch until Drake returns."*

Once Edith and Anthony join us, our group begins telling stories about the past. Bastian will wake if I speak, so I relax onto the blanket and listen. Anthony tells us about one of the times he caught up to my mother when he was still in the militia. I pull my fingers through Trish's hair and stifle a giggle when he gets to the part where my mother sliced his hand open. His blood made her arm too slick to hold, and she got away.

I like that Edith has started to tell us stories from her childhood. It's exhausting to always hear tales of the Luna. I love my mother, but I wonder if she ever grew tired of the pedestal. I wish I could wake up and just be a girl.

I look down at Bastian. My beautiful wolf stirs slightly as I slip my fingers through his fur. He rubs his nose against my belly until my shirt moves out of his way. Bastian's tongue slides over my skin, and his hum starts, but I'm pretty sure he hasn't woken.

So, maybe I wouldn't enjoy being a regular girl.

* * *

Matthew rubs his nose over my forehead to wake me in the morning. *"Luna,"* he says softly. *"You should leave soon."*

I don't remember falling asleep. Trish is still curled up beside me, but my Alpha is gone. "Where's Bastian?"

"In the house," Matthew answers. *"He's trying to put together a picnic. Tarq's helping. Ayls?"* He sits down beside me as I sit up. *"Bastian's lost a lot of weight."*

"I know," I snap, pushing myself to my feet. "Everyone has. We're doing what we can."

Matthew rubs his muzzle over my hip and bumps my elbow as I rub my eyes. *"We're all only worried about you,"* Matthew says sweetly. *"I will forfeit my rations for your Alpha. You need him more than you need me. He should be strong to defend you and your child."*

I fall to my knees and open my arms to him. "I'm sorry, Matthew," I whisper into his fur. "You didn't deserve that." His selflessness has somehow triggered the entire lake event to come crashing in. "My mother said she felt like she failed our wolves. My father was the one that helped her to understand that they would make mistakes."

"Sometimes even the mighty must be lifted," Matthew says.

"I feel like I've been going through life with my eyes closed," I continue. "When they opened, the world was horrible and cruel. We accepted him as one of our own. Why would he do that to us?"

Doc's life is the first I've taken out of anger. Daddy had me shooting Grandpa's bow as soon as I could walk, and I haven't missed a target since childhood. I have taken plenty of enemy lives when we were attacked. But this was the first life I took with my bare hands.

Although I may not regret my actions, I wish I had the answer to one question. It should be simple, yet no one has been able to provide it. *Why do they hate us so much?*

I don't cry at the drop of a hat like my mother had, but I accept that I am more emotional than most. However, I choose to blame my pregnancy when my father appears to pull me off Matthew and allow me to collapse into his arms. Daddy rocks and shushes me. When I hear him murmur, he's telling Matthew to get my Alpha.

It's only a few minutes before Bastian wraps around me from behind, sandwiching me between my father and himself. I'm fortunate to be surrounded by men who understand the emotions of being a Luna. My wolves might spend most of the time as a hum in the background, but they are all mine. I love them all, and their loss was determined to be recognized no matter how strong I pretended to be.

"This was a great loss," my father whispers. "There will always be someone who wants what we have. They have always attacked us, and we will never stop defending what is ours."

"Daddy," I say, still sobbing. "They took it. We lost what we had."

"Annalisa, Bastian, no one can take what we have," Daddy whispers. "We have love, family, and solidarity. We feel that in our hearts. So, as they beat, we have everything we need. No amount of hate, deceit, or treachery will ever take away what we have."

"Our house," I mumble, calmer but unwilling to pull away from them.

"Was just a house," Daddy responds. "You are my home. I will never lose you."

As my father silently sways us, I think of our remaining wolves. They are happy despite our losses. There is still danger, and we have lost a lot in the past week, but they are smiling and laughing. He's right, and I've neglected the bigger picture in my grief. I'm their Luna and must be strong enough to carry this pain for them.

Taking a deep breath and slowly letting it out, I lean against Bastian and cup my father's cheeks. "Thank you, Daddy."

"My pleasure, daughter," my father says, smiling. "Your mother was all crazy and hormonal and shit too."

Bastian chuckles as Daddy kisses my forehead and leaves us to retreat to the cottage. "I hope he'll feel comfortable enough to join Luna soon, but I'll miss him when he leaves." My Alpha pulls me back against his chest and cups my belly.

"He'll be back," I whisper. "Grandpa told me that all the Alphas return for the full moon. It's supposed to be a curse."

Bastian snickers. "Well, it will pull him away from Luna for a few hours," he says. "Perhaps that's the curse."

Turning to face him, I smile up at my Alpha. "I suppose you're right," I whisper. "Thank you for letting me fall apart when I need to."

"I will pick up your pieces and carry them around until you're ready to put them back together," Bastian replies.

"We should probably go before you make me cry again," I say, smirking.

"Yes, my Luna," Bastian says, kissing me gently.

A short time later, Bastian has packed some saddlebags with picnic supplies and readied Edith's gelding, Saint. He tosses me into the saddle and jumps up behind me. I lean back against Bastian's chest and bask in his embrace. My nerves have not reacted to his touch since the lake attack.

"Thank you for giving me this time," I say quietly, looking over my shoulder. "I wanted to be angry with you, but I understand why you did what you did. I wish you'd told me, but I would have stopped you if you had."

"I love you, Ayls," Bastian whispers. "I love our wolves, but you will always come first. You would have died trying to save them. Without a Luna, our pack would break apart again. As smaller packs, we are easier to control or eliminate. Tarq and Bruce have worked hard to educate me on the importance of a Luna."

Breathing out a laugh, I turn my thoughtful expression to the trail ahead. "My mother always stressed the importance of the pack," I say, recalling some of her lessons. "She always told me that everything I do must be for the benefit of the pack, and I cannot be selfish in my actions. But that's not really true, is it?"

"I guess not," Bastian agrees.

"If something were to happen to me without the Luna line of succession solidified, there would be no Luna," I say thoughtfully. "Grandpa and Uncle Miles were both Alphas. Were there more?"

Bastian chuckles and tightens his grip on me. "Many more, Love," he answers.

Drake slows ahead of us and waits for Saint to catch up before turning back toward the river. A minute later, he leads us to a raised bank with a 12-foot drop. *I think when the river was at its normal level, this was a bank, but now it's closer to the cliff your mother picnicked at the day before her wedding,"* Drake says, sounding quite shy.

Bastian helps me slide from my saddle, and I step toward the edge with Drake. "You did perfect, Drake," I whisper. "Thank you."

Drake slides his head under my outstretched hand. *"You're welcome, Luna. We'll leave you to enjoy your day."*

I turn back to Bastian and watch Drake and a few other guards move into the brush around us. "Leaving" does not actually mean they'll be going away. My guards will stay out of sight and leave us alone while we enjoy the day, but I will remain under their watchful protection.

My mother had once told Bastian that she hadn't been alone in over 15 years. I found that hard to believe until I became the Luna. It was strange and embarrassing initially, but Bastian barely noticed them, so he helped me feel at ease. He says they are the eyes in the back of his head, so he never has to worry about missing anything.

Bastian pulls a thin blanket from the saddlebags and lays it out before producing the food containers. "Come on, my Luna," he says, smiling. "Why don't you enjoy the day with me before I surrender you to your wedding prep?"

I lift my eyebrow. "Is this you not wanting a wedding now?"

"Oh no," Bastian says, shaking his head. "You're marrying me. You're not getting out of it now." Holding his hand out, he waits for me to join him on the blanket. When Bastian brushes his lips over mine, my nerves begin firing again. His eyes are soft and gentle with a loving gaze. "Tell me a story."

I roll my hips toward him, throwing my leg over his. "A story? What kind of story would you like?"

Bastian reaches for my thigh and pulls me against him. "Why did you teach Grease to bite Tarq's tail?"

I laugh as Bastian holds some of the sautéed beef before my mouth. I accept it and chew for a moment before answering him. "Mom was gone a lot," I start, piecing together my childhood. "Don't get me wrong, I loved her but was so mad that she always left me behind. Daddy and I got on each other's nerves, and Grandma had to get between us if Chase wasn't around."

"Uncle Chase normally went with Luna if Tarq didn't, right?" Bastian asks, holding out another piece of meat.

Wrinkling my nose, I shake my head. The meat isn't sitting well in my stomach now that Trish isn't near me. "Most of the time, he did," I answer. "Ash went on about half of her trips through the summer months. Some guy shot him one winter, so my mother refused to let him go with her once it snowed. His wolf sticks out against the white."

"Ash told me he helped Luna figure out who I was," Bastian says, pulling out some pork. "Anthony boiled this for you. It's not as tender but should sit better."

I smile and take a small bite of the pork. "I was training Grease and Bones at the same time. I had named the little black colt from her lesson Bones and wanted her to have him. I thought he would remind her of me. He was a bit of a loose cannon, and I was sure Daddy would demand Grease for her, so I taught Grease to bite him so he wouldn't."

"Your mother didn't need a horse to remind her of you," Bastian says, pushing my hair behind my ear. "Not many people were aware that you existed. I think she traveled so much to pull attention away from the lake. She stopped anyone from discovering you and kept you safe."

Frowning, I look up into Bastian's eyes. "I never thought about it that way," I say, nearly pouting. "When she came home, I would spend the entire first day scowling at her and being rude or whining. All that time I wasted."

Bastian wraps me up in his arms. "I didn't mean to point that out," he says. "I didn't have any friends when I was young. I was so strong that the other kids were scared of me. All I wanted to do was play, and they ran and hid from me. When my parents tried to have another kid, I was so mad. Obviously, they wanted to replace me."

I reach for his cheek. "You know that's not true."

"Well, back then, it felt true," Bastian responds, threading our fingers. "But Kade told me they thought I would have a friend if they had another kid like me. It took a while to forgive myself for hating them."

My tears spring to life as I look into Bastian's eyes. "That was actually really sweet of them," I whisper. "I know Daddy really struggled as a kid."

"Your father had Dax," Bastian says, lying back to stare at the cloudless sky. "I wish I had Miles, but I ended up with Tynan. I can't take back or change the past, but I am truly thankful he didn't realize who I was. He nearly killed me a few times. He would have succeeded had he known."

Bastian has fiercely protected the children in our pack because of his past. A small patrol of militia soldiers came near a field we'd traveled to for a game of ball once. Some young wolves were playing at the edge near the trail they were following. One of them aimed his rifle at the kids, and all seven soldiers lost their lives that day.

"We will use the past to find a brighter future," I say, smiling through my tears.

"We can do anything as long as we're together," Bastian whispers, closing his eyes. "Just don't ever think you'll be able to make peace with the militia. Your mother tried that for many years, and it killed her."

Bracing myself on my elbow, I look down at my Alpha. "I think the new life we build should be far away from them in a land they aren't interested in." I slide my hand over Bastian's face until he opens his eyes. "We will take our wolves into the mountains where they can play, hunt, and feast."

"I just want our daughter to be safe." Bastian pulls my fingers to his lips. "If she's safe, the rest will follow. The Luna's safety brings forth the pack's prosperity."

I wrinkle my nose. "Brains and brawn," I say, smiling wickedly. "I knew I kept you around for a reason."

Bastian's growl makes me laugh as he rolls over me, claiming my mouth and taking of me what he wants. I happily give in to him as my nerves fire from his attention.

We return to the cottage to find the grounds transformed. The dried grass wreaths and swags display various colors in the fading sunlight. They hang from every post and tree around the dock. Some have been twisted and tied together to create a walkway leading to the water.

A large arch of twisted sticks and limbs at the dock's entrance is decorated with assorted colored fabrics. Large bows with flowing tails seem to announce something special awaits beyond its gateway. Beside the walkway are blankets and sheets, with some younger wolves gathering on them to braid reeds from the riverbed.

"This is beautiful," I whisper.

"I've never been to a pack wedding," Clay announces excitedly as we slide from Saint's back before the cabin. "This should be fun."

"Sorry, Clay," my father says, stepping through the door. "Humans aren't allowed."

"Daddy, humans have been to pack weddings," I scoff, remembering Edith at most weddings, including Kade and Gaine's.

My father puts his arm around my shoulders. "We cannot bend the rules for a Luna's wedding, daughter," he says firmly. "Your wedding is as official as it is binding. All traditions are followed and honored. They can come to the reception right after, but not the ceremony."

"I'm the Luna," I grumble. "I should be able to say who attends my wedding."

"Annalisa, go inside and get ready with the ladies, please," Daddy growls. "You're not changing traditions that are as old as time itself. Not on my watch. Your mother would kill me."

I wrinkle my nose and cringe. He's probably right. My mother was firm about not offending the wolves and our traditions. "I don't have anyone to give me away," I say, frowning.

"And now you sound like her," Daddy says, laughing. "Just like then, I took care of that. Now, go." He holds the door open for me.

I look up at Bastian and see his broad smile. "What have you two done?"

Bastian laughs. "Get in there and let Edith pamper you," he says, leaning to kiss me. "I have to consider my vows 'cause 'woman, I fuckin' love you' doesn't seem to cover it."

"I will tear your head off and shove it up your ass if you even include that in your vows to my daughter," my father grumbles, glaring. "If I don't, you better believe her grandfather will."

I know what's about to happen by his tone, so I'm not surprised when the two shift out of their clothes and rear up at each other. It's hard to hear their shit-talk over their snarls and the snapping of their jaws.

"He better be pretty by the time I'm done, Daddy," I warn my father.

Bastian chuckles as he's pinned to the ground. *"You're in trouble now."*

"Shut up," my father grumbles.

I step into the cottage and close the door as Edith bounds toward me. She grabs my arm, pulling me toward a small room with a bed in the back. A strangely familiar girl sits on a chair beside a steaming basin.

"Myla says you two know each other," Edith says, moving me to the center of the room.

I scan the girl as she stands. "I expected you this morning," I tell her.

"I like to sleep in," she responds, shrugging.

"I was told you wanted to join the junior guard," I say, leading her to give me more information.

Myla reaches for my shirt as Edith lifts it over my head. "No," the young girl replies. "I'm here to join **your** guard."

Edith loosens my belt and pushes my shorts down my hips. "Ambitious one, isn't she?"

"Look," the girl grumbles. "Most of your guards would be dead if it wasn't for me. I'm the one that stopped them."

"What do you mean?" I ask, stepping out of my shorts and boots.

"They all thought you were in the fire," Myla says. "I was watching your house. I saw you ride away."

"Why were you watching her house?" Edith asks as I stare at the girl.

Myla shrugs. "Brock told me to stay at the bunkhouse, but those kids were annoying. They kept whining about being hungry. So, I followed him."

I remember Brock complaining about the little girl who pulled his whiskers. That same girl refused to stop following him around, demanding to join the guard. She's headstrong and wants a place of importance in our world but seems unwilling to play by the rules that would come with it.

"No," I say, lifting my arm for Edith to wash. "I don't think the guard is the right place for you. I have something else in mind, but you will need to stop arguing with Neala," I tell her.

The young girl smiles. "Yes, Luna," she replies. "Can I help?"

I sigh and look to Edith for the answer.

"Sure, kid," Edith says. "Grab one of those rags. You don't happen to know how to braid, do you?"

It turns out that Myla is quite skilled with braiding. She begins wetting and pulling my hair into layers of braids while Edith continues washing me. As they talk to each other, I relax into their soft pampering and tune them out to listen for my Alpha.

Bastian and my father have abundant energy because they've been eating well for the past few days and haven't done much work. Matthew is throwing a ball for them based on their trash talk. Edith and I are the only bow hunters in the pack, so they are just racing each other.

"Your Uncle Miles washed your mother's hair before her wedding," Edith says, pulling me away from my father's teasing of Bastian because he's not as fast. "Sometimes I think about how hard that had to be for him."

"Why would washing her hair be hard?" I ask, sitting in the chair they place behind me.

"He was bonded to your mother and quietly gave her to your father in the ceremony," she answers thoughtfully. "Miles was a ruthless Alpha. He took what he wanted. He had a fighting ring, according to some of his pack. You did what he said, or you fought—sometimes to the death."

Frowning, I shake my head. "I didn't really get that impression of him," I say slowly. "Even on Mom's birthday, when he was in the field with me, he was protective. He stayed between me and the wolves so I didn't get hurt."

"Your mother brought out the best in him," Edith says, nodding. "He was a different person after he spent time with her. I was with Miles on that last day. He told me that he'd never loved anyone as he loved your mother. He made me promise to make sure she was always happy."

"I wish she were here," I whisper, blinking back my tears.

"Me too, sweetheart," Edith says. Sighing, she turns to the wardrobe behind her and opens it slowly. "Anthony made me put her dress in the safe. He said you should have it when you were ready."

She turns around, holding a beautiful white dress with beads and ribbon sewn in the shape of flowers. It's floor length with two straps extending from the chest area to a choker collar. Edith holds it out and smiles sadly at it before turning it around. Myla gasps behind me.

I reach for it and run my fingers over the tiny reddish-orange beads along the area that will sit against the small of my back. They are sewn in a circle with a curved line through it and a green stem and leaf protruding from the top. My mother must have looked beautiful in this dress. I fear I will not do it justice.

"I couldn't do the whole dress," Edith says apologetically. "But I wanted it to have a little of you on it."

I stand up, pulling my hair from Myla's hands. "It's gorgeous, Edith," I whisper, slipping the fabric through my fingers.

Edith works it onto the floor so that it fluffs out and leaves a clear spot for me to step. She reaches out for my hand. "It's getting late. Dax will be here soon."

I pat my chest before taking Edith's hand. Bastian had taken Grandpa's medallion before we left the ridge. He said he wanted to talk to Grandpa before the ceremony. My mother's ashes still hang from my neck, though. I clutch them with one hand and offer Edith the other. She helps me step into the dress, and Myla assists her with lifting it around me.

Raising my chin, I take a deep breath and smile at Edith. "Would my mother be proud?"

Edith cups my cheeks. "Close your eyes and listen to your wolves for a moment." She watches as I do what I'm told.

The wolves that I can hear are happily talking about the ceremony. They ask about the food they smell and talk about music. They discuss when they will be off watch and able to join in. My wolves are miles from the home they knew and will never return to it. They lost many loved ones but are happier than I've heard in years.

Smiling, I open my eyes. "Thank you."

"You're welcome, honey," Edith says. "Your mother was happiest listening to her wolves enjoy themselves. She would be very proud of you."

I take a deep breath and try to blink back the threatening tears when someone knocks loudly on the door. Jumping, Edith furrows her brow, and Myla defensively steps around me.

"I didn't just run for two and a half days to stand outside a door, Luna," a voice yells, taking my breath away.

"Kade," I whisper.

Edith steps forward and opens the door. "You could've at least found clothes, Kade," she scoffs.

I don't care. I've seen naked men for most of my life. Kade is beautiful from head to toe, but his silver-blue eyes and playful grin capture all my attention. "I needed you," I whisper to him.

Kade saunters over and pulls me into his arms. "I know you did, sweetheart," he whispers back. "Your father promised a good meal if I got here on time. I smell lamb. I prefer mountain lion, but I'll live."

I shake my head as he keeps talking. I love Kade, but not nearly as much as he loves the sound of his own voice. I rub my hand over his chest and line my fingers with my mother's handprint.

"You're gonna have to stop fondling me one day," Kade continues. "You're about to be a married woman. I'm a married man. We can't keep doing this." He stops when he notices I'm giggling. "Quit laughing, woman. You know you want me." He straightens his back and puts his chin on my head. "Who's the kid?"

I lean back and hold Kade by the cheeks. "This is Myla," I announce. "She's your new apprentice. You have a unique way about you, Kade, and I believe you are the right kind of teacher for this young wolf."

"Oh, the wicked things I can teach you, kid," Kade says, smiling broadly.

"Kade," I start, sighing deeply. "I said teach, not corrupt. Behave."

Kade scoffs. "When have you ever known me to do a stupid thing like that?"

Edith allows me to have my moment with Kade, but she shakes some pants at him when there's a scratch at the door. "You better put something on," she tells him sternly. "That's probably her grandfather."

Kade winks at me before taking the pants. "But does the Luna want me to get dressed?"

Shaking my head, I smile and grab his face. "The Luna does indeed, Kade." I pull him to my lips.

Kade groans as he wraps his arms around me and holds his lips against mine. "Now that's what I'm talking about," he whispers, pulling back and licking his lips. "You taste different. What is that? Syrup?"

"She's pregnant, Kade," Edith scoffs, standing at the door. "Hands off."

Kade clicks his tongue. "Ah, that's why you were so weird for the full moon." He steps into me, erasing any distance between us. "He blew your mind, though, right? I mean, I've been with hundreds of women. Well, if Gaine asks, it was, like, three. But being with her. Wow." Kade makes a noise as if something is exploding.

The scratching on the door sounds again, but with greater urgency, and it's quickly followed by an insistent knock.

"Kade, I'm getting married," I whisper, pulling him from whatever thought is distracting him.

"Yeah," he says, taking a sharp breath. "Let's go do that."

Kade steps back to jump into the pants, and I turn to look in the mirror. Myla has created several small braids and twisted them with thin strips of white fabric to highlight her work in the moonlight. My chest is mashed, but the rest of the dress fits my body perfectly, flowing to the floor and covering my bare feet.

Edith moves as the door bursts open, and my father charges into the room, followed by Grandpa. "Easy, guys," she tells the Alphas. "You requested Kade's return for a reason, Tarq. Let them have their moment."

"That doesn't make her any less pregnant," Daddy growls.

"That Alpha of yours was a heartbeat away from charging in here himself," Grandpa says.

"I'm sorry," I say, sliding my arm around Kade's back. "I didn't realize how much I wanted him here. Thank you, Daddy."

"You're welcome," my father says, kissing my cheek. "You look beautiful." He pulls back to look at Kade. "You have about five minutes before that kid reaches his limit. I think that baby is affecting him more than her."

As Daddy leaves, I kneel to my grandfather. "I'm getting married, Grandpa," I whisper as he steps into my arms. "I wouldn't be without Mom's help. She should be here."

"Your mother is always with you," Grandpa says. He steps back and taps his nose on my chest. *"You carry her in your heart everywhere you go. And when you forget she's there, she shows up in the hearts of your wolves just when you need her."* He looks at Kade. *"She couldn't explain him. Something about that wolf captivated her too. He is one of a kind."*

"I'm quite sure you're the only wolf he respects," I whisper, giggling.

"He should," Grandpa grumbles. *"I'm gonna take your wolves to the altar. You should probably hurry. They may not be able to kill me, but they can get past me."*

Giggling, I kiss his nose and watch him leave the room. Kade reaches for my hand and helps me to my feet. I lead the small group into the main room of the cottage.

Clay smiles broadly. "You are just as beautiful as your mother," he gushes, kissing my knuckles.

"Thank you," I tell him. "You'll be allowed to attend the reception right after the ceremony. Myla?" I reach out to the young wolf and wait for her to step beside me. "You are Kade's charge, but he will be busy, so I ask you to wait here until he collects you."

When she tries to object, Kade steps forward. "Asking you to do something is the Luna's polite way of giving you an order," he snaps. "The proper response is, 'Yes, Luna.'"

"Yes, Luna," Myla mumbles, glaring at Kade.

Smiling, I cup her cheek. "Thank you, Myla."

Kade winks, extending his arm for me to hook mine through. "I brought you an elder so your wedding could be a little less crazy," he announces, opening the front door. "She just might be more beautiful than you tonight, though."

Gaine smiles at me from the porch. She does look lovely in the blue sundress that she's wearing. Her dark brown hair has bleached high-lights now, but her body shows no sign of life on the road or a lack of nutrients. I glance back at Kade and see his cheeks sunken. Clearly, he's been giving his wife all the food.

I squeeze Gaine's hand but look up at her husband. "Thank you for taking care of her," I whisper.

Kade kisses my cheek. "I always take care of what's mine," he says. "Why do you think I'm here?"

"The food," I answer.

"That is a delicious perk. I'm not gonna lie," Kade says, chuckling. "Alright, Luna. That kid survived hell to be your Alpha. We shouldn't keep him waiting any longer."

I smile when I glance toward the water. My wolves line the twisted twig walkway. Small candles sit atop each pillar that anchors the dock, but the large base at the end has lanterns hanging from its seven posts.

Bastian is standing with my father and grandfather, somehow more beautiful. They've washed him as they did with me. Bastian's hair mainly falls to the back of his head, but he has a few shorter tufts that always fall forward to touch his cheeks. He's dressed in a tan shirt with a black coat. The blue jeans fit him so perfectly that my lower lip slips between my teeth.

"Come on, Ayls," Kade whispers. "One small step at a time."

I tear my eyes away from Bastian to smile at my silver wolf. "Don't let me run to him, Kade."

Chuckling, Kade pats my hand. "No, ma'am," he says. "We're gonna do this all dignified like." He steps forward but stops and lifts his eyebrow when my arm jerks him back. "Ok, so we'll be dignified in just a minute."

I smile at Kade's words. My father had picked the perfect escort for me. I'm unsure if anyone else could have convinced my feet to move from this spot. But once I take the first step, Kade's momentum carries me forward. He rubs his hand over my fingers and quietly makes shushing noises that help block out everything else.

Bastian attempts to step forward as we walk under the arch. Daddy grabs his shoulder, and Grandpa curls around to block his legs. Anthony steps away from them as Bastian's growl shakes the dock. Daddy leans in to whisper into his ear, and his growl settles but doesn't disappear. He hasn't taken his eyes off me.

All I want is to feel Bastian's touch. His words would soothe my soul, his scent would ease my mind, and his kiss would calm my chest's tension. Kade stops me before we reach the base. His rubbing of my fingers is probably the only thing that's stopped me from running to Bastian.

Anthony clears his throat and steps back to the center of the dock's base. Out of the corner of my eye, I see his gaze flick between me and Bastian. I only hope he was expecting this tension after proceeding over my parents' wedding.

"Ladies and gentlemen," Anthony calls loudly, silencing my wolves. "We are here to join your Luna, Annalisa, and her Alpha, Bastian, in the union of marriage. Does the Elder bless this union?"

"I do," Gaine says from behind me.

"Do the Alphas bless this union?" Anthony continues.

My father grins. "I do."

Grandpa looks up at me when Anthony turns his gaze to him. *"You're confident that he's ready for the pack?"*

"I am, Grandpa," I tell him. *"He loves me and our pack. Even this one."* I shake Kade's arm, making him lift his eyebrow.

"Alright then," Grandpa says, nodding to Anthony. *"I do."*

After watching Anthony with my wolves for 22 years, it still amazes me how easily he understands their movements and expressions. He nods back to my grandfather and looks at Kade. "Who is here to escort this bride?"

Kade clears his throat, readying to be heard far and wide, undoubtedly pissing my father off. "The magnificent, honorable, and overly handsome Kade of the Luna's most trusted inner circle," he says with a firm air of seriousness.

By the time he's finished, Anthony's nose is wrinkled, Gaine's fingers are to her forehead, and all three Alphas are growling. I'm probably the only person laughing. I don't know what they expected him to do, but they were wrong. Kade can't take a funeral seriously. I didn't hear half his vows at his wedding over his guests' laughter.

I pull his cheek to my lips. "I love you," I whisper. "Thank you."

Kade winks. "I'm always here for you, baby girl."

"I'm almost afraid to ask this, but do you give this woman freely to the wolf she desires?" Anthony asks, cringing.

Kade winces. "Do I have a choice?" He turns me to face him. "Why don't you just stay with me? Gaine would share. You could have me every other day. Twice on Sunday if you behave yourself."

Bastian lunges, stopped only by my father's stealth. Grandpa steps forward with his teeth bared. Gaine hasn't stopped shaking her head since Kade opened his mouth.

Kade clicks his tongue, sighing with a pout. "Fine," he says, attempting to sound depressed. "He can have her."

I turn to my father. "You sent for him," I scoff, laughing. "What did you expect?"

"Someone who wanted to live through the night," Daddy grumbles.

"Luna, get over here before your father kills your escort," Anthony advises, rolling his eyes.

I smile broadly at Kade. "You are perfect just the way you are," I say, pulling him to my lips for a kiss. "Now get out of my way so I can marry my Alpha."

Kade bows with a grin and steps back to receive a smack from his wife. "What?" he scoffs.

I step forward to stand before Anthony and turn to my anxious Alpha. The muscles along his jaw are flexing from his tension. Anthony asks Bastian to step forward, and he's suddenly against my chest, holding my hands. Looking up, I blow gently onto his face until he noticeably relaxes.

"Easy, my Alpha," I whisper. "We're almost there."

"Bastian," Anthony whispers, leaning forward. "Your vows?"

My Alpha searches my face for something I'm not sure he'll find, but I don't think he's ready to talk yet.

"This is such a shit show," Anthony grumbles. He looks around me at Kade. "This is your damn fault."

Giggling, I reach for Bastian's face and slide my thumb over his lower lip. "It's just you and me, my perfect man," I whisper. "What do you want to say to me?"

"You are my world," Bastian starts. "I had given up on life when your mother found me. She reminded me that love wasn't painful. Your father taught me that I could be strong and gentle at the same time. I was ready to stand by their side, protecting them for the rest of my life."

Bastian takes a deep breath and steps into me so that he's against me from our chests to our feet. He smiles when he feels my bare feet underneath the folds of my dress.

"But then your mother told me I had a Luna of my own," Bastian whispers, searching my eyes. "You are perfect, beautiful, sweet... everything I wanted in my life, and I need you. You are the air in my lungs, the ground beneath my feet, and the breeze in my fur. I am yours. I've always been yours."

By the time Bastian stops talking, we're both heaving air. His lips nearly rub against mine in our closeness as we stare into each other's eyes. I jump when Anthony touches my shoulder, and Bastian growls.

"Your mother is gonna have a fit," Anthony grumbles. "I'm so glad I don't have to hear that."

"Yeah, I'd rather actually die than go back and listen to her for the next month," Grandpa adds.

"We're ready, Anthony," I say, rubbing my lips against Bastian's to soothe him.

"Then, Luna, you may say your vows," Anthony announces loudly for our guests.

"Bastian, you are so much more than my Alpha," I say, trying to project my voice without shouting in Bastian's face. "You are the most beautiful wolf I have ever seen. Your smile takes my breath away while your words breathe life back into me. You are in my soul and ground me when I need to find my center.

"I will honor you in every way, reminding you that you are loved daily. I feel blessed that you have given me your heart. I promise to protect it and keep it safe until the end of time. I will always be yours."

Bastian's holding my cheeks by the time I stop talking. My Alpha is highly emotional in general. After spending years feeling pain and shame, he does not view love lightly. His fingers hook painfully around my jaw.

"Grandpa, don't move," I say quickly while holding my finger up to Daddy. *"Bastian needs a minute."*

Smiling sweetly at my Alpha, I move my hands to his wrists. I stand still, rubbing his skin and softly blowing onto his face to allow the time he needs to collect himself. When his muscles stop twitching, I rub my lips over his until he gently kisses me.

"I don't deserve you," Bastian whispers.

"Yes, you do," I tell him. "You have always deserved me." I slide the back of my fingers over his cheek and shift my eyes toward our wolves. "It's time to accept them. Are you ready?"

Bastian takes a few deep breaths and nods.

"With the blessing of the Elder and Alpha, I bind you in this union," Anthony proclaims. "Bastian, will you accept this pack? Will you protect and guide them? Will you govern them in the way of those before you to promote solidarity and unity?"

Bastian leaves his eyes on mine as he reaches for my father's hand. Daddy accepts it while placing his other hand on Grandpa's shoulders. The three generations of Alphas stand as one solid unit, and the air seems momentarily electrified.

"I do," Bastian says, projecting his voice to our wolves. "I will accept every part of you," he whispers onto my lips as our wolves erupt with cheers. "Even that dumbass." Bastian smiles, flicking his eyes in Kade's direction.

"With the power vested in me, I bless this union," Anthony says quickly before anything else happens. "May your bond be unending, your love everlasting, and your voice heard as one. Hurry up and kiss her before Kade says something stupid."

Bastian breathes a quiet laugh and licks his lips. "I love you," he whispers before bending me backward and kissing me deeply. Moaning into his mouth, I answer his need with my own. Today is no different from yesterday, but declaring our love for each other before the pack has somehow ignited a spark within us.

12

y wolves talk excitedly as they look over tables lined with the food Edith and Clay are bringing out for them. We have limited clothes since the fire burned most of what we had, so only around half are in their human form. Plenty of hungry muzzles rub across the edge of the tables as they wait for their plates to be filled.

I nod toward the cottage when Kade catches my eye, reminding him that his student is still waiting inside. He winks and kisses Gaine's cheek before leaving to collect Myla. Bastian takes my hand and steps toward the blankets set out for picnicking since we don't have tables, but my fingers bump into Grandpa's fur.

"You go ahead, my Alpha," I say, smiling. "I want a moment with Grandpa."

"I'll save you a seat," Bastian says before kissing my cheek and leaving us.

While my wolves are distracted, I pull my grandfather back to the dock and sit on the edge. "It's all gone, Grandpa," I whisper, leaning against his shoulder as he sits beside me. "The house, the cabin, the sheds... they're all gone. The only thing left was the barn."

"Your father told me about Doc," Grandpa says, sighing. *"I'm sorry, Ayls. But the houses and such... Those are just things, kiddo. How are you doing?"*

"We lost Nate, Grandpa." I can't help the tears that stream out.

He turns to step into me so I can hide in his fur. *"I was 176 years old when I died, sweetheart,"* Grandpa says. *"I said goodbye to a lot of wolves over the years. Nate had a good life. He loved his job and you and your mother very much. He was happy being the old grumpy wolf and was so proud of Matthew."*

I wipe my tears away but stay against his neck. "I bet Matthew would like to hear that," I whisper. "Nate was like a father to him. He misses him."

"We always miss those that are gone. Through their memory, we're able to honor them." Grandpa backs up to look me in the eye. *"You will always carry them."*

"Am I doing the right thing?" I ask, gathering myself and wiping my face. "Was leaving the lake the right decision?"

"You're just like your mother," Grandpa grumbles. *"Honey, I can't see the future. My Luna told me that her wolves lived in the mountains, though. Maybe that's where your adventure is supposed to be."*

"The wolves used to live in the mountains?" I furrow my brow and think back to my mother's conversation with Edith and Daddy. I only heard her and Edith, but they were talking about westward travel. "Why did they leave?"

"After Aylee sacrificed herself, they fell apart. Fighting and such," Grandpa says, lying against my leg so I can rub my hands over him. His Luna has a habit of riling him up, and he enjoys the calming touch a little more than most. *"Lacking a destined leader, pack life turned into a battle of strength and divided loyalties. It became too dangerous to remain close to other packs as they split, so they started to spread out and leave the mountains for the safety of new lands."*

"Did she have any advice about the drought?" I ask, rubbing his leg as he holds it up.

"Aylee is a different kind of person, Ayls," Grandpa starts. *"I rarely get straight answers from her about the past. She said that you've ignored the signs for too long."*

"What signs?"

"I have no idea," Grandpa grumbles, annoyed.

I giggle, pulling his fur. "It's alright, Grandpa," I tell him. "Mom told me she was a special character. Maybe she'll tell you this month."

Grandpa nods. *"Speaking of your mother, she wanted me to tell you that she is proud of the Luna you've become."*

"No advice?"

"That's not her style, kiddo," he says, winking. *"She trusts you to be the Luna you're meant to be. She says she gave you all the tools you needed to protect your wolves. We are both very proud of your strength."*

I look out over the riverbed as he lays his head back down. "I spend most of the time wishing she was still their Luna," I admit quietly. "I wish she was here to make these decisions. I never questioned if she was right."

"Questions are important, daughter," Daddy says, joining us. He sits beside me, reaching across my back to pull Grandpa's fur. "She used to ask your grandfather for advice all the time. Sometimes, she listened. Other times, she rolled her eyes and told us all that she was the one in charge. We loved and honored her, just as we do with you, sweetheart."

Pulling my fingers through Grandpa's fur, I lean against my father, letting his heat comfort me. "You always know the right thing to say," I tell Daddy as he rests his chin on my head.

My father scoffs and points his finger toward a tree that's shading us from the moon. "They came and got me," he says, smirking. "Those two are who you should be listening to."

I look up where he's pointing to find Bastian and Kade leaning against the tree, watching us. Kade smiles broadly, but Bastian studies me intently. He's always curiously watched my interactions with Daddy and Grandpa. I can't decide if he's trying to learn how they support me or how to be a parent.

Daddy kisses my head. "Come on," he says to all of us. "Let's get back to the celebration. Maybe you two can sneak off and spend some more time together."

"See, Luna?" Kade starts excitedly. "Even your father knows we're meant to be."

Daddy clicks his tongue. "Not you, dumbass."

Kade laughs as Daddy stands and shoves him back toward the food tables, followed by my grandfather. Bastian extends his hand and lifts me to my feet once I accept it. He sighs as he looks me over before cupping my cheek and kissing the tip of my nose.

"Thank you for getting him," I whisper. "You should join us, though. Your thoughts are important too."

"I am truly your Alpha now, Ayls," Bastian responds. "Your father will be leaving, and you will wish for these moments with him. I want you to have them while you can."

"And here I thought you were afraid you'd say the wrong thing," I say, giggling.

Bastian lifts an eyebrow. "I might," he admits. "But so could he. You know what I picture when I think of you two? I remember when he would hold you in his lap and whisper to you. I close my eyes and watch you rub your fingers under his lip. I hear you giggling through tears as he calms you."

"Mom said we had a bond that she could never crack," I whisper.

"He will break that one day," Bastian responds, rubbing my cheek. "After that, all you'll have are the memories you make today."

Smiling, I press my lips to his. "How did I get so lucky?"

"Ayls, you were born to the best parents I have ever met," Bastian says, turning to link our arms. "They saved me from my past and shaped me into the man who will love and support their daughter until the end of time. That's where you got lucky."

I can only manage a stunned silence as Bastian escorts me among our wolves. Besides Grandpa and Clay, we are surrounded by the 72 wolves and two humans who survived the lake attack. They range from 3 years old to 78. Despite our trials and what we have lost, they all feel happy and excited over the feast before them and our festivities. Their smiles and laughter warm my heart and fill my soul.

Normally, we'd sit among family during our reception feast, but Bastian leads me straight to Trish, who's sitting with a few extra plates of meat. "You look beautiful, Ayls," Trish gushes as we sit. "But, Kade? That would have been perfect had he not spoken."

Smiling, I take the plate she offers. "I love Kade just as I love you," I tell her, making room for Bastian beside me. "Kade grew up under my Uncle Miles. Daddy says they are similar, and no one can explain how either ended up so deep in everyone's heart, but we can't help loving them."

Trish is barely paying attention to me. She's hungry and hasn't been able to eat much since I've been away with Bastian. I watch her pop a few chunks of lamb chop in her mouth and giggle when her eyes roll closed.

"Listen," Trish says when she swallows. "I'm not saying I don't like him. I just wish he wouldn't talk, especially when it's important." She looks toward a group over by the tables.

I follow her gaze and see Edith reprimanding Kade about something. He winks and blows me a kiss. "Kade was there for the worst night of my life. Now he's here for the best," I say, smiling. I turn to Trish. "He's always been the same person. The consistency of those around us grounds us to who we are. If he changed, it might alter me. So, I love and accept who Kade is without expecting him to be different."

"Kade has actually changed a lot," Bastian says, joining the conversation. "I suspect that was Gaine's doing, though. You never experienced who he was before he met her. You wouldn't like him so much if you had."

Bastian's eyes roll as he bites into a lamb chop smothered in a spice rub. The hums from the wolves around us become too overwhelming to ignore. When Bastian's starts, I can't control my giggling any longer. My wolves will usually hum in my presence, but this loud hum chorus is due to Anthony's extraordinary cooking and their full bellies.

Once upon a time, my mother told me that the wolf was the dominant trait of my pack. They have intense instincts, are fiercely passionate, and are hypersensitive to every feeling. To say that they love the sensation of a full stomach is a gross understatement.

"I'm gonna send your companion in for dinner, kiddo," Daddy says quietly, kneeling to kiss my head. "These guards aren't gonna make it back out there. We'll see about getting you two time alone soon, but tonight, hang out with Grandpa and get some sleep."

"I love you, Daddy," I whisper, cupping his cheek before he can stand. "Thank you for this."

I glance around as my father leaves, seeing my wolves beginning to stretch out over the blankets. Some younger wolves curl up with their parents, letting them lick their muzzles clean. I finally spot Kade and Gaine approaching us with Myla in tow. Kade's young charge is holding a plate stacked high with choice cuts of lamb and steak.

"Looks like you scored big," I say, smiling.

Myla blushes a deep enough red that I can see it in the moonlight. "Kade made me help the humans," she says, grinning. "I held back some cuts until I was allowed to eat."

"I never said you couldn't eat," Kade grumbles, helping Gaine down to the blanket.

Clay quietly strums on a guitar from the porch of his cottage. It's difficult to hear over the hum of my wolves, but his song is slow and sweet.

Bastian stands and extends his hand in my direction. "Come with me," he says quietly.

Tilting my head, I accept his hand and let him pull me to my feet. Bastian leads me near the porch and holds me against his body. I've only ever danced with Daddy, but Bastian handles my body like we've danced together daily. When he begins leading me through the grass, expertly guiding and twirling me, it's obvious that my family taught him.

"This was something Luna and I did while we stayed at the cabin," Bastian whispers. "Tarq made sure I knew how to lead. He said, 'If you're gonna marry my daughter, you better know how to handle her.' I don't think he was just talking about dancing."

I giggle and snuggle into his chest, letting him handle whatever he likes. My body fits perfectly against Bastian's. I tuck my face up into his neck and breathe him in as he gently twirls me to the soft, slow music coming from the guitar. My Alpha heats his body for me, and I press my stomach to him, easing my abdomen's ache.

Dancing has always been a healing experience for my family. Mom told me about the Alphas all dancing with her at her wedding.

Whenever I struggled, Daddy would find a way to make music so he could waltz me around until I found my center again. When I was six, Mom had the wolves howl a song in the flower fields for us to dance to.

"Grandpa used to dance with Grandma," I tell Bastian. "When he tried to distance himself, and she was missing him, Daddy would dance with her. He taught Mom." I reach for his cheek. "Grandpa Bruce took lessons from Daddy a few years ago. He told me not to tell anyone, but it was sweet that he wanted to do that for Grandma."

"He's a good man," Bastian says, smiling. "They all are." He sighs, resting his chin on my forehead. "Except for maybe Kade."

"Seriously?" Kade scoffs behind me. "After everything I do for you? Give me my woman."

I turn to look at him as Bastian stops dancing. Kade's grin is playful, but his hand is stretched to me, waiting for my response. I kiss Bastian and take Kade's offer. He twirls me before pulling me to his chest. Kade extends his hand to Bastian and nods before spinning me away.

I've spent a lot of time with Kade. Once I finally got him to start talking while he stayed at the lake with me, we would go swimming, fishing, riding, and sometimes just walking the trails for hours. I have never danced with him. I'm unsure why it surprises me how good he is. Kade has many hidden talents that I have yet to discover.

"Why did you refuse to dance at your wedding, Kade?" I ask, staying close to his body so he can guide me around the trees.

Kade slides his hand to my hip and pushes me into a spin before pinning me back to his hips. "I can't reveal all of my secrets to the public, Ayls," he whispers into my ear. "Gaine got what she deserved once we were alone."

"Why do you always make everything sound like a punishment?" I ask, giggling.

Kade breathes a quiet laugh. "I have an image to uphold," he whispers, winking.

"Did you two find anything good?" I ask, wondering if he has anything to report from his journey west. "Or am I leading our wolves to certain death?"

"So dramatic," Kade scoffs, clicking his tongue. "Your wolves love you and followed you willingly this far. Your companion and his mate traveled north to meet up with you because they love and trust you." He moves so that I can see Brock and Rachel have joined us after Daddy relieved them of watch. "You're the only one questioning this decision. Trust their faith in you. They'll tell you when you're overreaching."

I once asked Kade why he didn't kick Tynan's ass and take over as Alpha. He said being an asshole doesn't mean you'll make a good leader. He claimed he was too selfish to think about anyone but himself. I suspect that might have been true before he met Gaine. His need to win her turned him into the man who takes my breath away with his advice and wisdom.

Kade stops, leaning back to look into my eyes. "Seems my turn with you is over," he whispers, kissing my cheek. He spins me away and into my father's arms.

"Your husband wanted to give you a gift," Daddy says, smoothly spinning me along with Clay's new tune. "He's come a long way from the broken wolf that nearly gave up in your mother's arms."

"You both helped him," I say, snuggling into his chest. Bastian's words echo from deep within my heart. "You're not leaving, are you?"

My father breathes deeply, and I feel him look down at me. "No, baby," he murmurs. "I'm going to see this through with you." He groans a bit before continuing. "Besides, if your mother saw any of that wedding, I don't want to hear her thoughts. She might have liked Kade before, but I'm sure her opinion changed after that circus."

"I asked him what they found but didn't get an answer," I say, changing the subject before he starts listing all of Kade's annoying traits.

"I talked to Gaine while she was changing," Daddy tells me. "They reached the foot of the hills. I called them back at night, but they waited until morning to leave." He leans back and cups my cheeks. "They saw snow on the mountains," he says, smiling.

Grandma told me that the Rockies have an elevation that might be too high for us to live. But if there is snow up there, there's water. I've had a nervous pain in my chest since the fire. I had no idea what we would find once we crossed the flatlands and reached the mountains, where the militia could no longer attack us.

I close my eyes and breathe a sigh of relief. "Water," I whisper.

"And where there's water, there's food," Daddy responds. "We just have to get them there."

Turning to look at my wolves, I rest my head against his chest. "Those full stomachs are a good start," I say, grinning. "That will fuel them for a few days. If we let them finish the meat in the morning, we could leave immediately."

Daddy shakes his head. "Annalisa, that boy deserves some time alone with you," he says. "He's gonna spend a large chunk of his life missing you. He should have this time."

"What if we traveled beside the group?" I ask, thinking out loud. "We'd be alone but still moving forward."

"I don't know," my father grumbles, still shaking his head. "You need to talk to him about that. I'd be pissed, but he seems more understanding than I am." We stop dancing as Clay silences his strings. "Go on and lie down with your companion and Grandpa. I'll send Bastian back."

"Daddy?" I say, holding him before me. "I know you don't like Kade." I stop as he tries to disagree. I furrow my brow and nod, pretending to let him lie to me. "No, you don't like him. You've never tried to hide that. But I love you for calling him back for this."

"And tolerating his shit during the ceremony," Daddy leads.

"Yes," I agree, giggling. "That too." I wrap my arms around him, saddened by the thought that my days with him are numbered. Either he'll be leaving us, or we'll all die. "He really is a good guy, Daddy."

"I know he is, sweetheart," he whispers, kissing my head. "Go on, though. Grandpa will be leaving soon."

My father guides me back through my sleeping wolves to lie beside my grandfather. He leaves after promising again to send Bastian to me. I roll onto Grandpa's shoulder and curl my legs for him to rest his chin on. Edith describes him as an "old soul." I used to think she was just calling him old, but over the years, I've realized she was talking about how calm he is.

"You look beautiful tonight," Grandpa says as he settles into me. *"That young Alpha of yours is still pretty emotional, though, huh?"*

"In general, yes," I agree, rubbing my finger over his jaw. *"I got a little advice from Anthony and Daddy, and I'm figuring out how to help him. It's gotten a bit worse since I got pregnant."*

"Yeah, your father lost his damn mind from your scent," Grandpa says, chuckling. *"He was already a bit crazy, so your mother didn't notice until he was gone."*

"Anthony told me Mom connected to Daddy's wolf to convince him to return," I say.

"That man could always twist a story," Grandpa grumbles. *"The most important thing is that their child's scent will cause them to be extremely emotional. Your father shredded your mother's shoulder and took off on her. You need to be careful."*

"I knew about Mom's shoulder, but why didn't they tell me about Daddy leaving?" I ask as Edith approaches us with a plate of raw beef strips. When I lift my eyebrow, she points into the trees.

"Coming up behind you, my Luna," Bastian says. He lies beside me, pinning the sleeping Rachel between himself and Brock. *"Can you thank her for me?"*

"Edith knows you appreciate her," I tell him, smiling as I take the plate from the witch.

"Why don't you lie on him, kiddo," Grandpa suggests. *"I'll be leaving soon, and I don't want you to fall."*

"Daddy said Gaine reported they saw snow up on the mountains when they reached the foothills," I say, turning to lie against Bastian's shoulder. *"Grandpa, can you ask your Luna about the droughts again?"*

He groans, crawling beside me to lay his head over my lap. *"I'll try."*

"Has she ever mentioned unicorns?" I ask, feeling ridiculous for even saying it.

Grandpa lifts his head, tilting it curiously. *"I'm not sure she's much for fairy stories,"* he answers, confused. Bastian's hum starts, catching my grandfather's attention. *"Get your mouth off the Luna."* His growl is not playful.

Bastian is ignoring the food. His head is jammed between his front legs, and his jaw is wrapped around my arm. He's gently running his teeth and tongue over my skin. It's something he's always done but has gotten worse over the past month.

I push him out of hiding and give him a few fingers to chew on. *"It's fine, Grandpa,"* I say, scratching his whiskers. *"Daddy said Mom tasted good, but flowers were more for smelling than eating. He figures that my flavor is better than my scent since I smell like food. It has gotten worse since we bonded, though."*

"That's the baby," Grandpa grumbles. *"Mark my words, kiddo. He's gonna get worse."*

"I won't hurt you," Bastian says sweetly. He tucks to bump my belly with his nose. *"You're holding my favorite person."*

Grandpa shakes his head. *"What's this about a unicorn?"*

"You're not still thinking about that, are you?" Bastian asks.

Sighing, I hold up a cut of beef for him. *"It's been in enough of her visions that it might be worth asking Aylee about,"* I say, defending myself.

"I guess," Bastian grumbles. His eyes shift nervously between Grandpa and me before slowly tucking his nose under my arm for a quick taste before taking the meat.

Grandpa stares at him for a moment before turning to me. *"I can't watch this shit."* He rolls to put his back against me and stretches to lay his muzzle over my shoulder, using my chin to block his view of my Alpha mixing fruit with his meat.

"It's hard to explain, Dax," Bastian says, taking another cut of meat. *"I watched Tarq stick his nose to Luna for hours. She smelled good, but I thought he was crazy until I met Annalisa. I can't keep my mouth off her."*

Grandpa nuzzles my cheek. *"Her father was the same way when her mother first got pregnant,"* he says. *"That boy pissed me off. But I will tell you the same thing I told him. You need to remember that she is the Luna. Treat her with respect and dignity so that others don't think they can disrespect her."*

Grandpa's voice is firm. Although I am quite casual with my wolves and invite them into my space whenever they need me, my grandfather would prefer I stand on a pedestal and look down upon them as he did when he was Alpha. Bastian and I have a simple understanding regarding my grandfather. There is no arguing with Grandpa... ever.

"Yes, sir," Bastian answers. He gently licks my cheek before returning to his meat plate, forgoing the fruit flavoring while Grandpa is still here.

I lean against my grandfather's muzzle. *"My historian keeps seeing a unicorn when I ask her to look back on the drought,"* I tell him. *"Well, anything really. I asked her about the Alpha and Luna pregnancies, and she saw it again. She said it was hurt."*

"Alright," Grandpa states. *"I'll see what I can get out of her."* He takes a deep breath before rolling over to sit up. *"It's nearly time. I want you to be careful, Annalisa. This will be a hard journey. These wolves seem strong, but they lost a lot. They are distracted. You must be vigilant and stay strong enough for all of them."*

"I have Luna blood in my veins and two powerful Alphas by my side. How could I fail?" I slide my hand over his muzzle. *"I love you, Grandpa."*

"I love you too, kid." He nuzzles my cheek. *"Watch over your father."*

I sigh, leaning onto him just before he disappears.

Knowing me well, Bastian hooks his leg over my chest and pushes me back against his ribs. *"I've got you,"* he says softly. *"I will worry about everything for you tonight."*

13

❧

Once our wolves are well-fed in the morning, we bid farewell to
Clay and cross the river. Although the pack stays spread out to
avoid attracting attention, Bastian and I travel further to the north
than any of them to spend some time alone. Our seclusion reminds me
of when we would walk the mountain trails at home.

By the end of the third day, the pack reaches the area near the Ozark
that Kade had scouted. Bastian has taken too many liberties with my
body, and we are falling behind. I walk beside Edith's worn-out gelding
as Bastian chews on my fingers. While he's distracted, I listen to Daddy
position the guards for the night and yell at Kade for trying to sneak
off to find me.

"Ayls, I don't like you so far from the pack," Brock says. He and Rachel
are flanking us on one side while Ash and Drake are on the other.

I study Bastian for a moment before responding. *"My Alpha will spend
a large portion of the rest of his life missing me,"* I tell my guards, quoting
my father. *"He will have me tonight."* I rarely take a tone that demands
their silence, so when I'm firm with my wolves, they listen.

My Alpha shakes his head when I pull my fingers free. *"You ready to
stop?"* Bastian asks, looking around to get his bearings.

"Brock's not excited, but I think we've traveled far enough for one
day," I tell him, scratching his neck. "The pack has stopped for the
night, and the gelding is tired."

"You don't give Saint enough credit," Bastian says, chuckling. *"That horse
is a fabulous actor."* He stops suddenly, spreading his legs out to brace for

151

an attack, and snarls. Saint slings his head in the air, pricking his ears, listening for the danger. His tail is lifted, and I can feel his excitement.

"Well, he had me fooled," I say, grinning. I pat the horse's neck and move beside him to pull out some pants for Bastian. "Did you want to shift, my fierce protector?" I hold up the clothing with my eyebrow lifted.

"*I don't need clothes,*" Bastian says before shifting into my arms. "Neither do you."

I don't stand a chance. My nerves instantly reach out to him, set ablaze by his need, and I'm at their mercy. The pants fall to the ground as Bastian slides his hands firmly down my body. He rubs his cheek against mine and exhales over my ear. I love it when he glides his lips over my forehead to do the same on the other side.

Bastian pushes my shorts down and digs his fingers into my thighs to lift me to his hips. He presses me against a tree before I have the chance to latch onto him to stop from falling. Smiling, Bastian rubs his lips against mine and gently licks my top lip when I open my mouth to breathe more air.

"I can't get enough of you," Bastian growls. He pushes against my lips and slides his tongue over mine. Bastian's growl and hum mix while he slowly enjoys my taste. I hear my shirt tear when he tries to pull it off me.

"Was that necessary?" I ask, pushing him away by his cheeks.

Bastian smiles with his tongue between his teeth. He slowly pulls my shirt forward to slip my arms from the sleeves and drops it to the ground. Licking his lips, Bastian allows his eyes to trail across my freshly exposed skin. "Yes."

I gasp as I'm suddenly attacked by his teeth and tongue. Bastian chews on any part of me his mouth can reach, tasting my skin while claiming my body. My legs wrap around his waist, allowing me to accept all he's willing to give. I lay my head back against the tree to provide better access to my neck.

As his growl intensifies, Bastian lets go of my legs to grab onto the tree. He has become increasingly difficult to control and has done this a few times over the past few days. I tried calming him the first time. I won't make that mistake again.

I fight my body as my deepest nerves awaken, demanding attention. Bastian's hips match the rolling of his tongue on my neck. Biting my bottom lip, I desperately attempt to slow my breathing but only cause a whimper as my eyes roll closed.

Bastian pushes against me, rocking my hips and sending my body into a celebration like the fireworks in Daddy's movies. I call out to him as he bites my shoulder and growls so profoundly that I feel it in my chest. Our moment of release feels both painful and wonderful, but our bodies connecting for that brief experience is indescribable.

As his grip on my shoulder relaxes, my Alpha's growl simmers back to a hum. When his breathing evens, I slide my hands along his arms, sending small, unnoticeable bursts of heat to help him. Taking advantage of his exhaustion, I reach around his ribs to feel his muscles before he notices.

"Stop checking my body," Bastian grumbles against my neck.

I guess I'm not as sneaky as I thought.

"Bass, we need you strong right now," I whisper, slipping my fingers through his hair. "Your child and I are counting on you."

"No one will get near you," he promises. My nerves jump when he releases the tree to rub his hands over my sides. "My daughter will always be safe. No one will ever hurt her."

As I consider the bite behind Bastian's words, my grandfather's warning replays in my mind. I don't have anything to compare Bastian's behavior to, but his need for me is increasing, and I fear the moment he loses control.

"Are you ok?" Brock asks, stepping out from behind a tree.

I take a deep breath and lean my head against Bastian's. *"I am,"* I tell Brock. *"We'll be rejoining the pack tomorrow."*

Brock drops a log behind Bastian and works his jaw to spit out a piece of bark. *"I think that would be a good idea."*

I watch Brock slip back into the trees. I'm more thankful every day that he is with us. Chase was like a second father to me, and I remember a few times when my mother had to step between my father and her companion to keep the peace. I don't doubt Brock would get between me and my Alpha if needed.

It's dark when Bastian puts me down and turns to build a fire while I dress. My guards had been silently piling wood for us while he composed himself. My Alpha makes quick work of the kindling and lights a small fire so I can see. I remove Saint's cinch, but Bastian lifts his saddle from his back.

"Come sit by the fire, Ayls," Bastian says gently. "Are you hungry?"

My stomach turns slightly. I haven't eaten in the past few days, but I know whatever I try to put in my stomach will come back out. "I think I'll need to wait until we're back with Trish," I tell him, smiling weakly.

Bastian pulls on his pants and lays beside the fire. He pats his chest for me to join him. "Can I visit with my daughter?"

I lie on his chest and lean my hip out, allowing him to rub his fingers over my belly. "Edith helped my mother with her pregnancy," I murmur. "Maybe she has some advice for us."

Bastian sighs. "Advice about what?"

"Bass, I feel you struggling," I start, but I lift my head as voices that typically filter into the background become too loud to ignore. *"Kade? What's the matter?"*

"Luna, I need you," Kade shouts in my head. *"I need you now. Where are you? Please."*

Kade might be a pain in the ass, but he is the most emotionally balanced wolf I have in my pack. He has one emotion he can't process at all... fear.

"Kade needs me," I tell Bastian. I hold out my finger when he sits up to protest. *"Brock, call Kade."* I pull Bastian to face me. "Kade's skills make him dangerous when he's struggling with something. I am his Luna, and he's asking me for help."

"He couldn't wait one more day?" Bastian grumbles as Brock calls to Kade in the distance.

"Do you remember the morning we found Kade lying on our porch?" I ask. "He was broken. Daddy had to carry him inside because

I still couldn't get him to move after two days. That was fear. After he watched Daddy lose Mom, he was terrified of letting himself love Gaine because he didn't want to feel her loss."

Bastian narrows his eyes and looks off into the distance.

"Perhaps you'd like to shift and talk with us," I suggest.

"Alright," Bastian says, sighing.

Smiling, I cup his cheek. "Your daughter likes your heat, and your hum eases the ache a bit," I whisper, recalling some of Anthony's advice. "We love our wolf."

Bastian's expression softens as he leans on my hand. "You will always have me." His hum starts as he leans forward to gently kiss my lips.

I smile at his tenderness. "I love you, my Alpha," I whisper. "You are mine."

Bastian rubs his lips over my cheeks. "I am yours." He kisses the tip of my nose and removes his pants. His nerves are calling to mine, but he still shifts and shakes out his fur. *"I'll talk to Tarq before I shift again,"* Bastian says, nuzzling my neck before lying down. *"I'm sorry. You might be right."*

I settle against his shoulder and pull the fur on his throat. "I think Grandpa is the right one," I say, giggling. "But I'll take the credit."

Brock charges into our clearing with a snarl as Kade bursts through the brush, headed straight for us. I sit up and hold my hand out to Brock, stopping him. Kade slides to a stop beside me and jams his muzzle under Bastian's neck. My Alpha's eyes shift to me, confused.

Equally baffled, I shake my head and put my finger to my lips. I slide my fingers through Kade's fur as Gaine emerges from the woods. She rubs her muzzle over Brock's before sliding up my side opposite her husband. I wrap my arm around her neck as she sighs and lays her jaw on my shoulder.

Although Gaine's emotions are easy to feel, Kade's scar makes his challenging to access. Something has them both terrified, but Gaine is also sad. Kade's never put his muzzle under Bastian's neck. Since the rest of our pack is settled quietly in camp together, I can't imagine what might be going on with these two.

After a while, Bastian's body begins to heat as he falls asleep. Gaine continues to nuzzle my cheek, and although Kade hasn't moved, I know he's still awake.

"Gaine, would it be ok if I pull all of this so you can sleep?" I ask the brown wolf on my shoulder. *"I think it might be easier to talk after a good night's sleep."*

Gaine twists her neck to lay her muzzle across my throat. Her tears drip down my neck. *"He doesn't want me,"* she says sadly.

Sighing, I roll my eyes. *"Ok,"* I grumble. *"I know that's not true. Get some rest, Gaine. Things are always brighter in the sunlight."* I push my fingers into her fur, pulling her emotions as I rub her skin until her breathing evens.

"I do want her," Kade tells me quietly. *"I will always want her."*

"I know, Kade," I respond. *"I think it's important that you learn to talk to your wife. You're scaring her, and that's not fair."* I give Kade a chance to respond, but when he doesn't, I continue. *"It will take us two days to get around the lakes. Why don't you two stay with me during that time? Daddy can take the lead, and I can help you learn to open up to Gaine."*

Kade sighs. *"You have to help me protect her. Both of you."*

"I will protect all of my wolves, Kade," I promise him. *"That includes you and your wife. Sleep. We'll remind her in the morning how much you love her."*

I suffer through a restless night while comforting the pair. Kade jerks several times throughout the night but stays under Bastian's neck. Gaine wakes multiple times, dripping tears onto my chest and needing my help.

* * *

The next day is strange at best. Bastian and I exchange confused looks throughout most of the day as Kade yells at Gaine repeatedly, ordering her to stay with us. Although Gaine has access to my support and assistance, I'd asked her not to tell me what Kade is upset about. I know she's in pain, but the cycle will continue if her husband doesn't learn to communicate with her.

Traveling in front of us, Kade heads toward the northern flank of the pack. He brings Gaine any food he finds and stands by while she eats it before leaving again.

After he leaves the third time, I sit beside her, sliding my hand over her jaw. "I know he's making you very uncomfortable. I'm sorry," I whisper. "I will stop him if you want me to, but he has a process he needs to work through before he's ready to talk to us."

"Luna, you must be hungry too," Gaine says, touching her muzzle to my cheek. *"And Bastian hasn't eaten."*

"Why don't we focus on the sweetness of it?" I ask, thinking through Kade's actions. "He's clearly trying to take care of you. Why don't we thank him for his efforts and see if that will help him settle?"

"It's worth a shot, Gaine," Bastian says. *"I've never seen him this riled up."*

My heart breaks for her as she hangs her head. Gaine struggled at the schoolhouse when we were younger until she finally left for good. Before my mother became Luna, it was nearly unheard of for the wolves to find their mates. When she received her gift, our classmates wouldn't leave her alone and called her "the mate maker." Kade was her fresh start, and he was madly in love with her.

I stand and slide my fingers around Bastian's jaw. "Can we talk about your sister in the meantime? Has she found anything new?"

Gaine places her muzzle against my left hip as we begin walking again. *"That damn unicorn,"* she grumbles. *"I'm sorry, Luna."*

"Well, tell me what she says she's seeing," I say, sighing. "We have time. Maybe we can make sense of it."

"She described one with a flaxen mane," Gaine starts, narrowing her eyes. *"She said it was beautiful but hurt. When I asked her to concentrate on it, she screamed about blood and wouldn't talk to me for hours, so I stopped asking. The other is a bay."*

"Did she not like the bay?" I ask, confused about the difference.

"No," Gaine answers thoughtfully. *"There's a bright flash, and then she sees it run away. When the dust settles, a wolf is dead."*

Sighing, I slide my hand over her head. "Well, that doesn't sound pleasant, does it?"

"River doesn't talk about death," Gaine says. *"The moment someone dies, she refuses to look further."*

We walk in silence for a while. Bastian glances up at me a few times, but I'm struggling to make sense of my thoughts, so I'm unsure how to discuss them with him. My father had hoped I would one day have access to a historian as my mother did for a time. I fear he'll be horribly disappointed.

"I found a groundhog," Kade announces, stepping onto the trail.

I wait until he's closer before kneeling. "Will you stay with us?" I ask, reaching out for his jaw. "We could start a fire and cook it. You could eat a meal with your wife." I tilt my head and look over Kade's body, seeing blood in his coat from his recent kill.

"No," Kade says firmly. He drops the carcass before Gaine and sits with his head high, looking down at her.

Gaine hangs her head. *"Thank you, Kade,"* she says softly. *"But I would like to enjoy a meal with my mate."*

"You need it more," Kade responds. *"You eat it."*

When Gaine sits down and looks away in shame, I grab Kade's muzzle and pull it to me. "She would like to spend some time with you in thanks for the meals you've brought her," I snap. "Why won't you stay with her?"

"She's safer with you," Kade says, narrowing his eyes. *"She's staying with you while I scout ahead."*

"I am not," Gaine shouts.

"You've always traveled together, Kade," I say, sighing. "Why would you leave her behind?"

"She's pregnant," Kade growls.

I exhale heavily as I sit back on my heels. "Oh," I whisper. "Ok." I rub Gaine's hip where Kade can't see as he glares at her. "You're gonna be a father."

"Everyone is trying to kill us, and she chose now," Kade says, still growling. *"As if we need a bigger target than a shiny silver wolf. She's gonna walk around like a sale on wolf kills. Two for one!"*

Bastian looks away as he begins chuckling.

"Go ahead, laugh," Kade snarls, turning his attention to Bastian. *"Now you have two mothers to watch. Because if something happens to her, I will have nothing left to live for, and I will take you with me."*

Bastian's nonchalant gaze only fuels Kade's rage. I pull him back to me. "You're going to be a father," I state plainly.

"No, I'm going to be a widower," Kade growls.

I open my arms to him, tilting my head with a small smile. "Kade," I whisper. "You're going to be a father."

Kade takes a few sharp breaths before letting out a deep sigh and stepping into my arms. He slides his jaw down my back. *"I'm gonna be a father."*

I bury my face into his silver coat. Kade's fur is finer than any other wolf's. I assume it's another byproduct of his punishment. I slip my fingers through it, waiting for him to be ready. Kade's emotions are locked behind his scar, and he has to allow me to pull them. It makes helping him harder, but I think it's a form of control he needs in these situations.

When he begins humming, I see Gaine has moved to nuzzle her husband on my back. His emotions are overwhelming when I gain access to them. Kade never wanted to be a parent, but he has no choice as Gaine's mate. I'm sure some of this fear is of being a bad parent, but Kade would also fear for his wife's health and her ability to keep up as her pregnancy progresses.

I take deep breaths, releasing as much of his emotions as possible until Bastian steps forward and allows me to push them into him. He sets his jaw on Kade's shoulders as we all take a moment to enjoy this peace. I smile when Rachel steps out of the brush and sits beside Brock to rub her muzzle over his.

Kade traveled north with us after we escaped the train. He had taken us to my father, who was with Brock and the rest of our family. Kade was witty, sharp, and very much all about himself, but he was also Blood Pack and the enemy. Over the years, he won us all over with his unrelenting effort to win Gaine's heart. Their relationship affects us all and brings joy to our hearts.

"I do love you," Kade tells Gaine softly. *"I don't want to lose you. Why did this have to happen now? How on earth could you possibly feel safe?"*

I take a deep breath and straighten my back. "Bass, can you build us a small fire?" I ask, sitting back and folding my legs. "Edith told me a few things on the way to the river just to fill the time while Trish slept, and I think it's important information for Kade and Gaine."

Bastian steps back and shifts. "Sure, Love," he says, turning to dig through Saint's saddle bags.

"Come here, guys," I call to Brock and Rachel.

We brush the dried leaves away and clear a spot for Bastian to pile wood. He brings me my knife so I can skin the groundhog and a thick stick to skewer it with. I wait until the fire is lit before beginning the discussion.

"I know that most wolves have some control over when they bring a new life into this world," I start, slipping my hands over the cuddling wolves. "There are a few who do not, Kade. As the Luna, I have no choice. I become pregnant when I bond. I didn't know that until it was too late."

"Well, you do smell delicious now," Kade remarks. He licks my arm as Gaine scoffs. *"No. You need to taste her. Don't you have cravings? How aren't you craving the sweetness?"*

"That's humans, Kade," Gaine grumbles.

"Yeah, but you want to taste her, don't you?" Kade says, chuckling as he stares into her eyes and licks my arm again. *"You know you do."*

"Ok, yeah," Gaine admits as we stare at the pair. *"I kinda do."*

I hold my arm out to give them access and let them enjoy my peach and maple syrup taste as if I were one of Edith's popsicles. If it were anyone else, this behavior would not be tolerated, but Kade has always taken special liberties with me, and they have been extended to Gaine by association.

I giggle when Rachel licks her lips. "Come here, you two," I say, smiling. "You might as well have some too."

Bastian shakes his head but smiles, chuckling. Brock and Rachel jump up and approach my side to lick my other arm. They've only given me gentle licks on my cheek. It's a more meaningful kiss to the cheek versus rubbing their muzzle against it. Neither has dared to take a proper taste.

"Although Brock is my companion, he and Rachel are still just regular wolves," I say, starting the lesson. "When Rachel feels safe and in a stable environment, her body will react with the right hormones that will allow her to become pregnant."

Rachel nuzzles Brock before returning to my arm.

"*Whenever you're ready, dear,*" Brock mumbles whimsically.

"The mother of the Alpha and the historian's parents do not have a choice," I continue. "It happens when it is time, and it's our job to ensure she and her babies are safe."

"*Babies?*" Kade says, snapping his head up.

"Yes, Kade," I say, giggling. "You'll need to be a father to two children. The good news is that there will only be two. So, you know the number you must prepare for, and there will be no surprises."

"Incidentally, the Luna and Alpha's mothers can only have one child," Bastian adds, turning the carcass on the skewer to heat the other side. "My little Luna won't allow her mother to eat because she wants to be near her Alpha. You need to eat and get over yourself so we can get them back to each other."

"*That's who Trish is carrying?*" Gaine asks.

"Yes," I answer. "So, you see, Kade, Gaine is not safer with us." I move all the wolves off my arms and cup Kade's chin. "Bastian and Daddy, along with the rest of my guards, are tasked with protecting us. They would abandon Gaine if something happened to protect the future Alpha and Luna."

"*But my child is important too,*" Kade growls.

"I agree," I tell him. "All of my wolves are important to me. Whether they have been born yet or not, I love them. However, my guards have their priorities, and we cannot overlook them. So, as I've been trying to tell you, Gaine and your child will be much safer traveling ahead with you."

"I can shift until I'm four months along, Kade," Gaine assures him. *"We will have made it to the mountains by then. There is safety within the hills."*

Kade's eyes shift between me and his beautiful mate. I've never seen him look worried, but there's a first time for everything. Bastian lifts the meat away from the fire and holds both ends of the skewer so I can trim the carcass. I wink at him as we wait for Kade to absorb everything we've said. He is impossibly intelligent, but this is his wife and child.

"You will have another day or two to become comfortable with the idea, Kade," I remind him. "You'll be with us until we leave these hills. You don't have to make a decision now."

"But I can still feed her, right?" Kade asks, bumping his nose with his wife's.

"As long as you're nice about it," I warn him. "I've allowed you to continue to act like an ass, but that time has passed. This is the mother of your child, mate, and beautiful wife. I know you love her, so you'll show her that again. No more Mister Tough Guy."

"I would also like to eat with you," Gaine says hopefully. *"We all would."*

"Ok, well, probably not 'all,'" I say, laughing and rubbing Bastian's arm.

"I gotta say, I appreciate the man," Brock says, sneaking another taste of my arm. *"I don't know if I'd have ever gotten the balls to ask for a taste."*

Rachel giggles. *"You do taste wonderful right now, Luna,"* she says.

"I do envy my mother slightly," I say, grinning. "It must have been nice smelling like something that wasn't food."

"She still tasted pretty damn good," Bastian says, setting the remainder of the carcass on the ground. "The honeysuckle lingered." He kisses my cheek before standing to pull his pants off and shift.

"I wonder what these conversations would sound like to someone who didn't understand wolves," I say, passing Gaine a slice of meat. "Imagine just walking in on a conversation about how a person tastes. That would be awkward."

"But we're not people," Bastian says slyly. *"We're wolves. And we're hungry."*

He knocks me over onto my back and lunges at my neck, taking long, wet licks of my skin. The rest of the wolves laugh and join him, sliding their tongues over any skin they can find. I laugh and flail around uselessly.

"You guys are just making this shit weird," I shout through my laughter.

14

With Kade's added assistance, my guards don't complain too much about our distance from the pack for the next day and a half. Even Bastian settles into a routine of alternating positions with the silver wolf. Kade isn't used to working in hand, making every moment with him an adventure.

As we settle in for the second night, their rumbling stomachs become too much for me. "Bass, can you take Drake and see if you can find something to eat?" I ask, rubbing his jaw.

"Sure, but Ash is a better hunter," Bastian says, confused.

"Drake is new to our personal guard and could use some time learning to work with his Alpha," I respond, smiling.

"You're the Luna," he says, conceding. Bastian gently licks my cheek and calls to Drake before disappearing over the hill.

For the next few hours, Bastian reports that they haven't found much and calls Drake a noisy hunter. Kade isn't exactly guarding me, as he spends most of his time cuddling with Gaine and making her giggle with his flirting. Rachel stayed in camp with me while Brock left to take Drake's place patrolling with Ash.

It's well past dark when Bastian decides to give up. The trees aren't dead here like they were at home, but the lack of water has driven game elsewhere, and the small meals Kade had found have dried up since the groundhog. Sighing, I turn to deliver the news to our group.

"Luna! Luna, help!" Neala shouts to everyone, startling my guards. *"The kids! Timothy and Creto! They've been taken!"*

Jumping to my feet, I dash toward Saint. Neala continues crying out to me in her panic, breaking my heart. However, another voice demands my attention right now.

"Bass? Where are you going?" Drake shouts.

"Drake, stay with him!" I order. *"If you lose him, don't come back!"* I stop and wait for his acknowledgment, nodding when I hear it. *"Matthew?"*

"Yes, Luna?" Matthew answers instantly.

"Shoot him," I order.

"Ayls?" Matthew questions.

"You heard me," I bark, throwing my saddle over Saint's back.

"He won't get past me," Matthew responds.

My guards filter in from the woods as I slip Saint's bridle over his ears. I pull the horse with me and gather everyone by the small fire.

"Kade, I need you to come with me and Brock," I say apologetically.

"No, Luna," Kade says, shaking his head. *"Gaine –"*

"Will be safe with Ash and Rachel," I say, lifting an eyebrow. "Timothy is seven, and Creto is ten."

Kade clenches his jaw. *"Yeah, alright,"* he grumbles.

I kneel to Gaine. "Please stay here with them," I beg. "I know you are smart and powerful, but you and that baby are too important. I can't worry about you while trying to save those kids."

"Please bring him back to me," Gaine pleads. *"You convinced me to let him in."*

I smile and kiss her behind her whiskers. "I promise to bring your husband back to you safe and sound, Gaine." I look toward my aged guard. "With your life, Ash."

"You have my word, Luna," Ash vows.

Brock nuzzles Rachel as I swing into the saddle. I give them a moment of privacy to say goodbye and listen to Kade talk to Matthew about their position. I've never been this far west, so nothing they say makes sense to me, but Kade asks pointed questions and seems to know exactly where they are. I hold my chest as he gently licks Gaine's muzzle and bumps her belly with his nose.

"Alright, Luna," Kade grumbles. *"Quit staring. We have a long way to go and need to hurry. You ready?"*

Kade's not asking me. He stares at Brock and waits for him to nod.

"That is my life between you two," Kade snarls at Ash and Rachel.

"She will be safe with them, Kade," I tell him.

Nothing will stop him from worrying about her, but keeping her out of sight will prevent him from getting distracted. Kade looks back at Gaine one more time. They don't exchange words, but the moment seems too profound for such trivial things. He nods to me and takes off, leading Saint into the woods.

Brock stays beside me as we canter for hours. I lie against Saint's neck because, without a trail, low branches are everywhere, trying to pull me from my saddle. Kade had left Myla to guard Trish, but she is now trying to comfort Neala, who is also talking to Ash. Their voices begin blending as they panic and ask for my orders.

"STOP!" I shout at all of them. *"I am on my way. Not one of you is cleared to track those kids. You will all stop my Alpha. I will banish the wolf that lets him through."*

"I got him," my father responds.

I let them all filter to the back and listen for the kids. Not hearing them, I turn my attention back to my Alpha. Bastian talks to himself when he's struggling. There have been a few times when our kids have gotten into trouble. He's been tough to work with when that happens. Finally, I had Anthony shoot him in the hip the last time.

Bastian turns blindly violent when it comes to our young wolves. He injured Brock the first time because they crossed paths during the rescue. The second time, he killed a human teenager. I took drastic measures after that. His past renders him unable to think clearly when a child is in trouble. The string of obscenities he's yelling indicates this instance is no different.

I can hear Neala's tears in her words. She and Ash have cared for the junior guards for as long as I've known them. Mom called Neala "the child whisperer" because of how good she was with them. She is a second mother to them all. Her losses at the lake hit her extremely hard, and this has reignited that grief.

We finally slide to a stop beside a low rock wall. A fire burning against it is bigger than I'd like for a low-profile camp, but the growling and snarls filling the air indicate this is not the time to discuss that. Neala is lying near the fire with three children. She'd seemed to settle over time. I have no doubt these kids were the reason.

My pack releases a collective sigh of relief as Kade leads me around small clusters of nervous wolves. They love and trust me, but this ease of fear is Kade's doing. He was the Blood Pack's enforcer, but he's my fixer. I call Kade in when I have a situation that requires stealth, cunning, and surprise. His silver coat may have been a punishment, but he wears it as a badge, and the pack rarely sees it.

My father has pinned Bastian by the time we find them. I can filter one voice from the other, but with the two of them only shouting threats at each other, neither is worth listening to. My father has a cut down the side of his face, and Bastian's neck is bleeding from his grip.

I pull Kade's ear as he sits before the snarling Alphas. "Bastian?"

"Get him off me!" His volume makes me wince.

"Bastian?" I say again.

"Annalisa," he retorts.

"You can't be a part of this," I tell him.

Bastian kicks at my father, catching his face with his back claws again. *"The hell I can't!"*

When he twists his hips to kick at Daddy again, I straddle his gut and sit on him.

"Ayls," Bastian says with a building growl. *"Get off of me."* His anger flashes with every enunciated word.

"Bastian, my Alpha, can you please recall the events in which you have participated in a child's rescue?" I calmly ask. "Let us reflect on missions of the past. Shall we discuss the injuries that you inflicted on our companion? Do you remember the young girl's name that died when you charged into the wrong house?"

Bastian's snarl mutes. *"Alesha,"* he says quietly.

I slide my hands over his ribs and up his chest. "You are so strong," I start, leaning down to look my father in the eye. "You are the voice in my head, the force behind my heartbeat, and the courage in my soul." I slip my fingers into my father's mouth, prying him off Bastian. "But the past that you have endured renders you too dangerous for these rescues, my Alpha."

"*Annalisa,*" my father grumbles, pushing against me as I lift him.

"Give him to me, Daddy," I request, lifting him away from Bastian. I lean over my Alpha's chest and wrap my arms around his neck. "You are mine. I will not lose you. Trust me to bring these kids back no matter how far into the depths of hell I must go. I will bring them back to you."

Sighing, Bastian wraps his front legs around my ribs. For years, this was what I got whenever I needed a hug. *I loved every single one of them.* Bastian is my rock in a grass field, but his judgment cannot be trusted when kids are involved. We've never been able to completely overcome his past, and I would never expect him to forget it.

A rifle cocks behind me. "Which one am I shooting in the ass?" Anthony asks.

I laugh, suddenly realizing what we must look like. "Do not shoot me, Anthony." I lift off Bastian enough to look into his eyes, and he licks my cheek.

"*I don't deserve you,*" Bastian says.

"You will always deserve me," I whisper. "I belong to you. Always." I hold his muzzle to my cheek. "I need to go get those kids, though. I'll leave Daddy here with you just in case, ok?"

"*I don't need a babysitter,*" Bastian pouts.

I lift my eyebrow.

"*Fine,*" he grumbles. "*Come here.*"

Smiling, I lean in so he can give me a slobbery lick. "Don't get used to that," I say, wrinkling my nose as I wipe my face.

Bastian rolls over underneath me to lift me with his back. I stand up and look around, finding us surrounded by my guards. Anthony still has his rifle trained on my Alpha. I push the barrel down as Matthew approaches, followed by our usual team.

"Daddy, stay with Bastian," I start, pointing at my father, knowing he's not tremendously excited about my order. "Anthony, you can come with us or not, but decide quickly. Matthew, you're with Brock. Drake, same as last time. Hang back unless Matthew calls for you."

"*Myla will run with Drake*," Kade says. "*You told me to teach her*," he adds when I raise my eyebrow.

I shrug. "Yeah, alright," I respond, watching Edith lead two horses to us.

She hands their reins to Anthony and pulls me to the side by my arm. "You should not be going," Edith hisses. "Your mother didn't take unnecessary risks while she was pregnant."

"Edith, my father killed my mother while she was pregnant," I remind her. "I'm just taking a ride."

She hands me my bow and quiver, recently restocked with arrows. "Your mother would be proud," she responds, smiling. "But she will come back to life and kill us all if something happens to you, so be careful."

Smiling, I kiss her cheek. "Let's go," I call to my guards. I kneel as the Alphas step before me. "I will be right back, my beautiful Alpha," I say, kissing the tip of his nose before turning to do the same to my father. "Daddy, thank you for stopping him."

Anthony hands me his mare's reins as I stand and turn away from them. "Take her," he tells me. "She'll follow them." He points to the wolves before mounting a horse I've never seen. "We just grabbed this one yesterday."

I swing up into his saddle. "So, you guys were stealing horses?" I scoff angrily.

"Some of the kids," Anthony says. "They were hunting and found him."

"And you wonder why they came after us," I growl, shaking my head. "Kade?"

My silver wolf nods and darts into the woods, taking my horse with him.

* * *

The sun is just beginning to rise when Kade slows to a jog and starts sniffing the ground. Brock and Matthew fan out to help him find the scent. Anthony's horse is out of shape and breathes heavily as it catches up.

"How are you doing?" Anthony asks.

"I'm fine," I tell him, leaving my eyes on Kade. "They lost the trail." I nod in the direction of the wolves.

"I track with them a little more than you, kiddo," Anthony scoffs, lowering his canteen. "I don't need you to translate everything."

I turn my attention to the ex-soldier. "How are you doing with all of this, Anthony?" I ask, reaching for his shoulder. "You were close with Nate and some of the other guards."

Anthony sighs deeply, squinting into the distance. "To be honest, I miss Nate every day," he says, twisting his face to hide any trace of emotion. "He was a grumpy old man with so much life about him." He wipes his eyes and nods slightly. "He missed Mari, though. He should be with her, not kicking stones off the porch with me."

I slide my hand down his arm and thread our fingers when he gives me his hand. "But you'll let me know if it becomes too much, right?"

"I'm not a wolf, Annalisa," Anthony scoffs, shaking his head. "You don't need to watch over me."

Smiling, I squeeze his hand. "You were one of my mother's best friends," I tell him, winking. "By default, that makes you one of my wolves."

Anthony lifts my hand to his lips and kisses my knuckles as Kade reappears before us. "Looks like he's got something."

Kade sits as we dismount. *"I don't know why they'd shift, but they did,"* he says. *"The humans probably just thought they found some dogs. Now they know the boys are wolves."*

"Ok," I say, sighing. I kneel before him and look up at Anthony. "The boys shifted."

"That's not good," Anthony says, rubbing his forehead. "Do we know how long ago or how they're traveling?"

"The scent is fairly fresh, but they're on a wagon," Kade says. He slings his head to the side, and Anthony leaves us to inspect the ground in that direction. *"They'll know we're coming, Luna. You should call for your father."*

I shake my head. "If I do, Bastian will come," I remind him. "Whose blood shall be in his fur this time?"

"I'd prefer the people who took our kids," Kade grumbles.

"They won't get far," Anthony calls out. "The horse is lame." He's pointing to the ground in a few areas, probably trying to show us how he knows the horse is limping.

I always travel with some of the most powerful noses on earth. I don't care about a horse's limp. On the other hand, Brock loves learning Anthony's tracking techniques. My companion charges through the trees to see what he's pointing at, leaving Matthew to join me and Kade.

"How are we gonna do this?" Matthew looks between us a few times before sighing at our dumbfounded expressions. *"So, we're winging it as usual?"*

I nod with a grimace.

"Yep," Kade says, chuckling. *"Sounds about right."*

"There's a reason you two aren't allowed to work with my guards," Matthew grumbles.

I scoff. "Your guards work for me," I remind him.

"Come on," Anthony barks, approaching us quickly. "This land is sloped. They are probably headed toward water, which means more people."

We sling into our saddles as Kade darts forward, retaking the lead. We follow a wider trail before Matthew crosses our path to pull my horse into the woods. I listen to them calling their positions until Kade announces he's leaving the main trail.

When Matthew slows, his footfalls become careful and deliberate.

"Luna, come down here," he requests. He waits until I dismount to step toward some trees. *"They've stopped, but probably not for long."*

"What's up?" Anthony asks, hooking our arms.

I press my finger to my lips. "They've stopped."

Matthew swings his hips to block us, and we kneel to look through the brush. There's a long buckboard with a large draft horse pulling it. My chest tightens as I move around to take in the thick barred cages surrounded by six armed men in the back. Two more men are walking around the horse, feeling its legs.

"They knew," I whisper, slipping my fingers through Matthew's fur.

"You know, I will never understand how that shiny-ass wolf can sit right in front of people, and they don't even notice him," Anthony scoffs, confused.

I don't want to giggle, but I can't help myself. Anthony's right. Kade is sitting between two trees across the trail from us. He's in plain view of the men, and not one has noticed him. To be fair, the shine of his coat reflects the woods around us, so he's not as bright as he would be in the sunshine.

"But, yeah," Anthony continues. "It looks like they came for wolves. There are three cages. Wonder why they left early."

"Luna," Kade calls out. *"Climb the tree to your left. Have Anthony move to the front in case they try to escape. Brock and Matthew, as soon as I have their attention, you're on."*

"Drake and Myla, go with Anthony," I order. *"Do not leave him."*

"Yes, Luna," they respond in unison.

I can't see Brock, but he's normally trailing us, so he'll come in from the rear. We'll surround them and should have the kids out of there soon. I nod toward the front of the wagon for Anthony and look up at the tree Kade wants me in. It's a pine. He doesn't usually choose a soft wood tree for me to climb.

"You sure about this tree?" I ask him. *"Maybe I should —"*

"Luna," Kade growls. *"This is what I do."*

Rolling my eyes, I shrug and grab a low limb. The branches are thin and clumped closely together, making my ascent slow. My bow and arrows catch on nearly every branch, the sap makes the loose pieces of rippled bark stick to my hands, and the tiny shards of wood flaking off the limbs all seem to land in my eyes. If he was looking to render me useless, he's succeeding.

My wolves call out that they are set when I reach the area that made Kade want me to use this tree. The limbs are thin, and I'll need to be careful, but I'm high above the wagon in a bare spot of the tree.

"Any day now, Luna," Kade grumbles as I carefully turn to lean my back against the main trunk of the tree.

I rub my hands over my pants, trying to free them of some of the sap. I have a clear view of the boys from up here. My little wolves look scared and embarrassed in the small cages. They are naked except for the thick metal collars tightly locked around their necks.

That would explain why they'd shift. One of the rebel groups invented them. They lock them around the wolves' necks. If they are an actual wolf, they suffocate. If they are one of mine, they must shift to keep breathing. Until recently, these kids had never met humans other than Edith, Anthony, and Doc. They are getting a crash course in why that is.

The men in the wagon laugh as I pull my first arrow from its pouch. Creto reaches through the bars for Timothy's hand to comfort the younger boy. I look away just as one of the men violently kicks the cages. Creto screams, and I turn to see him bent over, holding a broken arm.

My jaw clenches, and my chest begins heaving air. *"Kade,"* I growl.

"Steady shots, Luna," Kade says in a forced calm tone. *"I need you to aim true, my beautiful woman. Take a breath."* He lifts his head enough to watch me as I let a few deep breaths out, trying to calm down enough to help him. *"Ok, sweet Luna,"* he starts again. *"Set that arrow somewhere just like I taught you."*

I follow Kade's orders as best as possible while listening to the men taunt my young wolf. Creto is trying not to make noise, but he's a little boy in pain, and the men continuously kick his cage, jarring his injured arm. When he throws up on himself, I nock my arrow, aiming for the man kicking the cage.

"The driver, Luna," Kade says, shifting my attention to the man climbing up to the lifted seat in the front of the wagon. *"Here we go, boys."*

When Kade stands, a ray of sunlight hits his back. His fur shimmers in the light, catching the humans' attention. They shout and jump up as the driver reaches for the reins. I release my arrow to hit him squarely in the back.

Matthew jumps out to take down the second man on the ground, but Kade stands still, capturing all the attention of the men in the wagon. Anthony laughs at how Kade can literally dazzle humans into a stupor. They view him as if he's as mythical as a unicorn.

One of the men shakes his head and begins yelling incoherently at the others as they all settle their rifles on Kade. Brock leaps onto the back of the wagon and jumps across the cages, rocking them and making Creto cry out. I let loose my second arrow, catching a man in the shoulder.

The man barking orders swings his rifle in my direction. "There she is!" he shouts.

I hear a few shots ring at once, and something slams me back against the tree. The eruption of pain in my shoulder causes me to double over. I reach out to steady myself with a branch, but it snaps under my weight, and my scream echoes through the woods as the ground rushes toward me.

* * *

"Would you look at that?" a woman's voice exclaims sarcastically. "It's the new baby Luna!"

It's dark, but I can see my hand, so my eyes aren't closed. *Right?*

"You two take screwing up to a new level," the woman sneers.

"Shut up, Aylee," my mother shouts, making me collapse. But then her hands reach toward me. "Hey, Sweets, come on up here."

"Mom, I died," I babble as she pulls me to my feet. "I got all our wolves killed, and then I died."

She pulls me into her arms and holds me tightly as I mourn my losses. "You can't take all the blame for the pack," Mom whispers. "I brought Doc in. I'm the reason everyone trusted him." She pulls her fingers through my hair. "I should've put it together on the train. Kade said he kept the soldiers off the river. How else would they have known where we were?"

I sniffle and pull away from her. "Then we'll both carry the blame," I say, smiling through my tears. "Half and half."

Mom smiles. "I'll take that deal." She pulls me in for another hug and kisses my cheek. "There will always be someone trying to kill your wolves."

Her words remind me of the man with the rifle. He'd yelled, "There she is!" They weren't after my wolves.

"Mom, they were after me," I say, confused. "They took the kids to trap me. Why do they want me?"

"Come on," Mom says calmly. "We've got a few minutes. Let's go home."

My vision changes from the dark curtain to our lake at home. Not the lake I left but the reflective blue water surrounded by lush green grass. "It really was beautiful, wasn't it?" I say sadly.

"It was," Mom whispers. "But Aylee showed me the mountains. They are beautiful too." She hooks our arms and begins to guide me around the lake. "Your wolves love you. They'll do anything to protect their Luna. That includes being a human's slave so they won't hurt you."

"It's never going to stop, is it?" I ask, frowning.

My mother shakes her head. "Probably not, Sweets," she says. "Our only job is to protect our wolves from these attacks."

"There should be more to life," I mutter.

"I always thought there could be," Mom says thoughtfully. "Maybe one day." She looks up as a shout calls out from far away. "We don't have much longer. They'll want to hunker down while you heal. It's not safe. Get them moving right away before anyone finds those bodies." She grabs my shoulders. "Do you hear me?"

My head feels foggy as voices begin filtering back in. "Mom, how do I save them?"

"You already did," she whispers, pressing her forehead to mine. "Now you just have to keep going. You can do this."

"How do you know?" I ask, clinging to her.

"I miss you, Sweets," Mom says as she slips away. "Tell Daddy I love him."

15

"She's awake," Bastian shouts much louder than what Mom and I heard, making me wince.

"What happened?" I mumble.

"You got shot, Love," Bastian whispers, brushing his lips over my forehead. "Then you fell out of a tree." He rubs his thumb over my cheek until I open my eyes. "Brock let Kade close your wounds, which I have feelings about, and then they brought you back to us."

"The kids?" I manage to ask before I start coughing.

Bastian holds a cup to my lips. "We got them back," he says. "Drink your tea. We'll get moving as soon as you're healed."

"No," I spout, shaking my throbbing head. "Leave. We have to go."

"Ayls, let us take care of you," Bastian starts, lifting my head slightly to help me drink.

I knock the cup out of his hand. "Get Daddy," I say, shaking my head. "I need to talk to my father."

Bastian frowns but jumps over the wagon's side and jolts my sore shoulder. Beside me, Trish holds Creto, who's still naked but wrapped in a blanket. He's shaking as he sobs. Timothy is fast asleep above me with his head on Edith's lap.

"I knocked him out," the witch whispers. "They both needed you, but this one..."

I slowly reach over my head and slide my hand over the boy's arm. I can't imagine these little wolves' terrified thoughts as they were collared and thrown into cages. I remember being afraid simply because the militia came near us.

"They were playing keep away with a stick," Edith continues as I turn my attention to Creto. "Kelsy was there, but the boys told her to run when they saw the men."

I nod, slipping my fingers through Creto's hair. "They're good boys," I whisper back.

Creto turns toward me, having heard my praise. His eyes are red and swollen from hours of crying. I imagine Anthony probably carried him back on his horse since he wouldn't have been able to shift and run on a broken leg. His pain and fear are more than any little boy should ever face.

"Come here, baby," I whisper, holding my arm out. "We'll be ok. Come lie with me."

My young wolf rolls away from Trish to curl up against me. I've never exchanged words with Creto, but I know him since he's one of my wolves. His parents died in the fire, and he's alone under Neala's care. He's sweet and has been watching over the younger orphans, which is how he found himself away from the older wolves. I also know that he's a good boy and quite polite.

I curl my arm around him, holding him to me as he lays his head on my uninjured shoulder. "I love you, sweetheart," I whisper. "No one will hurt you again. I promise."

The wagon rocks, and Daddy's muzzle rubs over my face. *"Hey, you,"* he says. *"You're quickly turning into your mother. Quit dying."*

I cough as he makes me giggle. "Daddy, shift," I tell him. "This needs to be a full meeting."

Tilting his head, he shifts and takes a pair of shorts from Edith. "Ok, what's up?"

"I talked to Mom," I say quietly.

Daddy's face twitches in an attempt to disguise his pain. He sits beside me and leans against the wagon's side, staring at the forest as his eyes glaze over.

"She told me to tell you she loves you very much," I start, knowing it's what he needs to hear. "She's ok, Daddy. She looked good. She yelled at Grandpa's Luna."

My father breathes out a small laugh. "Yeah," he says, nodding. "She's something."

"She said not to stay here," I tell him, squeezing his fingers as he takes my hand. "She told me not to let you wait. We're not safe here."

Daddy shakes his head as Bastian begins to protest from beside the wagon.

"Please hear me," I state plainly. "Mom had her reasons. We need to go."

My father straightens his back. I watch as his eyes dart around and his lips purse. He exhales deeply, nodding his head. Suddenly, commotion erupts around us. Matthew begins calling for horses and telling everyone to pack up. Parents call for their kids, and Neala runs through all the young wolves in her care.

Creto snuggles closer to me. "Can I stay with you, Luna?" he asks.

I wince as I turn to put my lips against his forehead. "I will stay with you for as long as you need me, sweetheart," I promise him. "How is your arm?"

Blushing, Creto tucks it between us, hiding that he's healed. "It's sore."

"You don't need to be injured to stay with me, Creto," I say, smiling. "You are my wolf. You're always welcome to spend time with me."

I remember my mother always smiling even after someone had tried to kill her. I asked her how she could forgive them so quickly. She gestured to our wolves and told me it was not her place to make them frown. They felt joy over her life, and that was enough for her.

I let my wolves' voices filter in as more shift to restart our journey west. They sound merry as they talk about the promise of wildlife and the fresh mountain springs. The families talk about large houses with wrap-around porches.

"Are you thinking about me?" Kade asks, hopping into the wagon.

I wrinkle my nose, realizing I'm smiling. "I was listening to the pack," I tell him.

Kade squeezes between me and the side of the wagon. "So, listen," he starts, sighing. "That blood of yours, it's like a damn delicacy. I know your Alpha probably didn't like me taking a taste…"

"*Correct,*" Bastian says, making me giggle.

"But I feel like it was my right…" Kade continues, oblivious to Bastian's proximity.

"*Incorrect.*"

"You know, based on the fact that you love me more than him," Kade finishes.

"*What the fuck?*" Bastian steps onto the wagon with his front paws.

"Hey, Bass," Kade says, casually acknowledging my Alpha. "I was just telling your wife what happened. I mentioned she might need to talk to you. Sharing is caring, man."

Bastian stares, dumbfounded. Even Creto seems confused by Kade's conversation. On the other hand, Kade nods slightly and looks at Bastian with a thoughtful expression as he sucks on his teeth.

"Come here, you ass," I spout, laughing. "I love you too."

Smiling, Kade leans down to kiss me. "My wife's nearly here," he tells me. "Then we'll get going."

"Two days, Kade," I tell him sternly. "Then I want you two out of here."

"Yeah, alright," he grumbles, leaning in for another kiss. "You should quit dying, but if you do, tell Luna I said 'hey.'" He groans quietly and kisses me before taking a long lick of my neck. "Mm. That's better than mountain lion."

Bastian glares at Kade as he jumps off the wagon. "*You don't have to encourage him,*" he grumbles, lying beside me.

"My sweet Alpha," I say, lifting my eyebrow. "Has Kade ever changed? Has my behavior made him worse?"

"*No,*" Bastian admits, sighing.

"So, what makes you think discouraging his actions would do anything?" I rub Creto's back as he relaxes on my shoulder. "Besides, I think he entertains everyone. He makes me giggle, and I've heard you laugh at him before."

Bastian rubs his muzzle over my cheeks and nuzzles into my neck for a taste. *"And I guess he does make some good points,"* he adds whimsically as his hum starts.

* * *

Daddy pushed our pack hard for two days straight. They weren't allowed to stop for food, water, or rest. I'd healed after a full day, but Bastian threatened to shoot me with Anthony's rifle if I stepped off the wagon. Creto thought that was funny until I made him shift to check on all the wolves I wasn't hearing. After a few hours, Timothy saw how much fun it was to work for me and asked permission to join him.

"You're gonna be a good mother," Edith remarks, grinning. "Those kids really took to you." She turns to look beside the wagon where Kade is jogging with his wife. "Now, I think you show some wolves a little too much love…"

Giggling, I turn to Edith. "I love them all," I tell her. "Each of them needs a different form of love. The kids need a mother's affection. And Kade, well… He just likes to be loved."

"What draws everyone to him?" Trish asks, sitting up. "He's an ass, but I like him. Why?"

Edith and I giggle at her as she shakes her head.

"I don't know that I could ever answer that," I tell them thoughtfully. "Kade was dark before he met Gaine. He was a player. Bastian said he had a different girl for each day of the week. He didn't even know their names. He'd call them the day of the week they were assigned. But look at him now."

They turn to watch Kade with me. I smile as he dotes on his wife, licking her muzzle and nipping at her chest playfully. Gaine's trying her absolute best to ignore him, but when Kade wants attention, he won't stop until he gets it.

"Anthony says he takes control when you call him in for things," Edith says curiously. She used to travel with my mother, but I don't feel comfortable putting her at risk like that.

"He does," I say, nodding. "That's the other side of Kade. He's deadly.

Our Alphas are powerful, fast, and unmatched in stamina, but Kade is cunning. He can kill off an entire squad one man at a time without them even noticing." I lift my eyebrow. "I've watched him do it. He's nothing short of amazing."

"And he is beautiful," Trish says, tilting her head, still watching him.

Edith sighs loudly. "Now I kinda want to marry him."

Trish and I turn away from Kade, giggling. As we settle back against the piles of blankets, the boys jump into the wagon with us. Timothy is quite small for his age, so Creto latches onto his scruff to pull him until his back paws can reach the wagon.

"Luna, Neala said to tell you we're out of food," Timothy says as he shakes Creto's slobber out of his coat.

"You kids had the last of our food," I tell him. "We have three days before your muscle starts to fade." I scratch their necks as they lie down with their heads in my lap. "You ate today, right?"

"Yes, Luna," they respond in unison.

"Good," I say, rubbing their muzzles. "You should take a nap. I think we'll need to start letting other wolves ride soon."

Trish helps me check their joints as they stretch out to sleep. She pulls at their claws and shows me that Creto's toes are becoming stiff. I nod as she moves to his tail and shakes her head at the burs in his fur. Trish gasps when he starts to hum.

I smile, sliding my fingers through his coat. "He's brave," I whisper. "But he was in a lot of pain. He misses his family."

"I get it," Trish says, frowning. "I miss Jinx. I wouldn't have survived that grief if I didn't have you and his baby. It's still there, but knowing my little boy will have a better life and we'll be free... That heals some of my heart." She reaches for my hand and squeezes my fingers. "You did that. You are giving us this chance."

The wagon jolts slightly before slowing to a stop. We look around to find we're at the edge of the woods. There are still trees, but they aren't as thick.

"We'll be at the flatlands soon, Luna," Kade says. *"We'll let the pack rest here tonight. There won't be many chances to stop after this."*

The boys wake up and jump from the wagon with me. "Go see if Neala needs anything," I tell them. "I need to talk to my guards."

They both nod and wait until I kneel so they can rub their muzzles over my cheeks as the grown-ups do. They giggle as I kiss their noses before sending them off.

"I wouldn't mind letting you babysit," Kade says, watching the kids bound away. He sits beside me, bumping his shoulder against mine. *"I'm gonna miss you. I like traveling with you."*

I hold my hand out for his paw. "I like having you around too," I tell him, pushing his pads and smiling as he groans. "You're not taking care of your paws, Kade."

My silver wolf winks. *"But Gaine's are beautifully smooth."*

"Thank you for being so good to her," I say, laughing.

"I feel lucky that she lets me," Kade says, rolling to his side to give me better access to his paws. *"I saw her at the edge of that basin and thought my heart stopped. It turns out that's when it started beating. Loving her is easy, and I don't deserve her."*

"I wish you got to spend more time with my mother," I tell him, doing my best to rub both of his front paws at once. "I rolled my eyes at her when she would kiss Brock or Bastian's nose. I even shook my head when they nuzzled her before bed." I sigh, thinking about my childish behavior. "And here I am, doing the same thing."

"I spent enough time with her to know you are just as amazing as she was," Kade says, nuzzling my leg. *"The love you showed me at the lake was everything I needed to learn how to love Gaine the way she deserves. That woman is worshiped, and you're the one who taught me how to do it."*

"I think you're giving me too much credit," I say, giggling.

"Whatever you say, Luna," Kade replies sleepily.

My beautiful silver wolf has been awake for two days, guiding the pack around human camps and clusters. He stayed beside the wagon with Gaine until a scout spotted humans. Then, he would run ahead and set a perimeter to keep everyone safe. Although he's very good at his job, his soft snore signals that he's reached his limit.

"Ah, so that's how you get him to sleep," Gaine says softly.

I smile, seeing her approach with Bastian. *"He's burned his candle at both ends,"* I tell her. *"But you make him so happy."*

Gaine lies by Kade's head, pushing against him until he stretches to slip his muzzle between her front legs, where she'll shield his eyes from the fading light. *"You were right about him,"* she says, laying her head on his shoulder. *"He is a good man. Or rather, he tries to be. He's flawed, but I love all he gives me."*

"Will you be ok to go on ahead with him?" I ask, eyeing her thinning frame. *"Do you know how far along you are?"*

"I will make it to the foothills, Luna," Gaine answers. *"I'm not sure how much further, but I can make it that far."*

"Ok," I respond, nodding. *"You should get some rest with your husband. I'm going to see what my father is doing."*

I gently set Kade's paws down so he doesn't wake, and Bastian hooks his front leg, helping me to my feet. He gives me an update on my guards as we walk through our wolves. I slide my hands over all I can reach and smile at their happiness. Our pack is tired, and most haven't eaten in days, but they are all happy to see me and feel my touch.

"Bass, please tell me we can do this," I whisper once we're beyond our group. "Because they are all counting on me, and I've been just winging it since we left the lake."

Bastian shifts, sliding his arms around my waist. "We could walk all the way around the world fueled only by your love," he whispers. His lips rub against my cheek, igniting every nerve within me at once.

I release a sigh of relief that is entirely involuntary. "I didn't know how much I missed you," I whisper, rubbing my lower lip over Bastian's ear.

My Alpha didn't need my encouragement. His growl rumbles as he pushes my pants over my hips and digs his fingers into my skin. Bastian rakes his teeth over me, working his way down my body while desperately pulling at my clothes. By the time my pants slip off, he's shaking.

"Easy, my Alpha," I whisper as he presses me against a tree.

Bastian lifts me to his hips and uses his weight to hold me in place. His hands slide over my jaw and grab the back of my neck. Bastian's growl intensifies as he rubs his lips over my face, causing my nerves to push painfully toward him, and I begin sweating.

My Alpha pulls away and licks his lips. "Come here," he growls.

Bastian presses his lips to mine, parting them to taste my tongue. His need is there, but there's a gentleness to him I wasn't expecting with the pressure I feel from my nerves. As his tongue slides over mine and his fingers dig into my neck, our bodies relax into each other. Bastian continues to lick and bite my lips and tongue until my head is blissfully stuck in a euphoric daze.

Finally, after what feels like hours, Bastian gives me his body. Every moment is sweet and tender as his growl settles into a hum, and he provides my nerves the attention they want. I call out to him repeatedly as he pushes me past my limits and causes explosions of enjoyment inside my body.

When he's unable to hold back any longer, Bastian pulls my leg to roll my hip and bites down onto my shoulder as he pushes himself deep inside me. Where I would normally be listening to his growl, I'm comforted by his hum. It's loud, but it is still gentle and loving.

"I love you," I whisper, pulling at his ear lobe with my lips.

Bastian lifts me from the tree and sits, leaning against it with me in his lap. "I know you do," he says, sighing with a smile. "And I love you enough to ask your father how to control myself around you."

I giggle, thinking about how that conversation must have gone. My father loved my mother with a fiery passion that any blind person could see. Mom loved him with just as much intensity but was better at hiding it. I knew better than to ever walk into their bedroom when the door was closed. But if anyone knew how to be gentle when everything in his core told him to take what he wanted, it would be my father.

"He was not happy, and you'll probably have to hear about it eventually," Bastian says, chuckling. "He did say Luna pushed him too far sometimes and that it was up to us to learn our limits." He pulls at the tips of my hair as they cascade down my back. "Gaine said they'll be leaving soon. Are you ok with that?"

Sighing, I rest my head on his shoulder. "I like having them with us,"

I admit. "I wish Kade would settle down enough to work with me. I enjoy his company."

"Don't send him away because of me," Bastian says.

"I don't send him away, Bass," I tell him, sitting up to look into his eyes. "Do you remember when Kade and I would go for walks at the house? Every time, he'd ask if he was ready to leave. I tried to convince him to stay with us. That's not his style."

"He's leaving Myla with you," Bastian whispers, knowing he told me something I won't like.

I shake my head. "No, he's not," I scoff. "He supposed to be teaching her."

"Gaine said he wants her to report how you're doing." Bastian chuckles. "She's to stay with you in case you need anything. You could use her in hand. Brock says she's quite the scrapper."

I relax back into him and trace my fingers over one of his deeper scars. "She's undisciplined," I remark. "Daddy would have a fit. He doesn't even like how relaxed Brock is in hand."

"Chase is meeting us at the foothills," Bastian reminds me. "Maybe he could help Tarq settle. Just having Brock here calms me somehow." He moves his hands to my sides and rubs his thumbs over my belly. "I'll feel better having Chase to care for you and check on my daughter."

"She's my kid too, Bass," I grumble, pushing myself to my feet. "Keep it up, and I will name her Boulder."

"Ok," he says, smiling. "There's no need to be mean."

Giggling, I pull my jeans on. "Come on, Love. You should rest before we leave." I pull him off the ground. "I fear the journey will be long, and your job is always much harder than the rest."

Bastian presses his back against the tree and crosses his ankles, watching me pull the rest of my clothes on. "You know, I grew up surrounded by so much hate, fear, and cruelty that our pack amazes me every day," he says, bewildered. "So much was taken from us. Our friends, family, and homes were annihilated in one fell swoop. Yet our pack is smiling."

"They are all focusing on the mountains and the freedom that comes with it." I pull my boots on and step into Bastian's chest. "The kids miss their parents, but they are excited by the chance to run and play without fear."

"The kids will be staying near us," Bastian says, shaking his head. "Look what happened the first time they came across humans. They don't need freedom."

"Bass, you don't mean that." I wrap my arms around his waist and press my ear to his heart. "Kids need to stretch their legs. Adults need to run and hunt together. We thought we were safe at the lake, but we were just hiding and hoping no one would breach our borders. Our wolves might have been in a large cage, but it was still a cage."

Bastian rubs my back, allowing his body to heat and comfort me. "I didn't think about it that way," he whispers. "I doubt they did either."

"Until we left," I say, smiling. "Suddenly, a whole world opened up to them. They are free of fear without walls and boundaries." I look up, cupping his cheek. "That's a life I want for my wolves."

Bastian sighs loudly. "Now it's just a matter of getting them there," he remarks.

"Therein lies my fears," I say, kissing his lips. "I know the life I want to give them and where they can have it. I just don't know if we can make it."

"Then let's get some sleep with our wolves and resume our journey," Bastian suggests. "I like seeing those kids smile and hearing their laughter."

"Hm, me too," I agree, nodding. "Maybe Myla would like to play with the boys. I'd feel more comfortable if she were with them for a while."

"Sure," Bastian says before kissing me again and stepping aside to shift. He rubs his muzzle over my hip and bumps my belly with his nose. *"Your Mom's pretty smart, kiddo."* He slides his jaw into my fingers and leads me back to the pack.

The boys fall in with us the moment we emerge from the trees. Hanging out with the Luna has become their favorite pastime since their kidnapping. I suppose it's easy to assume they feel safer surrounded by my guards, but they hardly pay attention to where those wolves are. The boys hold their heads high as they walk against my legs and Bastian's shoulder.

My Alpha has always fiercely protected the children in our pack and is remarkably gentle with them. He doesn't remember having a childhood, so he's unsure how to talk to them. He remains silent as he nuzzles them and carefully corrects them if they interfere with his job.

The kids shrink back a bit as Daddy approaches us. *"Annalisa, we've set up a bed under the wagon for you and Trish,"* he announces, hooking his jaw in my left hand. He tries to direct me toward the edge of my sleeping wolves where the wagon had been parked.

"No, Daddy," I say, stopping. "I want to spend this time with my wolves."

"Child, you'll be close enough," my father grumbles.

I kneel before the Alphas, rubbing their muzzles. "Guys, look at our pack," I say. "Do you see what I see?" I look over our wolves with them and smile as I spot Kade in the middle. "I see families tangling with each other. Neighbors are snuggled together. Kids are cuddled up with friends. Do you hear their hums? We should be a part of that love, not hiding from it."

"Brock and Rachel are lying with Kade," Bastian adds, nodding in their direction. The only part of Brock sticking out of the small pile near Kade is his shoulder. It is easy for our companion to blend in with the rest of our brown wolves, but Bastian will always recognize any part of him.

"Please come with us, Daddy," I request. "Let's be a true pack tonight. We all need sleep, and they need to feel our love. How could I be any safer than surrounded by my wolves?"

My father rolls his eyes and stands to help me navigate the wolf pile. As we approach the center, Kade sleepily pulls his head out from under Gaine's leg and yawns.

I kneel and curl his leg to make room. *"Hi, sleepyhead,"* I say, smiling. *"You've acquired quite the collection."*

"Where the hell did all these wolves come from?" Kade grumbles.

Giggling, I rub his jaw before rolling to lie against his ribs. *"Kade, you are well respected and loved by our pack,"* I tell him. *"You should probably just accept it."*

Kade groans and pokes my face with his nose. *"Come here, Luna,"* he says. *"Clearly, you need sleep."*

As he lays his head over Gaine's neck, Daddy and Bastian crawl up on either side of me to rest their chins on my shoulders. Between the chorus of hums and the heat radiating from all the wolves around me, I don't stand a chance. I fall asleep with a contented sigh, knowing my pack finally feels the love they deserve.

16

Kade's absence is felt as soon as he leaves. As a Luna, I must be self-less, but I've wanted my silver wolf to stay with us since we found him on our porch. Seeing Kade today, it's hard to imagine how broken he was. I laid on that porch with him for two days, never wanting him to leave my arms.

Kade taught me how to heal a broken heart and be a friend to my wolves, and when he was ready, he taught me how to let them go. I often wonder who taught my mother. I asked Daddy once. His answer was that a Luna knows her job, but I think Uncle Miles taught her. They had a special relationship we'd probably never understand.

Bastian has stayed by my side, helping me through this empty feeling. Brock joins us throughout the day but stands guard at night while Rachel rides in the wagon with us. We've been moving for three days, and my wolves are exhausted.

I have walked as much as Bastian would allow, but he was adamant that I ride at night. My wolves switched off, riding for a few hours to take small naps. I haven't heard from Neala or Ash since we left the campsite, but Creto reports they are carrying the younger wolves while they sleep.

"Daddy, we need to stop," I finally demand when Saint stumbles as he pulls the wagon with the new gelding.

"*Ayls*," my father starts with a sigh. He's about to tell me how wrong I am, and I'm not interested in hearing it.

"No, Daddy," I stop him. "Bringing our wolves where they can be safe and happy means nothing if they don't survive the journey. They're exhausted, and these horses won't last much longer."

"There's no food or water," my father growls. *"There's barely anything for the horses to eat. They won't last long anyway without water."*

"I'll take care of that," I retort. *"Brock, bring me the Belgian."*

"Ayls, what are you doing?" Daddy grumbles.

"Feeding my pack," I snap.

Brock jogs to me, pulling the large draft horse. Matthew took him from the kidnappers' wagon after we rescued the kids. Based on his teeth, he's only around ten years old but has limped off his back leg this entire time. It's rendered him useless to us for all but one purpose.

I pull my blade from my boot as they approach. Rubbing the horse's nose one last time, I whisper, "Thank you," before plunging my knife into his neck and twisting it to rip his windpipe open. His legs buckle, and I turn his head to help him fall onto his right side. Bastian shifts, grabbing my blade and jamming it behind the horse's elbow, deep into his heart to end his suffering.

I may have just ended a life, but ignoring the lips being licked around us is hard. My wolves are tired, but their hunger will keep them awake until they've had some meat. This large horse would only be enough to fill half of them at best, so they will share, and each only take enough to carry them for another day or two.

Bastian slides his arms around me so my tears fall on his chest. Every wolf was permitted to try the meat whenever we had to put a horse down, but none had acquired a taste for it. I would never deny my wolves their favorite meal, but they've opted for other prey because of my love of horses.

As I pull away, I see them still staring at the downed animal, moving carefully toward it. "Please," I start, sniffling. "This is for you. According to Kade's markers, we're only halfway. He's reporting dry conditions. This horse walked here to help you finish the journey. Please eat and then get some sleep."

Bastian ushers me away so I don't have to watch them. Horses have a special place in my heart, and watching them pull at the Belgian's hide would be too much for me. He scoops his arm across the back of my legs, lifting me to lie against his chest.

My wolves are talking about the meat, relishing its taste. The older wolves tell the kids where to eat to get the most fat. I want to filter them out but can't. There's nothing else to listen to until Bastian lays me down in the wagon. His lips brush over my jaw. My Alpha digs his fingers into my thigh to pull at my pants until they slide from my hips.

Closing my eyes, I moan quietly as I give in to my husband. His touch urges my nerves to reach for him and shuts out the voices. Bastian slowly enjoys my body for hours, tasting every inch of my skin and whispering about his love for me every step of the way. I'm exhausted by the time he releases for the last time.

Bastian covers us with a blanket as he wraps around me, burying my face in his chest. My wolves have finished their feast for the most part, and the boys jump into the wagon with us before I fall asleep.

* * *

The lack of reaction from my nerves causes me to jump when I wake, but my companion's gentle whispers settle me quickly. Knowing Brock's arms well, I relax and let him roll back over me.

"Where's Bass?" I ask.

Brock sighs. "He needed to eat," he whispers. "There's not much left, but he hasn't eaten in a while."

"I know," I whisper back. "Is there any marrow?"

"Anthony made sure the pack left that for Bass and Tarq," Brock says, lifting off me. "He split the bones for them this morning."

"Did you eat?" I ask, pushing his hair away from his face. Brock is my only wolf with different-colored eyes. One is green, while the other is brown. They hide behind his dark hair that spent the summer bleaching so much that it nearly matches Bastian's sandy blonde.

"We all had a little bit," Brock answers, pulling the blanket up to cover me. "A few of us had to trade off keeping the kids away from the wagon." He lifts his eyebrow and smirks.

I cringe with a sigh. "I appreciate that. Bastian was shielding me from having to listen to everyone enjoying the horse."

Brock pulls me back to his chest and rests his chin on my head. "His love knows no equal."

"I feel your love, Brock," I mumble, sliding my hand over his ribs. "It's different but still intense. I'm sure Rachel enjoys your love as I enjoy Bastian's."

My companion starts to hum as I rub my fingers over his back. "I can't decide which of you does that better," he murmurs, sighing. Many of my wolves enjoy relaxing under my touch. Brock hasn't needed me since he bonded with Rachel, but he enjoys having his back tickled.

"We'll both always be here for you, so you don't have to," I say, smiling. I wrap my arms around Brock and squeeze tightly. "You live in a world where you have two wives. One that will demand your heart, body, and soul and another who will demand your time, honor, and companionship."

"Hmm," Brock hums contentedly. "Which one are you?"

Giggling, I pull back from him to grab his cheeks. "The one who will replace both of them," I say, pulling him to my lips. "I love you, Brock. Forever in my heart."

"I love you too, Ayls," he says, chuckling. He kisses me one more time before pressing his lips to my forehead. "We should get the pack moving, though. It won't be long before they'll need another meal. Besides, one of those wives might be looking for me soon."

Kade says I spend an unhealthy amount of time in bed with Brock. Trish was my closest friend growing up, but I never felt as close to her as I do with my companion. I couldn't imagine having a physical relationship with anyone other than Bastian, but I can't deny that I enjoy my time in Brock's arms. I may not have survived many moments in our past without the comfort he provides.

"Annalisa, get up. We need to go," my father barks from beside the wagon.

I scowl. "You know I'm in charge, right, Daddy?"

"You're also naked in a wagon with three kids and your companion," he points out.

Brock shakes us both with his chuckle.

"Point taken," I grumble. "Out, kids. Luna needs to get dressed."

* * *

Within a few hours, we're back on the trail. A few of my guards work together to push and pull the wagon over the flat terrain as the kids herd the horses along small patches of grass to graze. While I listen to the morning report, Trish remains quiet with her arm hooked in mine but nearly bursts with thoughts once the guards finish.

"Edith said she'll teach me to make baby clothes for our kids," my friend says, patting my hand. "That will give me something to do while I watch the kids when you're off taking care of the pack."

Trish stops talking as Myla bounces by, followed by several kids. She has a large stick in her mouth that they found in the last grove we passed and is playing keep away with them. The kids laugh and bound joyfully, trying to catch her. Myla is only a few years older than the kids she's playing with, but her legs are much longer, making it easy for her to stay ahead of them.

"What's her deal?" Trish asks, eyeing Myla.

"She met my mother at a celebration during our last Christmas together," I tell her. "The militia killed her parents for their milking cow. She was eight when she met my mother and decided she wanted to be a Luna's guard."

"Everyone wanted to be your mother's guard," Trish says, breathing a laugh. "I couldn't wait to be old enough to travel with her like Ash. It sweetened the deal that I could go with you once you were Luna."

"You can still travel with me," I remind her. "Having a child, even the future Alpha, does not tie you to your home. While he's too young, you can leave him with the pack, and when he's old enough, he can come with us. Daddy says that he'll need plenty of exercise."

"Have you ever wondered what it would be like if our parents were still here?" Trish asks. "Do you think they'd make the same decisions?"

She's not really asking me for an answer. Her eyes are studying the setting sun as we end yet another day without finding water. I had thought about it a lot over the first few days of this trip, but my mother told me I was making the right decision. I haven't told anyone I'd questioned her about my choices.

"Luna, we found water," Chase announces loudly, causing an exaggerated sigh of relief to jump from my lungs. His southern group reached the foothills last night but had been without water for six days. He'd lost two older wolves, and the others struggled to slowly trudge along in the shade of the pines. *"Luna?"*

"I'm here, Chase," I answer. *"Did the rest make it?"*

"Even Grandma Pine," he proudly states. *"The kids have been pulling her on a dirt sled."*

I smile, looking for Myla. I suppose she'll be interested to know her old caretaker made it to the mountains.

"I haven't seen Kade," Chase tells me. *"He's not answering me."*

He won't. Chase's group is too big for Kade. He'll skirt them and watch over Chase's wolves but won't mingle. Luckily, Gaine also doesn't like crowds, so they'll stay together at a comfortable distance.

"I'll make sure he's close if you need him," I say. *"His markers put us two days from the foothills at our pace. We'll be there soon."*

"Annalisa?" Chase rarely uses my full name these days.

"Yeah?"

"You did the right thing," he tells me.

"Thanks, Chase."

Smiling, I look at Trish to find she's still lost in thought. "Why don't we have the kids hitch the horses back to the wagon," I suggest. "You look like you could use some rest."

I drop Trish at the wagon with Edith before leaving to search for my father. I find him lying in the shade of a lone pine while he waits for the horses to be hitched. "Hey, Daddy," I say, sitting beside him. "How are you holding up?"

"I'm tired, kiddo," he answers, yawning.

I don't know how the not-aging thing goes, but Daddy is older now.

I'd been worrying about my older wolves, especially after Chase lost a few, but it's easy to forget that Daddy is up there in age too. "We can stop if you need us to," I tell him.

"*Annalisa, I've been exhausted for years,*" Daddy grumbles. "*Keeping you Lunas alive is a full-time job. At least when your mother was alive, I got sex out of the deal.*"

I wince and shake my head. "Daddy, I don't want to hear about that," I scoff. "My ears. They've been violated."

My father rolls upright and sticks his nose in my face. "*I guarded that wagon while that kid enjoyed the benefits of being a Luna's Alpha. I believe I have earned the right to speak my mind.*" It's been a while, so I did not expect his slobbery tongue to slide impossibly slow over my face.

"Daddy! Gross!" I cry out as my father chuckles, lying back down. I wipe my face, trying to remove the layer of drool that seems to have found a home over my eyes. "Why?" I grumble. "Why do you guys feel the need to do that?"

"*I don't know,*" he answers dismissively. "*It entertains us.*"

"Why won't you talk to Chase?" I ask, irritated. "He's been calling out to us. They found water."

My father lifts his head. "*Was that what he wanted?*"

"Enough, Daddy," I say sharply. "He lost Mom too. We're all healing. Why do you keep pushing him away?"

My father rolls onto his side with a sigh. I've beat around this bush for years. Chase was my father's wing, his right hand. He was the wolf that took my father's place the moment he wasn't near my mother. They spent years together as Chase learned everything about my father so he could support my mother.

They moved Chase into our house after Bristol died, and I remember watching him struggle to pull himself up the stairs to slip into their room during his more difficult times. My father willingly shared his bed and my mother's love with their companion as he healed from that loss. But when it came to losing my mother, he shut him out. They were both hurting, and my father wanted nothing to do with him.

"When I lie in Brock's arms, I feel so much love radiating from him,"

I whisper, resting against his ribs. "I feel safe knowing he'll never let anything happen to me. The moment Bastian steps away, Brock is there, ready to fill in for him. Of course, he's a package deal with Rachel, but I believe it was the same for Chase and Mom."

"He loved her very much," my father says softly. *"He knew she was dying. He knew and kept that from me."* He slides his muzzle over the ground, attempting to hide his tears. *"He knew we would lose your mother and didn't give us a chance to save her."*

I take a moment to consider his words. Chase was acting as my mother's doctor while we were traveling. It would make sense that he knew. But I also know my mother. She would've made him promise not to tell us. She would've begged him. My mother wanted to give us that time with her to learn, laugh, and have fun.

"That wasn't his fault, Daddy," I respond, pulling the hair on his throat. "Mom was bigger than all of us. She was larger than life. Brock would do anything for me, and Chase taught him everything about being my companion. You can't keep holding this against him. He was only honoring Mom."

"He should've told me," my father insists.

"I imagine he wanted to," I say, staring off toward Brock and Bastian. They are sparring while they wait for me, rearing up at each other and trying to catch the other's muzzle in their mouth. "That probably ate at him. But you pushed him away when he came to you to heal."

Daddy sighs heavily. *"I need to heal too,"* he grumbles.

"Well, are you about done?" I ask, rolling my eyes.

"No," he answers sharply.

I had come over to talk about the direction we should travel and try to coordinate with Chase and Kade, but I got sidetracked. There's no hope of having that conversation now. I roll toward his shoulder and slide my hand over his front leg. "I wouldn't try to force you to forgive him, Daddy," I whisper. "But I think it would help you heal if you tried." My hand travels down to his paw, and I smile as he groans.

After a few minutes, Bastian joins us and jams his muzzle under my father's neck. I had a lot of trouble understanding why my Alpha would leave my mother on the train that night. I was furious at him. I even told him I wished it was him instead of her.

Bastian listened to me hate him for hours before I finally crumbled in a heap, crying my eyes out and screaming for my mother. He protectively crouched over me and nuzzled my cheeks. Bastian quietly told me how much she loved me and why she did what she had done. My Alpha explained that he begged her to come with us but pointed out that no one could tell my mother what to do. He reminded me that she was too strong for that.

Bastian seems to know exactly when my father needs his support. It's a skill Brock picked up quickly, and I'm delighted to see him jogging in my direction now.

I smile and roll to my back with my arm extended to him. "Now I have the three most important men in my life with me," I whisper as he slides his jaw over my shoulder.

"I won't tell Kade you said that," Brock says, chuckling.

I giggle, laying my cheek on his head. "I appreciate that."

We lie together as the rest of our wolves prepare for this evening's journey. Trish and the kids got the last of our tea yesterday. My young wolves have an incredible metabolism and require more food and water to keep their strength. They are suffering, so I couldn't justify keeping it from them.

Once the horses are hitched and the wagon packed, I shake the wolves beside me, and we head out. Myla has given her tea to Timothy, so my glare is quite cross until she jumps in the wagon.

"Kade told me to watch you," she states as she sits at attention on the back of the wagon.

"Yes, Myla," I respond. "But I doubt he advised you to neglect your well-being." I rub her chin before falling back to walk with some other kids.

Bastian and Daddy work as my wing guards once it's dark. Although Brock is close, he allows Creto to walk in my hand. The young wolf is shorter, so he jogs happily beside me with his head high, allowing me to hook my fingers under his jaw.

"How have you been, Creto?" I ask. "Are you feeling ok?"

"*Luna,*" Creto starts in the firm tone of a 10-year-old guard. "*I'm not allowed to talk to you while I guard you. Now, if you don't mind, I'll silently return to my job.*" His eyes never divert from the trail before us.

My cheeks hurt as I smile at him. Creto will be an unstoppable force when he's older. I open and close my hand to rub my fingers over his jaw. The young wolf has black hair and blue eyes, which become piercingly bright when he shifts. For some reason, his whiskers are white, and I find that adorable.

"He's turning into quite the young guard," Edith remarks beside me.

Giggling, I look up from the happy wolf. "He is quite formidable."

"You look tired, Annalisa," she continues her observations. "You should lie down."

Creto glances up at me. "*Luna?*"

I shake my head. "I'm fine," I tell them. "Let the kids ride for a little while. We still have a few more days." I hook arms with Edith and pull her close to whisper, "Chase found water."

Edith's bright smile is hard to miss. "Oh, that's a relief to hear!" she gushes, sighing heavily. Her gaze shifts up to the driver's seat of the wagon.

"When's the last time Anthony ate or drank?" I whisper.

Edith squeezes my arm. "I don't know," she responds sadly.

"Ok," I say quietly. "Is there anything you were holding back? A tea or something? He's human and needs more care than us, Edith."

She scowls, pulling a small vial from her pocket. "I have this. I was saving it for an emergency," Edith whispers.

Unhooking our arms, I hold out my hand. "Give it here," I tell her. "Let me see if I can convince him to drink it."

Edith scoffs. "Good luck," she grumbles. "Hardheaded man."

I smile and rub her back before looking down at Creto. "Let's go see Anthony," I suggest.

The happy young wolf jogs a bit faster to help me reach the front of the wagon. Creto stays with me as I move close enough to grab the handle and step onto the wheel's spoke. As the wheel turns, it lifts me to easily step onto the driver's ledge.

Anthony jumps when he sees me. "Hey, kiddo," he says, surprised. "Here. Let me help you." He reaches out for my hand and braces me as the wagon sways.

"Thank you," I say, smiling as I sit on the bench beside him. "I wanted to check in with you. It's been a while since we spoke."

"I'm old, kiddo. Nothing works as it's supposed to anymore," Anthony grumbles, patting my knee. "You don't need to worry about me."

I move closer to Anthony and hook our arms. "I talked to Mom," I whisper, watching his eyes widen. "When I died. It was just a moment, but she looked good. She told me we were doing the right thing and that the mountains are beautiful."

"Did she have anything about the unicorns that kid keeps seeing?" Anthony hisses.

I look out over the horses. I hadn't thought to ask Mom about that. I feel crazy just bringing it up, never mind questioning its validity. "I'll never experience a functional historian, Anthony," I finally mutter.

Anthony leans back in the seat and rubs my shoulder. "God, your mother," he starts, pulling air between his teeth. "She was a force of nature. Something was always happening with her—some new disaster, myth, or legend." Anthony stops and takes a deep breath before looking down at me. "And it pissed me off when she was right. Every damn time."

I shake my head. "What are you talking about?"

"If anyone can help you decode that crazy girl's rambling, it's your mother," Anthony advises. "You passed up a golden opportunity I hope you never get again." He shifts his legs and moves the horses' reins to lay them across his lap.

I slide my fingers over their smooth leather. "Even unicorns?" I ask.

Anthony chuckles. "Yes, kiddo. Even unicorns."

We ride silently for a moment before I remember why I'd climbed up here. "Edith was holding out on us," I say, holding out the small vial she'd given me.

"You have it," Anthony says. "You're more important."

"Why don't we share?" I counter.

"Fine," he grumbles, lifting his eyebrow. "You first. And I want to see actual swallowing."

Giggling, I pull the top off the vial. I tip it, pretending to take some into my mouth. To complete the act, I force my mouth to trigger a swallow. "Mm, that hits the spot," I exaggerate.

Anthony shakes his head and drains the vial before handing it back to me. "There," he spouts. "You can tell my wife you won the tea war."

Edith and Anthony married a few years after my parents. Anthony says Edith tricked him into it, but he is utterly devoted to her and made my father be his best man for the ceremony. I'm not exactly sure what that is, but Mom said it was a position of honor. She told me Anthony never stopped surprising her. That also seems to be my experience.

"Anthony," I say, lifting my eyebrow. "You are truly one of a kind."

"I believe that was supposed to be an insult," Anthony says, nodding. "However, I feel inclined to say thank you."

Giggling, I shake my head. "If that's how you want to play it," I tell him. "I think I'll go lay down for a while, though. Bastian will be upset if I look tired when he returns in the morning."

"Hmm," Anthony hums, still nodding. "That boy does like his Luna fresh." He squeezes my shoulders and kisses my forehead. "Get some sleep. We got this tonight."

"Good night," I whisper, climbing over the seat.

Trish lies among the blankets while Myla sits close to the back, facing me. I move some piles around to make more space than I need and reach my arm out for Myla. The young wolf hesitates.

"Come on," I whisper. "I've been watching you. You haven't slept in days."

She crawls beside me to lay her jaw over my shoulder. Myla's coat is long and hides her frame well. As I slip my fingers into it, I feel barely any muscle around her bones.

"We're reporting this to Neala in the morning," I tell her. "You've put on a good show but are too weak to guard me now."

"Yes, Luna," Myla responds sadly.

17

⸎

My wolves' warmth surrounds me when I wake. The lumpy blankets remind me I'm not at home, but I leave my eyes closed against the sunlight and pretend for a moment. I'm safe and warm, wrapped in blankets with my Alpha cuddled into my neck. My mother gently rubs my cheek to wake me. "It's time to wake up, Sweets," she whispers.

I jump awake. "Mom?!"

Several hands push me back down to the blankets in the wagon. The sun is so bright I can't open my eyes. With everyone yelling at once, I can't understand any of them. I flail around until teeth grab my arm, pinning it to the wagon beside me.

"Easy, Love," Bastian says soothingly. *"We can't waste any of this."*

I stop fighting at Bastian's request. The pressure holding me down releases, and I open my hand for his jaw, but it remains empty. I turn my head, trying to find shade so I can open my eyes. "Why is it so bright?" I mumble.

Bastian's muzzle slides over my face, shrouding it in darkness. His familiar scent fills my nostrils and helps me relax. *"I love you,"* my Alpha says quietly.

In the shadow of his head, I can open my eyes. I blink until I'm able to focus on the faces around me. Edith is fussing over the arm Bastian had held down, and my father holds tubes I know all too well. "Daddy?" I whisper. "Where's Mom?"

My father's brow wrinkles as he turns to face me. "Ayls, where's the tea Edith gave you?"

I shake my head. "I gave it to Anthony," I answer. "He needed it."

"We shared it," Anthony says from somewhere nearby. "That was my deal with her."

"Well, she obviously didn't drink any," Edith grumbles.

No one is answering my question. "Mom was here," I mumble. "Where is she?"

"Why isn't she making sense?" my father barks, his growl building.

"Tarq, she's losing blood faster than I can get it in her," Edith snaps back. "I'm doing the best I can. I'm not a damn doctor."

My head is foggy, but the pieces begin to make sense. They must be using the tubes Daddy's holding to give me Bastian's blood. I'm bleeding too much, and they can't stop it. Without help, I'm gonna die.

"Chase," I whisper. "Daddy. Chase."

The wagon lurches as my father springs from it. Bastian sways so violently that his shadow moves and forces me to close my eyes. Sighing, I smile weakly as I listen to Daddy call out to Chase for help. Chase reassures my father as they go over what has happened, and I try to reach for Bastian when Daddy says the blood is coming from between my legs.

* * *

"Hey, kid, it's not so great to see you," Grandpa's voice calls through my muddled thoughts.

I gasp and jump into his arms as he appears before me in the blackness. "Grandpa!" I exclaim. I've only been able to hug my grandfather once. I loved it but didn't fully grasp how precious that moment was until I lost my mother.

"Easy, kiddo," Grandpa grumbles, squeezing me. "I'm old."

Giggling, I release him and lean back. "I'm not dead, am I?" I would love to live in a world where my grandfather is with me, but I'm not ready to die to make that a reality.

Grandpa leans forward to sniff me. "No," he says thoughtfully. "You've been drugged. It's Edith's concoction."

"I'm bleeding," I tell him. "I heard Daddy say it's coming from the baby."

He rubs his hand over his beard scruff before cupping my cheek. "Your mother used to say making a Luna was hard. I don't think you ever tried to kill her, though."

"Grandpa, where's Mom?" I ask, watching him try to understand pregnancy.

He waves his hand dismissively. "She's keeping Aylee busy for me," he answers. "That woman is insufferable. I gotta take a break sometimes."

I lift my eyebrow in surprise. This is a whole new side of him that I've never seen. "Isn't she your mate?" I ask, confused. "How can you not love your mate?"

Grandpa scowls. "Nah," he starts, sighing heavily. "I love her. She's just a bit much."

"She might be able to help me," I say. "Where is she? Can I talk to her?"

"Oh, she'll show up," my grandfather says, rolling his eyes. "She doesn't let me take that long of a break." He pulls me back to his chest as I shake my head. "How's your dad doing? He seems lonely."

"He is," I say, sighing. "He misses Mom something fierce. I hope to help him reconnect with Chase."

Grandpa clicks his tongue and leans back. "Take them all fishing," he tells me. "Chase doesn't like playing in the water, but he likes something about doing it with Bass and your father." He rubs my arms as he steps back. "Take them fishing."

"There you are," Aylee gushes. "Stop leaving me with your little friend. You know she annoys me." The young woman steps around Grandpa and runs her eyes over me as if making a purchase. "Well, if it isn't screw-up-Luna number two," she scoffs.

"Aylee," my grandfather growls. "Be nice to my granddaughter."

"If she's here again, Dax, it's because she screwed up," Aylee barks. "What did you die of this time? A stubbed toe? You people can't even walk right."

I'm frozen as I stare at her. Grandpa seems quite cross with her, but I can't tell if she's being serious.

"What do you mean 'again?'" Grandpa questions. "She's been here before?" He's glaring at Aylee, but the young woman doesn't seem fazed by his anger.

She shrugs dismissively. "She was here a while ago," she says. "Your little friend yelled at me and told me to go away."

"Why didn't you tell me?" Grandpa's reaching a level of fury I'm not accustomed to seeing.

"It was need-to-know, Dax," Aylee says, lifting her eyebrow. "You're dead. Therefore, you did not need to know."

"I'm gonna need you to go far away, Aylee," Grandpa growls. "Very, very far away."

"Fine," she huffs before disappearing.

My grandfather closes his eyes and takes a moment to calm down. I watch as he sucks his teeth and wonder if I should try to leave. Looking around, I nearly laugh at myself, thinking about where I'd go in this darkness of doom.

"Come on," Grandpa finally says. "Let's go see your mom."

He throws his arm around my shoulders, and we're suddenly beside the wagon, watching Edith fuss over me. Mom is sitting beside her on the wagon's edge. We wait as she puts her finger to her lips. Edith is murmuring to Anthony while keeping her eyes on Daddy as if she wants to ensure he can't hear what she's saying.

She pulls the needle out of Bastian's leg and helps him tuck his paws against his body before he falls asleep. Anthony moves my legs while Edith changes the blankets under me. The bedding she pulls out is soaked with blood. I cover my mouth and try to blink back my tears before anyone notices.

"It's not as much as it seems, Sweets," my mother whispers.

"Darya," Grandpa scoffs. "They just drained that kid, and now they're looking at Tarq. I'd say that's a fair amount."

My mother glares at Grandpa for a moment. "Dax, maybe you could consider your audience," she snaps.

"Why didn't you tell me my audience had been here before?" Grandpa retorts.

"What good would that information do?" she replies. "You are making it very clear why Miles stayed away from you two."

They quiet down as Edith calls for Daddy, holding up the needle. Daddy shifts and stands beside the wagon, leaning against the side right next to my mother. She cups his cheek, and his eyes close as his hum starts. He reaches for his cheek and holds his hand where my mother's is. Daddy takes a deep breath before whispering, "Help's on the way, Dar. I'll save her."

"I know you will, My Love," she whispers, kissing his forehead.

"Mom?" I say quietly, hoping to find out what's going on.

She looks up and smiles. "Hang on, Sweets. We can't hear them when they're wolves. Let's listen to what Daddy has to say."

When she pulls her hand away from my father, he looks up at Edith. "Chase is on his way," he tells her. "Their healer is with him. They're bringing water to brew tea." He squints, looking down at Bastian. "Did you kill him?"

Edith clicks her tongue. "I gave you as much time as possible, Tarq," she scolds. "He'll just need rest." She moves my eyelid. "I knocked her out to slow her heart. It's slowed the bleeding, but not much."

"Alright," Daddy says, rubbing his forehead. "Don't drain me that much. We can't leave her without a guard." He shifts and crawls between my body and Bastian's before rolling to give Edith his front leg.

"Let's go," Mom says softly. "We need to talk to Aylee. Where is she?" She turns to Grandpa, who's watching Daddy nuzzle my cheek.

"I sent her away," he responds, sighing. "With any luck, she fell off that damn snowy cliff she pouts on."

"Dax, she never goes far," Mom scoffs. "Get out here, Aylee."

The young woman walks out from in front of the horses, scowling. Despite her sour appearance, Aylee is gorgeous. She's wearing furs still attached to the hides, clearly from another time. She has jewelry made of bone and quills hanging around her neck. Aylee looks younger than us yet still has a presence that demands respect.

Grandpa cups her cheeks when she steps before him. My grandfather's love for us is easy to see in his eyes, but the intensity of his gaze upon her is breathtaking. "You need to be honest with me about my family," he whispers.

Aylee reaches up on her toes to rub her lips against his as she whispers back. Wrinkling my nose, I turn to my mother for an explanation. She pulls my arm until we're far enough away that they shouldn't hear.

"Since a spell brought her back, she's pretty much a mythical creature," Mom says, sitting on a tree stump to watch them. "Her bond with Grandpa is quite strong. She doesn't have any magic left, but tread lightly because her words still sting."

"That reminds me," I spout. "Anthony told me to ask you about the unicorns."

Aylee blows her lips out. "You're a few centuries too late, kid," she says, turning her attention to us. "They were hunted to extinction long before you thought of them."

Lifting an eyebrow, Grandpa links their arms. "They were real?"

"Mm-hmm," she replies. "Here's the real kicker. Their blood could've healed your disaster of a Luna over there." She holds her hands out in a grand flourish. "But now you'll just have to watch her die."

Mom was right. Aylee's words definitely sting. I walk past them to stand beside the wagon. Daddy's head is over Bastian's neck as the two give everything they have to save me. "What's wrong with me?" I whisper.

"You're an idiot," Aylee replies. "Among other things."

"Can you please try to be remotely helpful?" I growl, turning to glare at her. "You don't have to be a bitch all the time. We came to you for help. So, pack up the bullshit attitude and say something useful!"

Aylee scowls but leans into Grandpa's chest in a possessive way. "Are you going to let her talk to me like that?"

Grandpa throws his hands in the air. "I talk to you like that," he says, laughing.

"Fine," Aylee scoffs. "I suspect the unborn Alpha is around here somewhere?" She points to the clusters of wolves nearby. "Probably that one, huh?" Aylee indicates Trish as the only obviously pregnant person.

"I think so, yeah," I answer.

"Being near you might make her feel better, but the moment your kid's heart started beating, she began demanding her Alpha." Aylee looks at the pile of blood-soaked blankets beside the wagon. "That kid's fine, but she's gonna tear you in half. When you die, so will she." She shakes her head. "Kids make the worst decisions."

I rub my stomach. "So, she's trying to be near him?" I ask. "What if I just stay near her all the time? Or maybe send her away so there's no chance of them being near each other?"

Aylee waves her hand as if brushing me away. "That damage is done, little girl," she says, shaking her head. "The salvation you need is extinct. You're screwed. Say your goodbyes, and we'll see you soon."

Before I realize what I'm doing, I've launched myself at my grandfather's Luna. I land against her, knocking her into Grandpa and latching onto her neck. I know it's not her fault, and I'm aware I can't kill her, but strangling her for a little while might make me feel better. Her bitchy smile only infuriates me more.

"Enough, you two," Grandpa growls.

Mom's laughter filters through my rage as she pulls me off Aylee. "I can't even count how many times I've done that," Mom says, laughing. "Come on, Sweets. Time moves differently here. We need to get going. You'll be waking up soon."

I release my emotions as she pulls me into her arms. "Mom," I sob. "I'm going to die." I close my eyes as the wagon disappears. "I just got married."

"Yeah," my mother says, drawing out the word. "About that." She digs her fingers into her eyes.

"Mom, don't start," I mutter. "I love Bastian. I love Kade. Nothing in my apparently short life will ever be normal or traditional."

I narrow my eyes as I look around. We've moved onto the side of a hill or something. The air seems crisp, and the view is clear without the constant kick-up of dust I've become accustomed to. There are pines below us, and the ground is littered with green shoots of timothy as I look up the rise. Something is rustling in one of the pines just below us.

"What is that?" I whisper.

Aylee scoffs. "A tree," she huffs, blowing out her lips. "Honestly, where do you find these people?"

"Dax, would you please?" Mom grumbles.

Grandpa rolls his eyes. "Come on, Aylee," he says before kissing my head. "I'll see you soon, kiddo."

Aylee tries to pull out of Grandpa's grip. "No," she states defiantly. "I wanna see how this ends."

Grandpa lifts his eyebrow. "I think you'll like this ending more."

His Luna perks up and smiles broadly. "Lead the way," she responds, winking.

My nose wrinkles as she hooks her legs around his waist and latches onto his lips before they disappear. "If that's what I'll have to deal with, I don't want to come here, Mom," I say, feeling like there should be vomit in my throat.

"You learn to appreciate their hormones," my mother says dismissively. "It's a porcupine, by the way." She nods toward the rustling in the tree. "Your wolves will want to play with it. Tell them not to," she adds, shaking her head.

"I miss you, Mom," I tell her as she hooks our arms and walks up the hill. "Everyone does. Anthony said you'd be able to help with the unicorn."

"I didn't, really," Mom says, shrugging. "That was Aylee."

Rolling my eyes, I kick at a rock. "I'd prefer to forget that I met her."

"Do you remember our lessons about give and take?" Mom asks, patting my hand. "Aylee made this world with the magic she received when she was brought back. She was inside of me, and I was kicking her out. While that fight was happening, she wanted to take a little of Grandpa with her. As a result of that desire, she has to do everything he says."

My eyes widen. "So, he can tell her to never speak again?" I ask hopefully. "And she'd be unable to talk?"

"Can you maybe not focus on yourself for a minute?" Mom asks, frowning. "Grandpa had his fun with it when she was in me, but he's good to her, or at least he tries to be. She's... difficult." Mom stops at the top of the hill and looks around. "She could fight it before she used the rest of her magic, allowing me to say goodbye to your father and uncle. I choose to be grateful for that."

Sighing, I follow her gaze and take in our surroundings. "Where are we?" I ask. The hills slope sharply down into gullies of pine trees. A soft breeze blows against our faces, pushing our hair away from our eyes.

"These are part of the Rockies, daughter," my mother says softly. "This is the beautiful land you are bringing our wolves to for a better future." She smiles and turns me slightly. "It's a land of wild horses and game that flourish in open spaces."

A large, well-fed, painted horse nearby lifts its head to stare into the distance. He's followed by a few mares and a colt. They are calm and don't mind the small elk herd behind them. I clutch my chest and approach them for a better look, but my mother catches my arm.

"We disturb the natural elements, so you'll want to leave them to their lunch," Mom says.

"I wish I could see them enjoy this," I say sadly.

Mom grabs my shoulders and turns me to face her. "Daddy stabbed me in the heart, and Edith's spell brought me back to life," she states, lifting her eyebrows. "Trust them. Love will always win if you just believe in its power."

I rub my eyes with my palms' heels, stopping my tears. "Mom, this isn't the same thing," I spout. "Love is what's gonna kill me. This kid wants her Alpha."

Biting her lip, Mom narrows her eyes at the wild horses. "When I was pregnant with you, your Daddy did some things," she says thoughtfully. "He's always been able to talk to you as a wolf, and he would lick my belly and tell you stories while I rubbed his pads."

I watch the horses with her for a moment, thinking about her words. "Daddy's always been able to talk to me?" I accidentally snap loudly.

It's my mother's turn to rub her eyes. "Focus, Sweets," she grumbles. "We're running out of time. You would push against my tummy like you were trying to pet him. Maybe Bastian can settle her a little. Ask Daddy to show him some things to try. Hell, maybe she'll like Daddy too."

"Mom, I can't do this," I whine.

She grabs my wrists and holds me before her. "I used to say that every time I hit a wall or bump," Mom whispers. "But then my wolves would smile or hug me. I knew I loved them so much that I would do anything for them, even if I had to brave the flames of hell. I survived for them."

I close my eyes to view my pack undisturbed. "They are pretty amazing, aren't they?"

"They have a breathtaking beauty that has no equal," my mother says so quietly that it seems she only breathes the words. "And they are free because of you." She cups my cheek. "It's time to continue your story, Sweets."

* * *

My body is rocked violently, waking me to find that it's nighttime. The wagon is moving quickly, and I can hear the clip-clop of trotting hooves. One of the horses is lame, but whoever is driving keeps pushing them.

When I lick my lips, I put my tongue on fur. Groaning, I try to move but must shield my face from the noses that suddenly begin rubbing over it. "What the...?" I scoff, trying not to end up with a nose in my mouth.

The noses retreat, and my Alpha appears in the starlight. *"Hi, Love,"* Bastian says softly. *"Don't leave me, ok?"*

"Where's Daddy?" I ask, unable to speak out loud with the lump in my throat as I try not to cry.

"I'm right here," he says, crawling along my body so I can see him.

"Mom said to teach Bass what you did with me," I tell him. *"How you would talk to me and nuzzle her belly. She thinks it will calm her."*

I'm weak. I don't have much left to give them, but if they can stop this kid from tearing at me, maybe I can survive until we reach Chase. My shirt is pushed up, and whiskers begin tickling my skin. I can hear them talking but can't understand what they're saying. Sighing, I smile as their tongues gently lap over my belly. Bastian's hum vibrates against me as I fall asleep.

* * *

"I won't let anything happen to you." Bastian's voice filters in as I wake. I nearly thank him but open my eyes and see that he's not talking to me. He's lying beside me with a needle in his leg and his muzzle propped to allow his nose to rub my belly. *"Your mother is so strong, but she needs your help, ok? I can't do this without both of you."*

A hand slides over my forehead. "Chase is just ahead of us," Daddy tells me when I turn to him. "He stopped to shift, so he'll be able to check you. Hang in there, ok?"

I try to pull my lips into a smile, but I don't think they move. I just stare into my father's eyes until the wagon slows. When he looks up to see why, I take a moment to appreciate him. My father is gorgeous, but his unwavering confidence has always been his greatest strength.

"There they are," he whispers, kissing my forehead.

I watch Daddy jump over the wagon's side and latch onto Chase. My father pulls at his companion, and the two bury their faces in each other's necks. It feels like the halves of my mother are finally back together.

Edith yells for a pot while Anthony starts calling for wood and brush. Bastian stays with me and murmurs to his daughter. I can't look away from my father. He hasn't been whole for a long time. A death tore him apart from his companion, and it seems another death will put them back together.

"Hey, sweetheart," Edith whispers, blocking my view of my father. "Just a little longer. I'm gonna let your wolf take a break, though. Tarq said he's talking to your daughter. That's sweet. Do you want me to get Trish?"

My eyes widen, and I shake my head as firmly as possible.

"Ok," she says, smiling. "Just tell me if you change your mind." Edith reaches over us to pull the needle from Bastian before removing it from my arm.

"Has she settled?" Bastian asks, closing the needle hole in my arm.

I frown. *"I don't know, Love,"* I answer.

I have never felt so exhausted. My blood was carrying me without food and water, but now I'm filled with more Alpha blood than my own. I wouldn't think something so impossibly small could be so much trouble.

Chase climbs into the wagon, rubbing his hands over Bastian and feeling his ribs. "The mountains look beautiful, Ayls," he whispers as he reaches over my Alpha to squeeze my hand. "I can't wait for you to see them."

Bastian tucks his legs in to give Chase room. He bumps my hand with his paw until I open it to hold hands with him. Chase's attention stays on my stomach, feeling the different areas. He pulls out his stethoscope and listens for a while. When he points to a spot, Bastian rests his head so that his ear is where he indicated. I smile when he starts humming.

"I hear you, my little one," Bastian says softly before licking the spot. *"Stay in there. We have all the time in the world."*

Chase smiles. "Tarq used to say he was cuddling with you when he did this to your mother," he tells me. Someone hands him a cup, and Bastian moves aside, allowing him closer to my head. "Here, Luna. It's hot, but we don't have time to let it cool."

He's right. The tea feels slightly below boiling point, but I'm so thirsty I don't care. He gives me a small taste before pulling it back to blow on it while I catch my breath and cool my mouth. The second sip is easier to swallow when Chase feeds me more.

"Did you see the horses?" I whisper. "The wild horses are beautiful, and the elk are huge." I lick my lips to find them dry and cracked. "More?"

Bastian sits up to nuzzle my cheek. *"Is it working?"*

"My Alpha, the tea works fast, but not instantly," I remind him, thinking more clearly.

Chase feeds me the remainder of the tea and smiles, cupping my cheek. "That's one strong Luna in there," he tells me. "She's gonna be just fine."

I take a deep breath. "She's doing this," I whisper. "She wants her Alpha. She's trying to get out of me somehow." Although in different forms, Bastian and Chase have matching confused looks. "We made a mistake. They can't be together."

"*I'll send her away,*" Bastian decides.

"It's too late, Love," I say. "She won't stop. We need a unicorn."

The confused looks become more pinched.

"Uh, sweetheart?" Daddy questions from beside the wagon. He feels my forehead as I turn in his direction. "Honey, you're talking crazy. Chase? Does she have a fever?"

"No," Chase says, mirroring my father's confused tone. "What's this about a unicorn?"

Bastian holds out his front leg. "*Give her some more of my blood,*" he orders. When the men ignore his gesture, he pushes Chase with his paw. "*Now! She obviously needs it!*"

"They're extinct," I mumble. Their words are coming too fast and jumbling up my thoughts. I'm unsure how much I've told them or if they heard me. "Love is my only hope. Aylee said I'm gonna die. I'm supposed to say goodbye."

Something slams into the wagon's side, and my father's growl vibrates the air. "That insufferable bitch," he snarls. "Pack this shit up. We need to leave." He softens, leaning to cup my cheek. "Edith, why don't you knock her back out? It'll give her a chance to heal."

A second cup is passed to Chase, but I turn away before he can place it to my lips. "Daddy, they're beautiful," I murmur, trying to tell him about the mountains. "You're gonna love them. Mom said not to touch the porcupines."

My father gives me a pained smile. "Sleep, my daughter," he whispers. "You can show them to me yourself when you've healed."

18

A few days later, I've earned the right to leave the wagon's bed and walk along the spring Chase found. Bastian is still sluggish from being nearly bled dry, so Myla walks with me while Kade watches from a distance. I decided not to share Aylee's advice with anyone since it seems the tea has worked, and with Bastian and Daddy taking turns talking to the baby, she's settled.

Listening to my wolves has provided me with an escape from my concerns. They are back to the joyful conversations they had at the river. So far, there hasn't been much game to hunt, but they've found a few groundhogs, rabbits, and a bobcat.

"You look happy, Luna," Chase says, linking our arms.

I didn't notice I was smiling. "They're happy," I reply, nodding toward some of our pack. "I can't wait to see them running freely in the mountains."

"We've been careful for so long," Chase says. "Some elders didn't think we'd ever see the day that we could let the kids roam without fearing they wouldn't come home."

He guides me along the creek as the kids dart between the trees, hunting chipmunks. Chase chuckles and points at a few boys clustered near a tree. A chipmunk jumps from the center of their group and dives for freedom. The young wolves fall over each other, trying to catch it. They roll around on the ground laughing.

"It's called a scurry," Chase says, stopping to watch. I lift my eyebrow, and he tips his chin in the kids' direction. "A group of chipmunks is called a scurry," he tells me, laughing. "Miles liked to read. Whenever we had to travel, he'd read to us at night. Mostly books about animals." He stops to take a deep breath. "He said we should respect our prey enough to learn about them."

"He was a very different wolf, wasn't he?" I ask, smiling.

Chase squints in thought. "Miles was rumored to be ruthless, but that wasn't exactly true," he says. "He encouraged us to be ourselves and to explore our strengths. It was good for most of us and allowed us to flourish within the pack. For others, well, you heard our reputation."

"Where did you go with him?" I ask. Uncle Miles always made my mother laugh, so he must have been fun to travel with.

"Ah, nowhere important," Chase says, turning me to resume our walk. "Sometimes Miles just needed air. We went to the city once, though. Miles took us to see the Sippi Fork and bought the blue blade Kade carries. He wanted to get him something for his birthday. He turned nine the spring before Miles died."

"Kade's one of the good guys, isn't he?" I turn to look up the hill where my silver wolf is sitting. Gaine lies sleeping beside him with her muzzle between his front legs. Kade dutifully watches over me but often leans to nuzzle and check on his wife.

"He had a different life before Miles died," Chase starts. He points to where Daddy is lying and turns in that direction. "He was a good kid. Miles liked him, and they spent a lot of time together. When life changes, you adapt and find a way to survive."

"I feel like that's all we've been doing," I admit. "We've just survived." We reach my father, and Myla gives me her shoulder to brace myself as I sit beside him. "I want to thrive, not just wait for the next attack or worry who will lose their life next. I want to build our world, not steal someone else's."

"Your mother did her best, Annalisa," Daddy grumbles. He puts his arms around me, pulling me to his shoulder.

I tuck my head under his chin and lean my forehead against his neck. There's an easy softness to him now that has been missing since Chase left, and I'm happy to have it back. If there was ever a time I needed my father to be comforting, it's now.

"Mom was the one who first had the idea to move west," I point out. "Do you remember that? I was almost asleep, but we were sitting by the river waiting for the boats. Edith was talking about the Fork and westward travel. Mom asked why he didn't do something and then had that look she got whenever she was cross with Grandpa about Grandma."

"I do," Daddy murmurs, reclining further against the tree. "She was asking why Grandpa never moved the pack to the mountains. Her focus was always on the health and safety of her wolves. She went on all the further trips, fought in all the battles, and oversaw the cleanup. Did you ever hear why Ash and Neala were put in charge of the junior guards?"

Sitting up, I watch Bastian approach us with a few plates of food. Brock sticks to his hip for support. "I haven't, Daddy," I respond. "I bet we'd all enjoy the story, though." I reach for the plates while my father braces my Alpha as he sits.

"Thanks, Tarq," Bastian says, sighing heavily. "I've had some tea, so I feel better but still exhausted."

"Yeah, it'll make you feel better but won't make blood," Daddy tells him. "We'll be ok here for a little while so you can build your strength back up."

Bastian lies beside Daddy and reaches out for my hand. I pick at the boiled meat he'd brought as Brock nudges my hips until I roll my belly toward him. Once he can rest his throat over my stomach, he begins to hum, soothing the ache I've become accustomed to over the past few days.

"That feels good," I whisper, rubbing my finger over his muzzle. "Thank you."

"It's been helping Trish," Brock tells me. *"I thought you might like it too."*

"Oh, is that where you've been?" I ask, smiling. "I've missed Trish, but this distance is probably for the best."

"We've been trying to soothe both kids," Daddy says. "If that tiny

Alpha has anything to do with what's going on with you, we thought calming him might help."

I selfishly didn't ask Aylee about him, so I have no idea. "Tell us the story, Daddy."

My father winces, clearly regretting bringing it up, but Chase chuckles as he relaxes against Daddy's tree. "Tarq, Darya hid many of her concerns from everyone," he whispers. "She always said she wasn't perfect and never expected the kids to be. Her fears were real and shouldn't be hidden from them. They should know."

Daddy sighs as he tucks my hair behind my ear. "It was about a year after you were born," he starts. "The scouts reported a unit surrounding Silverton. Mom and I went with our full guard unit, and most of the houses were already burning by the time we arrived. Nate ordered the junior guards to stay back and watch but didn't stay with them.

"Mom was normally our lookout and watched our backs, but she rode straight to the livery to help Micah with his horses. The kids thought their Luna would need protection and followed her. When a soldier found her and took a shot, he missed her but hit Drake's older brother, Lucas. Your mother was furious at Nate."

Daddy stops and leans his head back against the tree. Since I didn't know Drake had a brother, he probably didn't survive. My mother would have blamed herself for that. She would've felt it deep within her soul and come apart at the seams.

"Darya forbade Nate from working with the junior guards and appointed Neala their caretaker," Chase continues for Daddy. "She cared for them in the bunkhouse already, and your mother trusted her to keep them safe. She and Anthony developed a training schedule and established a hard rule that the kids had to stay within the inner boundaries until they were 19. She was not going to lose another child."

"She must have forgiven him at some point," I say. "I remember him training them when she took Neala on trips."

"It's not that she needed to forgive him," my father whispers. "She acknowledged her fear and realized neither was to blame." He squeezes my shoulders and kisses my forehead as I look at him. "The rule never changed, so the fear was still there, but she allowed Ash and Neala to convince her that the kids had a lot they could learn from Nate without leaving the lake."

"So, you see, she did everything within her power to keep our wolves safe," Chase says. He scratches Brock's shoulder. "As will you guys."

"I suppose relocating the numbers we were would've been extremely difficult," I say, moving my empty plate from Daddy's lap. "Especially with how spread out we were before the drought and fires." I yawn as I peek over at Bastian, finding him asleep. "I think I might need a nap."

My father takes a deep breath and kisses the top of my head. "Sure, kiddo," he whispers. "You guys rest. We'll watch over the pack for now."

"Thank you for telling me about the junior guards," I whisper before kissing his cheek. "I like it when you talk about Mom."

Daddy cups my cheek and wiggles out from between me and Bastian. I call for Timothy and Creto, who usually lie with me in the afternoon. Neala must be telling them to behave themselves because I hear them both say, "Yes, ma'am," before they join us.

Chase helps me pull Bastian onto my shoulder as Brock lays under my head. Once the boys arrive, he guides them to lie with their heads over my belly. They hum when they cuddle up with me, so the boys vibrate all the discomfort away when they lie down.

"*The water's so clean here, Luna,*" Creto says, nuzzling my belly. "*Do you think we could follow it downstream to see if there's a spot to swim?*"

"*It's not too cold?*" I ask, scratching his whiskers.

"*I know it's hard to believe, but I am actually a wolf, Luna,*" Creto informs me. He has turned into quite a character and often makes me laugh.

"*You don't say!*" I respond. "*What's that like?*"

"*Well, you see, I woke up one day and had fur,*" the young wolf tells me. "*The paws are a bit fun, but the tail took some getting used to.*"

"*I imagine that would be true,*" I tell him, continuing along with goofy seriousness. "*I would probably have trouble with the teeth. I'd be biting my tongue all the time.*"

Creto lifts his head to tilt it. "*You know? I've never bitten my tongue.*" He moves his tongue around to chew on it, and I giggle, shaking

Timothy and Bastian. *"I don't think that would feel good,"* he tells me, laying his head back down.

Brock nudges him with his paw. *"Your Luna needs a nap, Creto,"* he scolds the young wolf. *"I imagine you could rest after running around with Timothy all morning."*

"Yes, sir," Creto says quietly. He stretches to nuzzle my cheek, then lays his neck across my belly.

"He's a good kid," I tell Brock. *"And you work well with them."*

"Annalisa, I can't train the kids and be your companion," he grumbles.

"No, you can't," I agree. *"But you will make a wonderful father one day."*

"That might be true, but you'll never find out if you don't let me take a nap." Brock curls around to bump his nose against mine. *"I love you, Ayls."*

"I love you too, Brock."

* * *

I got everyone's permission to walk with the children along the stream a few days later. It amazes me how little control I have when I'm sick, but convincing four people that I am healthy enough to go for a walk has proven quite tricky. Accompanied by Bastian, Brock, Chase, Myla, and Kade, I'm thankful to go with the boys to find an area large enough to swim.

"From what I've heard, we'll need to build an enormous house," I remark, watching the kids.

Creto runs past us with a smaller fir tree in his mouth. He'd found it fallen over and decided it would be funny to drag it around. Myla and Timothy try to take it away from him, and they all laugh as they fall into the water in a jumble of fur and legs.

"Tell me again why everyone is moving in with us," Bastian says, confused.

"Well, I'm getting my own wing," Kade announces. *"I need my own space with my women."*

"Why does he think you're his?" Chase asks.

"Listen, Chase," Kade says, stepping beside me to rub his muzzle over my hip. *"Women just love me. I'm perfect and irresistible. Of course, the Luna is no exception. My bed is a desirable place to be."*

Giggling, I rub Bastian's jaw. "It appears we have too many cooks in our kitchen, Love," I tell him. I kneel to Kade and kiss his muzzle. "Kade, my sweet silver wolf, please stop confusing everyone. You and I both know your eyes only shine for your wife."

"A wolf can dream," he replies, licking my cheek.

I shake my head and stand, looking along the stream. I smile at the shimmer in the distance. "I think we found a pond," I tell my wolves. "Come on, just up here."

We cross the creek and cut through a thin section of trees to emerge beside a small, deep-looking body of water. Thick reeds grow along the edge, and the symphony of croaking frogs makes the kids laugh as they bound toward the water. All three dive in and lunge at the reeds, attempting to catch the frogs.

Bastian rubs his muzzle gently over my hip. *"I want to throw you in that,"* he admits quietly. *"Perhaps my little Luna should get used to it before it surprises her later in life."*

I look at him from the corner of my eye. "I believe we should allow her to remain blissfully unaware for now, Love," I suggest.

I've never been able to stop him before. I'm unsure why I thought this time would be any different. Bastian shifts before scooping me into his arms and running at the water. No one bothers to interfere as he jumps into the pond with me screaming, cradled against his chest. I'm surprised to find the water warm, but we've been walking since daybreak, and the water has mostly been in the sun.

I wrap my arms and legs around Bastian as we surface. "I still want to know why this is so fun for you two," I grumble, shaking water out of my ears.

The water is deep, so Bastian uses his arms and legs to keep us afloat. "I'm not sure," he whispers, rubbing his lips over my neck. "Perhaps it's just about getting you wet."

He licks my ear lobe, and the world around us suddenly means much less than it did a moment ago. My body instantly responds to him, and my chest forcefully pushes the air from my lungs as I rub my lips over his cheek. Bastian growls, pulling at the water with his arms until he reaches the bank.

Holding me against his chest, he claims my lips and marches toward the thin grove of trees. His need is strong, but he walks as far as his body allows before setting me down and shoving my pants over my hips. Bastian yanks my boots off with my bottoms and lifts me against a tree. My legs shake as he digs his fingers into my thighs.

Letting Bastian stay in control, I remain as still as possible while he tastes my lips and tongue. His growl settles into a hum, and I slide my hands up his arms. They move over his shoulders and down his back. Where I would generally hear Bastian's growl spike, I now listen to soft moans of enjoyment. I thread my fingers into his hair and hold him as I whimper for more.

My Alpha gently reintroduces his body to mine. I roll my hips, asking him to take more as my deepest nerves reach painfully for him, but he doesn't take what I've given. I twist my leg around Bastian's back to pull him to me, desperate to satisfy this need. Bastian licks my lips with a smile and pushes my legs to rock my hips away from him.

My nerves do not reach out on their own. They are reacting to Bastian. The force in which they are calling to him means he wants me in ways I could only imagine, but he stays slow and gentle, taking only what he needs to ease his instincts. Although my body shakes from its desire to feel more than Bastian allows, every part receives satisfaction as he slowly gives each nerve the attention it deserves.

When he finally acknowledges the deepest nerves, the explosion within me has him covering my mouth to mute my calls as he bites down on my shoulder to smother his. Pushing through my muscles' hold on him, Bastian enjoys the rest of what I've offered until he's had his fill. When he leans against me, catching his breath, my body falls into a state of relaxation that I'm not sure I've ever experienced.

"You are a pleasure that I'm glad I get to have," I whisper as he licks my neck.

Bastian rubs his face against mine. "I'm just glad I get to taste you," he says, barely loud enough to hear over his hum. "I would've never thought peaches and syrup could taste that good."

"I guess our next Alpha has a bit of a sweet tooth," I say, giggling.

"Mm-hmm," Bastian murmurs, taking another taste. "I appreciate his craving."

I pull him away from my neck and kiss his lips. "That's enough out of you, bottomless pit," I say, rolling my eyes. "We need to get back to the kids. There's no telling what Kade is teaching them."

Bastian sucks air through his teeth. "True."

I dress quickly, and Bastian shifts to escort me back to the small pond. Kade is lying beside the water while Chase naps in the shade of a tree nearby. I step down the bank toward my silver wolf, not seeing any of the kids.

"Kade, where are the kids?" I ask, raising my eyebrow.

"*Shh, Luna,*" Kade responds calmly. "*They're counting.*"

As Luna, I can hear everything my wolves say to each other. I can't hear the kids right now. "Kade?" I reach for his head. "Where are they?"

Kade sighs heavily and looks up at me. "*Is it my turn with you now?*"

I roll my eyes as Bastian growls. "Why do you have to do that? You know it makes him mad."

"*I was at that altar too,*" Kade says whimsically. "*I could say some beautiful vows and make you want me.*"

"Kade!" I snap. "Focus! Where are the kids?"

There's a commotion as Timothy surfaces and shakes his head. "*Did I do it?*" he shouts. "*Did I break your record?*"

"*They can't break his record,*" Chase tells me sleepily. "*Miles sat on his head until he passed out.*"

"Kade!" I scoff, running down to the water. "*Kids! Get up here, now!*"

Myla and Creto surface quickly, trying to get to me so fast they nearly leap through the water. "*Luna, are you ok?*" Myla shouts.

Creto quickly follows with, "*We're here, Luna.*"

"Kids, I am fine." I kneel as they run to me. "You can't hold your breath for as long as Kade did," I tell them, turning to scowl at Kade. "He was not conscious the entire time."

Kade chuckles and joins Chase by the trees. *"Quit leaving me with the kids."*

Bastian sits beside me and nudges the kids' jaws to pick their heads up. *"Kids, there's a reason Kade normally travels alone,"* my Alpha says gently. *"He'll behave a bit better once his child is born, but for now, it's probably best you don't take him up on his challenges."*

"Guys, Kade is fun," I start, smiling sweetly at them. "I love spending time with him because he always makes me laugh. He could teach you some amazing things and make you stronger than you ever thought possible." I raise my eyebrow, taking a deep breath. "But he can also be a pain in the ass."

The boys chuckle and rub their wet muzzles over my cheeks. *"Yes, Luna,"* they say in unison.

"Now go play," I tell them. "You only have a few hours because we'll need to make it back to the pack before we lose the light."

The boys nip at each other and rough house as they dash back to the water, but Myla stays beside me, staring off into the distance. She seems deep in thought as her eyes narrow.

"Myla?" I rub my hand over her shoulder. "What's on your mind?"

She glances back at Kade before responding. *"He's a good wolf, right?"*

Smiling, I open my arms to her. "Kade is the best of the best," I whisper as she accepts my hug. "He would not have let you hurt yourself but would enjoy a good laugh as you tried your heart out."

"Are you sure he's the right wolf to teach me?" she asks nervously.

"Think back to when the boys were taken," I tell her, backing up so she can see my face. "In your mind, see where Kade was when we caught up to him. Can you describe it?"

"He was up the hill a bit," Myla starts. *"In a thin grove. He was sitting on pine needles, but the trees were at a distance."*

"Right," I whisper. "Close your eyes and see your mentor. He was sitting as still as a statue just three or four yards away, and those humans didn't notice him in all his shining glory." I smile as Myla giggles. "Do you think he was worried about the boys?"

"Of course," she answers.

"Ok," I say slowly, trying to decide how to describe Kade's process. "What do you think he was doing?"

Bastian lies down beside me as we watch Myla consider her options. Her head tilts as she watches her mentor roll over to scratch his back. Kade never misses a word spoken in his proximity. He knows we're discussing him and that I'm about to introduce Myla to the inner workings of his highly complex mind.

"I think he was hoping they didn't notice him," Myla finally says. I can hear her frown as she faces the sad, selfish facts she believes to be true of her mentor.

"I can see why you would think that," I tell her. "But Kade actually stepped out into the open on purpose." I let her turn back to Kade to see him watching us. "His coat may shimmer, but he can stand as still as a statue."

"So why was he there?" Myla asks.

Smiling, I point at Kade, letting him take over.

"If the boys' lives were ever in danger, I only needed to move, and every rifle would turn in my direction," Kade tells her. *"I may be the present, but soon, I'll be the past. You kids are our future."*

"Kade is the master of doing the wrong things for the right reasons," I say, rubbing Myla's chin. "Your drum's beat might be different, but it's not unique. You asked if I made the right decision. Without a doubt, I chose the right teacher for you."

"Thank you, Luna," she says quietly, nuzzling my cheek.

"Don't thank me," I say, nodding toward Kade. "Thank him." I watch her jump up and jog toward her mentor before turning to Bastian. "How are you gonna handle having two rebels?" I giggle as he grumbles and rests his chin on his crossed paws.

The boys dart around the pond's edge and jump in the water nearby, splashing us.

"Boys!" Bastian shouts. *"Be careful of the Luna."*

I relax against his shoulder. "Let them play," I tell him. "Of all the kids, those two deserve to have some fun." The boys jump out of the water and shake their fur before running to me. They like to lie with their jaws on my shoulders, but neither has mastered the art of drying off. "Oh, boys, we need to teach you how to heat the water out of your fur."

They chuckle and rub their muzzles over my face, blessing me with wet whiskers. *"Luna, can we camp here tonight?"* Creto asks. *"So we can swim in the morning too? Like we did at the lake?"*

Timothy lifts his head, intrigued by the idea. The younger wolf had never been to the lake. His family lived further away, and his mother was often ill with a chronic cough. Edith believes she suffered an illness as a child that left lasting symptoms. Some of my guards dug a small paddling pool in their front yard that Timothy played in with his younger sister.

As the sole survivor in his family, I find giving him these new experiences keeps his mind off what he's lost. "We will need to check with a few wolves," I tell them, rubbing their cheeks. "Gaine is pregnant, and I'm sure Kade is missing her. We'll also need to check with my companion, who might also be missing his mate."

Timothy's ears tip back. *"Oh, Luna, please?"* the little wolf pleads. He rubs his whiskers over my face, trying to butter me up.

"We'll see," I say, smirking at them. "Why don't you boys go ask Kade? And I'll speak to Brock."

After they run toward my silver wolf and his student, Bastian curls around to look me in the eye. *"Ayls, I don't want you this far from the pack overnight,"* he admits. *"I'm quite sure your father will agree."*

"Bass, look at them," I whisper, watching the boys. Kade's making them list why they should be allowed to "camp out" for the night. He'd already decided they could and told Gaine that she better not leave my father's side, which made Daddy grumble. "They need this. I think we all do."

Brock emerges from his post at the edge of the trees with a log in his mouth. *"I suppose we should gather some firewood,"* he suggests.

"Thank you," I whisper, rubbing his cheek.

"You're welcome," Brock replies with a nod.

The boys whoop excitedly and bound back to me when Kade finally tells them we can stay the night. They slide back into my arms and lick my cheeks. Their hums fill my ears like a sweet symphony of joy. Before leaving to help Brock collect wood, they bump noses with Bastian.

At home, the kids weren't allowed to stay out at night, and since leaving the lake, we've been wandering as homeless vagrants. But tonight, we will be campers. Or perhaps for these children, we can be a family.

19

I wake to a soft muzzle rubbing over my forehead. I sigh happily and let a smile spread across my face. Although my Alpha is the most graceful wolf I have ever seen, there is one wolf that can maneuver his body around others without disturbing them. He slides his tongue over my cheeks and forehead before pushing his muzzle into my hair and taking a deep breath.

"I know you're awake," Kade tells me, licking my jaw. *"Damn, you taste good."*

I giggle and lean my cheek against his muzzle. *"Good morning, Kade."*

"Good morning, Ayls," he says quietly. *"These kids are hungry, and I smell cattle. Chase and I are going to see if we can nab a cow."*

"Be careful," I say, rubbing my cheek against his whiskers.

"For you, beautiful Luna, I will do anything," Kade professes. He slips his muzzle from under my face and bumps my nose before jogging away with Chase by his side.

Like Brock, Chase is an easygoing wolf. He can work with just about anyone. Kade might be an acquired taste for most, but Chase pairs well with him. They both spent a significant amount of time training under Uncle Miles, so the pair easily anticipates what the other will do.

"Where are they going?" Brock asks. He lifts his head from behind Creto.

I reach over to scratch his chin. *"They smelled cows,"* I tell him. *"They're gonna see if they can grab one."*

"That sounds good," Brock responds whimsically.

I slide my hands over the boys' heads. Life is full of favorites... Favorite foods, sights, smells. I have a favorite sound. My wolves don't just wake up. They always lick their lips and yawn as they stretch. I'm unsure which is my favorite part of their wake-up routine, but I love the gentle sweetness it leaves in my heart.

"Good morning, boys," I whisper. "How did you sleep?"

I wrinkle my nose as they both rub their whiskers over my cheeks. Their muzzles are warm from sleeping with them jammed between me and Bastian. My Alpha is awake but remains still so I can enjoy my snuggles. When Creto lays his head across my chest, Brock takes his place on my cheek, making me giggle.

Sitting up, I pull the boys with me and glance down at Brock. "It's time to shake the sleep off, my beautiful wolves," I tell them. The boys drowsily give me their muzzles for a kiss and step away to shake out their fur. "There we go," I whisper, scratching their necks. "Why don't you find us some wood for the fire, and then you can go for a swim. Just stay where we can see you."

Myla stands and stretches with a noisy yawn. *"Should I go with them?"*

"That might be a good idea," I respond. "Then you should have some time to play before Kade gets back. It won't be long before he restarts your training. I fear you may not have time for fun after that."

"Yes, Luna." She touches her nose to my cheek and jogs after the boys.

"It's hard telling them their childhood is over, huh?" Bastian says sadly, sitting up behind me.

I frown as he places his chin on my shoulder. "You didn't have one. Even yours was cut short, Brock," I say, reaching for my companion. "They need to play. We can't forget that they're still kids." I smile as Creto dashes past us with his tree from yesterday, followed by the other kids. "I love hearing them laugh."

"Love, I know you think these are games that only children play, but that's not exactly true," Bastian says, looking at me from the corner of his eye. He tips his muzzle toward Creto and his tree just before he and Brock take off after him.

Clapping and laughing, I watch as they latch onto his tree, drag him straight to the pond, and jump in, tree and all. Creto valiantly attempts to keep control of his tree, but he's no match against the adults. Once they've won the tree, Bastian and Brock try to catch the kids' muzzles in their mouths, getting nipped a few times since they're outnumbered.

After a while, I slip out of my boots and stick my feet in the water. My Alpha may not have had a childhood, but he's playing with the children like he never grew up. I don't believe I would have discovered this side of him if we'd stayed at the lake. I'm bonded to him, but I have never experienced the exhilaration I feel when I watch him crouch in full-play mode.

I hold my laughter as Myla slinks along the bank with a weathered stick she found underwater. She attempts to stay low in the reeds, hiding from the older wolves, but Bastian dives and swims in her direction undetected. The young wolf stays low until she's behind me, using me as cover.

I lose sight of Bastian momentarily, but then large air bubbles rise to the surface before me. I try to jump away, but he's too fast. His arms latch onto me and drag me into the pond. I scream and kick at him, but my Alpha only laughs in response as he pulls at the water, swimming away from the bank.

"You looked hot," Bastian says, smiling.

"I wasn't, and now my clothes are wet," I pout. I slide my arms around his shoulders and wrinkle my nose at his broad smile.

My Alpha gently kisses my pouting lips. "I love you, my Luna," he whispers.

"I love you too," I murmur against his lips.

"Are you ready?" Bastian rubs his face against mine.

I would normally play in the water with my father while Bastian joins in with the wolves. We have a few different games that we play. I won't join many of them because it would be considered disrespectful to dunk or throw water at me, but "Catching Kisses" is a favorite of the younger wolves. They enjoy trying to catch the Alpha for a chance to "kiss" the Luna.

I smile at Bastian's excitement and cup his cheek. "I am always ready, Love," I whisper.

With a smile, Bastian pulls me around to his back. "Who's gonna catch a Luna's kiss?"

The boys holler and jump through the water at us as Bastian dives forward. Myla quickly catches on to the game, and soon, all three kids are squealing and laughing as they try to catch us. With the yelps and splashing from the kids and my shrieking, Brock climbs the bank to watch over us in case anyone is close enough to hear.

Eventually, Bastian allows the kids to catch me, and I'm lovingly smothered with sloppy, wet kisses. When the kids become too excited, they shove me off Bastian's back, and he ends the game. I notice the boys are beginning to struggle to stay afloat.

"Come on, guys," I call them. "Let's stick to the shallow end and give your bodies a break."

My mother's research on their physique determined that the density of their muscles and the lack of fat tissue made it more difficult for our wolves to float. Their bodies try to sink every moment they are in the water, forcing them to swim constantly to stay above the surface. They can float for a short time on their back in their human form. Otherwise, it's constant work.

"*Coming in, Luna,*" Chase calls out as the kids join me in the shallow area. "*We've got company.*"

Chase would never bring someone dangerous into camp, but I still glance nervously at Bastian. "Love, come here," I say, reaching for his hand. "Kids, stay behind us." I put my arm out to hold them back as Brock slips quietly through the reeds to guard us from a hiding spot.

My eyes scan the trees and tall grass until I see them. Chase's nearly white coat appears first as he jogs out front, pushing a few small steers, quickly followed by a familiar chocolate brown wolf. Two horses emerge from the trees next, and I jump up as Bastian holds his arms out to Grandpa Bruce.

"Grandma!" I shout as she dismounts one of the horses. Running to her, I land in her arms. "I was getting worried. I didn't want to go into the mountains without you." I look up at the other riders as one more horse steps out of the trees. "Byron, Davis, I'm so happy to have you join us."

I wasn't sure if they could find him, so I hadn't told anyone I'd sent my grandparents to find Byron. I wanted Davis to come with us but didn't know if he would. Seeing him this far from the river sends a wave of relief over my body. Both were exiled from the pack, and I shouldn't care as much as I do about them, but I couldn't leave a wolf behind.

"Hi, Luna," Byron says, dismounting. "Amelia told me what happened. I'm so sorry. I hope I can help with my daughter, though."

I place my hand on his chest. "I'm happy to see you safe." I catch Davis by the arm. "Both of you."

"They got my boat," the captain grumbles. "Blew it up."

"We'll build you another," I promise, smiling. "This time, you can actually fish."

Davis chuckles and pats my hand. "Those kids look like they could use a good feast."

We all work together on the meal. Bastian uses my blade to take the smallest steer down, and Davis helps him skin it. Grandma smiles as she produces a pot to boil some meat for me. Byron seems a bit worthless when working with his hands but regales us with tales of his travels while we work.

"You moved around the rebel groups without them knowing who you were?" Bastian asks, pulling me away from a discussion with my father about how we won't be back until tomorrow.

"They are really just simple people," Byron says, shaking his head. "Most didn't even know what they were fighting about." He squints his eyes and frowns. "The rebel groups seemed quite primitive."

"They only check for the pack markings," Davis adds. "The militia are a bit more thorough." His face twists in thought. "The rebels won't cross the river. They talk of a mountain of bears."

"*I do like bear,*" Chase says whimsically.

Kade taps my leg with his paw. "*Ask him if there's a mountain of mountain lions.*"

Looking down, I furrow my brow at the silver wolf.

"*What?*" Kade asks.

"I love you," is all I manage to say.

"*I know you do,*" Kade scoffs. "*Now ask him. You know I love me some mountain lion.*" He taps my leg again and motions his nose toward Davis.

When I follow his gaze, Davis is staring at me with his eyebrow lifted. "Don't mind him," I tell the aged wolf. "We saw rebels on this side of the river. They took a few of our kids, trying to trap me."

"No," Davis replies thoughtfully. "That would've been bounty hunters. Most of them are prior rebels looking for a payout from the militia. The bounty on wolves and you especially, Luna, has increased significantly since the lake attack."

"Are the kids ok?" Byron asks.

"They are," Bastian answers, rubbing my back. "There were a few complications, but those two beside you were the boys taken." He points to Timothy and Creto, who are pulling at the ribs they've been given to snack on. "We keep them pretty close to us now. Their Luna has taken a shine to them." He kisses my temple.

"Oh, I heard we have a new little Luna on the way!" Byron announces, clasping his hands over his heart. "Congratulations! Your mother would be so happy."

"Thank you," I say, glancing back down at Kade. "I guess you haven't been told your daughter is also pregnant."

Byron gasps and smiles. "I'm going to be a grandfather!" he exclaims, latching onto Grandma's arm. His excited smile quickly fades as he casts his eyes down beside me. "I suppose it's yours?"

Bastian laughs as Kade sighs and rests his chin on my leg. I slide my hand over the sad wolf's head and rub his jaw. Kade's past has never sat well with the exiled wolf, and after Gaine disappeared with him during my mother's last winter, Byron has maintained a strong distaste for his son-in-law.

"He loves your daughter very much, Byron," I say, still frowning at Kade. "Please try to focus on his present and future for the sake of your grandchildren."

Byron grumbles, and Kade sighs again.

I pull his nose to my lips. "I love you and think you're wonderful," I tell him. "I see how much you love Gaine, and so does she. Isn't that all that matters?"

Kade licks my cheek. *"Thanks, Ayls,"* he says softly.

Sighing, I turn away from the meat we're cutting and lie down with Kade. He allows me to pull some of his depression as he hums over my belly, easing the ache my child is creating. "Byron, he's the wolf your daughter is very much in love with," I remind him. "He makes her quite happy, and they might be the cutest couple ever if it weren't for my grandparents."

Grandpa Bruce chuckles from his comfy cuddle spot on Grandma's lap.

"A mountain of bears, huh?" Bastian mutters, ignoring our conversation. "First, we had unicorns. Now, we have a scary mountain of bears. Next, you'll be telling me vampires are real."

"I remember something about unicorns," Byron says. "They hunted them or something." He rubs his forehead. "When you have access to all that knowledge, writing it down or remembering it doesn't seem all that important. I wish I'd written a journal now."

"Apparently, they were used for healing," I tell him. "I was told they were hunted to extinction long ago. Your daughter seems obsessed with them, though, and I'd like to get her past them if we could."

"I can try," Byron responds.

"Did we miss anything else?" Grandma asks.

"You know we said our vows," I start. "We had the issue with the boys. Turns out baby Luna and baby Alpha aren't supposed to be near each other, and I died a little bit."

The entire group erupts inside my head and out loud. I'd rather my grandparents fuss about my death away from the pack. They spend most of their time working away from home and generally hear about things long after they happen. Their reaction to bad news is never pleasant.

"Listen, all of you," I shout, snapping my fingers. "I am fine. We made a mistake, and Chase is giving me wonderful care. I am staying away from Trish so my child stops trying to be near her little Alpha. I want to enjoy a nice afternoon, feed these young wolves, and turn in early. We must be on the trail first thing in the morning, or my father will throw a fit."

"As his mother, I can tell you that's not something we want to experience," Grandma says, lifting her eyebrow.

Once I've pulled enough emotion from Kade, he moves away to accommodate the kids. Their full bellies will have them asleep soon, and I don't like them sleeping far from me. My grandparents and the exiled wolves had been eating off their herd while they traveled north, so they don't need much, but Bastian cuts the hips and a shoulder loose for him to share with Chase and Kade.

I take small bites of my boiled beef and listen to everyone discuss different experiences. Grandma brought up a family of giraffes they'd tracked. Davis figured they must have been in a zoo before the militia rose, and maybe they were set free. They all agreed they were too pretty to try to kill. I've seen pictures of them. They were probably too tall, and the older wolves couldn't be bothered.

My eyelids are heavy when Bastian passes me a thick bone. *"Can you split that, my Luna?"* he asks, nuzzling my cheek. *"I'd like the kids to have it."*

As I pull my knife back out, Creto sniffs the bone curiously. *"Luna? What are you doing?"* he asks.

"Bastian has asked me to split this for you," I tell him, winking. "The marrow is a good source of iron, protein, and fats, baby. You boys are a little on the small side, and this will help your bodies fill out a bit."

Creto rubs his muzzle over my face, blocking my view of the bone. The knife slips and slices my finger open. I suck air through my teeth and pull back from him, lifting my hand. Extending my fingers, I survey the damage. When Creto sniffs at the bone, Bastian snarls and snaps at him. The terrified youngster rolls back over his hip, instantly submitting to my Alpha.

"Stay there, Creto," I say calmly. "Let Bastian clean this up." I smile reassuringly at him before lifting my eyebrow at my Alpha. *"Was that necessary?"*

"Here, look," he says. He lowers his nose to the bone and shows me where my blood had dropped, mixing into the marrow. *"That boy was one lick away from a lifelong bond to you."*

Bastian closes my wounds and removes the bone with my blood on it. He carefully cleans my hand and the drops that had fallen. Grandma fires my knife's blade to remove any trace of my blood. Once I feel he is safe, I allow Creto back up.

"Come here, sweetheart," I say with my arm out. "You weren't in trouble, but you were in danger. Do you know what tasting the Luna's blood does to an unbonded wolf?"

Timothy approaches me, but Creto stays at a distance, holding his head low and eyeing Bastian. I might be the top dog, but my Alpha is the big, bad wolf whose snarl can't be ignored. Bastian can rip apart an entire militia unit on his own. To a ten-year-old, he's positively terrifying when he lifts his lips.

"Creto, sweet boy, he didn't want to hurt you," I reassure the young wolf. "Tasting my blood would have bonded you to me, and we do not want that for you." I hold my arm out again, and he crawls toward me until I can rub his neck. "I love you, but I want you to find happiness with a love of your own. We only wanted to give you that chance. I promise."

"Are you ok, Luna?" Creto asks quietly. He reaches his muzzle to my cheek but stops, looking nervous.

I lean down and wrap my arms around the boys' necks. "My Alpha has been protecting you this whole time," I whisper into their fur. "He loves you so much. Will you allow him to apologize for scaring you?"

The boys don't answer, but Bastian slips his muzzle under Creto's neck as I back up. I smile at Timothy as the young wolf rubs his nose over his friend's head reassuringly. They have seen Daddy and Bastian do this with each other a few times since starting to travel alongside me, but never to another wolf. My Alpha stays under Creto until the young wolf begins to hum before moving to give Timothy the same honor.

"I will always protect you," Bastian vows.

* * *

By morning, Bastian has won the children over, and they spend most of the trip back to the pack playing in the creek with him. Even Kade joins in their games a few times. I appreciate that Grandma decided to shift so I could ride her horse. Davis stays beside me, recalling stories about my mother while Byron studies his son-in-law.

"He seems different," the elder mutters, tipping his chin toward Kade. "Has he really cleaned up his act?" He turns to me with a thoughtful expression.

I reach for Davis's arm and smile before slowing my horse to ride beside Byron. "Kade will always have a past, just like the rest of us," I remind him. "He paid for that past and has worked hard to earn your daughter's hand. Kade is fiercely protective of her and their child. And now, he's learning to play with children for them. I'd like to think of that as growth."

"It's hard for me to forgive him, you know?" Byron says, still watching Kade. "People were going missing. Darius was dead. And he scoops my daughter up and takes off with her. All I could think was the horrible things that could've happened to her." Letting out a deep sigh, Byron looks down at his hands. "I don't know how to be ok with that."

I rub his arm, trying to provide some comfort. "If I were my mother, I would tell you to get over it," I say, smiling. "But I'm not my mother. I'm the Luna that spent weeks curled up with that wolf, waiting for him to be ready for my help. We sat on the porch swing for days, working through his pain. I walked miles of trails, listening to his fears. I think when you let him in, he'll surprise you just as he did me."

Byron narrows his eyes in thought. We watch as Kade teaches Timothy to crouch in the thick weeds and wait for the others to pass. Bastian pretends he can't see the young wolf and nips at Creto's legs as they jog along the stream together. Timothy and Kade leap out of the weeds, and Creto helps them tackle Bastian.

"You got me, boys," Bastian says, letting them catch his muzzle in their

mouths. He rolls over under them and lifts them over his back. The boys laugh and dart off while Kade bumps his shoulder into Bastian.

"*Those are some good boys*," Kade says, watching the kids run through the water. "*Do you think I can actually be a father?*"

"*With the love of a good woman, I think we can do anything*," Bastian responds, looking back at me.

I smile and clutch my chest. "*I love you too, my Alpha.*"

Although the kids continue to play throughout the afternoon, our journey is relatively quiet. Myla appears after a while to report what Chase had taught her. Kade does his best to pay attention, but Gaine is missing him, so she's unknowingly distracting him from his duties. Grandpa is being adorable with Grandma, making me feel like I'm intruding on them.

I let my wolves all filter into the background and step from my saddle to walk beside Bastian. "I think we're ready to head up into the mountains now," I tell him. "You've recovered, the baby has settled, and my grandparents have found us. It's time."

"*I agree*," he responds, sliding his muzzle into my hand. "*Access to water is important, but it can't be safe this close to the edge of the flatlands.*"

"We could follow the water for a while," I suggest.

"*This spring is coming from the north, Ayls*," Bastian says, looking up at me. "*We need to go west.*"

"I feel like I'm torn in two," I confess. "Half of me is walking straight into this, knowing what to do and standing tall, but the other half wants to question every step like it's a mistake." I pull Bastian to me and hook his jaw on my hip. "Which one is right?"

Bastian chuckles, gently rubbing his muzzle over my stomach. "*The one that is trying to protect her*," he answers.

"Well, that's helpful," I grumble. "Thanks."

"*Ayls, come here*," Bastian demands, stepping in my way. I kneel before him as he sits. "*Sometimes I think back on our trip south. I remember Luna was so confident in her decisions. She marched us down there with a purpose. She never questioned what we were doing. But then I remember our last moments with her. She had no idea how she would save us until the very end.*"

"So, I imagine she felt a lot like you do. She put on that brave face she let us see and kept moving forward until the rest made sense." He nuzzles my cheek, wiping away a tear. *"When it makes sense, you'll know you made the right decision."*

I wipe my face before reaching my arms out to him. "You were definitely the right decision," I whisper into his fur.

"Naturally," Bastian responds confidently. *"I am a stunning wolf."*

I giggle and sniffle, composing myself before I pull away from the fur on his neck. "You are the most beautiful thing I have ever seen," I tell him. "Your beauty will know no equal, and my eyes will always enjoy their view."

Bastian rubs his whiskers over my cheeks. *"Hmm, maybe we could convince everyone to take a break,"* he suggests, slipping his tongue gently over my skin. *"We could visit a few trees a little further in the woods."*

"So tempting, beautiful wolf," I whisper. "But Daddy would kill us if we survived Gaine's wrath."

Growling, Bastian backs away. *"Fine,"* he grumbles. *"Let's get Mister Shiny back to his woman."*

Kade stops beside us and stares at Bastian. *"My wife is talking about putting her tongue in some fascinating places,"* he states plainly, making me cover the pinched smile I can't contain. *"If I don't feel that very soon, your wife is gonna need to do it."*

I burst out laughing. "I love you both very much," I say through my laughter. "Let's get you back to Gaine, Kade. I know she's missing you."

20

After listening to my father's lecture on how my safety is more important than allowing children to play, I lie in the wagon's bed tucked into Bastian's gut. It's been a while since we've laid alone to simply enjoy each other's company. Even though I can feel the children's absence in my soul while they help Neala, I know this time is important for us too.

I slip my fingers through Bastian's fur and listen to our pack. There's a sweetness to them as they settle in for the night. A few smaller families and wolves without children have taken in some of the orphans, and listening to them put their little ones to bed is heartwarming. Ash makes the remaining children giggle as he tells them bedtime stories.

I'd taken Byron straight to River when we'd arrived at the main campsite, but he warned it might take a while to get through to her. I have a few guards watching them, and Matthew has given me reports of nothing new yet. Davis cannot be brought back into the pack, but my wolves know he left for a good reason and have all welcomed him with open arms.

Daddy stays nearby and reprimands the boys when they noisily bound toward the wagon after Neala gives them permission to return to me. *"Settle down, boys,"* he warns them. *"Our Luna's had some busy days and needs to rest."*

"Yes, Tarq," they respond in unison, carefully leaping into the wagon. They rub muzzles with their Alpha before moving to snuggle with me.

I roll onto my back, leaving my legs curled against Bastian. It feels significantly cooler tonight, and I need his heat. Creto allows Timothy to lie over my shoulder while he curls beside my hip and wraps his neck over my side to hum on my belly.

"*Luna?*" Timothy calls to me quietly.

"Yes, sweet boy?" I whisper.

"*I wish you were my mother,*" the young wolf says, filling me with emotions.

I take a deep breath and let it out before responding. "You have a mother, sweetheart," I tell him quietly. "She might not be with us anymore, but she's still your mother. You are my wolf, and I am your Luna. That makes us pretty important to each other, don't you think?"

"*I love you, Luna,*" Timothy says sweetly.

"Aw, I love you too, baby," I whisper before kissing his nose. "Let's get some sleep. Tomorrow we'll be climbing a mountain. We're all about to have a new adventure."

Timothy licks my cheek and nuzzles into my neck for the night. I hear Creto take a deep breath and know he's still awake, listening to me. He's been the strong older sibling for the younger kids, but I know he's missing his family just as much as they are. I can't reach him with how we're lying tonight, so I can only fall asleep hoping he knows he's loved.

* * *

I enjoy hearing the happy discussions over the next few days as we push further into the hills and away from the flatlands. Although not much higher in elevation, the change in terrain and gentle sloping provide enough difference to create a buzz among the younger wolves. Creto opts to stay with me, and Bastian helps teach him to work in my hand.

"He's starting to fill out," Gaine comments. "Myla's still a bit thin."

Sighing, I turn to watch her studying Creto. "She's been giving the boys some of her food," I tell her. "Kade told her to stop, but she listens just about as well as he does."

Gaine giggles and hooks our arms a little tighter. "She's been good for him," she remarks. "It's a relief when he's distracted and not always checking on me."

I wrinkle my nose and smile as Kade watches us from behind a tree. "I get the feeling he's not as distracted as you think," I tell her. "But he's quite nervous about being a father. Bastian's helping him." I glance down at my Alpha as he pushes Creto's chin up so he's not leaning on my fingers.

"Dad hasn't made much progress with River," Gaine says, changing the subject. "All I hear him doing is asking her questions about the unicorns. The two of them whisper like old ladies on a porch planning dinner. I love him, Luna, but I don't think he'll be much help."

"Grandpa's Luna said they were extinct, so it's pointless for them to focus on the damn things," I grumble. "However, the moon is full tonight. Perhaps my grandfather will have new information to share."

Creto jerks his head, yanking down on my hand.

"I think you better take a break, kiddo," Bastian suggests. *"Go run off some of that energy."*

"Luna, will that be ok?" Creto asks.

I slip my hand down his jaw and scratch his throat as I kneel beside him. "Neala's been playing hunting games with the other kids," I whisper. "Why don't you join them? Be a kid while you can, sweetheart. That is what I want for you."

"I love you, Luna," Creto says bashfully as he nuzzles my cheek. He rolls his head and pushes me over. *"Oh, Luna,"* the young wolf calls out, embarrassed. *"I'm so sorry."*

Giggling, I grab Bastian's front leg to pull myself back to my knees. "When my Alpha and I were still learning each other, he struggled at times," I assure Creto. "The Alphas are generally high-strung, and he was so nervous around me that it made remaining still difficult. He knocked me over a few times. It comes with the territory."

Bastian jumps down into a play crouch, and Creto responds by excitedly jumping around, nipping at his Alpha's muzzle. *"Go on, kiddo,"* Bastian says, chuckling. *"Go play."*

My Alpha slips his muzzle into my hand as Creto darts toward the other kids. He pushes my shirt up and slips his tongue over my belly a few times before settling enough to lead me forward. Gaine takes my arm and walks on, distracted.

"I've been thinking about what's happened on our journey," I tell them both. "Creto and Timothy have become a part of my family. They are more than my wolves. Gaine, you were an advisor I talked to sometimes before all of this." I turn to my dark-haired, distracted wolf. "I'm unsure what we are now, but we are more than that."

Gaine sighs deeply. "It has been cute watching the boys cuddle up with you," she admits. "And you both have been wonderful with them. They went through something horrible but came out of it with so much love in their hearts."

"They are both brave," Bastian remarks as Creto appears through some trees ahead of us. He's dragging a large vine that the other children seem to want. *"And have an endless supply of energy."*

I giggle, rubbing his jaw. "That I'll agree with." We watch them until they disappear over the next hill. "I wonder if these changed lives would have been better had they not changed. If the attack hadn't happened, would these new friendships have been formed, or would they be as happy without each other?"

"While I may not have that answer, I believe everything happens for a reason, Luna," Gaine says thoughtfully. "The attack at the lake was a horrible tragedy I wish hadn't happened. But I can't ignore how happy everyone is in their new lives and roles. Creto and Timothy suffered at the hands of those humans, but they are as close as brothers now. That experience made them family."

"We truly are seeing the silver linings, aren't we?" I ask, smiling.

"I choose to see the silver over the blood," Gaine responds. "Focusing on the pain won't take it away. That past won't change, but our future is an ever-evolving event. We all look ahead and see something brighter than the darkness we left behind."

I let my deep breath out slowly. "I'm glad to have you as a voice of reason," I whisper, patting Gaine's arm.

"Me too," Bastian adds.

We continue in silence for a while, reflecting on Gaine's words. Bastian's hum fills my ears, but the kids' laughter and the adults' joyful conversations fill my heart. When I think about our decisions since the attack, I often couple it with whether things would be better for us if it hadn't happened. But Gaine is right. There's no way of knowing how anything would be if our past had been different, so focusing on the brightness of our future just makes sense.

"I found a pond with fish in it, Luna," Drake calls out to me, making me gasp. This had quietly been his mission since my talk with Grandpa. There could not have been a more perfect time for him to get me this news.

"Where are we going?" I ask, smiling.

"There's a creek about two miles ahead of you," he says. *"Follow it north another mile, and you'll see it. Do you mind if I take down this buck?"*

"Not at all. Go ahead and eat," I answer Drake. *"We'll be up there in a little while."*

I rub Bastian's jaw until he looks up at me. *"What are you smiling about?"* he asks.

"Drake found a lake for our meeting tonight," I say. "Grandpa told me to take Chase and Daddy fishing."

"Oh, that'll do them some good," Gaine exclaims. "I heard they used to be nearly inseparable except when your mother traveled. Your grandmother has been remarking about their distance for years. They seem closer now, but something's missing."

"I'm afraid that might be my mother," I say, sighing. "I'm hoping to help them heal before Daddy leaves. I don't want him to have any regrets."

"Your father won't want to let you leave the pack again," Bastian says. *"He was pretty mad that we stayed away an extra day. And what about the boys? Luna tried to leave me behind before I was ready, and that didn't work out as she planned."*

I hadn't considered them in my excitement, but they've become a part of us, and I wasn't even thinking about leaving them behind.

"We'll take them with us," I decide. "They can sleep while we visit with Grandpa."

Bastian warns that my father won't like the kids joining us since he wants to discuss some of the things Aylee told me, but I'm not interested in hearing it. Regardless of anyone's feelings, he brought up the best point. I'd heard about the night my mother tried to leave Bastian at the cabin.

"Bastian, I hear you. I promise I do," I say, kneeling to him. "But those boys have slept with me every night since their abduction. I cannot leave them behind and expect them to accept it. They won't."

"We could try to keep them with us," Gaine offers. "Myla enjoys their company, and Kade makes her stay with me at night." I look up to catch her quizzical expression. "He sort of treats me like a prisoner, doesn't he?"

I giggle, pushing myself back to my feet. "I suppose that might be true if he didn't make plans around everything you want to do," I remind her. "He's just concerned for your safety. That poor man is overwhelmed with fear right now. He'll settle once we stop moving around so much."

Gaine scowls slightly. "I hope so," she grumbles. "I'm tired of pretending I don't see him watching me."

Laughing, I follow her eyes and see Kade duck behind a tree. The kids dash past him, chasing a squirrel. Their laughter and clumsy footfalls mean they are playing more than hunting. Bastian stops me as they dart across the path in front of us.

"Come on, kids," I shout to them. "There's a creek ahead. We'll race you."

They laugh and whoop excitedly. Creto gathers the smaller kids, and they all take off up the trail ahead of us.

"We're not actually gonna race them, are we?" Gaine asks. "I'm quite positive my husband will have a lot of words to say if I start running down the trail. They probably won't be kind and friendly."

"I assume they would be directed at me," I add, laughing. "No, Gaine, we'll not be racing the kids." I rub my fingers over Bastian's jaw. "I think my Alpha could use a good run, though."

Bastian sighs, pushing my shirt up to lick my belly again. *"Fine, I'll go play with the kids,"* he says, pretending to be grumbly. *"You be nice to your Mommy while I'm gone,"* he tells our daughter, scraping his teeth gently over my skin.

As he slips out of my hand, Brock takes his place. I look down when my companion pulls me forward. "Hello, my beautiful love," I say, smiling. "Did you hear about the creek?"

"Ayls, your guard reports to me," Brock says, leading me around a stump. *"The creek, the lake, and the mission you've had Drake on this whole time. I know it all. What I don't know is why you wanted it kept from Bastian."*

I pull his jaw until I can see the disapproving look in his eyes. "I'm trying to help Daddy and Chase reconnect," I say quietly. "I'm going to bring the three of them up to the lake tonight for the full moon, and I don't want any of them arguing with me about it."

"I think it would be nice to have a family gathering with your grandfather," Gaine comments. "Last month was the wedding, and you two had just bonded the month before. You were exhausted and didn't get any time with him. We can watch over the pack for the night."

I smile down at Brock. "You'll help, right?"

My companion sighs and lowers his head. *"Fine,"* he grumbles. *"Just stop making me hide things from Bass. I don't like the way it feels in my mouth."*

"You got it," I promise him before turning my attention to Gaine. "Would you like me to take Myla with us?"

"I would love some time alone with Kade, but he won't allow it right now," Gaine says sadly. "He'll want to lie with me and make her stand watch in case he falls asleep." She rolls her eyes and shakes her head.

"We just lost over a thousand wolves in a few different attacks, Gaine," I remind her. "He's got a right to be nervous."

"But Bastian isn't with you all the time. Why couldn't he relax enough for that?" she huffs.

I tap my ear with a smile. "My Alpha talks to Brock the whole time,"

I tell her. "He might not be beside me, but he knows exactly where I am, who's with me, how many times I've sighed, and which foot I'm taking a step with."

Gaine giggles. "Ok," she chokes out. "I see your point. I'll try to be more understanding."

* * *

It takes us another hour to reach the creek at our slow pace. The water is chilly, but there are a few fish in the deeper parts for the kids to test their fishing skills. Edith and Anthony fill the canteens and containers while some hunting parties set out for dinner. There's a bit of excitement as some of them pick up the scent of a boar.

My father had been working with the guards on the outskirts of the pack. I wait until I see him come in for water to call for Chase and the boys. As I approach him, all three fall in step with me. I kneel behind Daddy and wait for him to finish drinking.

"I want to go upstream for the full moon tonight," I tell them all. "I'd like to have a small gathering with Grandpa."

Daddy's eyes flick toward the boys. *"They need to stay here, Annalisa,"* he says firmly.

Timothy tucks his ears back and hides his nose behind my arm. Creto rests his jaw over the younger wolf's shoulders in support but eyes me nervously. Without a doubt, I've made the right decision to take them with us.

"They're not ready for that, Daddy," I state just as firmly. "They'll be coming with us."

My father's eyes roll as he sighs loudly. *"Annalisa,"* he starts.

"My job as Luna is not just to watch over my wolves and keep them safe," I say abruptly, stopping the argument before it starts. "I also need to learn from the past. Not long ago, you and Mom decided to leave a wolf behind who wasn't ready. If these children get hurt coming to me, it will be my fault because I know better."

The boys' eyes brighten, and Timothy licks the back of my arm where no one can see his appreciation. One day, these boys will be solid and fearless wolves who will jump in front of danger without thinking of their own safety, but today, they're children who depend on my love and support. They are happy kids with our current arrangement, so we'll stay the course.

"We'll leave once Bastian has finished setting the perimeter," I tell everyone.

My father grumbles, but Chase stays with him while I visit some families with the boys. The children are happy and allow me to run my hands over their bodies, checking their muscles. Of course, they're still thin but have put on weight since leaving the lake. The adults are sharing their meals with the kids, so as I progress through the older wolves, they aren't faring as well.

I continue through the groups, looking for one older wolf in particular. I can hear her, but I don't want her attempting to avoid me. The boys noisily bound around, playing with the children we come across and entertaining themselves as I quietly slip my hands over everyone within reach.

When my hand lands on Kade, he stops me. *"What are you up to, Luna?"*

Smiling, I put my finger to my lips and point ahead. I kneel beside Kade to watch Grandma Pine interact with Creto and Timothy. As my oldest wolf, her age shows in her solid gray coat and white muzzle. She is kind to the excited boys, rubbing muzzles with them and helping to knock some dirt off Timothy's shoulder. I listen to her ask questions about their day and talk to them about minding their manners with the Luna.

Grandma Pine gasps slightly when she looks up, seeing I'm with the boys. *"Oh, Luna, I'm sorry. I didn't realize you were there."* She stiffly curls her leg under her chest to lower into a full bow.

"That's not necessary, Grandma Pine," I say, smiling as I approach her. "I was just coming to check on you."

"These two are pretty special," she says in a way that allows me to hear her smile. *"I heard they suffered quite an ordeal."*

Kneeling before her, I sigh happily. "Indeed, they did," I say, nodding.

"But they are courageous and have recovered well. I enjoy their company very much." I scratch the boys' chins as they giggle and rub their muzzles over my cheeks. "Why don't you take Myla and play for a few minutes while Kade is distracted?" I whisper to them.

Kade sits beside me as the kids take off. *"I'm not distracted,"* he grumbles. *"How does she even know these kids?"*

"Grandma Pine makes a point of knowing all the children," I tell him, smiling at the older wolf. "She has cared for all the southern orphans and is a true treasure. I'm proud to call her my wolf." I hold my arms out and wait for her to step into them.

The old wolf hesitates. She knows I want to feel her body, but rejecting a hug from the Luna would be considered rude. Grandma Pine steps forward gingerly and slides her jaw down my back as I quickly slip my fingers into her fur. I frown, feeling only bones where muscle should be. Her skin feels thinner, which I assume is due to her age. I pull her leg until she lifts it and notice her joint grinding.

"I'd like Neala to look after your diet, Grandma Pine," I whisper as she steps back. "We still have a long way to go, and I'd like you to see the mountains with us."

"Oh, Luna," the older wolf says, slowly sitting before us. *"I'm fine. It's not easy getting old."*

"But you've done it so gracefully," I say, smiling. "Neala has cared for our junior guards for years. They all stayed with her throughout the winter so she could maintain their weight. She's assisted the children we rescued from bad situations and even worked with those two hooligans until I woke up." I nod in the boys' direction.

"They've told me about her," Grandma Pine comments. *"The children talk highly of her and her husband."*

I slide my hand under her jaw. "There are many orphans after the attack," I say sadly. "Perhaps you could help each other while she looks after your diet. I thought you might have some tips and tricks you could pass on."

Grandma Pine chuckles. *"I certainly have those,"* she tells me.

"I think we could use some too," I say, giggling. I bump my shoulder into Kade's and sit between them. "How did you start caring for orphans?" I ask.

"*My father died while my mother was pregnant,*" Grandma Pine starts, lying in the grass beside me. "*My mother didn't speak of it. She loved him very much. When I was about seven, we went hunting in the bayou, and she got caught in a trap. I howled for days, but no help came. The trap broke her leg.*"

At some point, my hand covered my mouth. Thinking of any of my wolves going through this is hard enough, but picturing this wonderfully caring older wolf calling for help and never receiving it is devastating. Kade nuzzles my cheek to wipe a tear and nudges my hand until I move it from my face.

"*It was a long time ago, Luna,*" the older wolf says. "*I wandered from family to family until I was old enough to care for myself. Luckily, I found my mate and settled further north of the bayou. Earl understood my need to get away from there. He was a good man.*"

"Did you have any children of your own?" I ask. I know all of my wolves and their lineage, but if they died before I became Luna, I can't see them or their family line.

"*My son died during birth,*" Grandma Pine answers, sighing. "*That was hard. We wanted a family more than anything.*" She stops with a faraway look in her eyes.

"*Is that why you started taking in orphans?*" Kade asks, rubbing his whiskers over her muzzle.

"It is," she replies, nodding. "*While we were healing, there was a fight with another pack, and a few wolves got killed. We took in their kids, and it grew from there.*"

"I haven't heard much about the old Alphas and pack wars," I tell her. "Were they bad?"

"*They could be. As they became harder to hide, there were fewer, but they never stopped,*" Grandma Pine says. "*Not until your mother, that is. The militia and those damn rebels kept us busy, though.*"

"Yeah, I get that," I say, smiling. "Myla has done well working with Kade." I slide my hand over the silver wolf's head and scratch his neck.

"It seems you helped her to embrace her differences. She's unique and independent, just like her mentor."

"Myla didn't talk for the first year she was with us," Grandma Pine says, turning toward the young wolf. We watch as she tries to catch Creto's muzzle in her mouth. *"Her family lived on the outskirts of our village. She was taught to always be quiet in an attempt not to draw attention to themselves. It didn't help them much."* She turns back to us. *"When she started talking, she had different ideas about how to live and didn't want to hide anymore."*

"I remember she had a strength about her when she met my mother," I recall. "Daddy led her around the cemetery, and she pulled my companion's whiskers." I laugh at the memory of Brock telling me the story. "He didn't like that much."

"I don't blame him," the old wolf says, chuckling. *"It hurts, and Myla knows that. She's always been strange."*

"Myla asserts her dominance in different ways," Kade tells us. *"See how she's lying with the boys? She keeps them along her left side and ensures she's lying uphill from them. She's playing with them, but she's also stationing herself as their guardian. Her dominant side faces away to shield them from danger."*

"Did you teach her that?" I whisper, watching the kids.

"Nope," Kade replies, tilting his head. *"I spend a lot of time just watching her with the other kids. She seems like she didn't have much of a childhood."*

"She didn't," Grandma Pine confirms. *"Right after she came to stay with me, a village was attacked nearby. Six children came to stay with us while their parents were with the healer. Myla helped us with the hunting and in the gardens nonstop to keep all the kids fed. She was just about their age but saw herself as their caretaker."*

"You did right by a lot of kids," I tell her, holding my hand out for her chin. "Will you let us care for you now?"

"I suppose that might be alright, Luna," she responds, placing her chin in my hand. *"You've given our pack hope. They are happier than I've ever seen them, and I've been watching over these wolves for a long time. We may have lost a lot, but what we are gaining helps to heal the hole left by those no longer with us."*

I feel a tear leak from my eye as I lean forward to kiss the old wolf's muzzle behind her whiskers. "You are all worth every struggle," I whisper. "I would do anything to see your smiles and hear your laughter."

"*That is why we will follow you anywhere, Luna.*" Grandma Pine stands and lowers into a bow. "*We feel your love deep within our hearts, and there's no way to ignore it. We know you will always do your best to protect us and brighten our future. I only wish Earl had lived to see the mountains.*"

"Thank you, Grandma Pine," I whisper. "I'm sorry to report that sometimes I must be reminded of that."

"*Rosalinda,*" she says, touching her muzzle to my cheek. "*My kids call me Grandma Pine. You, Luna, can call me Rosalinda.*"

Smiling, I open my arms to her. "I would be honored, Rosalinda."

21

Chase and Daddy walk ahead of us, talking the entire journey upstream to the lake. I enjoy listening as they recall some fun stories from their childhood. Uncle Miles seemed to have a soft spot for the kids in his pack. Chase tells of when they walked down the tracks to the next town, and Uncle Miles bought him his first pony. Daddy laughs and tells him about Grandpa running him over with his horse.

"It's nice to hear them laughing again," Bastian says, looking up as I swing from Saint's saddle.

"I keep kicking myself for not coming up with a plan to reconnect them before now, but I don't think this could've happened sooner," I tell him thoughtfully. *"Daddy needed to be ready to accept Chase back in his life."*

The boys dart past us toward the lake. I told them they couldn't swim until we reached it, so they bound happily into its depths. Chase doesn't like playing in the water like the others, but the boys' joy is contagious. When Daddy takes off after them, Chase doesn't hesitate to join the fun. They jump around in a shallow area, splashing and biting at each other.

Bastian helps me collect firewood while they play. He nudges me a few times when he catches me staring at them. Smiling at my thoughts, I return to our task. I don't know how old Chase is, but my father turned 49 this year. At nearly 50 years old, he'll still act like a kid in the right situations, and I love watching him play. Sometimes, it feels like my mother is beside him, shaking her head and begging him not to include her in something.

Once my arms are filled with branches, I return to the pile of small logs Bastian had brought back to the sloped bank. *"Why don't you take those two fishing, Bass?"* I suggest. *"I'll call the boys back to me, so you don't have to worry about them."*

Bastian rubs his muzzle over my hip. *"Are you sure?"* He glances at the water. *"You'll be ok?"* Looking at the hopeful expression in Bastian's eyes, I know Grandpa gave me the perfect suggestion. Bastian and Daddy are the wolves in this trio who love fishing. Like my grandfather, I have no idea why Chase will only fish with them, but I suspect I'm about to find out.

"Go on," I tell him, smiling. "Have fun with them. Your experiences with my father are limited now, too. You should have this to remember."

Bastian nuzzles my cheek as I crouch to arrange the firewood. *"I might not deserve you, but I'm glad you're mine."*

"I don't want to talk about my love for you," I say, wrinkling my nose with a smile. "I want to watch you have fun with my father."

Once he licks my cheek and excitedly bounds toward the water, I call for the boys. They slowly climb the bank and look back at the adults longingly. I hum quietly and break the kindling as they settle beside me. To their credit, the boys remain silent, allowing me to listen to my father and Chase as they dive into the deeper water with Bastian.

When they start the heavier trash talk, I turn to the boys. "If they can settle their playing, we should have some fish for dinner," I tell them, tugging their ears. "Are you hungry?"

"Yes, Luna," they answer together.

Creto lies with his nose against my knee. *"Why can't we play with them?"* he asks as the kindling catches fire around the edge of the logs.

I shift some of the wood and place my grandfather's medallion far enough away that he can safely appear. "You know that Brock is my companion, right?" I ask, holding my arm out as I lie back. "Do you understand what that means?"

"He's your best friend?" Timothy suggests.

"It's a little more than that," I say, tapping my chest to urge them to join me. "Brock is my Alpha when my Alpha is away. He's spent so much time with us that he knows how Bastian will answer a question or respond to a request. He will stay close to keep me warm or protect me with his life. Brock is a lifeline for me and eases the ache I feel for Bastian when we are apart."

Creto crawls along my side and rests his jaw on my shoulder. *"I'd like to think a best friend would do that for you, but he seems more like family,"* he says quietly. The young wolf nuzzles my neck sleepily.

"Family would be a good word for him," I agree, reaching for Timothy. "Come here, young one. Lay down for the story."

The smaller wolf lies against my other side to sandwich me between them. Timothy's still underweight and small for his age, so he curls into a small ball along my ribs and rests his jaw on my chest. He licks my chin when I look down at him, making me giggle.

"Before you were born, my mother was the Luna," I start. "Of course, my father was her Alpha, but Chase was her companion. He was like a second father. He even lived with us after his mate died. My mother loved him very much, and they were a strong team."

Both boys lift their heads to look toward the water. Neither would have been old enough to remember Chase since he left the lake within a year of my mother's death, but they both knew my father. As they study the nearly white wolf, I know they are wondering how this newcomer could have been closer than family in the past.

"When my mother died, it broke them both," I whisper, not wanting anyone else to hear the story I'm sharing with the children. "She was our world, and all felt her loss, but none more than my father and her companion. I think they struggled mostly because they felt the same pain and needed the same support, but neither could give it. So, Chase left, and they lost the last of their trio."

I close my eyes and listen to the adults while the boys consider the story. This is my first time hearing them while they fish. I watched a few times while we traveled that last winter, but I'm not sure it would've made sense if I hadn't had this experience. They aren't just fishing. They're racing. They choose a fish and race each other to it.

I giggle as Chase laughs at Daddy for trying to beat him. Chase seems to be a speedy swimmer, and neither Alpha can catch him. The Alphas can't be bested at many things, but Chase has found something that puts them all on an even playing field. It also seems we'll be going to bed hungry tonight because they are too busy playing to bring the fish back to shore.

"*I never thought I'd be happy to see that,*" Grandpa says, making the three of us jump. He rubs his whiskers over my forehead and looks out over the water. "*They've been missing each other for a while.*"

"They have," I agree. "Probably a little bit longer than we realized."

"*Yeah, probably.*" Grandpa lies by my head to use us as camouflage so the playing wolves won't see him. "*Your mother told you we can't hear them as wolves on the other plane. I never really knew what they were doing but could tell they were having fun.*"

"I don't know what I was expecting, but racing was not it," I respond, giggling. "I suppose after all those years together, though, Chase had to find something he was better at than Daddy."

"*I doubt either of them is better at fishing,*" Grandpa says, bumping his nose to mine as I turn to look up at him. "*Did you ever hear the story about when I tried to take him fishing as a boy?*"

"I did not," I answer, smiling broadly. I love hearing stories about when my father was little. He was such a rambunctious, opinionated child that every tale is an adventure of epic proportions. Even the boys prick their ears at the idea of hearing about their formidable Alpha when he was their age.

"*Your Grandma didn't allow me around your father much,*" Grandpa starts. "*She had it in her head that everyone would figure out he was mine because he was so different. That wasn't even my fault, but that's another story. I'd gotten pretty used to not being a father after 150 years, so I didn't know what to do anyway.*

"*We noticed he was different immediately, but his strength started showing up when he was about four. Grandma tried a few things, and Grandpa Bruce was there to help, but he seemed especially angry right before their wedding. We decided to try letting him stay with me for a few weeks after that.*"

Grandpa stops and looks over the water. Following his gaze, I can easily pick out Chase, but Bastian and Daddy have darker coats, so they blend in with the water and shadows better.

"*Exercise helped a lot,*" my grandfather starts again. "*He was seven when I took him fishing. I thought if the physical exertion let out the excess energy, perhaps the calm peacefulness of fishing would help him relax.*" Grandpa tugs Creto's ear with his teeth. "*I was wrong.*"

The boys giggle, and Creto's tail thumps the ground a few times as he lifts his head to rub whiskers with Grandpa. Neither boy has spent time with my grandfather. Even when I was a child, the immortal Alphas were magical in a way that their presence was an honor. Getting special attention from one is a real treat that doesn't go unnoticed.

"*It might surprise you to know that he annoyed the shit out of me with his constant fidgeting,*" Grandpa says. He chuckles when I raise my eyebrow. "*I know. It's weird, but he did.*"

I laugh and pull my hands from the boys' fur to rub my face. "Grandpa, stop," I choke out. "You two still bicker when he fidgets."

The grumpy Alpha huffs, shaking his head. "*I'm too old for such things,*" he grumbles. "*Anyway, as I said, it didn't work out as planned. Your father wouldn't shut up. He kept scaring off all the fish, so I told him we weren't leaving until we had a basket of fish for his mother.*"

"He told Mom you used to send him to the lake any time Grandma wanted fish for dinner," I say, watching Bastian lead the older wolves from the water.

"*Well, I can't deny that he was good at fishing,*" Grandpa says as Daddy lies beside him. "*But he got bored, so the next thing I knew, the furball was bounding past me and diving into the water. He had that basket full in 20 minutes.*" Grandpa looks at Daddy as he starts to chuckle. "*I threw the basket in the lake and refused to take him fishing again.*"

The boys snicker as quietly as possible, but Daddy still nuzzles them, acting like he'll nip them. Bastian tucks in beside Timothy to push him closer to me. The young wolf hums as he sleepily nuzzles his nose under my jaw.

We've made a point of bracing him between two warm bodies when he sleeps. Neala told us it takes a lot of calories to create his warmth, and he conserves energy if we heat his body for him. I haven't seen progress so far, but he's not losing weight even with all his running around, so I believe it's helping. Plus, he's adorable when he snuggles up with us.

"Did you guys bring back any food for the boys?" I ask, lifting my eyebrow.

"*Oh, um,*" Bastian stammers, looking at his uncle for help.

Chase scoffs. "*I won the races,*" he announces. "*Winner eats the fish.*" He lays his jaw on his crossed paws.

"*He does have a point,*" Daddy says, eyeing my Alpha. "*Loser goes hungry.*"

"*You lost too,*" Bastian whines.

"*Not as badly as you did,*" my father replies, tilting his head.

"*Fine,*" Bastian grumbles. "*I'll be right back.*"

"Thank you, my Alpha," I say, giggling. I kiss his nose when he gives it to me before leaning my cheek against Creto's muzzle. "Why don't you take his place, sweetheart? You can lie closer to the fire and help me keep Timothy warm."

"*Yes, Luna,*" the young wolf replies sadly. The boys both like to sleep against me. Bastian has been generous with them, allowing them to hog me while he lies on Timothy's other side. Creto acts as a big brother in every aspect of their daily lives, except when it comes to his Luna snuggles. I have become the equivalent of a teddy bear for both of them.

"*I'm still right here, sweet boy,*" I say so only Creto can hear me. "*I won't leave you.*"

Once Creto lies against Timothy's back and heats up, I roll to my side and slip my fingers through his fur. Chase and Daddy quietly fill Grandpa in on some things that have happened and what they've seen while I listen and settle the boys. Bastian brings back a few fish and pulls them apart for me before joining the conversation.

"*Do you know anything about the babies?*" he asks Grandpa. "*Is she safe now?*"

"*Aylee said she was gonna die, but she looks fine,*" Grandpa answers. He rubs his muzzle over my forehead as I feed a sliver of fish to Timothy, who's barely awake enough to chew. *She was only quoting myths and legends anyway.*"

"She was something," I comment. "*Maybe I just need to get used to her attitude.*"

"*There's no getting used to it,*" Grandpa grumbles.

Giggling, I pull a chunk of fish from its bone and feed it to Creto. "*She's your mate, Grandpa. There has to be something you love about her.*"

The old Alpha snorts. "*I do love to hate her,*" he grumbles. "*So, there's that.*"

Daddy chuckles and lays his head over Chase's shoulders. "*As long as you keep her away from me,*" he adds, still laughing.

I tune them out for a moment to focus on the kids. Creto is still hungrily watching my hands and quickly taking the chunks I offer, but Timothy is falling asleep between bites. He wakes when I pry his mouth open to put food in it but barely makes it through chewing before falling asleep. They played quite a bit today, but not to the point that would warrant this level of exhaustion.

Bastian sits up and studies the small wolf as I try to wake him for the last piece of fish, but he's not interested. I feed it to Creto and roll more of my body over Timothy. Slipping my hands over him, I notice he's cool to the touch. I glance toward Bastian with a furrowed brow.

"*Let me in there, Love,*" my Alpha says quietly. He steps carefully over Timothy, watching where his paws land so he doesn't cut us with his claws. Bastian crouches low over the young wolf and heats his body so much that I can feel the warmth without touching him. "*What has he been eating?*"

"*Lots of things, but Myla found a beaver before we left the foothills,*" Creto tells us. "*I'd gotten a squirrel earlier, so I let him have it.*" He pokes his nose under Bastian to nuzzle his little friend. "*We were always told they were dangerous, but it was easy to kill. It didn't make him sick, did it?*"

"Sorry, sweetheart," I whisper. "There's a reason you're supposed to stay away from beavers. They're normally infested with fleas and ticks. We'll need to get him back to Edith and Neala as soon as the sun comes up."

I push my finger into Timothy's mouth and feel a few lumps between the ridges on the roof of his mouth. Bastian nuzzles my forehead, and I nod in response. Timothy's mouth is full of ticks, and with the little wolf trying to recover from starvation and dehydration, he doesn't have the blood to spare. I search through the voices, looking for Neala, when I hear Daddy questioning Grandpa.

"*She doesn't know for sure that they're extinct,*" he states, questioning Aylee's information. "*The historians only said it was wounded.*"

"*I guess that's true,*" Grandpa says. "*That was nearly a hundred years before she was even born. She seemed pretty adamant, though.*"

"*She's also quite sure that she's a good person, and we all know that's a lie,*" Daddy grumbles.

"*Now you're talking crazy,*" I spout at my father. "*Daddy, there were movies and books and cars and planes... How would a unicorn ever hide from a world like that?*"

"*There is that,*" Grandpa agrees. "*Son, I hate the saying, but I think you're barking up the wrong tree. I was alive during all that time. Unicorns were just fantasy.*"

"*So were werewolves and witches,*" Daddy scoffs.

"*True,*" Grandpa grumbles.

"*We're right back where we started,*" Chase says, sighing. "*This is what it's like to talk in circles with your father, huh?*"

Daddy laughs while Grandpa snaps his teeth at Chase. "*Nobody asked you,*" my grandfather grumbles. The three of them lay their jaws on their paws.

Bastian licks his lips and nuzzles my cheek. "*You should rest, Love,*" he tells me. "*We will need to leave as soon as the sun comes up. He's pretty cold.*"

"*What's wrong with him?*" Daddy asks, lifting his head.

I reach to scratch his chin. "Timothy ate a beaver," I tell them all. "His mouth is full of ticks. I imagine he's donated a bit too much blood to them."

"*Ok,*" my father says. He groans as he rolls to his side and stretches his legs, pushing against Chase. "*We've got a few hours. You'll have to carry him on the horse with you.*" Daddy stands and orders Creto out of the way so he can help Bastian keep the little wolf warm.

Creto is sleepy, but he happily jogs to lie beside me again. I slip my fingers through his fur as he rests his jaw on my shoulder. He's pretty attached to Timothy, and his concern emits with each swipe.

"*We will get him back to the pack in the morning, sweetheart,*" I say quietly. "*He'll be ok. We didn't make it this far to lose him.*"

The young wolf rolls his head to rub it over my cheek. "*Do you promise?*"

"*Oh, sweet young wolf,*" I whisper to just him, rolling to put my back against Bastian and wrap my arms around Creto's neck. "*I will do any-thing to save my wolves. You are all precious to me, and I love you very much.*"

"*I love you too, Luna,*" he whispers back, licking my forehead.

Grandpa leans over to nuzzle my cheek as soon as the young wolf lays back down. "*Just keep doing what you're doing, kiddo,*" he tells me. "*It seems to be working. It's gonna start getting really cold soon. You need to get moving and find a steady food supply, or they'll all end up like this kid.*" He pokes Timothy.

"*Do you have any suggestions as to where we should go?*" I ask.

He stops to think for a moment, working his jaw. "*There was a national park to the north,*" Grandpa starts. "*They called it Yellow-something. Stone, maybe? I don't know. Anyway, there were enormous herds of buffalo and elk. If you can get up there before the snow becomes too deep, you could keep them fed through the winter.*"

"Thank you, Grandpa," I whisper.

"*You're welcome, kiddo,*" he says. "*Get some sleep. I'll always be back.*"

* * *

Preparation for the ride back to the pack begins at daybreak. We pull the stirrup leathers to fashion them as a sling because although the young wolf is relatively small, his dead weight is heavy. Bastian lifts him to me, and we work together to slip him into the straps so I won't drop him.

Once the little wolf is settled, I slide my hand over his face. He hasn't woken up since last night. His breathing has slowed, and his limbs are stiff. Bastian pulls a blanket from the saddle bag and wraps it around us. He ties it behind me, taking more of Timothy's weight off my arms.

"You might want to start working on the ticks in his gums, Ayls," Bastian says, pulling back the little wolf's lip. "This is gonna be slow. I won't take the chance of you falling off with him."

"I know," I whisper, forcing a smile. Timothy might be small, but he's still heavy and lanky. How we have him wrapped in my arms is causing me to feel off-balance. I don't have stirrups and can't grab the horn if I need help staying on. Not only would a fall possibly injure Timothy and me, but I have to think of the future Luna still growing in my belly. "Just stay with Creto. He's concerned about his friend."

Bastian leans over from the stump he'd stood on to hand me Timothy. "Of course, my Luna," he whispers before gently kissing my lips. "We will get them both back safe and sound." He cups my cheek with a grin and steps off the stump to shift. *Here we go.*

Creto stays beside Bastian in front of me for a while. He does his best to pay attention as my Alpha attempts to teach him how to lead the horse and control him for me, but the young wolf often glances worriedly in our direction. Daddy and Chase flank us, staying further behind but still within view. They distract themselves by discussing their adventures while Mom was pregnant with me.

I tip Timothy's head back slightly so his lip will fall away from his gums and start working on the ticks I can see. Edith has a few sets of tweezers that we got from Doc's office before we left. They'll work much better than my nails, but Bastian's right. I need to get out the ones I can reach to try to help him.

"Why won't he wake up, Luna?" Creto asks. I hadn't noticed he'd dropped back to walk beside me.

"He's fed them a lot of blood, honey," I tell the young wolf. "Normally, it would take much longer to cause these effects, but our little wolf here has been recovering from the drought. Being younger and living further away from the lake, I believe he struggled a little more than us."

"Luna, we're good kids, aren't we?" Creto asks, looking up at me.

I stop examining Timothy's mouth to study Creto. "Yes, baby," I assure him. "You are both wonderful boys. Why do you ask?"

"*Why does everyone hate us?*" Creto lowers his eyes and studies the trail before us.

I want to jump off Saint and wrap my arms around the young wolf. While at the lake, the kids never had these questions. They didn't hear about the hate unless someone close to them was killed in battle. Otherwise, our little ones lived a blissfully ignorant life. Maybe he wouldn't have thought of it had I not brought up the lake or Timothy's hunger. The worst part about this discussion is that I don't have an answer for him.

"I'm not sure, sweetheart," I say quietly, hoping I can ease his turmoil. "Perhaps they fear your strength or the bond we all share. Maybe the unconditional love we feel for each other is too foreign for them."

Creto looks back up at me with his head tilted. "*Why would they fear love?*"

"I find that people fear unknown things the most," I tell him. "That strange noise in the dark can be much scarier than a roaring lion in your face. Does that make sense?"

"*No,*" he answers, tilting his head the other way. "*We can see in the dark.*"

Giggling, I shift Timothy so his lip will cover his gums while Creto and I talk. "Ok, maybe that was a bad example," I agree. "We live in a world of deceit and distrust, sweetheart. The humans have trouble understanding our pack's fierce bond. You are all very powerful, and it's hard for them to believe you don't want to use that strength and bond to kill or conquer them."

"*Why can't we just tell them?*" Creto asks.

"Well, maybe they don't want to hear us," I answer thoughtfully. "You know when Neala is teaching you your lessons, and you're playing a little bit too much, she'll tell you to use your listening ears?"

"*Luna,*" Creto says in a way that I know something he shouldn't say is about to come out of him. "*If I wasn't listening, you know I didn't hear her say that.*"

"Creto, your lessons are important," I scold him. "You should be paying attention. That is something Neala says often, and now I know why. But, to continue what I was saying, perhaps humans don't know how to use their listening ears."

"Some humans do," the young wolf points out. *"Edith and Anthony are good humans, right?"*

"They are some of the good ones, yes," I say, smiling. "Maybe one day we'll find more. Until then, we'll be a strong family with an unrivaled love for each other."

22

Since I've been lying in the wagon with Trish to stay with Timothy for nearly two days, Edith has kept me on a diet of boiled fowl and healing tea. Pulling all the ticks from the little wolf's mouth took the witch hours. Many of them were so swollen that there was no way he didn't know they were there. Neala advised me to talk with him about the importance of honesty.

The little wolf mumbles his thoughts incoherently as he shifts his head over my chest. I roll back to give him more room to move around, but he just falls against me. His gums are still nearly white, but his body has started to heat itself, which Daddy says indicates he's beginning to rebuild his blood supply.

I move his nose so he can smell my scent as he rests. Being an undersized wolf, Timothy is easy to maneuver around, so I can comfortably hold my family's notebook and read through the confusing text. Anthony showed it to me a few years ago after my grandfather relayed my mother's permission. I was excited to hear he'd kept it in the safe with my mother's dress and it had survived the fires.

"Did you find anything?" Bastian asks, hopping over the back of the wagon to join us.

"Hello, Love," I whisper. "Can you grab that blanket? It's chilly in the shade."

Bastian pulls over a blanket to cover Timothy. *"How's he doing?"*

"He just woke up a little bit," I tell him, smiling. "I couldn't understand him, but I still count it as a good sign."

"Brock is tracking a small herd of deer," Bastian reports. *"We should have some meat for him soon. I'll make sure he gets a few of the bones."*

"Is Creto still with him?" I ask, closing the book with a yawn.

"Unhappily, yes," my Alpha answers.

Giggling, I slide my hand over his muzzle. "A few parts in that notebook mention the Luna's blood. It's what Doc was talking about." I stop as Bastian shimmies between me and the side of the wagon. I throw the blanket over him to trap his heat. "One section says that a Luna's blood would 'heal them all,' but it's talking about a Luna rebirth and sacrifice."

"Yeah, we're not doing that," Bastian quickly interjects.

I furrow my brow as he lifts his head to put his nose in my face. "Um, no," I say, confused. "I wasn't really planning that."

"Ayls, your mother planned it twice," Bastian states. *"I just want to be clear that I will not be happy if you try those shenanigans too."*

I stare at him for a moment, letting the awkwardness of his statement settle in deep before moving on. "As I was saying, that is one section," I continue. "Since my blood didn't heal humans, I'm wondering if it's meant to heal wolves."

"Why?" Bastian asks. *"What are you trying to do?"*

"Right now, Timothy is too weak to shift for tea," I say slowly. "I think there might be a way I can help him."

"All this from one damn beaver."

Bastian has repeatedly grumbled this statement over the past few days. I've explained that the little wolf's condition is much worse because of the state of his body, but that has not eased his anger. He wants someone to blame, and a dead beaver isn't good enough. I count us lucky that it was Timothy and not another child who isn't directly under my watchful eye. With their hunger, they are bound to break some rules to get food.

"We should take a walk once we have him back on his paws," I suggest. "It would be nice to spend some time alone."

Bastian sighs deeply as he switches gears. *"I would really like that."* He rubs the front of his muzzle over my cheeks and chin. His hum starts when I softly blow into his nostrils. *"Hmm, you smell good."*

"I love you very much, my Alpha," I whisper. I turn away from him as he tucks into my neck. His body heats, and he slowly laps his tongue over my skin.

Smiling, I close my eyes and listen to my wolves. Many adults are still conversing with the kids about which animals are safe to eat. Not many animals are too dangerous for my wolves, but there is prey that can have unhealthy repercussions, such as beavers, rats, skunks, and armadillos, for starters. Large game can be infested with different insects, but because they are bigger, my wolves don't put their mouths on the hide as much.

"I'm tired," I hear Creto whine. *"Can't I go lie down with Luna?"*

I search for Brock among the other voices. *"You need to help us bring this meat back, kid,"* he answers. *"Then you can lie down with her."*

Brock is firm but gentle with the kids. I know Creto's not ready to leave me, but his worry about Timothy was eating at him, and I wanted him to take a break. He left with Bastian, but being a pushover regarding the little wolves, my Alpha agreed to assign Creto to Brock when the youngster started asking to come back to me. I'm happy to hear they are on their way back, though. I feel the young wolf's absence.

I slip my fingers over Timothy's muzzle. "They're on their way, my little wolf," I whisper. "We'll have meat for you soon. You're so strong to keep hanging on."

The wagon pauses as Edith climbs into the bed with us. "Hey, Ayls," she whispers. "I have Timmy's water." She holds up a small canteen. Every hour or so, she checks the little wolf's mouth for missed ticks and helps me pour water down his throat.

"Brock and Creto have found some meat," I whisper. "Bastian said they were tracking a group of deer."

"That'll be good for him," she says, nodding. "I'll pull all the marrow I can and make a paste with the salve. If we wipe it on his tongue, he can medicate the roof of his mouth while he eats."

"That would work," I agree, rolling to move Timothy. I pull my arm from under Bastian, who moves with me to continue tasting my skin. I wrinkle my nose as his hum rumbles to life. "Is Chase coming to check him?"

"Yeah," Edith answers. "He'll be here in a little while. He's been checking on everyone today. Your two little ones aren't eating as much as the other kids because they can't hunt small meals while riding in the wagon with you."

Sighing, I frown at her. "I realize that now," I say sadly. "I'll walk more with them once we have this one healthy enough." I brace Timothy's head so she can examine his mouth thoroughly. I smile at her grin as the young wolf fights her when she pulls his tongue to the side. "That's a good sign."

"It is," Edith says, smiling. She leans down to put her cheek against Timothy's whiskers. "I have water for you, sweetheart," she whispers to him. "I'll make you some special food to help you feel better." He tries to lick her fingers, but his tongue flops out the side of his mouth. "Save your energy, baby."

I watch as Edith finishes the examination and pulls another tick she finds between his tooth and gums. "Why didn't you ever have any kids, Edith?" I ask quietly after she gives Timothy some water.

She shrugs. "I thought about it once," she answers thoughtfully. "But the timing never worked out, and there wasn't anyone I wanted to stick around." She turns to smile at her husband. "By the time Anthony and I were married, we had a whole pack of children who claimed our love. Besides, we were often traveling, and your parents always needed something."

"I'm sorry," I whisper, taking her hand.

"Don't be," Edith says, smiling and shaking her head. "I have a husband who loves me. I'm surrounded by wolves I adore and have been accepted as one of them. My life and heart are full, Annalisa. You and your mother have created this life for all of us, and we are thrilled to be a part of it."

"Do you regret anything?" I ask.

"Oh, honey, there's always regrets," she answers, sighing. "I can think of a million things I would do differently. But you know what? I might not be here with you and this little wolf if I did. Maybe I wouldn't be married to a wonderful man who used to be my enemy." Edith smiles and cups my cheek. "Even the smallest change could cause catastrophic differences, and I don't want to think about a world without the people I have now."

"I was thinking about the fires the same way recently," I admit. "I love having this little one and Creto with me, but I don't believe any form of this would have happened without the attack on the lake."

"But maybe he wouldn't have gotten a mouthful of ticks," Edith says, lifting her eyebrow.

"Or maybe he would have, and no one would've thought to check his mouth when he got sick," I retort.

Edith smiles. "See?" she asks. "Everything happens for a reason." She looks down at Timothy as he slowly licks his lips. "And whatever that reason may be, I am delighted to see your beautiful eyes, little wolf."

Edith feeds Timothy the rest of the water, and it's not long before Creto jumps into the wagon with us. He proudly drops a fawn beside us before nuzzling my cheek. The young wolf leans over me to ask Bastian for permission to snuggle with me, but my Alpha has fallen asleep and just grumbles at the disturbance.

"Come lie down and help keep Timothy warm while we get some steaks cut for you, sweetheart," I say, giggling.

Edith lifts the other side of the blanket for Creto to crawl into. Once Timothy is sandwiched between us, she holds her hand out for Creto's chin. "Come here, young man," she orders, lifting her eyebrow. "Open wide."

Although Creto swears he hadn't touched the beaver, Edith checks his mouth whenever he comes near her. He's polite and allows her to inspect him because he gets to snuggle with me when she's through. After he's declared tick-free, he rubs the front of his muzzle over my face and licks my cheek.

"Hi, sweetheart," I say, giggling. "I missed you too." I kiss the tip of his nose. "Did you eat anything while you were out?"

"No, Luna," Creto admits. *"I was busy."*

"No, you were in a rush," I scold him. "You need to eat. It won't do you any good to be near me if you still die of starvation. You need to find a balance." I give him a stern look. "Once Timothy has more energy, we will do more walking. You'll need to hunt through the day just like everyone else. You're not filling out, and that's my fault."

Creto tucks his ears back and hangs his head a bit. *"But you'll hunt with us, right?"*

"You have me for as long as you need me," I answer. "This is important, though. I need you both to be thick and strong to survive the winter. From the books I've read and the stories I've heard, it gets downright cold in these mountains during the winter, and that's coming very soon."

"Yes, Luna," Creto says, lifting his head as Edith passes me a flat board of meat cuts. He presses his nose against the wood as it travels past him.

Giggling, I set it down on Timothy's hip. "Even your body's telling you that things need to change," I say, slipping a sizable chunk into his mouth.

I settle into the blankets and feed the boys the raw meat. Edith shakes her head with mild disapproval. My mother would be stricter with these children, pushing the healthier little wolf out of the wagon and making him hunt his own food. Edith has the same beliefs and would prefer to foster the instincts that make them fierce hunters when they grow up. I lift my eyebrow at her and feed Creto another piece of meat.

* * *

I love having the boys with me, but after another day of riding in the wagon, Timothy is strong enough to start walking for some of the day. Sending him off with Neala so she can force him to track and hunt eases my mind enough to focus on my Alpha. Timothy quietly jogs beside Myla, who got Kade's permission to join the boys, but Creto hangs his head as he trudges behind them.

"They'll be ok, Ayls," Bastian assures me as he slips his muzzle into my hand to lead me away. *"They need this just as much as we do. They're little wolves, Ayls, not babies. What is it that you are always saying? Little wolves need exercise, food, and instincts."*

"I don't like it when you use my words against me," I grumble, letting him lead me to the top of a ridge.

We stop to look down at our pack. Most are traveling as wolves, so the tall yellow grass and green pine needles are disturbed by a sea of mainly brown and black coats. Children dart between small groups of adults as they play and occasionally hunt. I spot Timothy traveling quietly next to Neala while she talks to him about the importance of honesty again.

"My mother had her hands in every aspect of the pack," I whisper slowly. "She was better prepared when it came to the kids."

Bastian rubs his jaw over my hip. *"Luna never took the kids away from the lake,"* he reminds me. *"Why would she need to be concerned? Their food was brought back to the lake, and Neala cared for them all winter, ensuring they never spent a moment with a rumbly belly. You're comparing a bunny to a bull."* He shifts, pulling me against his chest and cupping my cheek. "But right now, can you be a bunny?"

Giggling, I rub my lips against his. "I will be whatever you want as long as you allow me to love you," I whisper as he licks my top lip.

My Alpha and my father handle many of the patrol rotations for me so that I can concentrate on the kids and more delicate matters, like monitoring the eldest wolves. However, anytime we step away from our pack, my guards move in and watch over them like overbearing stallions guarding their mares. When Bastian lifts me by my thighs and carries me into the trees, I know my wolves will be safe under the watchful protection of my guards.

I drape my arms over his shoulders with a smile. Bastian's hum drowns out the sound of the chirping birds as he rubs his face over mine. I could never explain what I love about this, but it causes air to rush from my lungs and pulls a moan from somewhere in my throat.

Before I'm ready for him to stop, I'm placed on my feet, and my clothes are slowly removed. The crisp autumn air leaves chills on my skin wherever it touches. Bastian removes my shirt last and gently trails his fingers over my belly before lifting me back to his hips. Sliding his arms around my back, he keeps me firmly against him as he drops to the ground and holds me in his lap.

Although he's heating up to keep me warm, Bastian's touch creates a fire that burns from within my body. I might not have any comparison, but I couldn't imagine ever wanting to experience another man. His lips leave a need behind that causes me to shift around to put the recently kissed portions of my body against him. I'm pretty sure he does it on purpose because I am still learning to give him the experience he shares with me.

Bastian rocks my hips to push himself into me as his tongue slides up my neck. He nibbles on my ear, allowing me to settle against him. "I love you," he whispers, exhaling over my skin.

I push him back to claim his lips and slowly rub my tongue over his. My father wasn't happy about teaching Bastian how to relax when we're together, but I'm thankful for him every time we are. As my Alpha's breathing eases into a study rhythm, I can enjoy the experience without pushing him past his limit.

I quietly moan into Bastian's mouth when my legs stiffen as I fight my body's need for him. He leans me back and lowers his mouth to my chest. Breathing out as his teeth scrape against me, Bastian introduces heat before leaving an exhilarating chill behind. My muscles shake from the shock of the experience.

When I'm sure I won't be able to handle anymore, Bastian lays me on my back. My muscles lock down on him as he claims the rest of me, causing me to cry out as my nerves celebrate his attention. Bastian pushes his shoulder into my face when my voice echoes back on us from the neighboring hills. I want to laugh, but my nerves pull my back into an arch, making gasping my only option until he's had enough.

Bastian slides off me and braces my back as my muscles relax. His hand lightly trails up my body and along my arm to pull my fingers to his lips. "So, these hills have quite the echo," he says, kissing my fingertips.

I finally let my laughter out. "I love you," I blurt out between gasps.

"I love you too, Ayls," he says. "I'm still gonna need you to keep it down. We wouldn't want Kade to get jealous."

I smile at Bastian. I love that he seems to settle more into the wolf he once was with each passing day. He struggled so much under the pressure when we first received my mother's permission that the fun side of our relationship suffered. Every smile and shared laughter excites me.

Bastian rolls my hips so my belly is against him and looks through the trees at the hill beyond. "It is beautiful here," he whispers. "It seems so untouched and innocent."

I twist to follow his gaze. The yellow grass sways as far as the eye can see, only disturbed by the pine trees and rock walls. There isn't even a plume of smoke from a fireplace to indicate any other soul in the area. "I only see safety," I confess. "The absence of the need to fight for something that's already ours." I turn back to Bastian and cup his cheek. "I feel welcomed here."

Bastian smiles down at me. "Everything happens for a reason."

I click my tongue and smack his shoulder. "You were awake," I scoff.

"I rarely sleep these days," he admits. "But I do want my quiet time to enjoy your flavor." He rushes at me, making me squeal as he bites my neck with a growl. "Mm, you taste good."

"Oh, I know," I say, lifting my eyebrow. "I've heard this story before." I trace his jaw and sigh deeply. "I want to try talking to Daddy again, Bass."

Bastian sighs with a frown. "Ayls, he'll go when he's ready."

"Do you think he'll ever feel 'ready?'" I ask, shaking my head. "Bass, he misses Mom but thinks we need him too much to follow his heart." I scan his face, not seeing any sign of agreeing with me. "Would you ever feel ready to leave our daughter if I died?"

"Every time my chest started to ache," he answers.

"He doesn't feel that anymore," I tell him, sighing. "Their bond on this plane broke when she died."

Bastian doesn't like to talk about this. The thought of our bond breaking upsets him in ways I will probably never understand. He sits up and pulls me into his lap, cradling me against his chest. I wait to see if he'll respond, but he only sets his chin on my head and envelops me in his arms.

"Grandpa told me the bond re-forms on the other plane," I whisper. We've already been over this, but he might need to hear it again. "Their love will never die, Bass. Neither will ours." I lightly rub my fingers over his chest. "I will always be yours—even beyond the day of our deaths."

Bastian sighs and kisses my head. "I know it's hard to imagine after a life filled with so much love, Ayls, but considering its absence is terrifying."

"You'll never be unloved, Bass," I say, leaning back to look into his eyes. "We can't erase the past, but our pack has loved you since they met you. First, my mother and father, then Neala and Brock. And what about your uncle? You already had their love, but then you blessed them by becoming their Alpha. Your heart will never be empty."

"But I will still miss you," Bastian whispers.

He's done talking. My mother once told me that Bastian would love me with a ferocity that would take my breath away. She was right about that, but she missed one vital part of his love that I would've appreciated a warning about. Bastian's love for me will cause him to shut down the moment he is forced to think about losing me. I love him and accept all his qualities, even those that make it impossible to discuss important subjects.

I nuzzle into his chest, asking for more of his warmth. I feel him relax with a sigh, and his body begins to heat as he rocks me like he's seen my father do for years. I love being with Bastian, but these are the moments I cherish. Our silence seems to scream how much we love each other. I turn it into a song and begin humming along until Bastian chuckles.

"Why do you always laugh when I hum?" I'm unsure why I've never asked, but now I want to know.

"Your mother used to hum to me," Bastian confesses, holding me a little tighter. "She hummed to Tarq when we traveled. She'd lay for hours humming while she rubbed his pads. It was calming and would settle the noise in my head. Not to mention how badly I wanted to feel a pad rub. Then, the long afternoons in the paddock with your horse."

His voice trails off. He's avoided mentioning Grease since we crossed the river and left any hope of finding her behind.

"Being a Luna is very emotional," I murmur, sliding my hand to his neck. "I help everyone deal with their thoughts and feelings. I can't do that without understanding my own. I miss my mare." I stop and narrow my eyes in thought. "I choose to hold hope that she made it far away from the blaze and is snuggled up with a stallion, ready to bless this world with beautiful fillies of her own in the future."

"That's why I'll always need you in my life," Bastian says, chuckling. "The moment I begin feeling bad about anything, you swoop in and remind me that there is light in darkness if only we take the time to open our eyes."

I smile into Bastian's kiss, holding him to me until his hum starts. "I will be your bright beacon whenever you need me," I whisper.

Bastian lifts his head and looks back over the hills. "Speaking of the pack, I think we got left behind," he says, scanning the terrain.

I close my eyes and listen to our wolves for a moment. A few voices come through, making me smile. "There are a few close by," I tell him. "They are stopping the boys from coming any closer."

"What are we gonna do with those kids?" Bastian grumbles with a smile as he pretends they annoy him.

My smile broadens as I cup his cheek and rub our noses together. "They are ours now," I announce. "For better or worse, those boys have adopted us. I hope you wanted a full house."

23

We slowly turn the pack north over the next few weeks. Chase and Daddy remembered seeing an old map that showed the national forest Grandpa mentioned pretty far to the north. I'm not sure we'll make it there this winter, but after talking with Grandma and Grandpa Bruce about their travels, I'm positive it's where we need to be. Food becomes more plentiful along the way, justifying the decision even more.

By the end of the third week, we meet our first precipitation since the beginning of the year. I wish it were rain, but it is winter, so snow is expected and still welcomed. Hunting has been bountiful, and my wolves have built up their mass for the most part. They bound happily through the few inches that cover the ground, scooping it with their front legs and burying their faces in the mound they create.

I smile as Bastian and Brock play with Creto, shaking limbs to dump their snow over him. Timothy has had a harder time leaving my side and lacks the thickness the others have built. I went hunting with him a few times to encourage him to try, but I might have coddled him too much throughout his issues. Creto still brings him around a third of his kills, and I sit in the wagon with the boys and Grandma Pine while they eat.

Once enough snow is on the ground, Anthony works a few fallen trees into flat drag sleds. As a rushed job, they're not smooth for sledding, but the small harness he fashions is designed to fit Timothy. "Let's try to give that kid a job, Ayls," Anthony whispers, handing me the harness. "He seems to see himself as your companion, but that job's taken. Let's give him a new one and see if he'll come out of his shell."

Timothy looks nervous when we call him off the wagon, but he stands proudly as we fit the harness. *I'm going to pull Luna,* he announces when Creto asks for one too.

I hadn't planned to ride in the sled. I thought we could start with a minimal weight since Timothy's still relatively small, but Anthony elbows me hard in the ribs when I try to protest. He tells the little wolf he forgot a piece of the harness in the wagon and drags me to the furthest corner of it so he won't be heard.

"Do not crush that little wolf," Anthony hisses. "I've never steered you wrong. I haven't seen that kid lift his head or stand proudly until now."

I lift my eyebrow curiously. "Anthony, how do you know what they're saying?"

He chuckles. "I've been around these wolves longer than you and your mother combined," he says. "Dax and I go way back, sweetheart. I don't need to hear them. They wear everything out in the open in their expressions and mannerisms." He turns me by my shoulders to face Timothy. "That little wolf has been a mouse until he got it in his head that he was gonna pull the Luna through the snow."

"Ok," I say, breathing out a sigh. "How do I do this without breaking him?"

"Everyone is having fun playing in the snow," Anthony answers. He squints as he looks around at my wolves. "We'll slow down and take more breaks. He should want to eat when we stop. We'll have Bastian or Brock bring food in for him. He shouldn't be hunting and pulling you. Not yet, anyway."

"He shouldn't be pulling me," I hiss, scowling.

Anthony grins and kisses my forehead. "You know the kid is smiling under that fur," he says, pulling me into his arms. "You don't want to take that away, do you?"

"Just because you're right doesn't mean I have to like it," I say, pouting.

Grabbing a random strip of leather, Anthony guides me back around the wagon and kneels beside Timothy. I watch as he pretends to adjust the harness and tucks the piece of leather in his pocket. He secures the small sled with a few chain links and lengths of rope. My small wolf stands as a proud statue while his gear is inspected several times.

"Are you feeling alright for this?" I ask, kneeling before Timothy.

The little wolf nuzzles my cheek. *"I will be fine, Luna,"* he responds. *"I'm your wolf."*

I hold his warm muzzle against my cold cheek. "You're my **little** wolf," I whisper, eyeing him pointedly. "I need you to be completely honest with me." I back away to ensure I have all his attention. "You **will** tell me if you need to rest or cannot do this job."

Timothy's cold, wet nose jams against mine. *"I promise."*

As he lifts his head to stand boldly, I think of my grandfather and the fit he would have about this young wolf treating me in such a general way. Grandpa stands on ceremony more than any other wolf I know. Accepting this little wolf into our fold will be difficult for him. I slip my hand over Timothy's chest while it's extended, getting a good feel of the area and sharpness of his breastbone.

"That is awesome," Kade remarks in awe, approaching from behind Timothy. *"Who do I need to bribe to make me one of those?"*

I catch Timothy's muzzle as he looks around nervously. "Kade, you cannot have this job," I say, smirking. "This little wolf has earned this position."

"Woman, I love you, but I want one to pull my wife," Kade says dismissively. *"It's getting harder for her to shift. Besides, I like keeping her close. You never know when I'll spontaneously need me some wife-time."*

Kade's flirtatious in general. He might be my shiny silver wolf, rubbing his whiskers on my cheeks, but I see the man's crooked grin and lifted eyebrow just as clearly. I smile as he turns his attention to his wife, who innocently jogs up to us, not having heard his request. Kade's hum isn't easy to detect, but I know it well and love that I can hear it as he gently rubs his muzzle over hers and mouths her lip lovingly.

"What are we doing?" Gaine asks, bumping her nose into Kade's.

"I'm loving on you," Kade says quietly. *"I don't know what they're doing."*

Gaine giggles and hooks necks with her husband. She'll do this when she needs to distract him since he likes to nibble at her shoulder blades. She glances up at me once he starts to nuzzle into her fur.

"Young Timothy here is going to give the horses a break and pull me on his sled for a little while," I tell her. "Kade has asked for a harness so he can pull you. He says it's getting harder for you to shift." I slide my hand over her jaw. "Can I feel?"

Gaine nods, and Kade pokes her belly with his nose. *"Of course, Luna,"* she responds. Her eyes still follow my hands as they slide along her side.

Gaine's three months pregnant at the most, but her belly is bigger than it should be. As wolves, their bodies are not equipped to carry the weight and size of a fetus in human form, and their babies can't shift. Once a mother-to-be is between four and five months, they lose the ability to shift, so we typically just have them stop once they are four months along to avoid issues. I've never seen a belly as distended as Gaine's on my pregnant wolves.

"Does any of this hurt?" I ask, reaching under her belly to feel the other side.

"It doesn't hurt, but I'm pretty uncomfortable," she admits quietly. *"Please don't tell Kade."* She pokes my shoulder with her nose and stares with pleading eyes.

"Ok," I say, sighing. "You're bigger than we're used to, so I'd like you to find a place to shift, and we'll have Chase check you over. It might be best if you stop shifting now, though." I scratch Kade's chin when he snaps his head up, looking worried. "Just as a precaution, my shiny wolf. We want your wife to be comfortable and healthy, right?"

Without speaking, Kade slips under my arm until my hand rests on his shoulder. He hums as he nuzzles his wife, and his emotions begin flowing freely through my touch. This pregnancy seems terrifying for Kade. Giving him this time to support Gaine, I silently pull all of his fear for him.

Once Kade's empty, I scratch his shoulder. "Why don't you find a place for her to shift?" I suggest. "She can ride in the wagon while Anthony makes you a harness. Then you can join us with a sled."

Both wolves nuzzle my cheeks before bowing and leaving. Timothy has learned to stay quiet while I work with other wolves. He's looking up the next hill when I glance in his direction. I follow his gaze to see my father and Bastian silently sitting together, watching us.

"*Luna?*" Timothy slowly says, turning to look at me. "*Why are they watching us?*" The little wolf tucks his ears.

"I am the Luna, sweetheart," I tell him, holding my hand out for his chin. "Our Alphas know to give me the space I need to assist my wolves without interruptions." I smile and rub my hand over his jaw. "If I am helping a little wolf overcome something, having my large Alpha standing over us might not be the best thing to ease that fear, right?"

"*I suppose not,*" Timothy says, returning his gaze to the hill. "*But Tarq and Bastian aren't scary.*"

"Not to you," I say, turning to the sled. "You've spent a lot of time with us and even heard them both snore."

"*They're loud,*" he pouts. "*I don't sleep well when they lie with us.*"

"The Alphas won't sleep anywhere but with me, young wolf. They need to rest but won't when they are too far away to protect me at a moment's notice." I consider our current situation and look at Timothy as I sit on the sled. "Perhaps when they are keeping you awake, you could join the other children to sleep."

"*No, Luna,*" he says calmly. "*I'll get used to it.*"

Well, it was worth a shot.

"*Come here, my Alpha,*" I call out to Bastian. "*This little wolf is quite excited about the job he gave himself, but I think he'll need some help.*"

Having watched the scene from above, Bastian doesn't ask questions as he joins us. He inspects the harness with Anthony and nods at every strap the older man tells him to keep an eye on. I watched a movie with Daddy when I was little that had dogsleds. I'm sure it's still a thing, but there were special harnesses for them. This looks more like a horse's harness and could cause sores.

We end up waiting quite a while for Gaine to return from shifting.

Kade will typically have a prancing bounce to his step when he's compromised her time, but he jogs calmly to ensure there is room for her on the wagon with Grandma Pine and Trish. I lift my eyebrow toward Gaine as she passes.

"He wanted to talk to his kid," she whispers, giggling.

"Oh, that must have been interesting," I say, wrinkling my nose. "I wish I'd listened."

"Nah, Luna," Gaine whispers, smiling. "He needed that time alone with his thoughts."

I shake my head. "Why do you pretend not to understand his craziness?"

Gaine winks. "Life's a little more fun when he thinks he's mysterious."

* * *

With only half a day left, Timothy doesn't notice how often we stop to let him rest. It doesn't take long to wear him out, even with Bastian pushing against my lower back to help. Neala took a few of the older children hunting when we stopped the first time. She brought him a goose and barely got the feathers out of the way before he tore into it. The small hunting party is specifically hunting swine.

The snow on the ground becomes thin as we reach the top of a ridge near the end of the day. The gully before us isn't deep but does have a few clusters of trees that offered cover when the snow fell, so the ground under them is dry. Bastian spreads the guard along the ridge to secure the area and directs our pack into the gully while I kneel beside Timothy.

"Kade will be happy that you've tried out Anthony's harness first," I tell the little wolf. "He doesn't think much of being uncomfortable."

"It's fine, Luna," Timothy says, slightly out of breath. His new job might have convinced him to eat, but it also takes a lot out of him. He's eaten three times his average amount for a full day in just this half day of pulling me.

I loosen a few of his harness straps. One has worn a good bit of his coat away, and another has pink skin underneath where it slipped through his fur. I frown, upset that he wouldn't tell us about having issues.

"Luna, I need that to get you to the camp," Timothy says, attempting to stop me from pulling his harness off.

"I can walk that far, sweetheart," I tell him, lifting the harness over his head. He tries to move with his gear. "You've eaten well today. How are you feeling?" I ask to distract him.

Timothy's head drops as he tucks his ears. *"I'm hungry,"* he admits.

Smiling, I lift his chin and kiss his nose. "That's good," I say. "Neala reports finding a boar. She says it's quite large, and they are bringing you some."

The little wolf licks his lips. I have yet to get him to tell me his preferred meat, but he'll claim anything as his favorite in his hunger right now. Timothy lifts his leg as he's seen my Alpha do many times, allowing me to use it to pull myself up. His muzzle quickly slips into my hand as I drop it after looping his harness over my shoulder.

"Alright, sweet boy," I say, breathing deeply. "Let's find a good spot for the night while we wait for your feast."

"You'll be eating too, right, Luna?" Timothy asks, looking up as he steps forward.

"Of course, my little wolf," I say, smiling. "I would be happy to dine with you."

I pull the sled as Timothy carefully guides me toward the trees. He's been paying close attention to our routine. The little wolf weaves through the thickest group of trees in the middle of everyone and pulls me to the center tree, which has been left empty. My wolves have saved it for me and those who stay with me at night.

Timothy stops us at the tree's base. *"I'll get you a blanket, Luna,"* he offers.

"No, baby," I say, holding my hand out for his jaw as I sit. "Another will bring us some bedding. I would like you to stay here and help me keep warm."

I open my arms, and Timothy rolls his eyes with a sigh. My little wolf thinks he's too old for this, but he's so small that he fits on my lap.

I guide his hips to lie across my legs and lean back so he rests his head on my chest. His hum starts the moment he hears my heartbeat. I slip my fingers through his fur as he rubs his nose over my collarbone.

"I still think I'm too old for you to be holding, Luna," Timothy whines.

"You are my little wolf," I inform him. "I will hold you until you are my medium wolf." I giggle and squeeze him tightly. "With all this hard work, those days are numbered."

"Luna?" the little wolf starts timidly.

"Yeah, baby?" I lean my jaw on his muzzle.

"Will you be my mother?" he asks, nearly taking my breath away.

It's not often that my wolves can completely shock me. I wasn't expecting this question since we've already had a similar conversation. I do my best to look down to see his eyes. "Why would you want to replace your mom, sweetheart?"

Timothy doesn't answer right away. He slides his muzzle up until the bridge of his nose rests against my neck. *"Some of the other kids are talking about families taking them in,"* he says sadly. *"Can I stay with you? I don't want to live with anyone else."*

"Is that why you won't leave me?" I ask, rubbing my hand over his whiskers.

"I don't want another family, Luna," he whispers.

I wrap my arms around him again and squeeze tightly. I don't remember Mom getting overly attached to any other wolf besides Chase. She was close and caring with Bastian and Brock during her last winter with us, but I don't believe it was this bad. I had never considered Timothy or Creto living with anyone but me. From the moment a house was mentioned, I assumed there would be a room with bunk beds for them.

"You are my family, little wolf," I whisper, bumping his nose with my finger. "I will not be your mother. You already have one of those. However, I would like you and Creto to stay with me if that is what you want."

Timothy lifts his head enough to rub his whiskers over my cheek. *"I want to stay with you,"* he proclaims happily.

Smiling, I kiss him behind his whiskers. "You'll need to start being honest with me," I say sternly. "I've never imagined you living with anyone else, sweetheart. You could've been playing with your friends instead of hanging around me all the time."

"I like my job, Luna," Timothy tells me. *"I don't want to stop."*

"Ok, but you'll still need to take time to be a child," I order.

Timothy chuckles but doesn't respond. We stay cuddled as the others join us. Anthony builds a small fire while Bastian piles blankets beside me. Edith begins heating snow to boil meat from a goose that one of the wolves had caught for me. When Creto joins us, I lose my little heater.

"Creto! Did you hear?" Timothy rolls off me in his excitement. *"Luna said she wants us to stay with her!"*

I wrap a blanket around my back as Creto bounds happily toward me. He slides to a stop, crashing his chest against me and his neck across my face. He was already humming when he reached me. Joy radiates from him at an overwhelming level.

"Easy, honey," I say, giggling. "Don't break the Luna."

"I was so worried you'd send us away," Creto admits.

"Where would I send you?" I ask, shaking my head. "You kids are crazy. Just try to leave me. I dare you."

The boys giggle and nuzzle my cheeks.

"I see why that young one wanted to challenge us to a race," Neala says, laughing. She bows as she enters the dry area under our tree.

Bastian sits beside me with another blanket as Timothy bounds excitedly toward Neala. He jumps around and happily reports that he'll be living with me. He rubs his muzzle over hers, catching the scent of her meal. The little wolf begins feverishly licking her lips to make her open her mouth as his tail thumps into everything close to him.

Neala tries to lift her head away from him, but he steps on her shoulder to match her height. *"Wait, little one,"* she begs.

"Timothy, stop!" Bastian growls, trying to pull the blanket over my face.

I reach out for his chest to calm him before he hurts Timothy, but catch the series of events they were trying to protect me from. Neala leans down and throws up a pile of large chunks of meat. Timothy instantly drops to the ground and pulls at one of the slabs while Neala ejects a few more pieces.

"No, Timothy!" I shout with a shocked expression. "What are you doing?"

The little wolf steps back with his head low and ears back. He slips the meat from his mouth and casts his eyes in shame. *"Oh, Luna,"* he pleads. *"I'm hungry."*

Bastian cups my cheeks and gently pulls at me so I'll look at him, but my eyes stay narrowed on Timothy. I can see everyone around us looking at each other. My only thought is how disrespectful Timothy had been to Neala and me.

"Hey, Love," Bastian whispers. "Ease up on him. That's his dinner."

I snap my eyes in Bastian's direction. "What?"

"There's never been a reason for you to see that," he whispers, nodding toward the ashamed little wolf. "But that meat is for him. Neala carried it a long way so he could benefit from its fattiness." Bastian's expression is apologetic as he studies my eyes. "Why don't I explain while we let him eat? He seems pretty hungry."

I open and close my mouth a few times. Words attempt to come out but just collapse into random sounds until I simply sigh. Bastian pulls me against his chest and nods to the wolves. Timothy's eyes remain nervous as he slides his jaw along the ground until he can reach the piece of meat closest to him. He quickly grabs it and slinks behind Neala to hide while he eats it.

"I don't understand," I mumble, looking back at Bastian.

"I know, Love," Bastian whispers, kissing my forehead. "I'm sorry about that. We've never had a reason to carry meat very far to bring it to another wolf."

My stomach isn't happy about the sight, but I rest my ear on Bastian's chest as I turn to study the event before me. The ravenous little wolf has finished the first piece of meat. Neala moves a few more to her other side, allowing him to eat them while remaining hidden from me.

"At the lake, our hunting parties used wagons to transport the carcasses back to the meat lockers and storage bunkers," Bastian starts quietly, brushing my hair behind my ear. "Out here, we can't store food, and we don't have pockets or bags. The easiest way to bring meat back to the pack from far away is in our stomachs."

My Alpha knows me well and allows me to consider his words. Not only do I need to accept this wolf custom, but I also have to find a way to apologize to them for finding it offensive.

I look at the mix of faces around us. Daddy has been stepping back more each day and hasn't attempted to stop me. Grandma and Grandpa Bruce have joined us tonight but remain silent and observe us from afar. Even Edith and Anthony seem to have expected this behavior and patiently wait for me to accept it.

I glance back down at Neala. She's moved all but one chunk of meat to her far side for my little wolf. She bows her head and uses her nose to push the remaining piece toward me. I reach for her jaw. *"I'm sorry,"* I say privately to her. *"Thank you for bringing that back for him. I will try very hard not to offend you again."*

Neala rubs her muzzle over my hand. *"Luna, that's not an easy behavior to stomach,"* she says. The older wolf chuckles before adding, *"Forgive the pun."*

I giggle and scoop the last piece of pork off the ground. Once Timothy finishes his meat, Neala stands and re-exposes him to me. He hangs his head, seeing that I have the only piece of meat left. The little wolf licks his lips as he eyes me nervously.

"Come here, sweet boy," I whisper with a small smile. "I'm sorry. I didn't know."

Timothy has never heard me be cross and is understandably cautious as he crawls on his belly to me. His eyes stay on mine as he slides up beside me, but his nose is drawn to the meat in my hand. I relax my grip, giving the little wolf permission to take it.

I slip my fingers through his fur as he finishes off the last of his pork. *"Was this all that you could bring back?"* I ask Neala, who's still watching over us. *"It doesn't seem like he's close to being full."*

"*There is more coming, Luna,*" she assures me. "*Luckily, the other carrier is a bit slower. She's opinionated and probably would've had something to say about him being reprimanded.*"

I giggle, knowing who must be coming. "It would seem there is more on its way, little wolf," I tell Timothy as he licks my fingers, having finished the last chunk. "Do you forgive me for being cross with you?"

Timothy rises to sit before us and bows his head to Bastian before brushing his whiskers over my cheek. "*Luna, I will gladly explain any strange custom we have to you,*" he says quietly. "*After I've eaten, though.*"

Smiling, I scratch his chin and kiss his nose. "You got it, small one," I whisper. "In the meantime, maybe you'd like to share some of my meal while we wait for Myla."

"*She has a bigger stomach,*" Timothy announces happily, licking his lips. "*I'll have plenty to eat. You should eat your goose, Luna.*"

I shake my head at the young wolf. "I hope that's not the only compliment you have for someone who travels miles with food in her belly for you."

"*She's the most beautiful wolf I've ever seen, Luna,*" he tells me bashfully.

"That is very sweet, Timothy," I say, taking my plate of goose meat from Edith. "I'm sure that will change when you meet your mate, but I bet Myla would enjoy the compliment now."

Timothy ducks his head slightly, tipping his ears. "*She is my mate, Luna.*"

24

The stone wall is cold against my back, but I appreciate it blocking the wind as the sun sets. Brock and Bastian work together to bring me wood as I arrange branches in the middle of a circle of rocks. Someone had set this up in the past, but it hasn't been used in quite a while. Timothy remains close, trying to help me stay warm while I light the fire.

"I don't know how much further we'll be able to make it, Ayls," Brock admits, dropping a log directly into the pit. *"There are still too many of us underweight to keep moving north without shelter."*

Bastian joins us and nuzzles my cheek. *"And you are not a wolf,"* he needlessly reminds me. I shiver most of the day, only finding relief when I can tuck into someone's gut. *"Neither is our baby."*

"Ok, I get it," I tell them through chattering teeth. "Let's see what Grandpa has for us tonight and decide from there."

I've been discussing the weather with Daddy for the past few days. He's trying to find shelter options because stopping to build a house is not feasible. My Alpha and companion aren't interested in hearing that. They want results and don't care how it happens.

The sparks from my stones start a small flame in the grass beside the kindling. Timothy leans close to blow gently with his nose until the thin wood catches fire. He gives me one log at a time to place in the pit until we have a good-sized fire. We relax together and soak in the heat.

"How are you doing, my little wolf?" I ask as Timothy curls beside me with his head on my lap.

"It's pretty cold, Luna," he responds, watching the flames. *"And I miss Creto."*

Anthony made Kade a harness to pull Gaine on her own sled, which left a hole in my guard unit. Brock has been training Creto to fill the opening. It's not a dangerous position, and he does stay close to me, but he's still too far to play with the other kids.

"We will find a place to settle for the winter soon, sweetheart," I say. "I'm worried about everyone in the cold right now." I slide my fingers through his fur and borrow some of his warmth while the flames warm my feet and legs.

"Do you know where we are?" Timothy asks, turning to me.

I cringe and wrinkle my nose. "No, baby," I admit. "I only know we've been moving northwest. Maybe we'll run into someone eventually who knows."

"What if they don't like us?" he asks fearfully.

We've traveled for months now without seeing a single person. While that does seem strange, it would appear that everyone was right about the mountains. They truly have been heaven for my wolves. There has been bountiful hunting, and we often stop because someone has taken down large game.

Meals are frequently brought to Timothy, and he is slowly filling out. Anthony complains daily about needing to adjust the little wolf's harness, but I've caught him pushing against places the straps don't touch and know he's checking the same muscles I do. These wolves are our life, and the little ones are our future. We all know that.

I look down at Timothy's nervous eyes. *Well, everyone but the kids.*

"Who wouldn't love a little wolf like you?" I ask, smiling.

Timothy places his chin in my hand. *"Humans,"* he mumbles.

I scowl. "We'll just have to meet some more good ones then," I tell him, winking.

We fall into our customary silence as a few more campfires spring to life around us. I was able to take the Alphas to a private area for the last full moon, but the weather has made that impossible this month. There is at least a foot of snow on the ground, and my wolves have disappeared in drifts that towered well over their heads. The kids thought it was funny, but it's dangerous as the temperature drops for the night.

My wolves will stay along the same rock wall within sight, so I know they are safe tonight. Everyone has been told to maintain their distance while Grandpa visits. I long for when anyone was welcome to spend time with us and get to know him, but I need his guidance, and Daddy doesn't want the pack to worry.

Timothy's jaw slides across my lap, and I turn in the same direction to see Myla approaching. Gaine tries to follow her, but Kade is in his human form and doting on his wife in adorable ways. He's holding a blanket around her and tucking into her neck. I can't tell what he's doing from here, but whatever it is makes her giggle.

"Good evening, Luna," Myla says, bowing to me before joining Timothy. Her behavior changed drastically in my presence after she was granted permission to stay with us at night. Since her mate is so young, their pull is different from what an adult feels. They desire each other's company and still snuggle, but none of the hormones that create the need to bond are present.

"Hello, Myla," I say, smiling. "How was your day?"

"It has been busy, Luna," she admits. Kade has been sending her to do all his work and deliver any messages he can think of. He can talk to anyone he wants but ignores everyone who tries to speak to him except Myla and my guards. He believes everyone will eventually leave him alone, which creates busy days for Myla.

"Kade sent you to get Chase?" I ask, knowing the answer. Kade had argued with me about the importance of this errand, and now that she's returned, I'm inclined to agree with him.

"Why wouldn't he just let you call for him?" she whines.

"I don't like that you're questioning your mentor, but I can understand why," I start, raising my eyebrow. "How long did it take you to reach Chase?"

"Six hours," Myla admits. *"Would it be alright if I give Timothy his meat?"*

"Of course, sweet girl," I answer, scratching her chin.

She opens her mouth, and Timothy helps to trigger the regurgitation that provides him with the meal she'd brought.

"I heard the trip back was much faster," I continue and smile when Myla giggles. "Sending you away from the bulk of the pack gave you access to many meals you would have missed out on staying so close to us. What did you find?"

Myla turns from me to Kade as he sits with Gaine on my other side. *"There were a few marmots,"* she starts, lying with her jaw across Timothy's shoulders. *"Then I found sheep with some of the biggest horns I've ever seen."*

"Like bulls?" I ask, furrowing my brow.

"No, they curled up on the side of their head," Myla tells me. *"They are quite delicious, too. You should try some, Luna."* She licks her lips, thinking about the meal. *"But this meat is from the elk Chase helped me take down."* Myla's nose pokes the last chunk of Timothy's meal.

"So, by sending you so far away, Kade was helping to take care of two of you," I say, sliding my hands over their heads. "Elk is a good meat for both of you. It's rich and fatty. I'm not familiar with marmot, though."

"There was a porcupine near the trail a while back," Brock says as he joins us. *"The kids listened and didn't touch it, but it smelled good. It was waving those quills like a flag."*

I giggle at the thought of them trailing it, trying to get a good sniff. "I'm sorry I missed that."

"Luna should've warned us how damn funny looking they are," Bastian adds. He sits beside me and leans over my legs to watch Timothy eat his final piece of elk meat. *"What did he have for dinner?"*

Kissing Bastian behind his whiskers, I move him aside to pull Grandpa's medallion from my neck. "Myla and Chase took down an elk before they came back," I tell him. "Chase will be doing a baby check in the morning, so make sure you don't take off too early."

Bastian lies beside me and rubs his nose against the layers of clothing covering my belly. I hand Kade the medallion before pulling up my shirt and coat to give Bastian access to my skin. He's told me countless times that he doesn't think our child can hear him unless he's touching me. I highly doubt that's why he needs to be against me when I feel his tongue gently slide over my skin.

"*He looks busy,*" Daddy grumbles.

I look up to spot him approaching with Chase. "I like seeing you two together again," I confess. Holding my hand out, I wait for his chin and kiss his nose when he gives it to me. "I love you, Daddy. Your happiness is important to me."

My father nuzzles my cheek. "*I know, kiddo,*" he responds quietly. "*I didn't know how to forgive him, but it turns out I didn't need to. Like the rest of us, he was doing as your mother wished. I might want to be mad at her, but I miss her too much for that.*"

"Mom's never far, Daddy," I whisper. "She told me that she disturbs the natural elements, so I imagine it's her every time a flock of birds takes off or a hawk cries out."

"*It would be great if she'd disturb a duck over this way,*" Daddy suggests.

"It's a little cold for that, but I'm sure she will as soon as she can," I say, giggling. I lean back and slide my hands over all four wolves around me. "We need to find a place to winter, Daddy. I want to talk to Grandpa about it, but I plan to send scouts to look for shelter. We can't continue to move north without a destination in sight."

"*I agree,*" my father says thoughtfully. "*We'll start with gathering any input from your grandfather and form a plan from there. The hunting has been great, even with the weather. The kids look good, and your guards are quite thick.*" He pokes Bastian with his nose. "*I'd like to see a little more on this one.*"

I tug Bastian's fur and scratch his jaw. "He's been busy," I say, defending him. "He'll get there."

"*If we make peach syrup, he'd eat whatever we put it on,*" Daddy grumbles, nipping my Alpha's ear.

Forgetting his place, Bastian snarls and whips his head around to snap at my father. I catch his face and blast him full of heat. Bastian's head falls limp in my hands, and Daddy eyes him as I roll him back to lie across my lap.

"Daddy," I start, irritated. "If you're gonna involve him in your grumpiness, let him hear you. You know he's sensitive."

"You were too when Darya was cooking little Luna," Grandpa says, appearing on the opposite side of the fire. *"Give the kid a break."*

I smile and hold my hand out, beckoning him to me. "Hi, Grandpa," I gush. My grandfather brings a sense of peaceful calmness that I've needed recently.

He walks around the fire, acknowledging each wolf in his customary way, including shoving Kade over and chuckling to himself about it. His muzzle slides over Chase's and then Daddy's before straining to reach me.

"Let me in there, son," Grandpa says. *"My granddaughter needs me tonight."* When Daddy moves, Grandpa's nose rubs over my cheek, catching a tear I didn't know was there. *"I'm here, little Luna. Whatever it is, we can figure it out."*

I hold his muzzle to my cheek while I attempt to organize my thoughts. I've been relying on my father's knowledge for so long that I'm unsure how to handle these situations where neither of us knows what we're doing. Grandma and Grandpa Bruce have been this far west, but it was during the summer. I know my grandfather has never been out here, but I'm hopeful he has some guidance either from my mother or his Luna.

"Grandpa, do you have any idea where we are?" I ask, choosing to cut everyone but Daddy from our conversation.

"I don't, kiddo," Grandpa answers, tucking his hips under him to lie as close as possible to Bastian. *"It's pretty cold, though."* He drapes his head over my Alpha's ribs so I can rub his ears between my fingers.

"We need to find shelter soon, Dad," my father says. *"We have a few wolves that won't make it much further up the trail in this cold."*

"How's that old wolf that ran the orphanage doing?" Grandpa asks. *"Darya said she was good to the kids in the south."*

Nodding, I smile slightly. *"She was,"* I agree. *"Her name is Rosalinda, and she's hanging in there. The kids like piling up in the sleigh with her. They call it a 'dog pile.'"*

The wagon became too hard to pull through the snow, so Anthony and Daddy worked together to turn it into a sleigh. Anthony and Edith have parked it next to the fire just up the trail. Grandma Pine has been their permanent passenger, and many kids pile in there with her at night to keep her warm.

Grandpa scoffs. *"You need to put a stop to that."*

"What? Why?" I ask, frowning. *"She likes having them all with her. She says that if she dies at night, she will be surrounded by the wolves who mean the most to her."*

"No, Ayls," Grandpa says, sighing. *"The 'dog pile.' They shouldn't be calling themselves dogs."*

"Oh, Grandpa," I start. I shake my head, unsure how to explain the kids' dialect. They are so young that they don't know how to be rude to each other. It's simply a term they'd heard Anthony say when he saw it for the first time, and it sounded fun. I smile, realizing I've just figured it out. *"It's Anthony's fault."*

"Hmm," Grandpa grumbles. *"That explains a lot."*

Daddy chuckles and pushes my hand with his nose. "Enough," he says, shaking his head. *"Do you have any advice for us, Dad? Has Dar been watching? Does she have anything?"*

"Will you both please understand that we can't see the future," Grandpa says sharply. *"I can offer you advice. I can give suggestions but can't walk ahead of you on the trail and find a destination for you. That's not how it works. This is your journey, not mine."*

I look down at Bastian, regretting blasting so much of my heat into him. I'm unsure when the kids dozed off, but they are both sound asleep on my other side. *"I'm sorry, Grandpa,"* I say quietly, wanting to hug him and ask for his forgiveness. *"I didn't mean to put so much on you. I think we're all just scared."*

"Of course you are, sweetheart," he replies, relaxing against Bastian. *"The world turned upside down for all of you just a few months ago. You battled the heat and drought to travel to a place of freedom and prosperity only to find yourselves stuck in a winter you could not have prepared for."*

"Do you have any advice?" I ask, hoping he has anything for us.

Grandpa's eyes narrow in thought. *"There used to be cliff dwellers long ago..."* he starts.

"Dad, we don't have time to build a house. You can't expect us to burrow into a cliff," Daddy grumbles, annoyed.

Grandpa lifts his head. *"He's getting a bit worse, huh?"* he asks, leaving his eyes on my father. *"You'll have to help him soon if he doesn't start sleeping."*

"I will, but he does have a point, Grandpa," I say.

"I remember reading about whole civilizations, but the early ranchers out here took a page from that book," my grandfather continues, ignoring our confusion. *"They carved large rooms into the side of these cliff walls for grain and food storage."* He turns back to lay his jaw over Bastian. *"It was easier to keep the wildlife out."*

"Like our bunkers, but with stone walls," I say slowly. *"There might be some around here?"*

"Yeah, maybe," Grandpa says. *"It's something to look for anyway. That storage might still exist even if a house is long gone."*

"It's something," I say, sighing. *"I'm sending out scouts starting tomorrow."*

Grandpa rocks Bastian with his jaw. *"How hard did you blast him?"*

I click my tongue. *"He needed a moment,"* I tell him.

My grandfather chuckles and rolls to push Daddy with his paw. *"I enjoy knowing you're suffering like I did with you."*

I giggle as Daddy pushes him back. Sometimes, I miss the old days when I could compromise Grandpa's time while my father played ball and harassed Uncle Miles for wanting to spend all his time with Mom. These days, I let Daddy reminisce with my grandfather more. It seems to lighten his heart when they talk about the old adventures. Grandpa always has a story that Mom tells him to mention so Daddy will talk about it.

We have time for it tonight, and I'm excited to hear my grandfather bring up the Christmas he spent with us. Although Grandpa was there for the end of the day, the daylight hours were entertaining, to say the least. I slip my fingers through Bastian's fur, hoping he'll wake up to hear Daddy's version of the story since I've already told him the truth.

"*She was not my daughter that day,*" Daddy grumbles, rolling onto his side as if he's going to sleep.

"I am your daughter every day, Father Dear," I spout sarcastically. "You should've stayed away from the tree."

On Christmas morning, our house was a free-for-all. Daddy would jump over the balcony to beat me to the tree and sit on my presents while he opened his. He never cared about what he got, nor did he ask for anything. It was just something we did together that became normal, and it was always fun.

The year Mom wants Dad to tell Grandpa about was very different. Chase had woken me up early, and I stood before the tree, blocking Daddy from getting near it. When he started getting pushy, I nocked my arrow and aimed it at him all day. I was stiff when Grandpa made it to the house, but it was worth it.

"*Woman, no,*" Daddy states. "*My daughter wanted me to have my presents. I don't know who that was shooting arrows at me all day.*"

Spit flies from my mouth as there is no time to swallow before my laughter bursts out. Timothy is used to us staying up to talk, and with a full belly, he's still deep asleep. But Myla isn't used to us, so she wakes, shaking her head to become more alert. I reach for her jaw and put my finger to my lips so she doesn't interrupt my father and his fun.

"*So, I woke up as I always do on Christmas morning—a loving, caring father,*" Daddy says whimsically. "*I delicately knocked on my ungrateful daughter's door and gently woke her with a kiss on the forehead.*"

"Daddy!" I shout, waking everyone else up. "I wasn't even in my bed!" Even Bastian stirs as I shake with laughter.

"*I know you weren't,*" Daddy scoffs. "*My sweet daughter was. You were some kind of demon who didn't deserve Christmas presents.*" My father shifts around so that he appears more serious. "*As I was saying... Gently and stuff. I slowly walked down the stairs to my loving wife. You remember her, of course. The beautiful and perfect Luna.*"

Bastian blows out his lips. "*What is your father talking about?*"

"Shh," I say privately to him. "*You'll recognize part of the story soon.*"

Having been sufficiently woken up by now, the kids inch their heads toward my lap to nuzzle my Alpha and receive their customary lick to the cheek before bed. My father has gone off on a tangent about how joyful the previous Christmases had been and that he doesn't understand what happened to his sweet daughter on this particular occasion. I shake my head when Timothy looks at me with a confused expression. Daddy might be trying to contain the conversation to just family, but I can include whoever I want.

"So, imagine my confusion as I stood braced for a day of love and family, but instead, faced an angry little elf with a bow and arrow," my father continues, getting on track. *"That angry elf yelled and threatened me throughout the day. She even poisoned my family into laughing and pointing maliciously at me as I clung dearly to the thought of happiness and joy."*

The kids look more confused with every word, but Bastian just rolls his eyes. *"Even if I hadn't heard the real story, I'd know this wasn't true,"* he says, chuckling.

Daddy quickly checks to be sure we're still paying attention before continuing. *"I asked and begged repeatedly for my presents and if the demon would return my sweet daughter,"* he says, sounding quite somber. *"My requests were denied. I cried multiple times but to no avail. Eventually, I was shot by many arrows and forced to endure a day of wounds and sorrow."*

"Prove it," I challenge him.

"Oh, I have scars, little girl," Daddy boasts. *"Are you interested in signing them?"*

"Daddy, I have never shot you," I say, lifting my eyebrow. "However, please remember that there is a first time for everything."

"You see?" Daddy asks, looking around at the group as he notices all the wolves looking at him. *"Everyone in this family shoots me. I'm a pincushion for their arrows."*

"Oh, stop," Grandpa grumbles. *"Every month, it's the same thing. Poor little Tarq."*

"You shot me the most, Dad," my father retorts, lying back down. *"I don't think this is a conversation that will prove your innocence."*

I leave them to their bickering. From what I've been told, this was how they spent most of their time when Grandpa was alive. Daddy's full of strange stories about how he was terribly innocent of all wrong-doing. He's one of the best storytellers I've ever heard.

I look down at my Alpha and the kids. "You should get some sleep," I tell them. "We have some long days ahead of us while we look for shelter."

"The northern guard found a trail marked by a buffalo herd," Bastian reports. *"We need to ask if anyone knows how to cure the hides. Edith could make clothes, and we need more blankets."*

"Agreed," I whisper, working my fingers through their fur. "Is Creto in the sleigh tonight?"

"Nah," Bastian responds. *"He asked to stay with Brock. They'll head out to help track the herd in the morning."*

"I don't want him going," I say, shaking my head. "I know he's excited to help, but he's ten. My answer's no."

"I don't remember anyone asking permission," Bastian says, lifting his head.

"Brock," I call out to my companion and await his response.

"What, Ayls?" Brock grumbles sleepily.

"That boy is not leaving my detail," I state plainly.

"Alright," he answers.

"Bastian, I know I can't protect them like we did at the lake, but we can't forget that these children have no training," I caution him. "The last strangers we encountered kidnapped and caged him. This fire pit proves that we are not alone out here. Let's ensure our children are not the first to encounter who we share this land with."

"Ok, you're right," Bastian agrees. *"They are itching to learn new things."*

"So, why don't you teach them some of your tracking and hunting skills closer to the pack?" I suggest. "You're still the best hunter, and I would love for the children to learn from you."

"Sure, Ayls," he says. *"I'll take him out with me tomorrow. We'll see about finding you some turkey."*

"That would be nice," I say, smiling. "Rest, my Alpha. Grandpa will leave soon, and I have a few more questions."

Bastian slips his tongue over my fingers as his eyes droop. He's never been one to stay up all night for the full moon. He works hard during the day and knows Daddy will watch over me while he sleeps. Kade throws more logs on the fire and lies down with his wife. I haven't slept in Bastian's arms in a long time. It's hard not to feel jealous.

"Hey, kiddo," Grandpa says, recapturing my attention. *"Aylee had some advice for you. She said your historian needs to shift."*

"River?" I ask. *"The crazy one, right?"*

"Isn't that the only one you have?" Grandpa tilts his head.

"Well, her father is with us, but yeah, it's just her," I answer, confused.

"Aylee says if she shifts, that should reset the information and give her control over it," Grandpa explains. *"That way, she'll be able to give you what you need instead of all the crap you don't."*

"I'm not gonna lie, that would be great," I say, sighing. *"How do I get her to shift?"*

Grandpa stands and allows Daddy to take his place beside Bastian. *"You and your mom have both been gentle with these wolves,"* he starts in a tone that warns me he's about to say something I won't like. *"This is too important. You need to order her to shift."*

I open my mouth to protest, but Grandpa disappears before I can. I hate not saying goodbye to him. His hugs remind me of easier times. Daddy rubs his muzzle over my hand until I look down at him.

"We'll figure it out, sweetheart," he promises.

I slide my fingers over his whiskers. "I like your stories, Daddy," I whisper.

"Me too, kiddo," he responds, laying his chin in my hand. *"I just wish some of them were true."*

25

Leaning against a tall pine, I listen to the breeze whistling through the dried grass. We've finally had a break in the weather. The snow has melted except for the higher drifts, and my wolves are having an easier time moving across the land. After a week, we are still searching for long-term shelter but found a collapsed rock wall dwelling two days ago.

"You feeling alright?" Brock asks, slipping his head under my hand.

Taking a deep breath, I look down at him. "I am," I say, smiling. "Everyone is healthy today, the kids are happily playing and hunting, the weather is beautiful, and I am surrounded by wolves I love with all my heart."

"Hmm," Brock starts thoughtfully. *"You do have quite the charmed life, don't you?"*

"I do," I whisper with a sigh.

"So, Gaine's having twins, huh?" Brock asks as the kids noisily play nearby.

"Chase says he heard two heartbeats," I reply, nodding. "It's taking the whole pack to raise these orphans. I can only imagine the work that goes into twins."

"I bet Kade is a damn mess," Brock remarks before looking up at me. *"Have there ever been twins born to a wolf?"*

I roll my eyes, scowling. "I don't know," I grumble. "I have a useless historian."

I watch Timothy and Myla run past and listen to their laughter.

He's grown an inch or two since we cleared the ticks out of his mouth, but more notably, his bones are all filled in and protected. Myla is still giving him half of her food, so she isn't as dense, but I understand her desire to help her mate build his body back to where it should be.

Creto is never far behind them when Brock lets him leave his post. Since he's still very young, he only stands a quarter of the watch rotation. Creto has also been hunting with Brock, so he's thick and easily dominates his playmates. The young wolf is arguably one of the best big brothers because he always lets Timothy win once he's ensured the smaller wolf has had ample exercise.

"Have you eaten?" I ask Brock, scratching his jaw.

"*Of course,*" he answers. "*I think we'll see what an overweight wolf looks like soon.*"

I tilt my head, lifting my eyebrow. "Has that ever happened?"

"*I don't think so,*" Brock says. "*We are in uncharted territory, so we're about to have a lot of firsts.*"

"Actually, before the Luna line of succession was broken, this is where the wolves lived," I tell him. "Grandpa told me at the wedding. He said they only left when the succession broke, and they used distance to protect themselves from the pack wars. So, in a way, we're coming home."

"*Well, we've enjoyed the homecoming feast,*" Brock remarks, chuckling. "*Just wish we had warmer weather.*"

Smiling, I look at my happy wolves again before pushing off the tree. "We did hot," I remind him. "You were all hungry. I'm fine with cold as long as I get to look at your healthy bodies."

"*Just don't stare at my butt,*" Brock says. "*Rachel might have an opinion.*"

I lift my eyebrow as I look down at Brock. After all these years, I still struggle to tell if he's joking most of the time. I'm never really sure if I'm supposed to laugh, and I usually just hope I don't offend him when I do. I want to laugh today but feel more compelled to thank him.

"*What's up, Ayls?*" Brock asks as I kneel.

I stretch my arms out to him and smile. "I owe you so much," I whisper as he slides into my embrace. "You have been solid in this bending world. You didn't have to take this on. You accepted the offer to be my companion, knowing how hard it would be and how much work you'd be taking on for the rest of your life. I love you."

Brock's jaw slides down my back. *"I love you too, Ayls."*

Closing my eyes, I rub my face into the fur on his neck. His words are nice, but I'm more comforted by the happiness emitting from him. Brock is an easy-going wolf but doesn't handle stress well. This happiness means he isn't bothered by our current circumstances. My wolves know they can survive anything when they have access to food.

I rub his shoulders and slide my hands down his legs. "Come on," I tell him, smiling. "Let's get everyone moving. I'm sure the horses have rested enough by now."

* * *

Although we are moving slowly from the lack of snow to slide the sleigh over, Daddy has us following the buffalo herd my guards were tracking. He says since they are native to the area, they will know where to find shelter from storms and food for grazing. When I mentioned that we don't eat grass, he reminded me that our prey does.

Humans have taught me many ways to hate and die, but my wolves have taught me how to love and live. My father has been my most supportive instructor. It's comforting to know that I will always have access to him, even after he decides to leave us. As my grandfather always says, he'll be just a full moon away.

Brock stays in my hand as we move forward. His guidance allows me to tune out my surroundings and focus on my wolves' voices as they talk to each other. Searching through the personal conversations, I hear my guards calling out their positions and findings. Chase and Daddy are goofing off toward the front, but Matthew sounds worried in the rear. He moves his unit closer to the pack and announces to them that he's leaving to talk to me.

"What's Matthew worried about?" I ask, looking down at Brock.

"I don't know," Brock answers. *"That unit has been asking him to go back there for a few days."*

"Weird," I mutter. "Should we call for Bastian?"

"*Yeah, I'll do it,*" Brock offers. "*He panics less when I ask for him.*"

I smile, knowing he's right. Bastian has gotten better over the years when he's closer to me, but he's monitoring the scouting wolves out front while my father and Chase play. He has always been the master of stealth. Bastian tracks and monitors the groups we feel need the most supervision without them detecting him.

I listen to the wolves in the rear while we wait for everyone to reach us. Nothing seems out of the ordinary with them. They discuss different scents, and one mentions footsteps, but then the conversation turns to playing ball. There has been growing excitement that they will be able to play again soon with all this prey and water available to them.

I shake my head. "You'd think they'd be exhausted by this constant movement," I say, rolling my eyes.

"*Not even a little bit, Ayls,*" Brock informs me. "*You put energy in, and we'll have to let it out. And I'm not gonna lie, I'm pretty excited about being able to play again.*"

He was having a separate conversation with Ash, but they were discussing the same thing. Brock has been on "Team Ash" for as long as I can remember. They work hard to beat Daddy and Bastian but haven't accomplished it yet. I'm glad they still have fun trying.

"*Luna, can we have a word?*" Matthew asks.

I stop Brock and turn to see the head guard and his second approaching us. Drake has relaxed a bit after the long months on the trail but still seems nervous. Brock turns as I kneel to the pair.

"Of course you can," I tell my guard. "You seem like something's bothering you." I reach my hand out for his chin. "What's on your mind?"

Matthew settles into my hand and hums, so Drake answers for him. "*We think someone's following us, Luna.*"

My hand accidentally clamps down on Matthew's jaw. "*Ow, Luna,*" he grumbles.

"I'm sorry, Matthew," I say quickly. "What do you mean, you 'think someone's following us?' How do you not know?"

My wolves have an unrivaled sense of smell. If something is out there, they know about it long before I do. Even their hearing has no comparison. Nothing gets past my guards, especially now that they are on high alert.

"*It has to be a wolf, Luna,*" Drake continues. "*We can smell them, but their scent is blending in with ours.*"

"*I didn't hear anyone, and I scouted behind the entire unit,*" Matthew adds. "*I could smell whoever it was but couldn't find them.*"

I sit back on my heels and consider the information. "Pull your unit in," I order Matthew. "You take over running point for my father. Drake, take my companion back there with you." I turn to Brock. "Stay together. I don't want you traveling alone." I rub my hand over his jaw. "Be careful."

"*Of course, Ayls,*" Brock promises, nuzzling my cheek.

I look at the three wolves and chew on my lip. Bastian hasn't made it here yet. He's not in a rush since Brock didn't make his message sound important. "*Daddy, Bastian, I'm not in danger, but I need you,*" I call out to them, hoping neither comes tearing in, trying to kill anyone. "*Chase, I'm sending Matthew to you.*" I catch the head guard's muzzle before he can leave. "Do you have any guesses?"

"*Luna, my only guess is that it's a wolf,*" Matthew answers. "*I refuse to believe anything else could be that cunning.*"

Breathing out a laugh, I smile at him. "I suppose you're right," I whisper. "You are quite superior." I pull his nose to my lips and can nearly see him blush in my mind as he pulls back. "Chase is waiting for you. I know he's been gone for a while, but he was the head of my mother's guard detail, which deserves respect."

"*Absolutely, Luna,*" he says, bowing. "*We'll find the herd.*"

Nodding, I turn to Drake and reach out for his chin. "When this is all done, and we've found a place to settle, I'd like you to spend some time under Kade," I tell him. "You have many skills that could be finely tuned by that silver wolf. I want to see what he can do with you."

Drake tilts his head. "*I'm not sure I know what you mean, Luna.*"

"You found a place for me and my Alpha when we needed time away before the wedding," I start. "You found the fishing lake for my father and his companion. And now you've tracked the untraceable. Kade won't leave Gaine right now, so I'll need you to keep doing what you're doing. But this time, you'll take Brock with you. He can silently flank you. Let's see what you find."

"What are you playing at?" Drake is as skeptical as he is curious.

"We have no outstanding wolves," I tell him. "We weren't followed here. If this is a wolf, they are a mountain wolf. Maybe there's an entire pack that can help us."

Brock's ears prick forward. *"You're keeping this from the Alphas?"*

"Yes," I answer. "They are high-strung as it is. We do not need them to panic over nothing if I'm wrong."

"I'm not happy about this," Brock grumbles.

"I know you're not, but let's keep them blissfully ignorant for now." I scratch his jaw in a place that always itches.

"I hate you," he says, letting me hear his frown.

"No, you don't," I reply, laughing.

Brock stares at me for a moment before sliding his incredibly wet tongue over my face. *"Yes, I do."* He backs away from me before I can swat at him. *"Come on, kid. Let's go catch your phantom."*

Drake watches Brock turn away from us and begin walking in the direction the guard had come from. *"I don't..."* he starts, sounding confused. *"Luna? Should I bite him?"*

"Oh, sweet wolf," I gush. "Brock is my closest friend. He has liberties no other wolf would dare to enjoy. But if you want to bite him, you can. Just tell him I gave you permission." I pull the fur on his neck with a wink.

Bastian charges out of the trees as I stand, sliding to a stop and eyeing Drake. *"What's wrong?"*

"Why does something have to be wrong?" I ask, reaching for his chin. "Can't I just want to spend time with you?"

"No," he answers. Bastian sits before me and nods to Drake. *"Weren't you leaving?"*

I click my tongue at him. "Bastian, try not to be rude," I scold, narrowing my eyes quizzically. "I'll be alright now, Drake."

The confused guard keeps his eyes on Bastian as he walks away. *"As you wish, Luna."*

Turning to walk in the opposite direction, I reach my hand out to my side. My fingers curl around Bastian's jaw as they find their happy place. "What's going on with you, my Alpha? You're getting quite sharp with our wolves lately."

He even snapped at Myla for waking Timothy last night. Bastian is not usually an angry wolf, and he's never been one to yell at the children. I was especially baffled by his timing since she needed to wake the little wolf to eat the dinner she'd brought.

"I have not," Bastian grumbles.

"You need to talk to him," Daddy says, stepping out of the woods beside us. *"He's clouded."*

That's Alpha code. I'd heard Chase say it a few times to my mother when my father acted particularly goofy. She took him somewhere private, and he was much calmer when he returned. I've known about bonds since I was a little girl, so it was normal to hear my mother yell when her nerves were set off. She apologized that I had to listen to it and said I would understand one day why it is impossible to stay quiet when it happens. She was right.

Frowning, I look down at Bastian. My nerves don't react to him when he's a wolf, but my chest still aches for him when he's away. As a wolf, his needs are muted but not gone. I wish I understood the cravings better. Perhaps when things slow down, he'll talk to me about them.

Daddy slips his muzzle into my left hand. *"It's alright, kiddo,"* he says soothingly. *"He'll learn that he's not stronger than this. Being an Alpha is hard. Your mother was my favorite part of the job, but you were a close second. Go remind him it's not all work."*

"Thank you, Daddy," I say, smiling down at him. *"I'm not sure I could've done this without you. I want you to know that I appreciate everything you've done."*

"I know, kiddo," he responds, rubbing his head on my hip. *"I got this. Go on."*

I turn my gaze to Bastian as my father slips from my hand. *"Let's take a walk, Love."* I stick my fingers into his mouth to help him settle as I turn him to the right and push him into the trees. I pull my fingers away once we're alone. "Bass, I know you're struggling. I wish you'd talk to me about it."

Bastian shifts into my arms. "I will never struggle a day as long as I know you're safe." He's made a point not to shift for a while, so his nerves' pull against mine is overwhelming. "You are my everything and carry a piece of perfection in your belly." His breath moves in hot waves over my skin.

I know we need to find a balance, but something about Bastian's need for me drives me crazy. My Alpha presses against me, causing me to step back until a tree blocks my path. I know better than to touch Bastian before he calms himself, so I reach back and hold the tree. My eyes close, and the quietest groan slips out when my Alpha's tongue tastes my lower lip. I stick it out for him, and he takes it gently between his teeth.

Bastian presses his body against mine as he moves on to taste my tongue and settles himself enough that I can move without triggering him. His hands stay cupped over my cheeks, giving me free access to run my fingers over his skin. It might be loud, but I love his hum. It's a sign of many things, but for Bastian, it's a sign of love and comfort. His fingers grip the back of my jaw when he's fully in control.

I curl into him, sliding my hands over his back, carefully avoiding the deeper scars. Bastian pushes my jacket from my shoulders and lets it fall to the ground. His fingers light my nerves along my waistband as he pulls my shirt loose before lifting it over my head. Leaning back, my Alpha slowly rubs his hand over my stomach. Our daughter only flutters when he touches my belly. They clearly already have a connection.

I reach for Bastian's cheek and hold the stray hairs back. "She loves you very much, my Alpha," I whisper. Bastian's smile could brighten the darkest nights, but I don't get to see it very often these days. I grin as his lips curl and his eyes meet mine. "You are everything to us too."

Bastian struggles to talk when he's emotional. I've learned not to urge him to try. I loosen my belt and let him push my pants out of our way.

Heating slightly, Bastian lifts me to him and releases a throaty sigh as he reacquaints himself with my body. As a wolf, he prefers to taste my skin, but in human form, he enjoys rubbing his lips over me. Every nerve near his mouth is excited by the attention it receives. Bastian's lips tickle my skin, his breath sends waves of hot and cold, and he leaves a feeling of wanting behind.

I close my eyes and relax into my Alpha's enjoyment of my body. Now that he's learned a few ways to control himself, his touch is sweet and gentle, giving me the same attention he's receiving. Bastian's teeth graze the edge of my ear before he leans his cheek against mine and exhales as he drags his lip over my skin. My hands slide over his arms, reaching for the back of his shoulders.

Bastian pushes against me to rock my hips and claims my lips as he ignites the rest of our nerves. Although I have to fight not to bite his tongue, this is the only way he's been able to mute my screams as he triggers my body's celebration of his release. The deepest nerves are the most sensitive, and there is no holding back the flood of air that noisily leaves my lungs.

When Bastian finally slows, he braces me against the tree that had stopped my retreat and tickles my thighs with his fingertips. I drape my arms around him and lay my cheek on his shoulder. I enjoy how calm he is after he has me. Grandpa Bruce told me a long time ago that Bastian was very emotional. Daddy says he's high-strung. But when I see him like this, I feel he just needs to be reminded of how much I love him more often.

With Bastian's body heating us, we stay together for a while, simply enjoying the moment. I keep as much of my skin against him as possible but still appreciate the extra heat when he lays his hands flat on my thighs. Pressing my face against his neck, I take a deep breath of his perfect scent.

"I love you," I whisper.

Bastian sighs and pulls away to look down at me. "I love you too," he says before kissing my forehead. "Are you warm enough?"

"I'm fine, Bass," I assure him. "Can we just stay here for a little longer? We keep forgetting that we're important too, and I want to spend some time with you." I curl some of his hair around my finger and tug it.

Bastian slides his hands over my legs. "Neala used to cut my hair at the lake," he says, leaning back against me. "Maybe she could teach you. It's getting long again."

Smiling, I lift off his shoulder to look into his eyes. "That would be nice," I say. "I like doing things with you." Missing Bastian has become an irritating pastime. I would happily work on his hair until he deemed it perfect if it meant I could spend more time with him. I hate to admit that I've grown accustomed to the ache in my chest his absence creates.

"You only have to ask for me, Love," Bastian whispers. "I will always come to you."

When my Alpha rubs his cheek against mine, I catch movement behind him. So that I don't alert him, I slide my arms around Bastian's back and run my fingers up his neck to lace them in his hair. He settles calmly into my embrace without noticing my attention has shifted. His nerves have relaxed their pull on me, so my wolves' voices have started to filter back in. I search for the voice of the wolf just inside the tree line.

"This is who was following us," Brock tells me, nodding toward the wolf beside him. *"She'd like to speak with you."*

I have to work hard to keep my body from reacting to my shock. The wolf beside Brock is beautiful. She sports a red coat like I've only seen on a fox. Her points are black, including the tips of her ears and tail. I have a few coal black wolves, but most have brown somewhere in their coats. This wolf is surprisingly void of any dull coloring.

She lowers into a full bow, keeping her eyes on the ground while I continue to study her.

"My Alpha, we have a visitor," I whisper, pulling back from his cheek. I smile at his narrowing eyes, sure he's figuring it must be the boys. "Brock is with her. He says she would like a word with me." I lean in to whisper into his ear. "I would like you to shift and participate in the conversation, please, Love."

"Who is it?" he whispers back, annoyed.

"I don't know yet," I answer, tracing my fingers over his jaw. "But she's been bowing for a few minutes, and I bet she's getting pretty stiff."

Pinning me to the tree with his hips, Bastian cups my cheek and rubs his thumb over my lower lip. "Will you stay behind me?" he asks. Pulling my chin, he gently kisses my lips. "I just want to know that you and my child are safe."

Sighing, I smile into his kisses. "Yes, my Alpha," I whisper when he stops. "I will stay with you so you know we're safe."

My Alpha kisses me once more before lifting me from his hips and setting me on the ground. He steps back to shift and turns toward our visitor. Bastian moves with me as I collect and put on my clothes. I scratch his chin and kiss the tip of his nose before turning to the red wolf, who has remained in a full bow.

"Please rise," I say, walking beside Bastian's hip as we approach the newcomer. "My companion tells me you wanted a word."

The red wolf stands and eyes Bastian. *We should speak alone.*

I rest my hand on my Alpha's hip as he begins growling. "That won't happen," I state plainly. "Why have you been following us?"

She ducks her head and looks away. *I've never had a mate,* she says quietly. *I was curious.*

Bastian and Brock look in my direction, confused.

"He's very honorable," I assure her.

The red wolf turns back to me and lifts her head high. *My mistress would like a word,* she announces. *And then you need to leave.*

"Leave? We just got here," I say, shaking my head. "There's nowhere else for us to go."

You need to find somewhere else, she replies. *West of here is a cave.*

It might hold all of your wolves. I will call for you there when my mistress is ready."

I step forward as she backs away. "Wait," I say, reaching out to her. "Please don't leave. Are there more of you?"

The red wolf stops and shifts her eyes between me and Bastian. *"There are."* She bows her head and attempts to leave again.

I rack my brain quickly, trying to find a reason for her to stay. "Would you like to meet Matthew?" I ask, stepping forward again. When she turns back to me, I drop to my knees before her. "I know he'd like to meet you."

"No," she responds abruptly. *"It's not safe here. You'll meet with my mistress and then leave."* She turns to go but stops. *"All of you."* She bows her head and jogs quickly from sight.

Although they were silent throughout the conversation, my Alpha and companion are not calm. Bastian moves to stand before me while Brock flanks him.

"What the hell was that, Ayls?" Bastian demands.

"She's Matthew's mate?" Brock asks.

"Who cares?" Bastian snaps. *"There's more of her? What's the danger? And what the hell is a 'mistress?'"*

They're both scared. They don't like me near anything considered unknown. Now, we are faced with a group of strange wolves, an unknown danger, and something or someone known as a "mistress."

"Maybe Daddy or Anthony will know," I suggest. "Come on, let's go talk to them." I rub my protectors' jaws before standing up. "At least she told us where we can find shelter. That was nice, right?"

26

"*I*t's *cold out here, Ayls,*" Bastian says. "*Can we please go inside?*"

"What if she comes for me, and I miss her, Bass?" I ask, pouting. "It's been a week. She's surely taking her time arranging this meeting for someone wanting us to leave."

"*Ayls?*" Bastian whines.

I push off the tree I'd been leaning against and kneel to him. "Can we just wait a little longer, please?" I ask, lifting my eyebrow.

I had forbidden Brock and Bastian from telling anyone about the red wolf. Without my mother to rein my father in, he would either try to hunt her down to kill her or attempt to move the pack south. We did ask him about what a mistress was. The subject made him very uncomfortable, and Anthony laughed about it. So, right now, we only know it's a person and probably a woman. *How bad could it be?*

"Bass, she has to be close," I whisper through my scarf, holding my hand out for his chin. "There is no other reason for the buffalo herd to return."

Bastian closes his eyes as I rub my hand over his cheek. "*Maybe they're so cold they would rather die.*"

I click my tongue and sigh. "She has to be pushing them back here," I tell him. "They scatter daily during the hunt. But the herd is back every morning, waiting to die."

"*I think Edith has some of the hides nearly dry enough to use,*" Bastian says, trying to change the subject. "*She's using the rugs that were here as examples.*"

313

"Aren't you curious?" I ask, pulling my scarf down to let his whiskers rub against my cheek. "She's a red wolf. That's weird enough, but she said there were more. Just think, a whole pack of beautiful red wolves. I want to meet them."

"*Annalisa,*" Bastian starts gruffly. "*Enough. You're bleeding again, and you need to get by the fire. Go.*"

I scowl, forgetting that my scarf isn't covering my face anymore.

"*Your father and I need our strength and can't keep giving you blood. Please, Ayls, go inside,*" my Alpha continues gently.

Sighing, I rise to my feet and allow him to pull me toward the cave. He can smell my blood the moment it starts. With Trish so close to delivering the next Alpha, our daughter has returned to her old tricks. Edith has been careful and only uses the tea when necessary, but she warned me we're running out. First, we lacked water to make it, and now we're running out of leaves.

Bastian leads me into the cave and straight to Edith. He stares at her as she scrapes a knife over the hide stretched out before her. Surrounded by wolves, Edith has become accustomed to them simply sitting next to her, so Bastian's actions don't distract her from her task. He nudges his nose toward her but shoves her with his paw when she doesn't acknowledge him.

Edith tumbles forward onto the hide, coating herself in the loose hairs she'd just scraped off. "What the hell, Bastian?" she shouts over my laughter.

"*She needs tea,*" he announces.

I love Bastian. He is mine and perfect in every way, but I will never understand why he talks to humans as a wolf and expects them to hear him. There's no containing my broad smile as I watch them stare at each other, both expecting a response. Edith rolls off the stretched hide and pushes Bastian back.

"What?" she asks, still staring at him.

"I love you two very much," I say, still laughing as I sit beside her. "Bastian says I've started bleeding again."

Edith furrows her brow. "Are you sure?" she asks. "It's happening more frequently now."

"*Yes,*" Bastian replies, bumping my cheek with his nose.

"He says he's sure," I tell her.

"Ok," she says, frowning. "Why don't you change, and I'll make a cup. The boys should be back soon."

I kiss Bastian behind his whiskers and leave to find clean bottoms in the sleigh deeper in the cave. Since arriving at the shelter, we've sent Creto and Timothy hunting with a different wolf each day. So far, Kade was their favorite, but he's only left Gaine's side once. Today, they are with Drake. I was pleasantly surprised by how gentle he was with them. He seems to be a well-rounded wolf.

I push my bottoms off and take note of the small blood spots before mashing them into the large jar we keep just for these moments. I jump into a pair of jeans and twist the lid of the jar closed as I hear the boys challenging each other to a race to see who can find me first. It won't take them long with the scent of my blood in the air.

Ignoring Bastian, they zip past where he's waiting with Edith and round the wagon to crash right into me. The side of my face hits the back gate, making the skin at my cheekbone sear.

"*Oh, Luna!*" Timothy shouts. "*I'm sorry. Are you ok?*"

I grab the side of my face and wince through the pain. "I know, sweetheart. I'll be ok." I pull my hand away and frown at the blood smeared across it.

"*Here, Luna. Let me help.*" Creto steps forward and slides his tongue across my cheek to clean it before I can stop him.

"*Creto!*" I shout to only him, shoving him back. I swipe my hand over my cheek, and my jaw slacks at the lack of fresh blood on my fingers. "*What have you done?*" I reach for his muzzle and wrench his jaw open. I brush my sleeve over his tongue as if that would help our situation.

"*It's ok, Luna,*" Creto says, nuzzling my cheek. "*I don't mind being bonded to you. My mate didn't make it through the attacks. Gaine said she couldn't see one for me.*"

Sighing, I roll back over my heels and sit with the boys. "It must have been hard seeing Timothy with Myla, huh?" I ask, reaching for Creto's jaw.

The young wolf sets his chin on my hand but tucks his ears back in shame. I open my arms and invite him closer. I saw no version of this coming. These sweet, happy boys loved having a mother to care for them. They got all the love and attention they needed and wanted, but somehow, that wasn't enough.

"I will always love you, Creto," I whisper. "You are my little wolf." I tighten my grip on his neck and prepare myself for what I'm about to say. "You have made the grown-up decision to tie yourself to me without knowing the full consequences, sweet child. This cannot be undone."

I allow Creto to stay in my arms with his jaw on my back. I know at ten years old, he's not feeling the pull of the bond the way he will as an adult. However, I have no idea what will happen once he's old enough. The only wolf besides Daddy that bonded to Mom was Uncle Miles, and he handled it well as a wolf. I sigh, realizing I'm out of my league again.

Timothy's eyeing me nervously when I look up. "It's ok, sweetheart," I whisper to the little wolf. "No one is in trouble. We have a pretty scary road in front of us, and I need everyone to have a clear head."

"*Yes, Luna,*" my little wolf says quietly as he bows his head.

"Myla should be with Kade," I say, scratching his chin. "I'm sure she'd like to visit with you."

Timothy lets me kiss his nose before bowing to excuse himself.

I rub Creto's shoulders and slip my hands down his legs to signal the end of the hug. He backs away to face me, trying to act like nothing has changed. Behind him, I see Bastian approaching with a steaming tea cup for me.

Handing me the cup, he sits beside me with a curious expression. "What's going on?" he asks, flicking his eyes between me and Creto.

"We had a little accident," I say, sighing. "I fell and hit my cheek."

Bastian grabs my jaw more firmly than I'd like and turns my head a few times, lifting his eyebrow when he doesn't see a wound. "What did you hit it on? A cloud?"

Creto's ears tuck again, and he looks away, dropping his head.

"Our young wolf here cleaned the wound for me," I say gently.

"He did what?" Bastian snarls. His growl builds quickly, causing Creto to cower.

My Alpha won't hurt Creto, but he obviously has feelings about this. Bastian doesn't need to speak to reprimand the young wolf. His growl echoes around the cave, causing everyone to watch as he stares Creto down. The young wolf crouches, still hanging his head, but swings it from side to side, showing his shame. It breaks my heart, but I know Bastian has to establish his dominance from the beginning before any lines can be crossed.

Once his growl simmers, I take a small sip of the tea. My movement catches Bastian's attention, and his eyes flick away from Creto.

"Timothy?" he asks.

Gently smiling, I shake my head. "Just Creto," I answer. "Our young wolf was a little sad watching Timothy and Myla. It seems Gaine told him she couldn't see a mate for him."

"Kid, you're 10!" Bastian spouts, turning back to Creto. "Those two are nearly that many years apart. Your mate could be one of these babies about to be born."

The young wolf rests his chin on his paws, sighing. I had the same thought as Bastian but had decided not to remind Creto. He made the decision to bond to me hastily. He didn't need to hear that he still could have found his mate and had just destroyed that chance.

I rub Bastian's arm. "Creto understands what has happened," I whisper. "He doesn't need to be reminded of this right now. Let's take a moment to think this through, and then we'll find a way to move forward as a family, ok?"

Bastian leans his head on my shoulder while I finish my tea. After setting my cup down, I reach for Creto and lift him until his jaw rests on my other shoulder. Pulling my fingers through Bastian's hair and rubbing Creto's ribs, I wonder what my mother would do. Perhaps this is why she kept her distance from the kids.

Regardless of what happened or what could have been, we'll need to find a way to move forward. "We'll figure this out, guys," I whisper to them. "Mom, Dad, and Uncle Miles somehow made their situation work. We'll find our way, too."

My mother spoke to me often about the blood bonds. She wanted me to know how important it was to guard my blood and be sure that our wolves stayed clear of it so that this situation didn't happen. She told me that it was the strongest bond there was since it could stop our wolves from recognizing their mate and deny them the ability to bond. She built a healthy fear of it, so I would always be careful, especially since all my friends were wolves.

I take a deep breath and lean back to look Bastian and Creto in the eye. "Because we are a family, we will find a way." I turn my attention to Creto. "I want you to be honest with me about everything. Tell me if you are feeling things or have any questions. You need to communicate with me as things change."

Creto nods and touches his nose to my cheek. *"I will, Luna."* He turns to Bastian, dropping his ears. *"I'm sorry, Bastian. I just wanted to know what was so great about it."*

I shake my head. "He says he's sorry, Bass."

Bastian opens his arms to Creto. "You are our wolf, small one," he whispers. "We will do our best to help you through this and find a way for us to be a family." Bastian's eyes flick toward me before he adds his final request. "Just talk to us before you decide to do something stupid again, ok?"

Creto giggles as he pulls back. *"Yes, Bass,"* he says, bowing. *"I promise."* Overcome with happiness, the young wolf jumps forward to bump his nose into Bastian's cheek. It's not a traditional way to greet an Alpha, but it's how a wolf would show affection to their father.

Bastian scratches his chin with a grin. "I love you too, kiddo." He stands and pulls me to my feet. "I think we should keep this between us for now. I don't want any of the other kids to get ideas."

* * *

I'm startled awake in the morning by a loud shout in my head. I bolt upright, looking around at the pile of sleeping wolves. Now that I'm in the middle of it, I can understand why they call it a dog pile. Although I can recognize all of them, they are still just a jumbled-up pile of legs, tails, and noses.

I smile at the significance of this moment. Our numbers may not be what they once were, but these wolves are mine. They are closer than family. Some of them had never met until we joined together at the foothills. Yet here we all are, piled together in a cave to stay warm during a cold winter night. Each wolf will wake up snuggled and warm because of their love for one another.

"Luna? Are you there?"

That's right. Someone woke me up. I replay the words a few times in my head. The voice is familiar but still strange to me. I run back through conversations, trying to place it. My wolves' faces come to me when they talk. It's like looking through glass with the image reflecting against it. This one isn't coming to me, though.

"Luna, I need your guards' assistance," the voice says, a bit calmer.

I've got it. The red wolf.

"Where are you?" I ask.

"I'm outside the cave," she answers.

I curl Creto's legs into his chest so I can stand without disturbing him. Bastian is on my other side. There is no way I'm getting out of here without waking him. I scratch his belly and put my finger to my lips when he opens his eyes.

"The red wolf is back," I tell him. *"She's outside."*

There isn't a wolf on the planet with my Alpha's grace. He rolls forward and stands without disturbing a hair of anyone's coat. He crouches slightly to give me his shoulders to push myself to my feet. We carefully move around the wolves at the edge of the pile and exit the cave in the early morning light.

I'm relieved to see that it didn't snow again last night as I look around for the red wolf. "Do you see her?" I whisper.

Bastian slips his muzzle into my hand and pulls me to the right. *"She's over here,"* he says, leading me toward a thick group of pine trees.

The snow drift at the edge of the trees is so firm that I can walk on top of it. Bastian pulls me up the mound but then stops, trying to yank me back. I squint through the shadows and see that our visitor has brought friends this time. I scratch Bastian's jaw to stop his retreat but don't move forward as I look over the group.

"I see you've brought friends," I say, smiling. "Did we cause you concern last time?"

They are nearly identical, with only slight size differences. I assume the wolf that steps forward is our previous visitor, but I can't be sure. Bastian carefully braces me as I step down the drift and stands by as I kneel before the wolves.

"How can we help?" I ask.

"*Our mistress has fallen,*" the wolf before me states. This wolf is a man, not my previous visitor.

I furrow my brow. "And she needs help standing up?"

"*This human is an imbecile, Aine. She can't help us,*" the wolf snaps, turning away. "*We're wasting time.*"

Bastian jerks out of my hand, snarling at the wolf before us. "*That is the Luna you are speaking of,*" he growls. "*You will honor her as such!*"

The wolf turns back and lets his eyes travel over Bastian. "*She's no Luna of mine,*" he grumbles before walking away.

My Alpha attempts to lunge at him, but I grab his nose. The wolf that addressed me continues to walk away. One other turns to follow him, but the third approaches me.

"*Our mistress is hurt, and we've been unable to locate her,*" the wolf says, letting me know she is the visitor from before.

The other red wolves stop and turn back toward us. I trail my finger-nails through Bastian's fur while studying the three wolves. Now that they are quiet and still, giving me a moment to observe them, there is definitely something older about them. Or perhaps timeless. They have an air of wisdom far more significant than any elder in my pack.

I turn all of my attention to the wolf before me. "Is your name Aine?" I ask, holding my hand out.

"Yes," she answers. "*We are Defenders, and we need your help. You have the numbers we lack. There are thousands of miles to cover, and we are running out of time.*" Desperation builds in her voice with every word. "*Ruairi might be right, but I don't think we have any other choice.*"

The Guardians uphold the first laws of the original wolves. I've never heard of "Defenders." I look down at my empty hand, still waiting for the red wolf's chin. "What do you defend?" I ask.

"*Light,*" Aine replies, still not acknowledging my hand.

Bastian snorts and sits, no longer interested in a formal meeting. "*Red wolves, 'Defenders of Light,'*" he lists, chuckling. "*And this fool wants to treat you like you're the village idiot? I think we're done here.*" He adjusts his front paws and raises his muzzle while licking his lips. This is a wolf display to show their disinterest and that they're above what is happening around them.

Ignoring him, I move on. "Is it just the three of you?"

"*Enough, Aine,*" the wolf, I assume is Ruairi, says, stepping forward. "*They need to leave, not help us. I told you this was a stupid idea.*"

"Wait," I say abruptly. "We'll help you."

The grumpy wolf stops and narrows his eyes in response.

"Will you answer my questions if we help you find your mistress?" I ask hopefully.

Ruairi critically studies me for a moment before he releases a deep sigh. "*No.*" He turns away from me and disappears with the silent red wolf over the snow bank.

I lift my eyebrow to Aine. "So, he doesn't like me," I say. "But am I still helping?"

"*Please,*" Aine begs, finally stepping forward to place her chin on my hand. "*Please help us.*"

My breath catches as she steps forward, sliding her jaw and throat over my hand. There are no accurate words to describe how she feels. Her coat is somehow both warm and cold. My fingers slip into her fur but still look like they are on top of it. I curl my hand into a fist, attempting to grab her coat, but it easily slips right out of my grip. She feels like water but reminds me of smoke.

"What are you?" I whisper.

"Dead if you don't help me," is her answer. She steps back, letting me study her again now that I've felt her.

The Guardians are the Alphas of the past who have avenged their fallen Luna. They are a type of mythical creature. The Defenders must be something like them. Aine doesn't feel real, yet she is before me, speaking to me and asking for my help.

I take a deep breath and lean back on my heels. "What do you need us to do?"

Bastian has been eerily quiet throughout our exchange. When I glance in his direction, he nods in approval. I remember my father manipulating situations like this when Mom and I argued. My Alpha has been paying attention.

"My mistress doesn't normally leave our sides, but she said she needed to think," Aine tells us. *"That was two days ago. We've been scouring the range looking for her, but we can't cover enough of the territory."*

"You can't track her scent?" Everything about these wolves confuses me, and none of them seem interested in giving me answers.

Aine tucks her nose and shifts her eyes away from us. *"We can't smell,"* she whispers in my head.

Bastian and I sit up, confused. "What?" I spout without meaning to. "You can't...? Wh-why can't you smell?" I stammer. I'll never claim to be the most intelligent person in the world, and I have many people who help me work through any problem, but a whole pack of wolves that can't smell makes absolutely no sense.

"Will you please send your guards to help us search?" Aine asks, ignoring my confusion.

"You realize your mate is my head guard, right?" I ask, switching subjects with her for now. "His unit will not be going without him."

"Will you order him to leave me alone?" Aine asks, turning her eyes away again.

"No," I answer. "He's a good wolf. His name is Matthew, and I've known him my whole life. You'd like him."

"No, I wouldn't," she responds sharply. *"Send your guards northwest."*

"Wait, Aine," I call to her as she tries to leave. "What are they looking for?"

"*A bay horse,*" she answers before bowing and jumping over the bank.

I'm frozen as I stare after her. Bastian's jaw is slack, and his tongue is sticking out slightly. My first movement is to tug the tip of his tongue, triggering him to pull it in and swallow.

"*All this for a horse?*" my Alpha asks, sounding as confused as I feel.

"Maybe the mistress was riding it?" I suggest. "Did you see how her fur reacted to my hand?"

"*It moved away from you,*" Bastian says thoughtfully. "*Ayls? What the hell are those things?*"

"I don't know," I answer, pushing myself to my feet. "Wake the guards. Maybe if we help them, they'll let us stay."

* * *

Saint stumbles through the snow a few days later, trying to follow Bastian to the top of the next ridge. It snowed again yesterday. My Alpha forcefully made me stay in the cave for the day, saying it was too dangerous for his child to be exposed to such cold weather. I tried to remind him that I would be the cold one, not his child, but he growled at me, and I couldn't stop giggling long enough to argue with him.

"*That horse needs a break, Ayls,*" Bastian says, cresting the ridge. "*Come down here. This ledge will block the wind.*"

"Do you get the feeling that we're wasting our time?" I ask, stepping from the saddle. "No horse would just stay here through these storms, and if it's hurt, it wouldn't have survived."

"*Why are we out here looking for a damn horse anyway?*" he grumbles. "*What the hell is so special about this horse?*"

"Matthew's been asking questions," I say, bringing up another point. "He doesn't understand why you've taken command of his wolves."

"*Well, I refuse to tell him his mate doesn't want anything to do with him,*" Bastian mutters. "*That was my biggest fear once I knew you were mine. I was so afraid you wouldn't want me.*" Bastian starts chuckling. "*Did you know I asked your mother what would happen if you refused to bond with me?*"

Giggling, I crouch to put my back against the ledge and extend my arms. "You did have a close yet strange relationship with my mother," I say, closing my arms around his neck. "She knew the truth, though. There was no way I could've said no to you. You are mine."

Bastian hums, pushing his jaw against my back. *"It's not fair. Matthew should have this too,"* he says sadly.

"Alright," I say, sighing. "Let's worry about that later. We've nearly searched the entire area Aine mapped out for today. It's time to start rounding everyone up."

"Kade's got the kids," Bastian tells me, backing out of my arms. *"He's having trouble with Creto."*

I've listened to them argue all day, so I know the issues. Creto has been trying to come back to me. He's used nearly every excuse in the book. Edith has been looking through her journals to see if a potion would subdue the effects of the bond. So far, she hasn't found anything.

I stand and step toward the edge of the ridge to look over the wolves searching nearby. "I'm going to let him stay with me for a while," I announce. "Until we can figure this out, the arguing must stop. I don't want any other kids thinking it's ok to argue with their superiors."

"I agree," Bastian responds. *"I want Matthew to meet Aine."* Bastian sits and looks up at me quite sternly. He has powerful feelings about mates and their right to be with each other. I've never disagreed with him... until now.

"Bass, she's not a normal wolf," I remind him for the tenth time since we met her. "She could disappear into thin air when we find her horse. Maybe she'll kill us all. Perhaps she's a ghost. How would he ever survive her turning him away? We can't walk into this blindly. We must protect our wolves from all threats, even the unknown ones."

"Annalisa," Bastian says with a heavy sigh.

"Bastian, we are too far away from anything that could heal him if she breaks his heart," I say sternly. "If she doesn't want to meet him, we will honor that for now."

"I don't want to," he snaps.

"I know, Love," I whisper. "Just for now."

I pull my fingers through the fur on his neck as I listen to my guards calling their final position. They've reached the edge of their search radius and are nearly done for the day. Today, a large elk herd ran through the area, and most groups picked off at least one. We might not have found what we sought, but well-fed wolves are a nice consolation prize.

27

My wolves surround me as I slowly ride down the trail they cut for Saint. Another unsuccessful day of searching comes to a close as the light begins to fade from the cloudy sky. The red wolves didn't seek me out tonight to gain a report as they typically do. *They're probably assuming we didn't find anything.*

Bastian is trying to push Saint, but the older horse hasn't had anything to eat for a few days with this deep snow, so he's weak. All of our horses are in the same condition. It won't be long before we'll have to find a different place to winter if the snow doesn't let up. I reach forward to scratch his neck under his mane. His ear flicks back to me as I murmur quiet words of encouragement.

We descend into a valley of pines and skirt a rocky ledge before finding smooth dirt. My wolves stop under a tree where some old trampled grass lies under the curtain of limbs. It's not the healthiest of grasses, but Saint doesn't care. He yanks the reins from my hand and greedily pulls at it. Drake digs in the snow nearby to find more for the hungry horse.

I close my eyes and listen to the guard units still further out. I count them as they report in, ensuring each is accounted for, but I have trouble understanding Kade's team. They aren't fighting, but they're shouting at each other.

"Kade?" I call out. *"What's wrong?"*

"Shit, Luna!" he shouts, making me wince now that it's aimed directly at me. *"She smells like a fucking celebration!"*

I open my eyes and look around. My wolves are all at attention, listening to Kade broadcast his shouting. I can typically control this, but his excitement is overwhelming, and his entire unit is shouting similar things.

"*Easy, Kade,*" I call out, hoping to calm him. "*What are you talking about?*"

"*The horse, Luna,*" he responds excitedly. "*She's got a broken leg. I can eat her, right? She's like steak!*"

"*She smells like cake!*" Creto chimes in.

"*Right!*" Kade agrees. "*A steak cake! Oh, just a taste. I'll share her. I promise! Hey! Don't you dare, kid! I found her, so I get the first bite.*"

With my jaw slacked, I look down at Bastian. "They found the horse?" I mumble, shocked. "How the hell is that thing still alive?"

"*It won't be for long, by the sound of it,*" Bastian grumbles. "*I'm pretty sure the red wolves would have something to say about that.*" He stares up at me, waiting for my orders.

"Alright," I start, reaching for my reins. "She smells like steak or cake, but she might be dangerous. Let's form up and find them."

"*Kade, call it out,*" Bastian orders.

It takes a moment as I'm sure Kade is considering his options, but eventually, his call rings through the air. The guards traveling with me take off in its direction, leaving me behind with Bastian. My Alpha tries to shout over them, but they aren't listening. Kade's made this meal sound delicious, and their dominant trait has taken over.

When Kade's second call sounds, a frail voice rings in my head. "*Please don't let them eat me,*" a woman barely whispers.

Bastian bumps his hip into Saint's head to make him pick it up and looks up at me. "*You ready?*"

"Bass," I say with wide eyes. "I'm pretty sure that horse just talked to me."

"*What?*" he scoffs, tilting his head. "*Ayls, horses can't talk.*"

"Neither can wolves," I snap back at him. "But some woman just begged me not to let them eat her."

"*What the hell did they find?*" Bastian asks, matching my wide eyes.

"I don't know, but you need to get us there before they eat her," I say, spinning Saint around in the direction my wolves had gone.

Bastian leads us as fast as Saint can follow. The trail is narrow and slick, two types of footing that don't work well under hooves. The excited shouts in my head turn to yelling and fighting. There are so many loud voices that I'm forced to push them all to the back of my mind to concentrate on my horse.

We hit an obvious trail that shows most of my wolves traveled along a rock wall. Bastian follows it around a bend and into a clearing where they are all jumping around. The red wolves are trying to defend a brown mound in the middle. My wolves are persistent. No matter what my Alpha threatens, they aren't listening. They will fight to the death to put whatever that mound is into their stomachs.

I stop Saint safely outside of their tight circle and scan my pack. Daddy is circling them, trying to calm them, but they aren't listening to him either. Swinging out of my saddle, I drop to the ground as he approaches us.

"Ayls, that thing has a broken leg," Daddy says. *"I'm inclined to let them have her."*

Sighing, I kneel and kiss him behind his whiskers. "Daddy, I believe she spoke to me," I whisper. "She begged me not to let them eat her."

"Stop," my father grumbles, sitting before me. *"Now you're just making shit up. Horses don't talk."*

I rub my fingers over my forehead. "For werewolves, you two have small minds," I scoff. "There's obviously something different about the horse. She has impossibly colored wolves guarding her. She smells like... I can't believe I'm about to say this... 'steak cake.' Don't you think she could have talked to me?"

"Alright, well, how are we doing this?" Daddy asks, looking back at our jumping wolves.

"We can't hurt them," Bastian says quickly. *"We can't use the tea. Ayls needs it."* He tucks under my arm to poke my belly.

I sit back on my heels and look past my father. Bastian is right. I've been needing the tea daily now. Trish is due soon, and our little Luna wants out. Edith has warned me that I must keep everyone safe because there wasn't enough tea to treat anyone else.

Using Bastian's shoulders, I push myself to my feet and take in my wolves again. They are getting more agitated by the minute. As I step forward, Daddy and Bastian flank me, staying against my hips to shield me from the jumping wolves.

I swipe my hands over any wolf that comes near enough, pulling large bursts of emotions from them and fueling my fire touch. "You need to calm down," I yell over their excited whimpering and panting.

Their voices settle to something closer to a whisper in the back of my mind. We reach the center where the red wolves have created a perimeter around the horse. Bastian stays with me as I walk around the circle between the red wolves and our pack, sliding my hand over the muzzles within reach.

"Easy, my wolves," I sing calmly into their heads. *"Be gentle, my wolves. Easy."*

They aren't calming, though. The wolves from behind are pushing harder against those closest to us. Our circle is becoming smaller with each passing moment. I've never lost control of my wolves. They have loved and honored me through everything. Something about this horse is overwhelming them.

I can feel my anger building within me. I don't know where to point it. I'm angry at this horse for whatever it's doing to my wolves. I'm mad at the red wolves for not being completely honest with me, as there is clearly something else going on here. I'm most ashamed of the anger I feel toward my wolves and the loss of control they are experiencing.

I stumble slightly as Bastian is shoved into me. He regains his footing and lunges at Kade. I step back toward the horse and swing my arms to my sides. With my hands charged, I clap them together above my head as hard as possible.

My hands sound louder than any clap of thunder I have ever heard. A rush of air sweeps across me, and some invisible force throws my wolves back away from us. Even the snow they had trampled down has been swept back to expose the dirt below. The Alphas' wide eyes match mine in our shock.

"I know this is overwhelming for everyone," I start calmly, speaking to all of them at once. *"I don't know what just happened, but I need your attention."* I step slowly around the larger circle my hands created. *"I will get answers for you, but this is no ordinary horse, and you cannot eat her."*

My wolves slowly climb to their feet, hanging their heads. It surprises me to see some of the wolves that have collected here and been driven mad by the scent of this horse. I watch Neala help some of the children to their feet. Timothy and Myla bury their muzzles in each other's necks, attempting to hide from me. The most surprising is Grandma Pine, who I didn't think could make the trip this far from the cave on foot.

I hold my hand with my palm up as I continue walking. My wolves reach their chins out and allow me to rub my hand under them, pulling any excess emotions. *"Are we in control now?"* I ask them, raising my eyebrow. *"The sun will be setting soon, and I want the children in the cave by then. They have a strict bedtime."* My eyes lock on Neala, the caretaker who proposed the curfew.

There is a chorus of affirmations and apologies. Every wolf stops by to see me before they leave. The red wolves are relentless with their patrol, not allowing anyone close to the fallen horse. While I say goodnight to Timothy and Myla, Creto asks Bastian if he can stay. The young wolf attempts to argue when his request is denied and receives a nip on the muzzle in reprimand.

I kiss his cut when he stops before me as the last wolf to leave. "We need to find a way, little wolf," I whisper. "You can't always be with me. I need you to guide the younger children toward a better future."

Creto nuzzles my cheek and joins Neala and the rest of the kids. My guard unit stands back as I watch the children disappear around the bend. The guards are fidgeting, but Matthew catches my attention. He's frozen to my left, staring at Aine while she does her best to ignore him.

Blowing out a deep breath, I scratch my father's chin. "Daddy, watch the guards for me," I whisper. As he moves away, I turn to the red wolves. "Aine, would you please come here?" I hold out my hand for her. Matthew raises his head, and Aine hesitates. "It's ok," I whisper to her. "Give him a chance."

The red wolf gingerly steps forward and slides her jaw over my fingers. Aine tries to keep her eyes on me, but they keep flicking nervously toward Matthew.

"I know you said you didn't want to meet him," I start in a whisper. "He's not going to be able to walk away. He's waited a long time for you." I stop and give her a moment. I've learned over the years that pushing any of my wolves never ends well. Allowing her to make this decision on her own is best. "Are you ready for this, Aine?"

The red wolf's breathing speeds up as she swallows hard. *What do I say to him?* she asks quietly.

Smiling gently, I shake my head. "I don't think you'll need words," I whisper back. I curl my fingers to urge her forward and rest her muzzle against my cheek. She still feels strange, but I don't think Matthew will mind. "Here we go."

I hold my other hand out to Matthew while keeping Aine against my cheek. My guard's movements are slow and exaggerated. His head is lifted so high that he cannot see where his feet land, so he lifts them much more than necessary.

"She's mine, right?" Matthew timidly asks me, sliding his jaw over my hand.

Sighing, I lift my eyebrow. "Matthew, this is Aine," I say quietly. "She is a wolf, not a possession." Matthew licks his lips and nudges his nose toward Aine a few times, but she remains hidden behind my cheek. "Aine, this young guard is Matthew."

"Ayls, she's beautiful," Matthew whispers in my head as he gently touches his nose to the tip of her neck's fur. *"Tell her she's beautiful."*

I've never been part of a mate introduction. I remember my mother doing this with me and Bastian, but I didn't know who Bastian was. I'm unsure how it would've gone had I known. Aine had been firm and forceful about not meeting Matthew, but now she almost seems afraid.

I ignore the watery feel of her fur and rub my hand over her shoulder, giving her the freedom to move in any direction.

Matthew pokes his nose against my cheek before moving past me. He nuzzles Aine's neck and slides his muzzle over her head. When she doesn't move away, he gently licks her ear, then twists his head to slip under my chin, looking for her cheek. My poor guard pulls his head back, looking for any acknowledgment from Aine, but tucks his ears when there's no response.

As a kid, he was relentless in his pursuit of me. I was only practice for this moment. Matthew licks his lips and adjusts his front paws to allow him to slide his muzzle over my back. If she won't come to him, he'll go to her. He tries to reach her through my hair, but she stays securely hidden, so he burrows along my neck to touch her.

I smile when I feel his tongue slide over my skin, knowing I'm not his intended target. Aine's whiskers move over my neck as Matthew pulls at her lip with his tongue. He rolls his head to give his nose better access to her muzzle and pushes against me, trying to reach her cheek. If it were any other wolf, I don't believe I would tolerate his behavior. But Matthew has been my friend for as long as I can remember, and he's quite smitten.

Aine shifts slightly, not returning his affection but allowing him to reach her cheek. *"Please, ma'am?"* she requests quietly.

My brow furrows, and I look up at Bastian as he tilts his head, equally confused.

But then the frail voice responds, *"Very well."*

Aine steps around me. I clutch my chest and watch her slide her muzzle over Matthew's. They lower their heads, rubbing whiskers and licking each other's lips. Aine pushes against Matthew's chest until he rolls over his hip and lies down for her to curl up against.

"Ok, that was pretty cute," Bastian admits, making me giggle.

I turn my attention to the horse on the ground—the one who apparently is a mistress and goes by the name Ma'am. Bastian gives me his shoulder to rise to my feet. After a quick scan, I see her front leg is broken, but otherwise, she seems in good condition even after being out here for so long.

"What are you?" I ask sharply, narrowing my eyes. The horse doesn't move or make any attempt to respond to me. "I stopped my wolves from killing you. You will answer me, or we will leave you here to die."

The horse takes a deep breath and groans as she rolls upright, pulling her head out of the snow. My jaw drops, and my hand slaps over my mouth too late to hide any of my surprise. Turning her head toward us, she reveals the beautiful shimmering silver horn in the middle of her forehead. It seems to glow, yet I'm sure I can see through it.

"Is that...?" I start without knowing where I'm going. "But how? What? You're a..." I'm babbling like an idiot, frozen in front of this creature that was supposed to be either a fairytale or extinct.

"Yes," she whispers. *"I'm a unicorn. The last of my kind."*

I glance down at Bastian to see he's slightly more frozen than I am. My father is creeping up to my right side, unsure if he should defend me from this horned being.

"Daddy, go get Anthony and the sleigh," I say quietly, slipping my hand over his head.

"Annalisa," my father snaps. *"She could stop what's happening to you. Ask her how to stop it. Tell her to save you."*

Bastian whips his head around, knocking me off balance. I fall back to my knees, braced against my father. Wrapping my hands around their muzzles, I pull them to me and take a moment to absorb our situation. I consider the future I had hoped my wolves could have in these mountains.

"Not now, Daddy," I say privately to him. *"Please, just go get the sleigh."*

My father keeps his strong opinion to himself as he bows and leaves us.

I move toward the unicorn on my knees. "Do you mind if I check your leg?" I ask, reaching toward her limb.

"I don't need you to," she whispers gruffly. *"I can see it's broken."*

Frowning, I sit back on my heels. "Maybe I could make it more comfortable until the sleigh gets here," I offer. "Are you cold? My wolves could help keep you warm."

"*When did I ask for your help?*" she snaps.

"Your Defenders requested my assistance," I snap back. "My wolves have been out here for days looking for you. So, I would say we've been helping you for a while, whether you wanted it or not."

"*What is your name, young one?*" she asks, taking a good look at me.

"Annalisa," I answer. "I'm their Luna."

"*Hmm,*" she huffs. "*If you say so.*"

"Didn't you want a meeting with me?" I ask, reminding her why we are still here.

"*Yes, I did,*" she answers, lying back down. "*I wanted to tell you to leave and never return, but that seems inappropriate right now.*"

Giggling, I move toward her head. "It would seem so," I say. "Come here. You shouldn't lay your head in the snow. You'll get frostbite on your ears." I slide my arm under her face and lift her head so I can sit under it.

"*What are you doing, human?*" the unicorn scoffs.

"I am not a human," I reply. "I'm a Luna, and I'm helping you." I lay her head over my lap while Bastian tucks behind me to heat as much of my body as possible. "Let's get you warmed up." I smile as I gesture to my wolves, asking them to lie around her. "If you taste her, you'll answer to me," I warn them.

The red wolves lie against her stomach and neck. Matthew doesn't provide much assistance when he balls his body to curl up with Aine, not touching a single part of the unicorn. I smile as he gently dotes on his mate, licking her jaw and cheeks. I like that I can recognize everything Bastian does to me. It has helped me to understand the different ways they interact with each other.

I slide my hand along the unicorn's neck and turn my attention to her horn. "How do you keep that hidden?" I ask, watching how it shimmers in the moonlight. "Can I touch it?"

"*No,*" she responds.

"Oh," I say, stopping my hand from reaching for it.

"I mean, you can't," she says, groaning slightly. *"It's not really there. Your hand will go right through it."*

"Do you mind if I try?" I ask, intrigued.

"If you must," she grumbles.

I rub my hand down her face, between her eyes, and slip right through where her horn looks like it is. The light leaves a sensation on my hand that is unlike anything I've ever felt. "What is that?" I whisper.

"Essence," the unicorn responds. *"Long ago, my kind was honored. We were loved, and life was good. But then the world turned on us. They wanted what was ours even though it wasn't something we could give. We hid but were found and slaughtered like livestock. One by one, my family and friends fell until I was alone. All that I have left is my essence."*

Abandoning her horn, I move my hand to her cheek and slide my thumb over her fur. "We know a little bit about that," I whisper. "I'm sorry about your family. I think your essence is beautiful, but I don't want to take it. It looks good on you."

"You're not what I expected," she says.

"I rarely am," I say, smiling. "What's your name?"

"Aisling," she whispers. *"Thank you for helping my wolves, but you are pregnant and shouldn't be out here."*

"But I am the one that agreed to help them," I tell her. "I can't ask my wolves to do something I'm unwilling to do myself. My child is tucked safely inside me. While I am safe, so is she."

"My guard can't go with your wolf," Aisling says, closing her eyes. *"They are bound by blood to me. She can't leave the mountains."*

"Oh, that's ok," I reply, smiling. "We aren't leaving."

"Yes, you are," Aisling states, ending our conversation.

* * *

It takes Daddy a few hours to drive the sleigh up to us. Bastian shifts and pulls on clothes my father had brought for him. Together, they line the back of the sleigh up with Aisling's body and stop, unsure how to proceed.

"How the hell are we gonna get that damn horse on here?" Anthony asks, sitting on the sleigh bed. "More importantly, why are we doing all this for a horse? Just let the wolves have it. It's cold."

I click my tongue. "Anthony, this is Aisling, and my wolves won't be eating her," I scoff.

"Why are those wolves red?" he continues his inquisition. "Annalisa, what the hell have you gotten yourself into?"

"He can't see her horn," Ruairi tells me.

"Well, that would've been nice to know," I grumble. "You guys are great at only giving minimal information." I turn to Anthony. "Aisling is a unicorn, and these wolves are somehow tied to her as guards. I don't know how or why because they've conveniently left that information out, too."

"She's a what?" he says, furrowing his brow. "If you wanna help this horse, fine. You don't need to make shit up." He stomps toward the front of the sleigh.

A muted chuckle comes from Aisling. *"Your human entertains me,"* she says. *"If you have a blanket, I can shift."*

"You can shift?" I spout louder than intended in my shock.

"Maybe you could just get me a blanket instead of shouting at me," Aisling suggests.

Giggling, I tug her mane. "You're right, I'm sorry," I say. "Is there a blanket in the sleigh? Aisling would like to cover up."

Daddy brings us a blanket and a wooden dowel. "We bite down on these when we have to shift injured," he says, holding out the dowel. "Do you want to use it?"

"No, this will be quick," Aisling responds.

"Just the blanket, Daddy," I answer for her, smiling. I help spread the blanket over her body and watch her shift seamlessly as the Alphas do.

Her beauty takes my breath away even when she winces as she adjusts her broken arm. Her flawless skin is dark against mine, and her hair is smooth on my fingers. It is so dark that it appears blue in the moonlight. I risk turning the moment awkward by sliding my fingers through it to enjoy its feel a little more. Aisling's unicorn has brown eyes, but when she glares at me for petting her head, they're purple.

"Oh," I whisper, clutching my chest. "You're beautiful."

"You're not my type," Aisling grumbles.

Daddy chuckles as he scoops her off the ground. "I assume your wolves can guide us back to your house," he says, adjusting her position so I can tuck the blanket around her.

Aine offers to guide us while Ruairi and the silent red wolf join us in the sleigh. I spot Matthew sitting far out front with her. I assume Aine's offer had nothing to do with finding the house and everything to do with spending time with her smitten mate.

Settling in for the ride, I smile down at Aisling. "They are quite cute together," I say as the sleigh jerks forward. "Matthew is a good friend and a solid wolf."

Aisling watches Bastian pull me into his lap and wrap his arms around me to keep me warm. "He's welcome to join their ranks if he wishes, but I doubt any of these wolves would recommend it." The two red wolves in the wagon turn their eyes away from us. "Didn't think so," she adds in a huff.

"I've never seen a red wolf," I whisper, reaching for Ruairi's fur. He shies away from my hand. "Where do they come from?"

"Here and there," Aisling says. "Not sure I ever asked or cared. They were other colors when they bit me."

I inhale sharply, unsure of who I should be comforting. "So, it's a punishment?"

"Curse, actually," she replies. "'Born of blood, they will forever guard the bitten, reminding those who try to follow of the price they paid.' I think that's how it went." Aisling moves around and tips her chin toward Aine. "That one's been with me nearly 400 years. She's never known a mate. Kinda sad that she can't keep him."

"Aisling, why can't we stay?" I ask, desperate for the answer.

"You saw your wolves," she responds. "You'll lose them all if you stay. And honestly, I don't want them. These three annoy me."

We ride in silence for a while. When I listen to Matthew, he's telling Aine what it was like growing up with me and my mother as Lunas.

I look down and see Aisling staring at me. "You're not like the other Lunas," she states. "Why did you call your wolves off?"

"Because you asked me to," I whisper. "I wouldn't deny them food, but you're no ordinary prey, are you?"

The sleigh slides over a crest and begins descending toward a quaint cabin below. It's dark, but in no way does it look abandoned. It has beautiful cloth hung over the windows to keep snow off them. The porch has comfortable-looking rocking chairs with colorful cushions, and the tables contain painted vases that probably hold flowers in the summer months.

Bastian helps me move around to see over Anthony's driving bench. "This is cute," I say, smiling. "This is your home?" I glance back at Aisling to see she's still studying me. "What is it?" I ask.

"Aine tells me you are different," she says, narrowing her eyes. "She will show you to the southern barn. There is a hay shed attached. You can stay there while your horses recover. Then I want you gone."

28

The southern barn is enormous, with towering rafters and stalls along one wall for the horses. Beyond its sliding doors, a shed stands with bundles of hay stacked to the ceiling. The multiple walls and doors in the building stop the wind from reaching us, and with my wolves all heating up at once, it's comfortable for a remote barn.

Aine is allowed to visit with us during the day but is ordered to return home each night. I let her spend most of her time alone with Matthew, but we speak and ask questions daily. She seems especially curious about the hierarchy and how I can control my wolves.

My father continuously urges me to press the red wolf about using Aisling to fix what is happening to me. "The full moon is in five days," Daddy hisses to me as we watch the red wolf approach from the north. "Your grandfather will shit out your mother if he finds out that we have a unicorn and you're still sick."

I wrinkle my nose. "Daddy, that is a horrible image," I groan.

"Wait till you see it," he replies, raising his eyebrow.

"I don't see how that would even be possible," Bastian says, confused.

"Neither do I," I grumble, watching my father walk away.

Matthew bounds past me in a blur to meet Aine in the snowy field. Even at a distance, her nervousness about his first touch is apparent, but she relaxes after just a few moments of his affection. I can only hear her when she allows me to, but Matthew told me she's anxious about how her coat feels even though he doesn't care.

"She normally takes her time coming here," I remark as Aine urges Matthew toward us.

"*Maybe she's finally ready to help,*" Bastian mutters.

So far, Aine has asked many questions but refused to offer much by way of answers. I heard Matthew explaining how the guard units work and the hunting rotations. He has told her about our battles and Timothy and Creto being taken. I cringed through the story of how I died rescuing them.

When Aine talks to me, she asks about my mother and how she became a Luna. She was intrigued by my grandfather's story and the love my mother showed to everyone. I blame my pregnancy for my crying while telling her what I knew of the day she died and Uncle Miles' sacrifice for my parents. Aine stared at me curiously as if trying to figure out if my sorrow was genuine.

Today, she seems to have a plan. Although Matthew walks steadily beside her, nuzzling and licking her muzzle, her eyes are fixed on me. I lower to my knee as she approaches and reach for her jaw.

"*I bit her,*" Aine states as her chin slides over my fingers. "*I bit my mistress.*"

My jaw drops. "What? Why?" I stammer. "Is she ok?"

"*That's why I'm cursed,*" she says. "*I was sent to find the unicorn for my ailing Luna. I led my unit of fierce hunters over the mountain. We found her— the last one. Oh, she smelled so good.*" She stops and closes her eyes as she remembers. "*I only wanted a small taste. I caught up to her and bit her back leg. Her blood... That's why I wear this coat.*"

Armed with this new information, the feeling makes sense. The fur is still there, but it has a liquid-type feel and is blood-red. These red wolves are wearing blood coats.

"Aisling said you've been with her for around 400 years," I say, tilting my head. "How old are you, Aine?"

"*I don't know, Luna,*" she says quietly. "*When you've lived this long, time doesn't matter.*"

"Ok," I whisper. I rub my hand over her throat and let Matthew comfort her momentarily. I enjoy watching him love on her, but it often raises a question I have yet to ask. "Aine, can you shift?"

The red wolf looks away and tucks her chin. *"My sense of smell and beautiful coat are not the only things I lost that day,"* she admits.

"I don't mind," Matthew whispers to her. *"You are beautiful in every way to me."*

I smile at my guard. "You were always a mushy one," I say, tugging his ear. Once Aine finishes enjoying his affection, I push her for more information. "You said you were doing this for your ailing Luna. Why?"

"Her pregnancy was failing," Aine tells me. *"It was too soon for the baby to come. The unicorn could heal them both. I was sent to find it."*

"If her blood does this, how could she heal them?" I ask, confused.

"I don't know, Luna," she whispers.

I frown, sighing. "What happened to the Luna?"

"She died giving birth," Aine says. *"The baby barely survived. Mistress took us away after that. I'm not sure what happened to the pack."*

"Were Ruairi and the other wolf already with her?" I ask, changing the subject as Bastian pushes under my arm to poke my belly and talk to his daughter. "What is his name anyway?"

Aine breathes a quiet laugh. *"We don't know,"* she answers. *"He's never spoken."*

"Oh," I say, giggling. "He did seem like the strong, silent type."

"They were both with her," she continues. *"They were holding my unit back, but I broke through. They all died."* Aine lowers her head but closes her eyes and curls into Matthew when he nuzzles her. *"I used to think they were the lucky ones."*

"Matthew's pretty special," I say, smiling. "I think you're both lucky." Matthew pokes my cheek with his nose, and his happiness bursts through me like a lightning bolt. I catch his muzzle and kiss the tip of his nose. "Why don't you two spend some time together? I know Aisling doesn't let you stay too long."

"No, Luna," Aine says, stopping me from pushing to my feet. *"I actually came for you today."*

I relax back onto my heels. "Did you have more questions?" I ask, furrowing my brow.

"I was hoping your doctor could look at my mistress," she tells me. *"She has been ill and getting worse. She wasn't able to get out of bed this morning."*

"Ok," I whisper, twisting my face in thought. "We'll grab Chase and a horse. Matthew here could use some exercise." I scratch his chin as he chuckles.

* * *

It's not long before I'm riding through the snow, following the red wolf and her mate. Bastian and Chase are the only other wolves joining us after the pack's previous reaction to Aisling. I expected my father to argue, but he agreed that he should stay and keep an eye on our restless pack while I was away.

I lean against Chase's chest and let his heat soak through my clothes. "I bet you never thought you'd be doctoring a unicorn, huh?" I say, smiling over my shoulder.

Chase chuckles. "I definitely did not," he answers. "But throughout this whole thing, I can't help wondering what your mother must be thinking."

Sighing, I turn to watch Matthew and Aine. "I doubt she knows," I tell him. Chase tries to object, but I shake my head. "Mom's work is done, Chase. She taught me well and trusted me to care for all of you. Don't you think she's earned a little 'me time?'"

"Hm," Chase huffs thoughtfully. "I suppose you're right." Although it starts small, his laughter builds until I turn back around with a confused expression. "I doubt she'll get much 'me time' once your father joins her."

"He does miss her quite a bit," I say, giggling.

"There's the house, Ayls," Bastian announces beside us.

I look down at my beautiful Alpha. He's still the gorgeous wolf that took my breath away in Grandpa's field many years ago. The picture is slightly different now that he has a white rabbit hanging from his mouth.

"I love you very much," I say, dropping from my saddle. "I just don't understand why you had to carry that here."

"It would be impolite not to bring a gift," Bastian says, as if anyone would gladly accept his slobbery rabbit. *"We are about to beg her to let us stay."*

"I believe you should leave that outside for now," I tell him, giggling. "Aine told me she raises cattle, so I think she's good on meat."

"If she says no because we didn't bring her a gift, you only have yourself to blame," Bastian warns playfully.

I scratch his chin after he drops the rabbit on her porch step. "I will accept full responsibility if that happens."

"You remind me more and more of your mother every day," Chase says, leaning to kiss my temple.

We follow Aine onto the porch, but she stops us at the door. *"Please wait here,"* she requests. *"I did not ask permission to bring you. She needs convincing."*

I click my tongue and scowl but stay quiet as Aine pulls the latch down with her teeth and pushes the door closed behind her. "We'll freeze to death out here before she agrees to see us," I grumble once Aine's gone.

I turn to inspect the rocking chairs. They remind me of Grandpa's chairs that sat in the main bedroom of our house at the lake. I watched my father rock my sick mother in front of the fire the fall before she died. He had cried into her blankets afterward, telling stories about her rocking me in them for hours when I was a baby. I always thought I would rock my daughter in them too.

Picking up a semi-frozen pillow, I sit in the closest chair and let it rock a few times. My hands slide over the arms, feeling their smooth, worn wood. This rocking chair is loved and used often. I imagine Aisling has spent long hours on this porch. From the difference between the two chairs, I assume they were lonely hours.

Lost in my thoughts, I jump when the door opens. *"Please come in,"* Aine says, bowing once I stand. *"You'll have to stay here,"* she adds when Bastian tries to join me. *"The Luna and her physician only, Bastian."*

My Alpha's dismay is unmistakable. He shakes his head and bites my sleeve. *"No, Ayls."*

"Bass, we need this," I whisper. "Chase will be with me. I'll be ok." I slip my finger between his teeth so he'll release my sleeve. "Go eat your rabbit. You know you didn't bring that here for her." I kiss his nose and step through the door, quickly closing it behind me. I turn to Aine. "Don't make me regret that."

The red wolf tips her head in a gentle bow and leads us through the small living room to a door. She peeks in before pushing it open with her shoulders. Chase attempts to enter first, but snarls erupt from inside the room. When he steps back, I slip past him. Ruairi and the other red wolf are lying on the bed with Aisling as she shivers under her blankets.

"It's ok, guys," I say gently. "Let Chase look at her. How long has she been like this?"

My wolves' teeth can't puncture my skin, so there's no need to fear them. But these wolves are different. One huge difference is that they seem above the wolf-killing law. As we move forward, I keep myself between Chase and the two wolves on the bed.

Aisling's teeth chatter, but sweat is beading on her brow. Her skin is hot to the touch. My jaw drops when I lift the blanket and see her swollen hand.

"Guys, please," I beg the red wolves. "We need to get in here."

"You can help her in just a moment, gentlemen," Chase says soothingly. "We're going to pull this heat down from her head."

The wolves lift off Aisling and allow us to pull back the blanket. Chase had trained under Will for years. The doctor may have been trying to find a way to kill us off but was genuine in teaching Chase. However, we've never needed to treat an injury like this because we had tea. Aisling's arm is horribly discolored from the break and clearly infected.

Sitting on the edge of the bed, I hold the hand of the uninjured arm while Chase removes the blankets and positions Ruairi over Aisling's feet. The unicorn groans as he moves her arm to examine the break. I squeeze her hand as she screams when he realigns the bones.

"We need to collect some snow," Chase whispers. "We'll pack it around your arm to reduce the swelling." He nods toward the door as he stands. "Luna, I could use your help."

I smile down at the wincing patient. "I'll be right back, Aisling," I promise. "Ruairi will stay with you and keep heating your feet."

She only weakly squeezes my hand in response. I reach for Ruairi's muzzle, but he pulls his lips back.

"I'll win you over one of these days, grumpy wolf," I say, winking.

I nod to the silent red wolf before ducking from the room. Chase takes my hand and drags me straight out the front door. Matthew and Aine are lying in the snow beside the porch near Bastian, who's finishing off his rabbit. Chase leans against the wall and pulls me to him.

"She's not going to make it," he hisses to me, not intending for anyone else to hear. "That infection is in her bone. She has a day, two tops. There's nothing I can do." His eyes search mine. I don't know what he's looking for, but he doesn't find it, judging by his reaction. "Ayls, we just need to make her comfortable and wait until she's gone."

I hear what he's saying, and I understand his meaning. Let her die, and we can have the mountains. There would be no one to run us off. The red wolves would be free of their curse. We could even take over the ranch and have a large herd of cattle. *Wouldn't that be great?* I sigh. *So why do I feel dirty?*

"Make her comfortable, Chase," I order, looking into his eyes. "It's the least we can do."

My mother's companion nods and leaves with a vase from the table. I watch him pack snow into it before pulling some supplies from my saddle bags. The wolves stay where they are but keep their eyes on me while I move to sit in the rocking chair again. I reach for the other chair's arm and slip my fingers over the rough wood.

"I think she always hoped someone would sit there," Aine tells me. *"She would rock for hours just staring into the distance."* She nudges Matthew's

muzzle before looking back at me. *I don't know who she was looking for, but they never came."*

I recall the countless times I'd climbed the stairs at home to find Daddy sitting in Mom's rocking chair. I imagine he hoped Mom would sit in his lap one more time. Leaving to join my mother on the other plane would make my father happy. Perhaps Aisling's death would allow her to be with her mate. She did say she was the last of her kind.

Looking down at my hands, I think of the life I took with them. I felt nothing with all the enemy lives I've taken over the years, but Doc's death stained my soul. He deserved it. I might go as far as to say he earned it. But that doesn't make my hands any cleaner. I had him taken to that room with the full intention of murdering him. My anger took hold, and I stole his last breath.

Chase pats my shoulder on his way past with the supplies, making me jump. "You coming?"

"I'll be there in a minute," I say, smiling at him.

He nods and disappears through the door.

I turn back to Aine once I hear the door click. "Ruairi seems to care about your mistress," I say, trying to lead her to open up.

Aine only lays her head in the snow. Her red fur mixes with the white snow, making it appear pink.

I twist to look at the door again. The handle is unlike any I've ever seen. Squinting my eyes, I study its curved shape and flat hook at the end, which looks heavily welded into place. The rope bolted to the bottom corner looks to have been replaced a few times. I'd seen Aine tug it to pull the door away from the wall before she closed it.

"The house seems to be set up for you guys to get around without Aisling," I mention casually, relaxing back into the chair. Bastian tilts his head, obviously wanting to know what I'm doing. "She seems strict, but she's done her best to care for you." I wink at Bastian and put my finger to my lips.

"I don't always like her orders, but she is good to us," Aine says. *"We are her constant companions. I think we used to annoy her because she yelled at us a lot. After a while, we somehow became a weird group of friends."*

"Does she normally go off on her own?" I ask.

"*No,*" Aine answers. "*It's dangerous, and we tried to talk her out of it, especially with your pack so close. She said she just needed to clear her head. Mistress is faster than us. We slow her down.*"

"She didn't say what was bothering her?" I ask, pulling a rag from the inside pocket of my jacket. I stand and descend the steps to crouch before Bastian. "It does seem careless with how attracted they are to her scent." I hold the rag open for my Alpha's muzzle.

"*She did not,*" Aine answers, watching me rub the rabbit fur and bits of meat from Bastian's muzzle.

"Ok," I say, sighing. "Let me get back in there to help Chase." I tuck the rag back in my pocket and kiss Bastian's nose. "I love you, my Alpha."

"*I love you too, Ayls,*" Bastian responds as I stand.

I slowly walk back through the house and into the bedroom. Chase has set Aisling's arm over a pan and packed snow around it. It looks more swollen than it did when I left. He's asking her questions, but she just stares at him. Ruairi and the other wolf are curled at the foot of the bed, staring at their mistress.

Chase shakes his head at me when I rub his shoulder. He wrings the rag that was on her forehead out and replaces it with one that had been sitting on the snow. "Can you grab that pot on the stove, Ayls?" Chase asks. "We'll clean this sweat off and make her more comfortable."

After retrieving the pot, I turn back to a very apprehensive-looking Aisling. Chase is peeling back the layers of blankets to reveal her bed-clothes plastered to her skin with sweat. My wolf couldn't care less that the white fabric has turned see-through, but Aisling clearly has an opinion about him seeing it.

"Why don't you guys give us some privacy?" I suggest, smiling. "I believe this is something we ladies can handle on our own."

Chase stands and opens the door for the red wolves, but they don't seem interested in leaving until Aisling nods to them. They watch her as they exit, waiting to see if she'll change her mind.

I smile as I sit on the edge of the bed, placing the pot on the bedside table. "They're an interesting bunch," I say, wringing out the rag Chase had left in the water. I eye her thin bed clothes. "We should probably try to remove these."

Aisling groans as she shakes her head.

"Ok," I say, narrowing my eyes in thought. "We'll just do our best then."

I take my time, slowly wiping the warm rag over her skin to clean away the multiple days' worth of sweat. The unicorn becomes visibly more comfortable with my presence as her skin loses its sticky grime and gains a soft smoothness.

"Why are you helping me?" Aisling asks in a hoarse whisper.

Smiling, I slide the rag over her leg. "Because you need it," I answer. "I'd like to think, if I needed help, that you might offer assistance too."

"You'd be wrong," Aisling states.

I laugh and rinse the rag out. "Maybe."

We continue through the afternoon in silence. Aisling lets me lift her clothes away from her skin to clean under them. The clothing dries in the arid environment but still feels thick from the sweat. I lift the towel I'd draped over her broken arm to see no reduction in her swelling and frown.

"Who was the other rocking chair for?" I ask, placing the towel back over her arm. "It doesn't look like it got much use."

Aisling's eyes wander critically over me before she answers. "No one."

"My grandfather made rocking chairs for my grandmother," I tell her, recleaning her uninjured arm. "They were in my parents' room when I was growing up. There were two, but I often found my mother curled up in my father's lap as they rocked in front of the fireplace."

"I'm sorry about your home," Aisling whispers.

Smiling faintly, I'm relieved Aine shared that story so I don't have to repeat it. "We came west because we'd heard stories of the game and freedom we would find out here. I just want my wolves to be safe from the hate they've endured."

"I made those chairs many years ago," Aisling starts slowly, still hoarsely whispering. "We have mates too. I had hoped to find mine one day." She sighs and looks toward the stove. "I should've burned it long ago."

"How do you know that you are the last?" I ask. "You've stayed hidden all these years. Why wouldn't you think someone else has too?"

"I'm 476 years old," Aisling grumbles. "Can you blame me for giving up?"

"I suppose not," I say, frowning. "I'd sit with you, though."

"You won't have to," she responds, wincing as she coughs. "I won't survive this."

"Why did you leave your guards?" I ask.

Aisling sighs deeply, frowning. "I'm not immortal, obviously," she says, indicating her arm. "Like you, I don't age, but I also can't kill myself. I thought I'd let your wolves do it for me." She looks away for a moment before turning back to study me. "But your wolves are different. I watched you work with them and show them love. I stood on top of that ridge and watched them play."

"Yeah," I say, smiling. "They do that a lot. They're good wolves."

"I knew better than to run in the snow," Aisling grumbles. "But this old pony felt the need to kick up her heels and broke her damn leg slipping on some buried ice."

"It happens," I say, giggling.

"I think we could've been good friends, Annalisa," Aisling says, taking my hand in her own. "Maybe in a different life." She groans, trying to adjust her infected arm.

I study her before pulling a vial from underneath Bastian's muzzle rag. "Aisling, I'd like the chance to find out," I whisper, holding the tea out for her to see. "I don't think this is how your story ends."

* * *

"What happened to the one I gave you?" Edith asks two days later. She holds out a vial of tea and a clean pair of jeans.

Smiling, I accept the items and pop the vial's cork off. "I must have dropped it," I lie. I believe in honesty and hate lying, but admitting I'd shared the vial with Aisling would cause too many issues.

"I told you we were running out, Annalisa," Edith scolds me. "We're down to two. That is not enough to get you to term, and that baby will not live if she's born now."

I put my finger to my lips and push my pants over my hips. "Edith, my father is going to speak with Aylee," I whisper. "Let him leave. He needs this." I pull the clean pants on before stepping into my boots. "I've been trying to get him to go to Mom for years. So please don't share that information with him and change his mind."

"You're as bad as your mother," she scoffs. "Can't you just be selfish for once?" She storms off with my pants as I catch my father bounding across the snow in front of the barn.

Joining Bastian, I lean against the large sliding door to watch my father say his goodbyes to the wolves he's closest to. He'll be back in a few days but will never again see these wolves daily. He's sad, but there is still a spring in his step.

"I am gonna miss him," Bastian whispers. "I know he misses Luna, but he's the only real father I've ever known." He pulls me to his chest as my father turns to us.

Daddy slides to a stop and shifts, taking the pants Bastian had been holding. "Come here, you two," he says, reaching for us. "I wish I could leave you in a better situation, but that damn creature survived somehow, so now I want to know how she can save you." He reaches around my neck and pushes my chin up so I'll look into his eyes. "I will find out how to save you if I have to torture it out of that annoying bitch."

"I just want you to be happy," I say, smiling. "You have been here long enough, and we are ready to take on the pack alone. I will protect them. They'll be safe with me."

Daddy smiles as he wipes a tear from my cheek. "I love you very much," he whispers. "I am so proud of both of you." He kisses Bastian's forehead and squeezes him as we hold each other. "I'll see you in a few days." He kisses my cheek and lets out a deep, shaky breath. "I'm ready," my father whispers before disappearing from our arms and leaving us with an unexpected emptiness.

29

Like when my mother died, my father's leaving packed a punch. I honestly thought I was ready for him to go. But Daddy touched every life within our pack somehow, and everywhere I turned, a wolf needed my help. The night before the full moon, I'm relieved when Aine announces Aisling's requested a meeting in the morning.

I wake feeling excited to make the trip to the unicorn's small cabin, leaving behind my mourning wolves to experience my own sorrow for a moment. Aine had been given permission to spend the night with us, which meant Matthew could cuddle with her while he slept.

"Are you two ready?" I whisper to them in the morning. Bastian and I sleep in a stall away from the pack. Matthew and Aine had joined us so they could have some privacy. I giggle as Matthew sleepily opens his eyes. "I'm very happy for you."

Matthew yawns and licks Aine's ear as she tucks her nose further under his chest. *"I'm not going to leave her, Ayls,"* he says quietly. *"I can't."*

"I know," I say, sighing. "I would never ask you to." I reach for his chin. "Just let me talk to Aisling before you do anything drastic, ok?"

"I promise, Ayls," Matthew says, tucking back into his mate.

Bastian pulls at me and kisses my neck until I turn to face him. "Good morning," he whispers, kissing the tip of my nose. "I could live in a barn for the rest of my life as long as you're in my arms."

"You are my favorite part about being the Luna," I whisper, rubbing my lips against his to trigger his hum. I snuggle a bit closer to put my belly against him. As wolves, their hum comes from their chest, but as humans, it comes from just below their ribs. Bastian's lines up perfectly with his daughter when we lie in each other's arms.

"What do you think Aisling wants to talk about?" my Alpha asks, tucking my hair behind my ear.

"I'm hoping that she's finally succumbed to the pull of my beautiful wolves," I respond, smiling.

"Hmm," Bastian groans. "We are pretty special."

I sigh noisily and slide my arms around his neck. "I completely agree," I whisper, pulling him to me.

Bastian is incredibly gentle with our child between us but still hungrily plunges his tongue between my lips. I would giggle when Matthew grumbles if Bastian didn't captivate so much of my attention. Aisling will just have to wait a little longer.

*   *   *

Later than intended, Aine and Matthew lead Saint through the thick snow to Aisling's house. Admittedly, nothing looks the same to me with every new day. The snow falls and melts, making it all look like a different land. I can't be sure we're going in the right direction until we climb the hill that towers over the quaint, decorative cabin.

"It looks so small from up here," Bastian comments. He pulls the buffalo hide blanket tighter around us. Between its insulation and his heat, my jacket is nearly overkill. "She's been waiting for us." Bastian nods toward the house.

I look up to see a tiny dot sitting on her front porch and smile. "Rocking on the porch is a perfect way to spend this day," I whisper with a sigh.

The wolves guide us down the hill, and I'm delighted to hear Aine laugh heartily when Matthew trips over a buried limb and falls face-first in the snow. It's our turn to laugh when he stands and rubs his face full of snow all over her. She whines, but I can easily hear her smile.

"Gaine was out for a walk yesterday and watched them for a while," Bastian tells me. "She said the red wolf looked like wet red paint in her vision."

"That makes sense since her coat is 'born of blood,'" I say thoughtfully. "Mom and Dad broke their curse. There must be a way to free them of theirs."

Bastian tucks near my ear as we approach the porch. "Maybe we should figure out how to be her friend before we steal her wolves," he suggests quietly.

"You're probably right," I murmur, smiling. "Aisling," I say, raising my voice for the unicorn. "It's wonderful to see you out. How are you feeling?"

"Well enough to ask you here," she answers. "I expected you earlier. Your coffee's cold."

I giggle as Bastian helps me from my saddle. "I got a little distracted," I reply, winking.

Aisling orders Aine to take Saint around back to a hay trough before reluctantly permitting Matthew to accompany her. I duck to kiss his muzzle and whisper a warning to behave himself before he quickly jogs after his mate. Aisling shakes her head as he disappears around the corner.

"He's sweet to her," I say, smiling as I step onto the porch.

Aisling motions to the other rocking chair. She's removed some of the cushions and added a thick blanket across the seat that extends over the arms. I smile and wipe my tears, recognizing it as exactly how I'd described my mother's chair. The blanket over the arms protected her back while Daddy cradled her.

"I heard about your father," Aisling says quietly, nodding at Bastian as he passes her to sit in the chair. "I'm sorry."

Bastian settles in the rocking chair with our buffalo hide blanket and reaches for me. "We'll see him tonight," he tells Aisling. "We miss him quite a bit, though."

"Aine tried to tell me about that, but it didn't quite make sense," Aisling remarks. "How do your dead come back to life?"

I explain the curse and how the Alphas return for the full moon. For a unicorn, she has a lot of knowledge about wolves and how the hierarchy works. "Did you know the last Luna? The Annalisa that I'm named after?" I ask.

"I knew of her, but going near the packs was never good back then," Aisling answers. "That little brat brought down an entire empire."

We listen to the story of how the Luna line died. Aisling tells us of the wolves' ruthlessness and how Aylee had riled them into a frenzy, inciting wars and brutality. I shiver from the cold, and Bastian excuses himself to make me something warm. He returns with a pot of hot tea, a few cups, and the other red wolves.

As we settle back into the rocking chair, I pull out my great-grandmother's notebook. "I wonder if you could help me with some of this," I say, opening it to the part about my blood. "I've been trying to finish the translation, but it seems inconsistent."

Aisling raises her eyebrow. "It definitely is," she scoffs. "Who translated this? It's horrible."

I shake my head. "I don't know," I answer. I relax into Bastian and sip my tea. It's a type I've never had before, but it's nice. "What is this?" I ask, looking up at him.

"I don't know," Bastian says, shrugging. "The quiet one pulled it out for me."

I look down at the wolf who's never spoken. He's sitting close enough that I can rub my fingers under his chin. "Are you ever going to talk to me?" I ask. The wolf only stares at me in response. "Ok," I whisper. "But we'll have to decide on a name you like if you won't tell me yours."

"His name is Lorcan, and that is an Earl Grey tea," Aisling informs us. "It's his favorite. He'd probably like to have a cup." She nods toward the small bowl on the table. "This part that says it's talking about blood is wrong," she continues as if she hadn't just dropped all that question-creating information on me. "It's about how bringing the Luna back would cause the return of other shifters." She looks up and catches my shocked expression. "What?"

I stammer through noises more than words before finding something intelligent to say. "Did he used to talk? Or does he just talk to you?" I start but quickly follow up with, "Other shifters? There are others?"

"Well, I suppose we could sit here for months talking about the past, but you said you wanted to see your father tonight," Aisling says. "Lorcan bit me when I was a foal. You might say we grew up together. He got mad at me and said he'd never speak again." She lifts her eyebrow and looks down at him. "Let's just say he's a man of his word."

Giggling, I lean over with Bastian's help and kiss the red wolf's nose. "How very honorable of you." Lorcan's nod makes me laugh harder.

Aisling taps the notebook. "This part is not talking about blood at all," she tells us. "It says, 'With thy Luna rebirth, her fate shall raise them all.' When the line ended, I lost my shift. Our existence is tied. Without you, I am simply a human who doesn't age. But when I got my shift back... I love to feel the wind in my mane. I suppose I have your mother to thank for that."

"There are stories about bears in the mountains," I say, smiling. "Do you know anything about that?"

Smiling, Aisling rests her head against the back of her chair. "Well, they wouldn't be too scared of a unicorn, would they?" She laughs, staring into the distance. "How do you not know any of this?" the unicorn asks, turning back toward us. "Don't you people have a historian?"

I groan, but Bastian begins growling. "We recognize you as a unicorn," he grumbles. "We are wolves."

I slide my finger along Bastian's jaw and blow gently onto his face, trying to calm him.

"You're right, Bastian," Aisling says, eyeing us. "Apologies. But generally, a historian would never be far from the Luna."

"Ours is broken," Bastian grumbles. "Apparently, she went crazy when her father passed his gift to her when she was little."

Aisling shakes her head, making sounds of disapproval. "From what I gathered over the years, they have to shift into the gift," she says thoughtfully. "If she didn't when it was passed, you'll need to wait until the next one."

I scowl, but Aisling seems to have so much knowledge that I decide to press on with other things. "I have a young wolf that accidentally bonded himself to me," I say, changing the subject. "Have you heard of anything that could be done to help him?"

"There were a few Lunas that loved to be worshipped and pleasured over the centuries," she starts, squinting. "You'll have to send him away until he's old enough that you can satisfy his needs."

Bastian tenses under me, and I send a blast of heat straight into his face. It doesn't affect him much with the intensity of his anger and irritation, but it stops him from attacking Aisling. I don't like what she said, but I can't blame her after the centuries of hateful wolves she experienced. We are very different from what she is used to, and it will take time for her to understand us.

"We don't really have the option to send him away," I say sadly. "We have the whole pack with us. After everything that's happened, I don't feel comfortable splitting them up."

"Well, keep your eye on him," Aisling advises. "He's gonna do something stupid. Kids always do."

We spend the rest of the afternoon telling each other stories about our wolves and the past. Bastian stays calm and even surprises me by catching a quick nap. Aisling notices but just giggles and continues her story of when Ruairi bit her. I'm sure I hear Lorcan chuckle when she gets to the part about him throwing the wayward wolf in the pond by his scruff, attempting to stop him.

* * *

Edith knocks before entering the stall where Bastian and I sleep later that night. "Bass said you were bleeding again," she says, closing the door behind her. She sighs as she crouches beside me. "I fear this will only happen more often. Trish has gone into labor."

I take the jeans she'd just washed yesterday with a huff. "She's my best friend, and I can't even go near her," I whine.

"Let's hope your father has answers for us," Edith says, handing me the tea vial. "After this, there's just one more. I've never been without tea."

I close my eyes and consider the weight of everything on us. The future Alpha is about to be born, and the future Luna is becoming more insistent about wanting out of me to be with him. Creto fights with everyone I send him with, wanting to be near me. My sweet wolf has turned quite rude due to this blood bond. Aisling hasn't agreed to let us stay, but I've enjoyed our time together.

Edith is still angry with me for "losing" the vial of tea that I shared with the unicorn. In reality, though, one more vial of tea wouldn't have saved my child or me. I need a miracle.

"Everything will be fine, Edith," I tell her, opening my eyes. "We've found a way to carry on through everything so far. We can do this."

Trish yells from somewhere in the barn.

"Alright, I need to go help Chase with her," Edith grumbles, taking the dirty pants from me. "Your Alpha said you were meeting with your family in the hay shed tonight."

"Everyone misses Daddy and will want to see him," I whisper. "I want to make sure we have time to talk."

"That makes sense," she says. "I have missed watching him strut around." She bites her lip and stares at the wall as I stand awkwardly beside her. "Anyway," Edith starts again, opening the stall door. "You should probably get going."

I follow her through the door, and Bastian catches my hand, swinging me toward the large sliding door. "The Alphas will be here soon, and you have one more thing to deal with." He turns my face by my jaw to show Creto sitting beside the hay shed.

Sighing, I rub my eyes. "Clearly, Aisling was right about him," I grumble. "The worst part is that he doesn't know he's doing anything wrong." I let Bastian escort me to Creto and kiss his cheek before kneeling to the young wolf. "Creto, sweetheart, you have to go in the barn now. The sun is setting."

"I heard we were meeting the Alphas in the hay shed, though," he responds.

"Sweetheart," I say gently. "This will just be family tonight."

"Sure," Creto says, standing. *"You ready?"*

"I mean, just me and Bastian, Creto," I say, furrowing my brow. "You'll have to go lie down in the barn."

"But we're family," the young wolf nearly shouts. *"You said so yourself."*

"Creto, I love you, and you are my family," I say, attempting to capture his jaw. "But you're still a child, sweetheart. And this is a crucial meeting with a very grown-up topic."

The young wolf continues to hold his head out of my reach. Bastian's chin slides over my shoulder as he exits the hay shed. He towers over Creto to assert his dominance, as he must do daily with him now. The young wolf lowers his head and lets me kiss his nose before slinking toward the barn door.

"Thank you for that," I whisper, leaning against Bastian's shoulder.

"I was gonna shift anyway so I could hear Tarq," he responds. *"I don't know how else to get through to that kid. Why would they do this on purpose in the old days?"*

Groaning, I use his shoulders to push to my feet. "You heard Aisling," I remind him. "The Luna's were a bit free with the love, apparently." I rub my hand over Bastian's jaw as he leads me into the hay shed. "I grew up watching my mother and father and wanting what they had. My father looked at Mom like she was everything, and Mom knew and understood Daddy like he was the breath that gave her life."

Bastian wipes away my tears with his muzzle as I sit beside a crate holding a lantern. *"Their love knows no equal,"* he says quietly.

"Yes, it does, my Alpha," I whisper, reaching out to him. "I wouldn't enjoy being Luna if the job didn't come with you."

Bastian chuckles. *"You make being an Alpha easy."*

When he steps back, I kiss his nose and lift my necklace over my head. "Did you check on Trish?"

"Yeah," Bastian answers, pushing my necklace to the middle of the shed. *"She looked uncomfortable but fine."*

"Who's that?" Grandpa's voice rings through my head.

I reach my arms out to him as he appears before us. "Trish," I answer. "She's gone into labor." I hold onto him momentarily and rub my face against his shiny black coat. "Grandpa, where's Daddy?" I ask, pulling away and looking around.

"*He missed your mom quite a bit, and it's his first time leaving her,*" he says. "*Give him a minute.*"

"*I thought the curse forced you to come here for the full moon,*" Bastian questions, confused.

"It does," Grandpa says, lying beside me. "*It's a pull you can fight for a while but lose in the end.*"

I lift my eyebrow. "You and Uncle Miles always came at the same time."

"*Ayls,*" Grandpa says, sighing. "*I've never wanted to fight it. I appreciate the break from my Luna.*"

Giggling, I roll down to lay my head on his shoulder. "I can understand that."

We relax on the floor of the hay shed, filling Grandpa in on the pack happenings while we wait. When my father arrives, Bastian jumps up to hook necks with him. I smile as I watch them through misty eyes. Bastian's bond with my parents is a beautiful thing.

I try not to listen and give them privacy, but I've wanted to hear my father's voice more desperately than I care to admit. "*I've missed you too, kiddo,*" he tells Bastian. "*But we need to talk, and I don't want to run out of time.*"

When he steps back from Bastian, I open my arms. "We can take another minute for a hug, Daddy," I whisper. "I might not have been as ready as I thought."

Daddy steps into my arms and slides his jaw down my back. "*No one is ever ready for goodbye, Ayls,*" he tells me quietly. "*We do our best. Your mother sends her love and wants me to remind you that your baby is more important than anything. Without that baby, the line will die.*"

"We're doing our best to keep her where she is, Daddy," I say as he backs away.

"*I've got a feeling you're not gonna like this, but I got everything I could out of that pain in the ass,*" my father tells us, watching Bastian sit beside me. "*She said you need the unicorn's blood.*"

I furrow my brow. "Daddy, her blood causes the curse that tied the red wolves to her," I say, confused. "How would that help anyone?"

"*You have to kill her,*" he responds, placing his paw in my lap.

My deep breath seems to echo in our stunned silence. I turn my hands over and stare at their stained palms. Bastian promises it's all in my mind, but they haven't been the same color since Doc's death. His murder was revenge. Aisling's would be for gain. How could I ever clean that off?

"*Tarq, there has to be another way,*" Bastian begs. "*Maybe a week ago, I would have been fine ripping her throat out, but we've spent time with her.*"

"*You spent time with Doc too,*" Daddy grumbles. "*Yet that didn't save him.*"

"He killed Mom," I spout angrily. "And I still can't forgive myself for what I did to him. Aisling hasn't done anything to any of us."

"*Yet,*" my father mutters.

"What?" I snap.

"*Annalisa, the world will always hate us,*" Daddy says, sitting up to face Bastian and me. "*You want to see a brighter future, but that's not reality. We will cease to exist if you don't take what you need.*"

"I refuse to believe that's true, Daddy," I say through my tears. "Aisling is kind. Unicorns have been hunted until she is the last one left. I can't kill her."

"*You have to,*" my father demands. "*It's her or us, Annalisa.*"

"Then our wolves will find another way," I sob. "We've always found another way. The past has never led us down the right path. Why would it start now?"

My father tries a few different approaches but always has the same advice: kill my friend. Even if she were our enemy, I would have reservations. She's the last of her kind. Ending an entire species would leave a stain on anyone's soul. I would have to carry that into the other plane and accept it as part of my existence, unable to escape its presence.

By the time they leave, I'm more emotionally exhausted than ever. Now I understand why Daddy started our conversation with my mother's advice. I don't know if he believed anything he said as he used every technique he could, trying to convince me to kill Aisling. Grandpa did his best to moderate the argument, but in the end, they both disappeared, watching me bawl like a baby.

Bastian hooks his leg over my shoulder and pulls me down with him. I curl up to his gut and cry into his chest. Usually, his whiskers sliding over my skin would comfort me, but now it only makes me wonder just how long I'll be able to feel them if I don't kill my friend.

I'm nearly asleep when someone knocks on the door. "Hey, you two," Edith whispers. "Not that it's a surprise, but I thought you might like to know it's a boy." She pauses, waiting for a response that won't come before changing the subject. "It looks like this little one has been out here for a while. I think he wants to come in."

Sighing, I mumble, "Whatever."

* * *

"Mistress was asking after you again last night, Luna," Aine says quietly as she approaches my hay bed. *"She would like you to visit."* She looks around the hay shed, confused. *"Why are you out here?"*

"It's fine, Aine," I answer. "My child just wants to meet her Alpha a little early. The distance helps." I rub my fingers over her jaw. "You should spend time with Matthew instead of worrying about me. You've waited quite a while to meet him and shouldn't waste time in here."

I've avoided Aisling since speaking to my father. I didn't want my Alpha to get any ideas and wasn't sure if I could lie if she asked how our visit went. Her invitations have become more insistent over time.

"Why don't we waste time together then," Aine responds sweetly.

Matthew rubs his muzzle over hers. *"That sounds nice,"* he agrees. *"Bastian could stretch his legs while we watch over you, Ayls."*

Bastian and Creto haven't left my side for more than a minute over the past week. We waited until the last tea was essential, but a few days ago, I was bleeding steadily. Chase and Edith agreed that it was time to use the last of my salvation.

Matthew helps me convince them to go out for a hunt. My Alpha is the only wolf Creto occasionally listens to anymore, and when he doesn't, Bastian isn't shy about reprimanding him. Matthew climbs into the hay bed with me to keep me warm as they leave. I close my eyes and listen to Aine describe the wedding she's always wanted.

* * *

Yelling causes me to jump awake after what feels like only minutes. I'm wrapped in a buffalo hide, and Matthew is nowhere to be found. Creto's muzzle is in my face. He's repeating the same phrase, but I can't hear it over the yelling. When I roll, I notice my pants have been removed.

Bastian appears upon my movement. "Hang on, Love," he shouts. "We'll fix this." He looks away and begins yelling again.

I follow his eyes to see Chase and Edith are also here. I swat at Creto, attempting to silence him so I can hear what's going on.

"Bass, her water broke," Chase shouts. "We're out of options."

"We can try hooking you up to her," Edith suggests. "We might be able to save her if we can get the kid out."

"What about distance?" Bastian pleads. "It's helped before."

"It's too late, Bass," Chase tells him, looking down at me.

When Bastian turns back to me, his face shines in the lantern light from his tears. "What do I do?" he asks, wanting me to have the answers.

I try to reach out to him, but my arm is too weak to leave my side. I shake my head slightly as tears slide from my eyes. The miracle I had hoped for never came.

Bastian wipes his face and takes a few deep breaths. "Hook us up," he orders. "I'll take her out of here." He holds his arm out.

Edith springs into action, setting Bastian's needle in his arm before working on me. "Listen to me, sweetheart," she whispers down by my ear. "You need to say your goodbyes. Your body will reject this blood. Help him by saying goodbye."

Creto's muzzle rubs over my forehead. If I had the energy, I'd be screaming at Edith. My death will break Creto much more than it would affect any other. She finishes hooking me up and announces she'll get Saint for us.

My head is foggy, but the introduction of Bastian's blood gives me some of my strength back. I reach for his neck as he cradles me in his arms. "Don't trust..." I get out, trying to warn him that Creto knows about everything.

"Come on, Ayls," Bastian whispers, pushing past Chase to follow Edith from the hay shed. "We'll go south. It'll be warmer down there." He kisses my forehead and lifts his eyes to look around. "Christmas in the South like old times."

Trotting hooves interrupt his whispering. Bastian steps onto the stump I use to mount the horses and carefully swings onto Saint with me still cradled in his arms. He tries to reach for the horse's rope, but his arms are buried in the hides with me.

"Just take it off," he orders. "South, Creto. Lead him south."

I try to stop what's about to happen, but the sudden rush of cold air as Saint takes off after the heartbroken little wolf takes my breath away. Creto ignored my orders to go to bed and stayed outside the hay shed all night for my meeting with the Alphas. He knows killing Aisling would save me. Bastian begins yelling at Creto when he realizes we're not going south.

"Creto! Stop!" he shouts. "You're going the wrong way!"

We could never have planned for this. That little wolf won't listen. He's trying to save my life, and Bastian had Edith remove the one thing that might have allowed him to stop Saint. I trained this horse. He will follow Creto over the side of a cliff. We can't risk jumping from his back in our weakened state at this speed.

I turn my head to see in front of the horse. The meager moonlight causes the snow to shine but highlights some moving dark blobs. My chest aches as I pull in the cold air, trying to make sense of the masses. My arm jerks as I realize what they are, pulling the needle out of my vein. I try to warn Bastian about the buffalo stampede, but it's too late as some burst through the trees beside us.

Creto screams as they trample over the top of him. Saint's stride falters before he grunts and falls under us. Bastian grabs me tightly and pushes away from the horse, rolling to the ground. He braces himself over me and jerks a few times until the thundering hooves fade.

Breathing out a groan, Bastian rolls us to our sides and looks into my eyes. "I love you," he whispers as blood pours from his mouth. "Please live."

I open my mouth but can hardly form words. "Don't you leave me," I sob, watching the blood run from my Alpha's mouth and nose. "I love you." I wiggle enough to kiss his lips.

Bastian weakly returns my kiss. "I'll see you again," he whispers, closing his eyes. His last breath tickles my lips, and his body falls limp beside me.

Breathing between the blood loss and my tears is difficult, but I take a few shallow breaths and pool my strength as hooves begin thundering around me again. "I'm ready!" I scream.

30

❧

Twenty-Four Years Later

My name is Charlotte, and I am the Luna of wolves. Twenty-four years ago, my family suffered a tragic accident while trying to save me from myself. Tonight, I will marry the Alpha I was desperate to be with. I've never felt my father's arms, but I love spending time with him every full moon and can't wait for him to bless my union tonight.

I stand before the mirror and watch Aisling pull my hair aside to fasten the choker collar of my dress. My grandmother's beaded flowers cascade throughout the white fabric and lace, while my mother's peach lies across the back, out of sight at this angle. Trish wanted to put a piece of me in the design, but I begged her not to. It's perfect, just the way it is.

"Do you think I'll make them proud?" I whisper, staring at my reflection.

"You already do, young Luna," Aisling responds, quickly twisting some of my hair into small braids. "You've done well with these wolves."

There's a commotion on the stairs, causing us to furrow our brows and the young red wolf, Creto, to tilt his head. Kade bursts through the door without knocking, quickly followed by my mother.

"I told you she wasn't naked," Kade shouts, laughing. He spins my mother until she lands in his arms. "You owe me a dance now."

"Kade, I didn't bet you anything," my mother spouts. "I told you to do your damn job and leave my daughter alone. The rest of this was all in your head."

I pull Aisling aside as Kade walks my mother backward until he pushes her onto the bed. He crawls over her with his butt in the air. This is normal for them. Kade is the oddest wolf in our pack and somehow has these weird freedoms with Lunas. *Yep, he does this with me too.*

"What are you doing?" my mother grumbles.

Kade lifts off my mother's neck to look down at her. "You two are delicious," he says, laughing. "That's never gonna change."

Gaine enters my room in a gorgeous red dress, holding my bouquet, which she uses to smack Kade's rear end. "Get off her," she snaps, laughing. "You have somewhere to be."

My mother laughs and grabs his face. "Now you're in trouble," she says, pulling him to her lips. "Go get dressed so you can marry these kids. I miss my Alpha."

Kade's hum starts as he presses his lips to hers again. "Mm," he murmurs. "Love me some Luna." He pushes off Mom and snags his wife, leaning her over backward. He kisses her deeply before straightening her again. "And some wife," he adds before turning to me.

"Kade, it's my wedding day," I whine pointlessly. There is no stopping Kade.

He smiles broadly as his arms slide around my back. I cup his cheeks and grin into his kiss. Kade's team are the misfits of the pack, and they all act exactly as he does, but we depend on them in a crisis.

"I love you, Kade," I whisper to the wayward wolf.

"Baby, everybody loves me," he replies. When Aisling scoffs beside me, he turns to the unicorn. "Come on, Ash," he says, holding his arms out with a big grin. "Give me some love."

"Wolf, I will stab you in the throat," Aisling growls.

Kade laughs as he walks toward the door. "One day, unicorn," he says, pointing at her. "You're gonna love me one day!"

Gaine shakes her head as he disappears down the hall. "I know you want him, but he's all mine," she states frankly, raising her eyebrow.

"Well, darn," I say, laughing.

She kisses my cheek and hands me my bouquet. "You look beautiful," she says before exiting the room.

Mom fixes her sun dress and cups my cheek. "I'm glad you two grew up with Kade," she says, smiling. "Your father never did get used to him."

"Is he really the best choice to officiate this wedding?" Aisling asks.

Mom and I laugh as she might be the hundredth person to ask us.

"He's the only one Anthony taught how," Mom tells her. "I think it was a final joke on us before he passed."

"Anthony played a joke on us, but Edith stopped an argument we've had my whole life," I tell my mother, putting my arm around her.

Mom leans her head on my shoulder. "All you had to do was ask," she says. "I would've told you why I chose your name. I had my reasons."

My mother told me once that everything happens for a reason. I've always hated the saying, but I understand it now. Creto was bonded to my mother through the misguided actions of a 10-year-old. His desperation to fix my mother caused my father's death but ultimately saved my mother's life.

Aisling was on her way to see why my mother would not visit her and found her nearly dead in my father's limp arms. I recently learned that Mom tried to follow my father to the other plane. Creto was also mortally wounded and dying, but Aisling raked his teeth over her leg to curse him, which healed his wounds and bound him to her.

A unicorn's blood can only heal a Luna due to the magical bond between our powers. Aisling nearly died pumping enough blood into my mother to heal her, but they'd become friends, and she would do anything to save her. So, although I wish my father could dance with me at my wedding, the events that killed him allowed my mother to raise and teach me how to be a Luna to my wolves.

Mom says she will join my father once Jinx and I return from our short holiday after the ceremony. I've never experienced them as a human couple, but their love is obvious when they are together for the full moon. When she leaves, it will be with my blessing. My mother has been alone long enough, waiting for me to be ready to take the pack from her.

A scratch at the door pulls me out of my head. I look out the window to see the shadows are gone, and night has taken over. Aisling opens the door to let the Alphas in. My father runs straight into my mother's arms while I kneel to greet Grandpa and Grandfather Dax. Once my mother releases him, I turn to my father with my arms out. He slips into them and gently slides his jaw down my back.

"*Hello, Chair,*" Daddy whispers, making Grandpa scoff and Grandfather Dax chuckle. "*I have missed you.*"